ONE-EYED ROYALS

SEVEN OF SPADES #4

CORDELIA KINGSBRIDGE

RIPTIDE
PUBLISHING

Riptide Publishing
PO Box 1537
Burnsville, NC 28714
www.riptidepublishing.com

One-Eyed Royals
Copyright © 2018 by Cordelia Kingsbridge

Cover art: Garrett Leigh, blackjazzdesign.com
Editors: Rachel Haimowitz, Veronica Vega
Layout: L.C. Chase, lcchase.com/design.htm

ISBN: 978-1-62649-640-8

First edition
September, 2018

Also available in ebook:
ISBN: 978-1-62649-639-2

ONE-EYED ROYALS

SEVEN OF SPADES #4

CORDELIA
KINGSBRIDGE

RIPTIDE PUBLISHING

J.J.Q.T.C.P.
Cousins by blood, siblings in spirit.

TABLE OF CONTENTS

CHAPTER 1

Dominic groaned as sirens split the air and flickering red and blue lights filled his rearview mirror. He kept driving for a few seconds, hoping the cop would pass him, but no such luck.

He pulled his pickup truck over to the side of the road and glanced at the dashboard clock. Goddamn it, he was going to be late. *Again*.

The cop who approached his car was a young white woman whose blonde hair was braided beneath her cap. Dominic adjusted his jacket to better hide the shape of his shoulder holster—he had a concealed carry permit, but there was no point in taking risks around cops. Then he put his hands back on the wheel and gave her the most disarming smile he could muster, which was no easy feat these days.

"Is there a problem, Officer?" He knew for a fact he hadn't been speeding.

"Your right taillight is broken, sir."

Dominic's hands tightened on the wheel so hard it creaked beneath his grip. The cop noticed and raised her eyebrows.

"I'm aware of that," he said, struggling to keep his voice even. "This is the third time I've been pulled over for that light in the past five days."

"Then you should probably get it fixed."

"I will. It's just that money is a little tight right now."

She gave him an unimpressed look. "Money's going to be tighter if someone rear-ends you because they can't see you're hitting your brakes."

"Is a broken taillight really the best use of your time?" he said despite his better judgment. "How about the serial killer that's been stalking the city for almost a year? Or the neo-Nazis running wild around the Valley?"

He nodded to the building nearest them. The symbol of Utopia—a white supremacist group swiftly escalating in scope from street gang to outright homegrown militia—was graffitied in stark black paint on the wall.

The cop turned her face aside, and he could see he'd hit a nerve. As he studied her in profile, he realized something else.

"We've met before," he said, taken aback. "You're that rookie cop Levi Abrams liked—Kelly Marin, right? The one who got busted for leaking the Seven of Spades story to the *Review-Journal* last April?"

She blinked, retreating a step. He seized on her moment of hesitation.

"Levi put you up to this, didn't he? He asked you to harass me."

"The LVMPD doesn't harass civilians, sir," she said stiffly.

Dominic snorted. "So it's just a coincidence that I've gotten more tickets and warnings from cops in the three months and change since Levi and I broke up than I'd gotten in my entire life? One of your buddies gave me a ticket for *jaywalking* last month, in the middle of a crowd of people doing the exact same thing. You can't expect me to believe Levi didn't put out some kind of covert BOLO, asking you all to keep your eyes peeled for me and my truck and find any possible reason to hassle me."

Kelly didn't answer, but he didn't need her to. When their relationship had gone down in flames in November, Levi had promised to make Dominic's life a living hell—and he'd been living up to that promise. Not only was Dominic hounded by cops every time he turned around, he was pretty sure it was Levi who'd broken his taillight. He'd left his apartment one morning to find the light deliberately smashed, and no further damage to his truck or the other cars in the lot.

"Look, are you gonna give me a ticket or not?" Dominic asked. "I'm running late for a work meeting."

The truth was, he would have been late even if Kelly hadn't pulled him over. But that was Levi's fault too. Since their breakup, the bastard had been steadily blackballing Dominic from every casino one by one. When Dominic had resorted to not-so-legal venues, each operation had been mysteriously raided by the LVMPD the very next day.

In a matter of weeks, Dominic had found himself persona non grata at almost every gambling establishment in and around Las Vegas. The only place Levi's influence didn't extend was the Railroad Pass in Henderson, a half-hour drive from the Strip. So unless Dominic was content with gambling online—which just wasn't the same—he had to haul his ass all the way out there, and he always underestimated traffic driving back into the city.

"I'll let you off with a warning this time," said Kelly. "Make sure you get that taillight fixed."

"Of course."

Dominic turned the key in the ignition. He knew Levi believed he was doing the right thing. This wasn't like the other times Dominic's gambling had gotten out of control, though. He'd learned from his past mistakes; he had a handle on the gambling now. It wasn't a problem, but Levi was too bullheaded to accept that.

"By the way," he said to Kelly as she backed away from the truck, "you might want to remind Detective Abrams that he left his phone charger at my place when I fucked him last Saturday."

Dominic slid smoothly back into traffic, leaving her gaping behind him.

"This is a new low for us," Levi said as he took in the Seven of Spades's latest crime scene.

"It doesn't reflect well on building security, that's for sure," said Martine.

They were standing in the chambers of District Court Judge Cameron Harding, who had been murdered in the city's Regional Justice Center—a building full of people, cameras, and armed guards—in the middle of the afternoon, with nobody noticing anything amiss until hours later.

Like the vast majority of the Seven of Spades's now twenty-two victims, Harding had been drugged into paralysis before his throat was slit from behind. A half-empty coffee cup on his desk was the most likely source of the killer's drug of choice, ketamine, though they'd have to test it to confirm.

Harding himself was seated at his desk, but it was the objects on the surface that caught and held Levi's attention. Two statuettes of Lady Justice, sword in one hand and scales in the other, had been set up on either side, angled to face Harding. Little craft eyes had been glued over their blindfolds so it looked like they were staring at him.

At the top edge of the desk was a bronzed model of the scales of justice, with a seven of spades card carefully balanced on each scale. Finally, a sheet of paper sat in the center of the desk, right in front of Harding, with one of his bloody hands resting on top of it. Levi could tell from the displacement of the blood around Harding's chest and neck that the killer had pressed Harding's hand to his own throat wound before laying it atop the paper.

When Levi and Martine stood side by side, he had to look down to meet her eyes—she was a petite woman, though her commanding presence effortlessly filled a room. "You know anything about this guy?"

"Nope."

Steering clear of the crime scene photographer, Levi circled the desk with his gloved hands in his pockets. The CSIs were still working the room and the coroner investigator hadn't arrived yet, so it was even more important that he not disturb anything.

By leaning over Harding's shoulder, Levi was just able to make out the words at the top of the blood-stained piece of paper beneath the man's hand.

"It's the oath of office Clark County district judges take," he said to Martine.

She snorted. "The Seven of Spades is so extra."

He shot her a bewildered look.

"That's Mikayla's assessment," she said, referring to one of her teenage daughters.

Mikayla wasn't wrong. The Seven of Spades styled themselves a vigilante, targeting only betrayers of trust—people who had committed some form of treachery and gotten away with it. The killer took particular delight in staging the scenes to emphasize the victims' guilt.

The setting and details of Harding's murder sent a clear message. Levi just didn't know how Harding had violated his oath as a judge; he'd never met the man and wasn't familiar with his career.

Martine came around the other side of the desk, studying Harding's body. "At least the killer is still sticking with their usual MO. No signs of struggle or violence."

Levi nodded. The Seven of Spades—who was quickly racking up one of the most prolific, uninterrupted strings of serial murders in modern history—had a distinct killing style. They were able to appear trustworthy enough to incapacitate their victims with drugged beverages without raising any alarms, then administered a single passionless knife stroke to the throat.

The Seven of Spades had only broken from that MO three times. They had once hired a sniper to kill a man on the steps of this very building, in retaliation for that man trying to frame them for his wife's murder. On another occasion, they had slaughtered five human traffickers at the same time, then flown into a rage and mutilated the bodies postmortem. And once—only once—they had killed a single victim without bothering to take him unawares, instead subduing him with a stun gun and a forceful injection of ketamine.

Afterward, the Seven of Spades had confessed to Levi that they'd enjoyed using such active violence, and there had been concern for a while that the killer would become more aggressive. But each of the murders since then had been faithful to the original MO. The only thing that varied was the elaborate staging.

Levi turned to the responding officer, who was hovering a few feet away. "This building is covered in cameras. How did the killer manage to slip in and out without drawing any attention?"

"The head of security already looked into that," the officer said. "The building's entire system was hacked and put on a sophisticated loop that nobody noticed. They haven't even been able to fix it yet—they had to call in specialists."

"Carmen," Martine muttered.

Levi closed his eyes and rubbed the bridge of his nose. Not long after their debut, the Seven of Spades had cultivated a mole in the Las Vegas Metropolitan Police Department—Carmen Rivera, a brilliant young technical specialist. She'd been arrested a few months ago when Levi and Martine had discovered her betrayal, but she'd escaped within days thanks to the street gang Los Avispones, another ally of the Seven of Spades. Wherever she was now, her assistance continued to provide the killer access and information they wouldn't have been able to obtain on their own.

"Okay, we need to—"

"Levi Abrams!" snapped an ice-cold voice.

He winced before he even turned around.

Deputy District Attorney Leila Rashid was standing on the other side of the crime scene tape strung across the office doorway, her arms crossed. As always, her black hair was pulled into a fuss-free ponytail, and her simple pantsuit flattered the hard, lean lines of her athletic body. She crooked her index finger at him, gesturing for him to come over.

Despite his irritation at being summoned like a dog, Levi walked up to the tape. Martine accompanied him, a curious look on her face.

"Did you maybe forget to do something today?" Leila said, laying the sarcasm on so thick it would've crushed a lesser man's spirit.

"For God's sake, Leila, a city judge has been murdered—"

"Cameron Harding?" She peered past him at the body, then waved a dismissive hand, apparently unfazed by the grisly scene. "Everyone hated that douchebag; his sentencing was blatantly racist. I'm only surprised the Seven of Spades didn't get to him sooner." Pointing a finger at Levi, she said, "You were supposed to be in *my* office half an hour ago for trial prep."

He opened his mouth, but she barreled on without giving him a chance to speak.

"Jason Wilson's new defense attorney is a total slimeball. You cannot go into that cross-examination unprepared, especially with your anger-management problems."

"Jason Wilson?" Martine said, while Levi bristled all over. "Isn't he one of the Utopia gangbangers who was arrested for the assault on Sergei Volkov's underground casino? I thought those trials were supposed to start a couple weeks ago."

"Don't even get me started," said Leila. "All the Utopia assholes we have in jail or on bond keep getting their trials postponed because their legal teams are in constant flux, and the court schedule's a mess. Their attorneys keep quitting."

Martine hummed thoughtfully. "I think I read something about that. They've been getting death threats, right?"

"Yeah. Even worse, as far as lawyers are concerned, big-ticket clients have been threatening to pull out of their firms if they represent Nazis."

"You're a lawyer," Levi said.

"I'm a prosecutor. There's a difference. And don't try to change the subject." Leila stepped closer to the tape. "You didn't even call to tell me you weren't showing up, nor did you answer any of *my* calls or texts, which meant I had to waste time tracking you down."

Levi suppressed a cringe. That *had* been shitty of him, though he had an explanation. "I know, I'm sorry. My phone died hours ago. I lost my charger and haven't had time to buy a new one."

If it had only been Leila, that might've worked. But Martine knew him too well. She was his partner, his best friend, a sister far superior to his biological one, and she wasn't so easily fooled.

She narrowed her eyes. "You don't lose things. Which means you know where your charger is but you can't get it for some reason . . ." Her eyes went wide. "Oh my God, you left it at Dominic's apartment!"

"You're the worst," said Levi.

"You slept with him *again*?" Leila said, loudly enough to catch the attention of the uniformed officer standing guard at the doorway.

Levi glowered at the man until he hastily backed out of earshot. "I didn't plan on it! It just happened. We ran into each other at the grocery store—"

"You don't live anywhere near each other—"

"And one thing led to another," he continued, steadfastly ignoring that comment. "I thought . . . Well, it doesn't matter what I thought. I was wrong."

This wasn't the first time he'd found himself in this predicament. He and Dominic would cross paths—and all right, sometimes it was because he'd engineered the circumstances and sometimes because Dominic had. They'd start talking, and if they made it through the first five minutes without fighting, things would start feeling normal again. Dominic would seem like the same charming, thoughtful, easygoing man Levi had fallen in love with, Levi would believe there was hope for their relationship after all, and they'd end up in bed.

Then, inevitably, something would happen to smack Levi in the face with the harsh truth—Dominic was a compulsive gambler in a full-blown relapse, refusing any and all offers of help. That hadn't changed, and until it did, they couldn't be together in any meaningful way.

"You know," Martine said, "when a couple breaks up, they usually stop having sex with each other."

"What the hell do you know about it?" Levi retorted. Martine had only been in one relationship her entire life. She and her husband, Antoine, had been childhood sweethearts who'd grown up in the same Flatbush neighborhood of Haitian immigrant families, and they'd gotten married during college.

"Hey, don't take your angst out on her," Leila said. "She's not the one who keeps jumping on Russo's dick."

Martine made an exasperated noise. "It makes sense that you and Dominic are drawn to each other. You're still in love; breaking up didn't change that. But this is not a healthy way to deal with your separation."

"And *this* is not the time or the place to have this discussion." Levi gestured to the corpse fifteen feet away. "A city official was murdered in a government building in broad daylight. The mayor is going to have a nuclear meltdown."

"Like things weren't already bad enough," Martine said glumly.

Tourism in Las Vegas had plummeted ever since the Seven of Spades had become a nationwide phenomenon, even though they'd never actually killed a tourist. Utopia's explosive growth had only made matters worse, and the combined pressures had ignited a political firestorm in which the mayor, the city council, and the sheriff were more interested in slinging blame at each other than solving the problems.

Martine and Leila fell into a debate about damage control, and Levi breathed a quiet sigh of relief. As far as he was concerned, there *was* no right time or place to discuss his relationship with Dominic. He could barely stand thinking about it.

Dominic was his *bashert*, his soul mate. Without him, Levi felt like he'd been gut-shot and it was taking months to bleed out.

"Detective Abrams?" one of the CSIs said as she approached him from behind. "There's something you should look at over here."

He and Martine followed her across the office. Leila, who hadn't signed into the scene, stayed behind the tape.

"This seemed out of place, so we took a closer look. And . . . well, you'll see." The CSI gestured to a greeting card set on a sideboard decorated with framed photographs of Harding's family. "It's already been tagged and photographed."

Levi picked the card up carefully with the tips of his gloved fingers. The front was a shimmery ombré design with the words *Sorry I missed it* in silver foil. Inside, *Happy Belated Birthday!* was printed above a typed message.

Dear Detective Abrams,

I know your birthday was in January, but the perfect gift takes time to prepare. Rest assured I haven't forgotten. I'll have something special for you soon.

An imprint of a seven of spades card had been left with a rubber stamp at the bottom of the page.

Goose bumps prickled across Levi's skin, and he was gripped with the sudden irrational urge to tear the card to shreds. Instead, he looked to Martine, who was eyeing the card the way she would a tarantula.

"What the hell does that mean?" she said.

"I have no idea," said Levi. "But I'm pretty sure I'm not going to like it."

CHAPTER 2

ominic walked into the Double Down Saloon, a raucous dive bar whose official motto was *Shut Up and Drink!*, and had to immediately dodge a stumbling drunk puking his way out the door. He rolled his eyes and squinted through the chaos, spotting his client in less than five seconds.

The Double D attracted a rowdy punk-rock crowd, and Nathan Royce stood out like the sole diamond in a hand full of spades. He was a preppy white silver fox wearing a nice suit and fancy watch that screamed *upper middle class*, not exactly the bar's usual clientele. It didn't help that he was twitchy as hell, glancing around nervously, tapping his foot against the floor, drumming his fingers on the high-top table he was standing beside.

Dominic bulldozed his way through the mob—not a difficult proposition for a man of his towering height and muscular build—until he reached Royce. "We could have met somewhere else," he said, leaning close to be heard over the incoherent yet wildly enthusiastic band.

Royce shook his head. "No risk of seeing someone I know here."

"You're the client," Dominic said with a shrug. He hefted his messenger bag onto the table; in this environment, it was less likely to attract attention than a briefcase.

"Have you found anything?"

"You know, I could do my job a lot faster if you'd be more specific about what I'm looking for."

"I've told you enough," Royce said impatiently. "Highly valuable proprietary information has been compromised in a way that's caused my company severe financial losses in a suspiciously short period of time. It's either a conspiracy to commit insurance fraud, or corporate sabotage by a competing agency. What more do you need to know?"

"The nature of the compromised information, for starters."

"I can't tell you that."

Dominic stifled a sigh. Royce was the director of Management Liability Insurance at Kensington Insurance Group, a national firm catering to high-net-worth individuals and Fortune 500 companies. He'd hired McBride Investigations three weeks ago, and while it was a juicy contract, his refusal to disclose the full extent of the problem meant it was also unnecessarily frustrating.

Tilting his head, Dominic put Royce under closer scrutiny. It was hot in the Double D, like any other bar packed to capacity with drunk horny idiots, but Royce was sweating far more profusely than was warranted. There was a fine tremor in his hands as well.

"Something else went wrong," Dominic said. "Today. That's why you wanted to meet last-minute."

"I . . ." Royce gave him a startled look. "Yes. There have been, ah . . . concerning new developments. But that's all I can say."

"All right." Dominic withdrew a thick stack of bound folders from his messenger bag and pushed them across the table. "I've been conducting exhaustive background checks on all the names you gave me. I'm still working my way down the list, but so far everyone is clean."

"You haven't gone through everyone yet?"

"It's a long list, Mr. Royce."

The pool of potential suspects Royce had provided was divided into two camps: KIG clients who could be involved in insurance fraud, and executives at competing agencies who might be working a corporate sabotage angle. Judging by the sheer number of names, Royce was either extremely paranoid or in deep shit.

When he was sure Royce was done interrupting, Dominic continued. "I haven't found any of the red flags you'd expect to see in cases of fraud or sabotage. No connections to criminal elements. No sudden financial windfalls or unusual excessive spending. No evidence of recent erratic behavior like unexplained absences from work or uncharacteristic anxiety. There was only one thing even slightly out of the ordinary. You had me check out Ethan Deering, the CFO of Aphelion Innovations?"

Royce nodded, his eyes round.

"Two weeks ago, their CEO Rose Nguyen went on an unexpected medical leave for a few days. Deering had to scramble to cover for her at some important client meetings. But she's back at work now, and it's business as usual, so it doesn't seem suspicious."

Royce licked his lips and looked away, avoiding Dominic's gaze. He was gripping the stack of folders so tightly Dominic could see his knuckles whitening even through the gloom of the dark bar.

Now it seemed suspicious.

"What about the local KIG employees?" Royce asked.

Erring on the side of discretion, Dominic pretended he didn't know Royce was changing the subject on purpose. "There haven't been any alerts from the spyware you had us install on their computers—though you may want to consider blocking Facebook. McBride had a technical specialist comb through your system, and he couldn't find any backdoors or other weaknesses an average hacker could exploit. Would you like me to do another technical surveillance countermeasure sweep of your office?"

"Not yet. I got too many questions the first time you did one." Royce dug his phone out of his jacket pocket. "I'm going to email you another name to add to the list—she needs to be prioritized over anyone else you have left."

"Understood."

Patting the folders, Royce said, "I can keep these?"

"Sure. They're just copies of my original research."

"Great, thanks. Keep in touch."

"Mr. Royce—"

Too late. Royce had already scooped up the folders and was hightailing it out of the bar, shouldering his way through the boisterous crowd.

His skin crawling with irritation, Dominic briefly considered following Royce and putting *him* under surveillance for a while, just to get some straight answers for once. The only thing that decided him against it was his concern that his boss would find out. Ever since his gambling had critically endangered an investigation several months ago, he'd been skating on thin ice with her.

He had the gambling compartmentalized now, and he never allowed it to interfere with his work as a PI. But McBride was not renowned for her forgiving nature, so he couldn't risk another slipup.

Heaving a sigh, he slung his messenger bag over his shoulder. He'd had enough of Royce's case for one day; he'd start looking into the new name tomorrow morning. In the meantime, he'd go home and get some dinner, maybe take Rebel out for a run, and play a little online poker.

The blackjack tables at the Railroad Pass had been hot tonight, though. He'd had to tear himself away from a winning streak to make it to this meeting. If he went back, he could keep riding that wave and clean house—

No. No way. He'd just come from spending hours at the casino; he wasn't going to drive all the way *back* out to Henderson at this time of night. It would be too ridiculous.

He *wouldn't*.

Dominic's blaring alarm dragged him out of sleep at six the next morning. He moaned in protest and flailed one arm out, slapping blindly at his phone until it stopped.

He was so groggy his head felt stuffed with cotton. He hadn't gotten home from the Railroad Pass until . . . two a.m.? Three? Most of the night was a blur.

The only thing that stopped him from immediately falling back to sleep was a quiet whine beside the bed. He opened his eyes to find Rebel, his German Shepherd–Rottweiler mix, staring at him from inches away with a sad, soulful gaze.

Guilt crashed through him and twisted his guts into knots. He reached out with one hand to scruff Rebel's ears, leaning forward so she could lick his face.

When he'd supported himself through bounty hunting, he'd brought her on almost every job. She'd been by his side practically twenty-four hours a day for years. But he'd started leaving her home for longer periods of time once he'd gotten an internship at McBride, and these days she spent more time alone or with his next-door neighbors than she did with him.

He had taken her out a few hours ago when he got home, so he knew she didn't have to relieve herself. She was probably just lonely.

God, could he be a more worthless piece of shit?

"You want to go for a run?" he asked. Rebel's enthusiastic tail wag shook her entire body, and he laughed before throwing back the covers. "Okay, let's go."

They drove out to the University of Nevada, Las Vegas to run their usual five-mile route through the campus. As their feet pounded the sidewalk side by side, Dominic used the opportunity to clear his head and refocus on the Royce investigation.

One of the major stumbling blocks that prevented Dominic from working at full efficiency was that he didn't know what kind of insurance fraud Royce's clients might be perpetrating. Royce refused to disclose the nature of their policies.

The clients he'd had Dominic investigate were all high-ranking executives in successful companies with local Vegas offices. The name he'd given Dominic last night, for example, was Cindy Barnes, Director of Administration at a Vegas-based investment firm.

So Dominic could deduce that the policies were corporate in nature. But he'd looked into all those companies, and not one of them showed evidence of recent problems—no thefts, lawsuits, disgruntled employees, or anything of the kind. There was no reason for them to file claims against any corporate insurance policy.

Then again, it might not be insurance fraud at all. Royce seemed convinced that corporate sabotage was an equally likely possibility. The fact that Royce didn't know which problem he was facing made the whole situation even more bewildering.

By the time Dominic and Rebel returned to their apartment building, both of them pleasantly worn out by the hard run, he was no closer to finding a satisfactory answer. He let Rebel off her leash when they entered the chain-link fence surrounding the property. As they walked past the pool at the center of the U-shaped building, they ran into Jasmine Anderson, one of his next-door neighbors and closest friends.

"Hey," he said, bending down to kiss her cheek. "Sorry, I'm all sweaty."

"That's okay." Jasmine had her dozens of multicolored braids bound in a giant bun the way she did when she meant business. She crouched to give Rebel an ear scratch. "I'm just on my way to the final meeting with the wedding DJ."

"Want me to come with?"

"Nah, my mom's meeting me. Thanks though." She straightened back up. "Is everything set for Carlos's bachelor party?"

Like many couples these days, Carlos and Jasmine had decided to have their bachelor and bachelorette parties weeks in advance of the actual wedding. Dominic was determined not to drop the ball as Carlos's best man as badly as he had earlier in their engagement, so when Carlos had confided how it important it was for him to have the quintessential American experience of a classic bachelor party—minus anything skanky—Dominic had pulled out all the stops.

"Yep. We'll start the night with a traditional steak dinner, then a party bike pub crawl of some of Vegas's most outrageous bars, and we'll hook up with you and your girlfriends at Stingray to cap things off. I told all the guys to keep the details secret from Carlos."

"Sounds great. So . . ." Jasmine glanced up at him through her thick eyelashes, chewing on her lip ring. "We thought we heard Levi's voice Saturday night."

Oh, they'd heard Levi, all right. Dominic's bedroom shared a wall with Carlos and Jasmine's, and Levi screamed like a motherfucking banshee during sex.

"He came over, yeah."

"Are you guys getting back together?"

Dominic stiffened. Rebel, who had perked up at the mention of Levi's name, sat at attention and panted happily.

"I don't think so," he said tightly. It had been incredible having Levi in his arms again, watching Levi relax and light up with pleasure, hearing Levi's gasped declarations of love while Dominic surged inside of him and returned them in kind.

But the very next morning they'd had a knock-down, drag-out fight as bad as any that had come before it—a confrontation that ended with Levi throwing a plate at a wall and storming out. The whole thing had been very mature and classy.

Levi would never accept that Dominic could control his gambling; he believed Dominic was too weak. Dominic had to come to terms with that reality sooner or later.

"You know we invited Levi to the wedding," Jasmine said. "He already RSVP'd yes. Is that okay with you?"

"It's fine," said Dominic, pretending the thought of Levi at his best friends' wedding wasn't more painful than the bullet he'd taken in Afghanistan.

"Great. And, um . . . *you're* doing okay, right?"

Dominic's hackles rose further and he scowled at her. He, Jasmine, and Carlos had arrived at an unspoken understanding: he didn't let his gambling affect his relationships with them, and they didn't bring it up. *Ever.*

"Is there a reason I wouldn't be?" he said, his voice pitched low in warning.

She backed off at once. "Nope. Look, I gotta run. See you later?"

"Sure. Have fun."

He watched her walk out to the parking lot, squashing his rising remorse. Feelings of shame and guilt only intensified his urge to gamble, but he was in charge this time. He wouldn't let it control him anymore.

Whistling to Rebel, he headed for the stairs.

CHAPTER 3

The slam of Levi's car door was swallowed up by the vast open space surrounding him. He'd parked along the curb in a suburban housing tract at the very northwestern edge of the Las Vegas Valley. At the end of the street a few blocks north, civilization abruptly gave way to miles of desert and mountains, with a couple of lonely roads meandering off into the distance.

The houses here were Southwestern ranches on large square lots, but one lot on the neighborhood's perimeter was vacant—just an empty expanse of sand and scrub, now swarming with LVMPD personnel. Though this area lay outside the Vegas city limits, the LVMPD was a police department and sheriff's department in one, and therefore responsible for investigating homicides that occurred in unincorporated areas of Clark County as well as the city itself.

This wasn't necessarily a homicide, though; the responding officer had called it in as a suspicious death. That meant it couldn't be the work of the Seven of Spades, which was a huge relief. Levi had been obsessing over the killer's threatening promise for days, trying to anticipate what fresh horrors they had in store, flinching every time his phone rang—

STOP, he thought. He shoved his anxious thoughts aside and concentrated instead on the image of a stop sign, picturing every detail. *Stop it now.*

Thought-stopping was a technique his therapist Alana had taught him. His friend Natasha, also a clinical social worker, had referred him to Alana several months ago to try cognitive behavioral therapy for depression and anger management. It was helping, although it seemed to be a process of two steps forward and one step back.

Travel mug in hand, he started across the street, but he halted when another car pulled up behind his. He gulped some coffee while he waited for Martine to get out. Though they usually drove to crime scenes together, they'd been called to this one so early that they'd come from their respective homes instead of the substation.

"Beautiful day for a homicide," she said as she joined him.

He snorted. It was actually shaping up to be a gorgeous spring day—the sky clear and blue, the air pleasantly cool. Memories of weather like this were what he hung on to during the months Vegas became a suffocating hellscape and he wondered what had possessed him to move to the middle of the desert.

"Have you eaten?" she asked, because it wasn't enough for Levi to have *one* mother constantly badgering him about his lean frame.

"Right before I walk into a crime scene? No." They both knew that wasn't why he'd skipped breakfast, but it made a good excuse.

She took his mug, sipped from it, and pushed it back into his hand with a grimace. "I swear to God your heart runs on pure caffeine. One of these days it's just going to explode."

Ordinarily he would have returned her banter with a snappy comeback, but he didn't have it in him this morning. He shrugged and started across the street.

Catching his elbow, she gave him a closer look and then said, "Shit. Nightmare again?"

"Yeah," he muttered.

For most of his life, he'd been plagued by recurring nightmares about being trapped and helpless while pursued by a relentless, unseen enemy. A few months ago, however, the tone of those dreams had shifted. Now *he* was the hunter stalking the terrified prey, every single time.

Martine and Alana were the only people who knew about the change in his nightmares. He'd never even told Dominic.

"I'm fine," he said, hating the concern he'd put on her face. He wiggled his mug. "Just sleep-deprived. Hence the triple Red Eye."

"Blech," she said—and offered no further judgment or commentary, which was one of the many things he loved about her.

They crossed the street and were approached by a uniformed officer named Daley while they were signing the crime scene log and pulling on gloves and booties. "Morning, Detectives," he said.

"Morning, Daley," said Levi. "You're the responding officer?"

"Yep." He held up the tape so Levi and Martine could duck underneath. "Victim was found about two hours ago by the people living in the house next door. They let their dog out in the morning like usual, and he ran straight for the body. Messed around with it a little before they pulled him off, but he didn't do any physical damage."

Levi followed the direction of Daley's pointing finger to a middle-aged couple at the far edge of the lot, deep in conversation with a pair of uniforms. A Golden Retriever paced around at the end of a leash, looking intrigued by all the activity. "We'll need hair and saliva samples from the dog."

Martine nodded. "I'll interview the witnesses, you check out the body?"

"Sounds good."

She headed off, and Levi followed Daley across the sand.

The victim was a white male in his late forties to early fifties, average height and build, lying on his back. He was dressed casually in a T-shirt, sweatpants, and sneakers, and there were no obvious injuries or immediately apparent cause of death. The only remarkable thing about the body was that his left eye was heavily bandaged.

"Victim's name is Joel Buckner," Daley said. "Aged 51, Summerlin address."

"He had ID on him?"

"Yeah. Wallet was full of cash and credit cards, too."

That ruled out robbery as a motive, and meant the killer wasn't concerned about Buckner's identity being discovered. Assuming, of course, that there was a killer at all.

Levi was leaning toward homicide, though, because Buckner's body had clearly been dumped here. This area was nothing but sand and gritty, dusty soil, but the soles of his sneakers were squeaky clean. In fact, the shoes looked like they'd never been worn before.

"Cell phone?" he asked.

"Not that we've been able to find."

"Thanks." He broke away from Daley and moved closer to the body, kneeling on the opposite side from the coroner investigator, who was hard at work.

After they exchanged pleasantries, she said, "I'd estimate he died within the past twelve hours. It's impossible to determine cause of death without a full autopsy, but I suspect some kind of overdose or poisoning. I'd almost say it could even be natural causes, if not for the location and, well . . ." She pointed to the bandaged eye.

"Yeah, I was going to ask about that. What's going on there?"

She grasped the edge of the bandage, hesitated, and said, "Did you eat breakfast?"

She wasn't asking for the same reason Martine had. "No," he said warily.

"Good idea." She peeled back the thick bandage, revealing an eyeless socket containing nothing but a half-open eyelid that exposed the empty cavity beneath.

"Ugh," Levi said, recoiling. This was far from the worst thing he'd seen in his years as a cop, but there was just something about a hollowed-out eye socket that was deeply repugnant.

"Enucleation." The coroner investigator left the bandage pulled aside. "Total removal of the entire eyeball. Definitely done premortem, but very recent—within the past twenty-four to forty-eight hours, judging by the stage of the healing process."

"Torture?"

"I doubt it. His eye wasn't gouged out; it was surgically removed by someone who knew what they were doing. The wound's been cleaned and bandaged properly too, and there are no signs of infection."

In someone who'd been tortured, Levi would also expect to see signs of a struggle, defensive wounds, and bruises and abrasions from being bound. There was no evidence of that on Buckner—Levi would have to get a closer look underneath the man's clothing, but his bare arms were unmarked. There was just some minor irritation and slight bruising on the back of his right hand.

"Have you seen this?" he asked.

"Yeah. It's almost certainly from an IV line. It could have been used to sedate the victim during the procedure, or to administer pain medication or antibiotics afterward. Or it could have been used to kill him."

This was just getting weirder and weirder. Levi thanked the coroner investigator for her time, stood up, and backed away from the body so he could take in the scene at large.

The choice of dumping ground had been deliberate. This was an isolated spot with no cameras around; it would be easy for a vehicle to drive through and drop a body off undetected.

But it wasn't so isolated that the body wouldn't be quickly discovered. The killer could have dumped Buckner in the adjacent desert; instead, they'd chosen to leave him in this neighborhood with his ID still on him. They'd *wanted* him found, which could have been a message for someone, or even a sign of respect for the deceased or his family.

Why remove someone's eye if you weren't torturing them, though? Levi had never seen mutilation unaccompanied by other signs of rage or hatred toward the victim. What was the point in doing something like this so dispassionately? Organ theft, maybe, but that was unlikely with the rest of the body intact.

The coroner investigator had suggested there was a gap of a day or two between the removal of the eye and Buckner's death, so . . . maybe the threat had been used as leverage against a third party, or against Buckner himself? If someone wanted something from Buckner they weren't getting, slicing out an eye was a good way to prove they weren't fucking around. If that were the case, though, things must have gone sideways for Buckner to end up dead.

One thing was certain—this wasn't a random act of violence. Somebody somewhere had a personal motive for killing Buckner. All Levi had to do was find out who that was.

Hours later, Levi leaned back in his chair at the substation and rubbed his dry eyes. He'd finally made some progress—incremental, but progress nonetheless.

Joel Buckner was the founder and managing partner of Buckner Partners LLC, a Las Vegas–based investment firm with multiple overseas enterprises. He had no criminal history and no known association with any criminal organizations, nor did any members of his immediate family. His company had also never fallen under any suspicion of wrongdoing; Levi had checked with Financial Crimes and the SEC to be sure.

Despite his illustrious position, however, Buckner had been in debt up to his . . . well, eyeball. His firm, while operating within the bounds of law and ethics, was failing. He and his wife were months behind on their mortgage, and all their credit cards were maxed out.

Was it possible Buckner had gotten in too deep with a loan shark? Debt made people desperate, and desperate people made bad decisions. Vegas loan sharks weren't above snatching people up and dishing out pain if they didn't get their money, though Levi had never heard of one putting a guy's eye out. In fact, he'd never seen this brand of mutilation in the Valley before. It also seemed unlikely that a loan shark would kill a man who could now never pay them back.

One step at a time. As much as Levi hated dealing with the arrogant pricks in Organized Crime, they'd be more up-to-date with the rumblings among the local loan sharks. He heaved a sigh and reached for his desk phone.

His cell phone rang, giving him a good excuse to put off the unpalatable call for another few minutes. Seeing Martine's name on the screen, he said, "How's it going over there?"

Martine had spent the morning with Buckner's family, breaking the news of his death and then interviewing them one by one. "They're giving me nothing," she said, her voice thrumming with frustration. "Stonewalling me at every turn. It's obvious they're hiding something."

"Really?" he said, his curiosity piqued. "Like what?"

"I'm not sure. When I told them Buckner was dead, they seemed genuinely devastated, but . . . I don't know. It's like they already knew what I was going to say. They weren't surprised at all."

"You think they were involved?"

"Hmm . . ." Martine was a good detective, and she wouldn't dismiss a theory out of hand no matter how implausible it seemed. "I doubt it. The kids are nine and seven, and they reacted the same way their mom did. I can't imagine her pulling them into a plot to kill their dad."

Levi agreed. He told Martine about Buckner's debts, and she made a soft sound of surprise.

"Before I called you, I checked in with the kids' school. They've been out for three days. Mom told the school they have the flu, but I didn't see any evidence of that."

"Well, we know from the gap between Buckner's death and his eye being removed that whoever killed him had him for at least twenty-four hours, maybe more." Levi gazed blankly into space, his fingers tapping his desk. "His family had to have known he was gone, and maybe they also know why. If they know who killed him, they may be too afraid of retaliation to say anything."

"Could explain their jumpy behavior. Look, I'm not gonna get anything more out of these people today. I'll head over to Buckner's company and talk to his colleagues, see if they know anything helpful. If I push them on his debts, maybe something will pop up."

"Good thinking. I'm about to check in with OC about the loan shark angle. I'll let you know what I find."

They ended their call just in time for Levi to hear a voice say, "This is Detective Abrams right here."

He looked up. A uniformed officer was approaching his desk, escorting a young, casually dressed Asian woman with a visitor's badge pinned to her hoodie. Her long black hair was styled in a way that concealed the entire left side of her face; it was so clearly deliberate that Levi assumed it was an attempt to hide some kind of scarring.

The officer nodded to Levi and went on his way. "I'm Detective Abrams," Levi said, getting to his feet and extending his hand. "You needed to see me?"

"Yes. Rose Nguyen." She shook his hand briskly. "I'm sorry to just show up like this, but I didn't know how else to contact you."

Martine's desk adjoined Levi's so the two were facing each other. Since she wasn't here, Levi stole her chair and wheeled it around to the side for Nguyen. He gestured for her to take a seat, and sat down as well.

"How can I help you?" he asked, bracing himself. If Nguyen had come here looking for him by name, it had to be related to the Seven of Spades.

Which brand of nutjob would it be this time? Conspiracy theorist convinced that her boyfriend/coworker/neighbor was the Seven of Spades? Serial killer groupie hoping to learn more by pretending to have helpful information? Angry citizen who held Levi personally responsible for the Seven of Spades's continued rampage?

"I just read about Joel Buckner's death online," Nguyen said. "A blogger with a contact in the coroner's office leaked the details."

Wait. What? Levi gave his head a slight shake to clear it. "Did you know Mr. Buckner?"

"Not at all, but I think I may know what happened to him."

"How?" Levi said, nonplussed.

She shifted her hair aside, displaying an unscarred face and a bandaged left eye. "Because the same thing happened to me."

CHAPTER 4

"**C**an I get you anything?" Levi asked as he shut the door to the more comfortable—and private—interview room adjacent to the bullpen. "Water, coffee?"

"No, thanks," said Nguyen, who had settled onto the same overstuffed couch that had graced this room since the early 1990s.

Levi sat across from her, pulling out a notepad and pen. "Why don't you start at the beginning?"

"It happened almost a month ago, on February 20th," she said. "I was the last one at the office, like usual, and I left work pretty late. On my way home, I got funneled into some kind of detour for road work. I ended up on this little side street. There was a stretch where huge construction equipment was parked on either side, and as soon as my car was between those machines, large black SUVs pulled up in front of and behind me and boxed me in."

A standard kidnapping technique, though one requiring strategy and precision. He nodded for her to continue.

"Masked men jumped out of the SUVs, dragged me from my car, and injected me with something that knocked me unconscious. It all happened so fast I didn't even have time to process it. When I woke up, I was blindfolded and tied to a bed." She stopped to take an unsteady breath.

"Were you harmed in any way besides your eye?" Levi asked as gently as he could.

"No. I mean, I was terrified that they were going to . . . well, I'm sure you have an idea. But once they'd taken me, they barely touched me. They mostly left me alone, and when they did talk to me, they were . . . polite. Businesslike, I'd say."

Professionals, then, with no stake in Nguyen beyond their payday.

"As soon as I was awake, they told me I was being held for ransom and would be safely released once it was paid," she went on. "Then they removed the restraints and let me have free rein of the room I was locked in."

Levi frowned. Kidnapping an adult and holding them without torture or sexual assault for a straightforward ransom? While that was an everyday occurrence in some parts of the world, it was unusual in the United States. "Did you take off the blindfold?"

"I couldn't. It was locked somehow; if I had to guess, I'd say it was some kind of fetish gear." She cracked her neck from side to side and said, "You know, I think I will take a water, please."

He got up to fetch a bottle of water from the fridge in the corner. She took a few shallow sips before soldiering on.

"I've had kidnapping safety training, so I knew to stay calm and follow directions. But I also did what I could to learn the layout of the room and listen at the door as much as possible. So I heard right away when they found out my company had refused to negotiate."

"Your company?"

"Aphelion Innovations. We're still pretty small, but we recently signed a huge contract with the Department of Defense. I'm the CEO and chief engineer. The kidnappers went straight to my board of directors for the ransom."

"But they refused to pay?"

"Yeah. I found out later they thought it was a hoax and cut off all contact with the kidnappers. After that, I heard a lot of tense whispering and discussion through the door, but I couldn't make out most of it. Then the kidnappers got a phone call. A few minutes later, they came into my room and told me they needed to sedate me. I was afraid they'd do something worse if I refused, so I cooperated. They injected something in my arm, and when I regained consciousness..." She swallowed hard, her breathing speeding up. "My... my eye was gone. I guess they wanted to send a message that couldn't be ignored."

She sucked in a shuddering breath, and tears trickled from her remaining eye. Levi handed her a box of tissues and waited quietly while she collected herself.

He knew what it was like to be victimized—not just the pain and fear, but the *shame*, the deep sense of helplessness and all the bitter self-blame that accompanied it. Those things left behind a gritty slime that couldn't be scrubbed away by other people's platitudes, no matter how many times they said, *It's not your fault* or *There's nothing you could have done.*

Words like that had never helped Levi, so he didn't say them now.

Eventually, her tears stopped and she seemed calmer. "Sorry about that."

"No need to apologize. It was brave for you to come here and tell me this at all."

She smiled faintly, balling the tissues in her fist.

"Could you tell me about what happened after . . ." He gestured vaguely toward her eye.

"After they took my eye, they kept me drugged, so the rest of it is a blur. I know they gave me pain meds, and the doctors I saw later said they must have given me antibiotics too." She shredded the tissues as she spoke, fluffy white bits raining onto the couch. "About a day later, they told me the ransom had been paid and they were taking me back to the city, but they'd come back for me if anyone reported the kidnapping to the police. They knocked me out again. This time, I woke up in a wheelchair outside an emergency room."

Levi leaned forward. "Did the kidnappers use those words exactly? That they were taking you 'back to the city'?"

"Um . . ." She gave it some thought before nodding. "Yeah, that's what they said verbatim. I remember because I was so relieved."

Meaning the kidnappers had held Nguyen *outside* the city. They would have wanted to stay close, though, to make for easier transport and communication. Levi's mind flashed back to the desert roads ribboning through the sand near Buckner's dump site.

"You mentioned you've had kidnapping safety training. Is that because of your company's contract with the DoD?"

"No, actually. Aphelion has always done a lot of work improving information systems infrastructure in developing nations. Places where kidnap for ransom is a genuine industry—Central America, certain areas in Asia and the Middle East. Once the company started making a name for itself, the board insisted I go through the training just in case. And as I found out later, it's why they bought a kidnap-and-ransom policy for me."

He lifted his head from his notes. "A what?"

"An insurance policy against kidnap and ransom," she said. "You don't hear about them a lot, but they exist. And thank God they do, or this ransom would have bankrupted my company. I obsessed over that the whole time those men had me. At least it was a relief to find out we'd still be solvent."

Trying to wrap his brain around this new information, Levi said, "So you didn't know your board had purchased this policy for you until after the kidnapping?"

She shrugged. "They couldn't tell me. Apparently, it's a precondition of the policy that the subject doesn't know it exists—at least, that's how it is at KIG. Something about preventing insurance fraud."

"How does it work?"

"When the policyholders receive a ransom demand, KIG sends out a professional crisis response team so law enforcement doesn't have to get involved. After the exchange is made, they reimburse you for everything—not just the ransom, but time lost from work, even medical care." Nguyen brushed a self-conscious hand against her bandages. "They're paying for me to get a prosthetic eye. So far I've had an ocular implant put in, and once it's had a few months to heal, they can fit me for the actual prosthesis."

Levi jotted down notes in shorthand, his mind racing. He could see the need for measures like this in other countries, but he'd bet money the insurance company had never expected this policy to be activated on US soil.

"You said your policy was through KIG—that's Kensington Insurance Group, right?"

She nodded. He scribbled down the name and underlined it several times.

"If the kidnappers threatened you to keep you from going to the police, why did you decide to come forward?" he asked.

"I didn't know they'd done this to anyone else, but then I found out they killed one of their victims. That means something went wrong, right?" She spread her hands. "Who knows what else they might do, how many other people they might hurt? I can't have that on my conscience."

Levi admired her courage even more now. "We can set up a protective detail for you, just in case."

She gratefully agreed, and after that, he walked her through her story again, probing for more detail. Nguyen believed she'd been kidnapped by a team of five or six men. She'd never seen their faces and they hadn't used names, but she was sure she'd recognize their voices if she heard them again. From what she'd learned through eavesdropping, the men had been receiving instructions via phone from someone who wasn't present.

Because she'd been unconscious both times she'd been transported, she had no idea where she'd been held. However, she had noticed a distinct lack of ambient noise in the environment— no traffic, neighbors, or anything beyond the sounds of the men in the next room and a constant rumbling she was sure was a generator. There had been no running water, so her captors had provided her with bottled water to drink and bathe with.

Once Levi was satisfied he had everything, he got Nguyen's contact information and gave her his card. As they stood, one last question occurred to him. "What exactly did the kidnappers do with your eye?"

She was quiet for a moment, then said, "They sent it to the chairman of the board."

That was more or less what he'd expected. He thanked her again, then set her up with an administrator to arrange the protective detail before he returned to his desk in the bullpen.

Staring at his notes, he mulled over the implications of Nguyen's story. Professional mercenary teams kidnapping adults for a simple ransom just didn't *happen* in America. Then again, he never would have known about Nguyen's experience if she hadn't come forward, so maybe it did happen and law enforcement agencies were just never consulted.

Either way, it was no coincidence that the kidnappers had chosen a victim with this type of insurance policy.

He grabbed his phone and texted Martine. *Ask Buckner's colleagues if he had a kidnap-and-ransom policy with KIG.*

While he waited for her to respond, he researched the insurance company. Turned out they had a local office right in Summerlin, an upscale suburb west of the Strip.

She texted back ten minutes later. *He did, and you would have thought I shot my gun off in here by the way they reacted. WTF? What's going on?*

Satisfaction bloomed in Levi's chest. *Meet me at KIG's Summerlin office. I'll call you on the way.*

"This is a weird one," Martine said when she and Levi met in KIG's parking lot.

He nodded without comment. They'd been on the phone most of the drive, filling each other in on their respective aspects of the investigation.

Just like Buckner's family, his colleagues had rebuffed Martine at first; only when she brought up the insurance policy had their resistance cracked. The policyholder—Cindy Barnes, the company's director of Administration—had confessed that their failing company had been unable to come up with the funds to pay the ransom demanded by Buckner's kidnappers. She had then directed Martine to a man at KIG named Nathan Royce and refused to answer any further questions.

They hadn't called ahead. Levi wanted to take Royce by surprise.

The excitement of the hunt had Levi's blood up, the thrill of a strong lead keeping him focused and energized. Though the Seven of Spades case had shaken his confidence, dimmed his enthusiasm for a job he'd once loved, it was times like this that he remembered why he enjoyed being a detective.

So he was feeling pretty good, right up to the point where he and Martine walked into KIG's reception area and saw Dominic standing at the front desk.

CHAPTER 5 ♠

While waiting impatiently for the receptionist to let Royce know he was here, Dominic kept his body angled so he could see the front door in his peripheral vision. It wasn't a conscious decision so much as a reflex, the need to keep an exit in sight at all times left over from his days with the Army Rangers.

When Levi and Martine walked in, there was a moment when Dominic genuinely thought he was hallucinating.

He turned around to stare. Levi and Martine stopped short and stared back.

Christ, every atom in Dominic's body and soul longed to be closer to Levi. It took all his willpower not to sway forward.

He ran hungry eyes over Levi's familiar form, lean and wiry and wound tight with unceasing tension. Levi's cheekbones were so incredibly sharp that they gave his face a striking, hollow-cheeked look Dominic had always found fascinating. After they'd broken up, Levi had cut his curly black hair short again—which had been pure spite, done only because he knew how much Dominic liked it longer. A jagged scar sliced diagonally across his forehead, courtesy of the trip he'd taken through a window at Volkov's compound in November.

Dominic knew from covert conversations with Martine that Levi was in therapy, but he wasn't sure it was helping. The dark circles under Levi's eyes, the way his ribs and hip bones had pushed against his skin when Dominic had seen him undressed on Saturday night, made it clear he wasn't taking care of himself—not eating enough, not sleeping right—

"What are you doing here?" Levi snapped. His gray eyes were frosty with disdain.

Immediately on the defensive, Dominic said, "That's privileged information. What are *you* two doing here?"

"None of your business."

"No? Let me tell you, then. You guys caught the Buckner homicide."

Levi stepped closer. Unable to back down from a challenge, Dominic met the advance with one of his own.

"That was reported as a suspicious death, not a homicide," Levi said.

Dominic rolled his eyes. "Come on. Guy's been missing since Tuesday, turns up dead with an eye removed? Someone killed him."

A hint of surprise crossed Levi's face before melting into a smirk. "And why would you know any of this unless you were here for the exact same reason?"

On Wednesday, it had taken Dominic about two minutes to realize there was something very wrong at Buckner Partners LLC. After spending the morning doing his usual thorough background research on Cindy Barnes, he'd gone to the office in person to gather surveillance. He'd found the place in total chaos, like a wasp nest split open with a baseball bat.

Out of pure curiosity, he'd gone inside and asked to speak with Barnes, just to see what would happen. The harried receptionist had shut him down at once, not even checking his story about having an appointment before having him escorted out. While he was inside, he'd overheard enough to know there was some kind of emergency with the company's managing partner.

Joel Buckner wasn't the name Royce had given him, but Dominic couldn't resist the lure of a hot lead. He'd gone to Buckner's house next and found it in a similar state—kids home from school, grandparents over, strangers rushing in and out looking furtive and anxious.

The next two days had been spent splitting his time between staking out Buckner's home and office. He'd quickly figured out that Buckner was missing, though because he hadn't planted any listening devices, he didn't know why. But after using the time to do more research and discovering Buckner's dilemma—deeply in debt, company floundering at the brink of financial ruin—his best guess had been that Buckner had absconded with what remained of the company funds and left a huge mess behind.

Then he'd remembered Rose Nguyen's unexpected medical leave. He'd taken another look at the other three client companies Royce had told him about, and finally spotted the pattern: at all five companies, the top-ranking executives had recently been absent without explanation for a few days. But all of those executives were back at work now, and besides, they weren't the people Royce had asked him to investigate. Their colleagues were.

McBride had called him in to assist with another case this morning, but he'd set up a Google alert for Buckner's name. When the man's odd death had been leaked, he'd decided enough was enough. He'd come straight to KIG to confront Royce and demand the truth.

Levi intruded farther into Dominic's personal space. "Or are you just following me around?" he asked with a taunting note in his voice. "Flattering, but I already have one creepy stalker, thanks."

There were only inches between their bodies now. Dominic wanted to grab Levi and shake him, pull him close, kiss the ever-loving fuck out of him until he stopped being such a goddamn *bastard*—

"All right, guys, put your dicks away." Martine stepped between them and pushed them apart, unperturbed by the fact that she was half a foot shorter than Levi and over a full foot shorter than Dominic. "Let's remember we're in a public forum."

Scowling at each other, Dominic and Levi reluctantly separated.

The receptionist at the front desk cleared her throat, and they all turned around to find her watching them with wide eyes. "I'm sorry, Mr. Russo, but Mr. Royce is unavailable all day. I can schedule you an appointment for next week—"

Before Dominic could come up with a professional way to tell her to get that sketchy little weasel out here or else, Levi flashed his badge.

"Why don't you tell Mr. Royce there are two homicide detectives from the LVMPD waiting to speak to him, and we'd be just as happy to do that at the station if he prefers."

The receptionist paled and nodded, reaching for her phone again. Lust swooped low in Dominic's belly as he watched Levi all steely and authoritative, something that never failed to get him going. He wanted to drop to his knees and worship Levi's cock before bending him right over that desk and nailing him hard until he screamed in ecstasy.

Levi glanced sideways at Dominic, who didn't bother hiding the desire he knew was plain as day on his face. Instead of responding with irritation, Levi hastily looked away with a flush on his cheeks. A quiet growl crawled up the back of Dominic's throat.

Royce chose that moment to hurry out from the back office, his eyes bloodshot and his cheeks dusted with stubble. "I'm sorry, Detectives, but—" He faltered as he caught sight of Levi and blinked rapidly. "Oh my God, you're Levi Abrams."

Thanks to the Seven of Spades case and a viral YouTube video, Levi was a notorious public figure these days, easily recognized by most of the city's residents—despite the fact that he flatly refused to be interviewed or provide official statements of any kind.

Levi inclined his head. "I am, and this is my partner, Detective Valcourt. We need to speak with you regarding a recent homicide."

"Ah . . . now isn't a good time."

"I'm not surprised," said Levi. "Tell me, how many claims against hefty kidnap-and-ransom insurance policies have been filed against your company recently?"

Royce's jaw dropped.

"'Kidnap and ransom'?" Dominic said, and then groaned as the last elusive piece of the puzzle clicked into place.

"I don't know what you mean," Royce said.

Levi wasn't having that. "Sure you do. How many kidnappings have there been, Mr. Royce? I know of at least two, but I have a hunch there were more. How many?"

"Five." Dominic glared at Royce. "There've been five."

Royce's eyes flicked between Dominic and Levi, then traveled to Martine as if in appeal. She arched one eloquent eyebrow.

Shoulders slumping, Royce said, "Maybe you should come on back."

"You don't understand," Royce said as they settled around an oval table in a cushy conference room. "These policies were intended to protect executives and high-net-worth individuals while traveling through dangerous areas where kidnappings are an everyday occurrence. We never expected our beneficiaries to need them in the United States."

"But nothing in the policy language prevents that?" Martine said.

"No."

Dominic's chair was too small for his frame; he shifted around, trying to get comfortable. Levi had attempted to prevent him from attending this meeting at all, but Royce—seeming to sense that Dominic could be used as a buffer—had insisted he be included.

"When was the first kidnapping?" Levi asked.

"January 31st—about six weeks ago. Hamza Nadir doesn't live in Nevada, but he visits Vegas often on business. He was snatched on his way from the airport to his hotel, the ransom demand was sent to his company's director of Risk Management a couple hours later, and they contacted us. We were surprised something like this would happen here, but we did everything we would in another country: sent out the crisis team, facilitated the ransom exchange, got Mr. Nadir back unharmed without needing to call the police. We thought it was an isolated incident."

"But it wasn't." Dominic was having trouble wrapping his head around this—a kidnap-for-ransom ring in the Las Vegas Valley?

"No." Royce rubbed a hand over his face. "Joanna Shaffer was kidnapped a little over a week later in exactly the same way, which is just . . . impossible."

Levi frowned. "Why?"

"The content of our K&R policies is some of our most highly protected information. Even the subjects of the policies don't know they exist. But we had two taken within a week and a half in the same area, and not only did the kidnappers know who to target, they knew who to contact with the ransom demands. They never even bothered with the victims' families. They went straight to the people who'd purchased the policies to begin with. There's no way they could know that information unless they'd accessed the policies somehow."

Martine jotted that down, then said, "When did you hire Mr. Russo?"

"After the third kidnapping. Rose Nguyen. It—it went wrong. Her company refused to negotiate at first, and . . ."

"The kidnappers cut out her eye and sent it to the chairman of the board," Levi said coldly.

Dominic made an involuntary noise of disgust. Royce hunched his shoulders, looking down at his hands.

Levi turned to Dominic. "You said five victims. Buckner must have been the fifth, so who was the fourth?"

"Walter Randolph. He's back at work now and he definitely has both eyes, so everything must have gone smoothly with that one."

Royce confirmed that with a nod.

"You seriously think this is insurance fraud?" Dominic asked him. He'd seen some crazy fraud scams in his time, but this would mean the victims' trusted colleagues had betrayed them. The victims couldn't be in on it, not when one kidnapping had ended in mutilation and another in murder.

"It can't be a coincidence!" Royce exclaimed. "Look, after Ms. Nguyen's kidnapping, my superiors took notice of how many large claims had been filed so quickly and demanded an explanation. Either the policyholders conspired with each other to kidnap their policies' subjects, or a competing agency got a hold of our client information and is sabotaging us by overloading us with enormous claims. What else could it be?"

"KIG is a national agency with hundreds of offices all over the country," Levi said. "But you—you're the director of Management Liability Insurance for the entire company, right? Meaning you're directly responsible for the K&R policies."

"Yes . . ."

"And you hold those policies on people throughout the United States?"

"Of course."

"But the only ones who were kidnapped were living in or visiting the Vegas area—where you, the one person who *definitely* has access to the policy information, quite conveniently has his home office?" Levi leaned back. "That's a little suspicious, don't you think?"

Royce blanched, then drew himself up with air of flustered self-righteousness. "I don't know what you're implying—"

A knock sounded on the door, and it opened to admit a stunning young woman who could have walked straight off a Hollywood red carpet—Juliette Dubois, Royce's executive assistant. Dominic had met her twice before in his previous visits to the office.

"Sorry to interrupt," she said. "I have your coffee here, Mr. Royce."

She tossed her lustrous bronze hair behind one shoulder and sauntered over to set a mug by Royce's hand. His entire demeanor softened as he watched her like she was the only person in the room.

"Can I get your guests anything?" she asked, scanning the table with perceptive eyes. "Coffee, water?"

Royce brushed his hand against her arm. "We're fine, Juliette, thank you."

She graced him with a dazzling smile and stepped out, quietly shutting the door. Already rolling his eyes, Dominic looked to see if Levi and Martine had arrived at the same conclusion he'd drawn the very first time he'd observed Royce and Juliette interact. He wasn't disappointed.

"You're pretty sanctimonious for a guy having an affair with his assistant," Levi said.

"*What*?" Royce blinked rapidly, fiddling with his wedding ring as if by reflex. "I—I'm not— You don't— How *dare*—"

He took in their expressions, seemed to remember he was facing two experienced detectives and a private investigator, and gave up.

"It's not what you think. My wife and I aren't monogamous. We just . . . keep things discreet." With a frustrated grunt, he waved both hands. "But that's neither here nor there. I would *never* have any part in these terrible crimes. And even if I were that kind of person— which I'm not—it would make no sense for me to sabotage my own company. My job's on the line."

Levi only smiled. Dominic knew what he was thinking. The payout from five huge ransoms could be more than worth a lost job—especially if Royce was considering riding off into the sunset with his beautiful young girlfriend.

"Mr. Royce," Martine said, "once you realized that subjects of your K&R policies were being targeted, why didn't you warn them?"

"*Warn* them?" He looked honestly shocked by the suggestion. "I can't do that. It would void the policies."

The room went silent as they all stared at him.

Dominic was the first to speak. "Are you serious?"

"Very serious. The K&R language explicitly states that the subject cannot know of the policy's existence, or it's immediately voided. Even if we only alerted the policyholders to the threat, they would tell the subjects—it's human nature. It would look like KIG was trying to deliberately sabotage the policies to avoid claims. We'd be opening ourselves up to huge lawsuits."

His voice thrumming with poorly controlled rage, Levi said, "So you're willing to put God knows how many people at risk of kidnapping, mutilation, and *murder* just to protect your company's bottom line?"

Martine put a hand on his arm. He took a deep breath but didn't appear to get any calmer.

Royce had shrunk back in his seat. "No, I . . . It's not like I did *nothing*. This is why I hired a private investigator. To fix things quietly behind the scenes without anyone needing to know."

"Except you didn't tell me the full story," said Dominic. His own anger was mounting quickly. "If I'd known the truth from the beginning, I may have been able to stop this. Joel Buckner might still be alive."

"Why *isn't* he alive?" Martine asked. "Ms. Barnes told me they couldn't pay the ransom. Why would that matter if they had insurance?"

"Um . . ." Royce wrung his hands, his gaze darting everywhere around the room except their faces. "Mr. Buckner's company has been struggling financially for some time, and the premiums for kidnap-and-ransom insurance are quite expensive. At the time of his kidnapping, his policyholder had missed several payments, and his company couldn't put together the money to cover those overdue premiums. You have to understand, we can't honor a lapsed policy."

This new deathly silence was even worse than the one before. The only sound Dominic could hear was Levi's labored breathing. He'd seen Levi like this before—unmoving except for a fine tremor of rage, eyes fixed unblinking on the target of his wrath—and it always meant Levi was about to explode.

Martine was as dumbfounded as Dominic had ever seen her. "So you knew Buckner would die and did nothing to help?"

"That's not how insurance works—"

Levi shot to his feet and slammed both hands on the table so hard the entire thing rattled. "You piece of shit."

"Levi!" Dominic and Martine said at the same time, though in different tones—Dominic astonished, Martine stern.

Levi's nostrils flared as he reined himself in, though he didn't sit down. Martine shot him a worried glance, then turned to Royce and said, "Why don't you give us a list of your K&R policyholders, and we'll warn them ourselves? It'll still void the policies, but it should remove the question of liability on KIG's part."

"That's proprietary information," Royce said, displaying his first sign of backbone despite the wary way he was eyeing Levi. "I'm not authorized to share those names."

"Right," Dominic said with a snort. "And I'm sure the millions of dollars in annual premiums you'd be losing has nothing to do with your decision."

Royce clenched his jaw.

"You . . ." Levi stopped and swallowed harshly. When he spoke again, his voice was unsteady with the effort of curbing his anger. "Let me be clear. This is now an official homicide investigation. If you insist on a court order, we can get one, but if anyone else is taken while we're waiting, that'll be on you."

Guilt flashed across Royce's face, but he said nothing.

"In the meantime, if you're not going to help us, stay the fuck out of our way." Levi arched an eyebrow at Dominic. "That means amateur hour is over."

Dominic had been on board with Levi's tirade until that point. "Whoa, hey! You have no right to tell a private citizen he can't hire an independent investigator, as long as I don't obstruct law enforcement."

"You can't walk down a sidewalk without obstructing it," Levi retorted.

Dominic opened his mouth but could only splutter indignantly.

"Do you two know each other?" Royce asked.

Martine stood as well, put a hand on Levi's back, and said, "It's time for you to step outside."

Levi walked out of the conference room without another word.

Because Martine had turned away from Royce to watch Levi go, Dominic was the only one who saw the shattering exhaustion that seized her. By the time she returned her attention to Royce, her expression was as professionally neutral as ever.

"He's right, you know. We will get a court order for those names, and if you do anything to hinder our investigation, I have no problem charging you with obstruction." She passed him her business card. "This is all going to come out sooner or later. It might be best for you and your company to get out ahead of it. We'll be in touch."

She squeezed Dominic's shoulder on her way out. Royce gave Dominic a helpless look, and Dominic scowled back.

"Stay here," he said. "You and I aren't finished."

Leaving Royce alone in the conference room, Dominic dug in his messenger bag as he pursued Levi and Martine. He caught up with them in the parking lot right outside the office.

"Levi!"

When Levi turned, Dominic tossed him his phone charger. Levi caught it, stared at it blankly for a second, and then went absolutely *incandescent* with fury.

The aggrieved glare Martine sent Dominic could have drawn blood, but he barely noticed. He only had eyes for Levi.

Sure, it was petty, but Dominic couldn't bear for Levi to walk away without acknowledging him. Even Levi's anger was preferable to his indifference.

Levi didn't shout, though it seemed to be causing him a significant amount of strain. "Have you just been carrying this around with you?"

"I knew we'd run into each other eventually."

Levi flung the charger at Dominic's face; he just managed to catch it in time.

"I already bought a new one," Levi said.

"Must be nice to just write off a perfectly good charger and buy a new one without a care in the world," Dominic shot back. "Some of us can't be so casual about how we spend our money. Maybe you'd like to reimburse me for the taillight you smashed on my truck?"

"You did *what*?" Martine said.

Levi gave Dominic a smile that was pure malice. Dominic's breath stumbled and his cock stirred.

The thing was, Dominic had always loved Levi's hard edges, his acid tongue, his ruthless streak. Underneath all that prickly sarcasm lay an achingly compassionate heart—a man who was unflinchingly loyal and fiercely protective. Dominic had enjoyed peeling away all those layers, had relished the knowledge that he was one of the few people in the world Levi trusted enough to be vulnerable with.

Except . . . Dominic had violated that trust. In an effort to hide his relapse, he'd hurt Levi on purpose, and more than once. Levi didn't trust him anymore.

Remembering that was as good as a slap in the face. Dominic faltered and took a shuffling step back.

Levi watched Dominic for a second, his vicious smirk slipping away. "I'll pay for the taillight," he said quietly, before he turned on his heel and headed for his car.

Dominic stared after him, his tongue heavy with all the things he wanted to say but couldn't.

Martine dropped her eyes to the charger in his hand, then lifted them to his face. "Really?"

Suddenly embarrassed, he stuffed the charger back into his bag. "You told me Levi's therapy was helping, but his anger is still totally out of control."

She shrugged. "A few weeks ago, I would have had to physically stop him from flipping the table in there. It's progress. Incremental, but better than nothing." She gave him a pointed look and added, "At least he had the balls to admit he needed help and ask for it."

The familiar cascade of shame-anger-defensiveness rippled through Dominic like toppled dominoes. Levi had told Martine about the gambling—which Dominic didn't resent, because there had been no other way for Levi to explain their breakup to his closest friend—but Dominic wouldn't tolerate her throwing it in his face.

"I'm fine," he said, his voice tight. "Levi just can't accept that I'm competent enough to handle myself. I have everything under control."

"You know, back in Brooklyn, I had an uncle with an alcohol problem. He used to say the same thing—that he had everything under control. Every time he started drinking again, he'd repeat that mantra over and over, right up until his esophageal varices ruptured and he died of internal bleeding at the age of fifty-two."

Dominic briefly closed his eyes.

"If you gave Levi the smallest sign you were willing to get help, tossed him the tiniest bread crumb, he would have your back in seconds and you know it," she said. "But you can't expect him to keep bashing his head against the same brick wall. It's not fair. Loving someone doesn't mean you have to let them treat you like shit, no matter what they're going through."

A muscle jumped in Dominic's jaw; he couldn't bring himself to speak. Martine sighed.

"Take care of yourself, Dom," she said, and walked away.

"It's not him," was the first thing Martine said when they settled at their adjoining desks in the substation bullpen.

"It *is* him, Martine," Levi said tiredly. "It's just the worst parts of him. And it's not like I don't understand. When my anger runs away with me and I say or do things I shouldn't, that's still me. An alien doesn't take over my body and force me to be an asshole."

"He—"

"I don't want to talk about it," Levi said, then softened his request with a smile. "Please."

Martine let it go, and they got to work.

At least Levi had an interesting case to distract himself with. While their official mandate was to solve Buckner's homicide, that would require investigating all five kidnappings. He and Martine would need to interview all the victims and their families, friends, and coworkers, searching for commonalities and discrepancies between everyone's stories so they could create a timeline of the kidnappings and establish the perpetrators' MO.

Then they'd need to obtain traffic camera footage for every area the victims had been taken from and returned, plus GPS data from the victims' cell phones and cars—though the kidnappers had returned Nguyen's car to her home with her phone on the dashboard, so he didn't anticipate that the latter would be very helpful. It would also be a good idea to reach out to their criminal contacts; a mercenary kidnapping ring couldn't have moved into the Valley without causing some kind of ripple effect.

Finally, Levi was going to make it his personal mission to not only get his hands on the names of KIG's policyholders, but to thoroughly investigate Nathan Royce. For one thing, the guy was shady as hell, but Levi could admit his determination was born from spite as much as anything else.

Royce was a selfish coward who had put his job above innocent people's lives. Levi was going to make him regret that.

Levi worked late into the night, hours after Martine had left, though he didn't begrudge her departure—after all, she had a husband and two daughters to go home to. There was nobody waiting for Levi, not even a pet.

Tomorrow was Saturday, and Levi planned to continue working the new case even though it was his day off. Martine had agreed to meet up with him after her daughter's softball game. However, that plan was derailed by the message waiting for him when he got out of the shower on Saturday morning:

The Seven of Spades had struck again.

Levi paced the lobby of Caesars Palace while he waited for Martine, ignoring the sideways looks from the tourists who gave him a wide berth as they walked past. There was no guarantee that this murder was connected to the "gift" the Seven of Spades had promised him, but a sick pit in his stomach assured him that it was.

Everything the Seven of Spades did was meticulously planned down to the tiniest detail. They had left him that birthday card to fuck with his head, and the timing of their next murder wasn't an accident—it had been long enough for Levi to stew in anxious anticipation of the possibilities, but not long enough to take the edge off his apprehension. This was sure to be the next stage in their scheme.

"It just *had* to be a Saturday, didn't it?" Martine groused when she showed up. "Simone's so pissed I'm missing another game."

"At least Antoine will be there."

"Yeah, but I'm getting pretty sick of having to tell my girls I can't show up to support them because a serial killer is rampaging around the city slitting throats left and right."

As they proceeded to the elevator, Levi said, "Why here? The Seven of Spades doesn't kill tourists."

"Maybe it's an employee."

They rode up to the twentieth floor and entered one of the hotel's lavish three-bedroom suites. Levi wrinkled his nose in distaste as he glanced around—this entire place was a garish, over-the-top Roman Empire fantasy extravaganza. It looked like a cheesy porn set.

No sooner had they stepped inside than they were greeted by Jonah Gibbs, a stout, ruddy-faced officer with a volatile temper—though Levi was giving him a run for his money these days.

"Hey, Detectives. I gotta say, this is a bizarre one, even for the Seven of Spades."

Levi and Martine followed Gibbs through the main room of the suite. There were busy people crowding the large space—uniformed officers, CSIs, the crime scene photographer—but there were also six civilians who Levi noticed right away. They were all men, ethnically diverse but in the same age group—early thirties, like Levi himself.

Most appeared to be in shock, motionless and glassy-eyed, but one man was crying and another was shouting angrily into his cell phone by the window, almost incoherent in his grief.

"Bachelor party weekend," Gibbs said, gesturing to the men. "Their buddy won some kind of all-expenses-paid getaway. Bet they're wishing they'd stayed home now."

"*Gibbs*," Martine said sharply, impatient as always with his lack of tact.

They entered the master bedroom, and for Levi, time screeched to a halt.

A white man was zip-tied to a chair, his throat slit in a gaping arc. His mouth was duct-taped shut, and the playing card was stuck horizontally to the tape right over his lips. An enormous red ribbon had been wrapped around his chest and tied into a giant bow like he'd been gift-wrapped. Half a dozen gaily patterned balloons were attached to the back and arms of the chair, all bearing the slogan *HAPPY BIRTHDAY!* along with smiley faces and colorful stars.

But Levi's brain only cataloged those details on autopilot, because the rest of him was paralyzed. Every movement in the room seemed to happen in slow motion, every sound around him a prolonged, distant echo.

"Meet the groom-to-be," said Gibbs. "His friends found him like this when they woke up. Poor bastards."

Time came unstuck. Levi reeled backward, stumbled, and crashed into the wall hard enough to rattle a nearby painting. He hadn't breathed for at least ten seconds, so when he finally sucked in air, his loud gasp echoed through the bedroom.

Everyone stopped what they were doing to stare at him. Martine hurried to his side.

"Levi, what's wrong?"

"He's one of them," Levi croaked. He couldn't take his eyes off the victim.

Though the man's face was a decade older, Levi would never forget it. The image was seared into his memory like a cigarette burn—those same features twisted into a hateful sneer, spewing homophobic bile at him while he was beaten to within an inch of his life. Those hands had choked him, punched him, held him down. Those feet had kicked him again and again, until he felt his ribs break and puncture his lungs and he knew he was going to die right there on the dirty asphalt of the parking lot—

"One of who?" Martine asked.

A violent shudder racked Levi's body. "He's one of the men who attacked me in college."

CHAPTER 6

Martine didn't react at first, so Levi wondered if he hadn't said it out loud. He forced himself to turn his head, and found her staring at him in utter incomprehension.

Then she blinked once, looked at the victim, and her face twisted with horror.

"What's going on?" Gibbs moved closer. "Abrams, you okay, man?"

Levi coughed, clutching his chest. He knew he was breathing, but none of that oxygen was reaching his lungs. Crushing pressure squeezed around his heart—was it possible to have a heart attack from the shock of something like this?

God, this man was going to be the death of him after all, just ten years later—

Martine grabbed his elbow, dragged him into the en suite bathroom, and slammed the door shut. He caught a glimpse of his chalk-white face in the mirror before she pushed him onto the closed toilet seat and crouched in front of him.

"Levi," she said in a calm, measured voice, "you're having a panic attack."

He shook his head blankly. He'd never had a panic attack in his life. His problem had always been rage, not anxiety.

His heart throbbed, and he doubled over with a groan. The lack of air had his vision graying out. "I can't breathe."

"I know it feels that way, but you *can*. Try breathing in through your nose and out through your mouth, nice and slow."

He gave it a shot, but all his breaths were raspy wheezes. He made a thin, frightened animal noise he hadn't heard himself make since—since that night—

"Levi!" She gripped his knee. "You're safe here. I'm not gonna let anything happen to you."

That was true. He grabbed that thought with both hands and held it tight.

"Now, I want you to count upward in multiples of eight, okay? Just do the best you can."

He had to swallow several times before he could start. "Eight," he said through gritted teeth. "Sixteen. T-twenty-four . . ."

The count gave him something to focus on besides his fear, but he still made it all the way to 120 before the pressure in his chest eased and he could breathe normally again. He abandoned the count, buried his head in his gloved hands, and said a silent prayer for strength.

He heard Martine stand up and move away. "You okay?" she asked.

"Yeah." He took one more deep breath, then stood on shaky legs. Though he desperately wanted to drink some water, maybe splash some on his face, this entire hotel suite was an active crime scene. It was bad enough that he'd sat down.

She looked him over. "Let's get you out of here."

He couldn't have agreed more.

They returned to the bedroom, Levi already flushing at the thought of how all these people had seen him freaking out. Most cast curious glances his way but continued going about their business. Gibbs was the only one to spread his hands and say, "What the hell?"

"Detective Abrams has to recuse himself," said Martine. "He knows the victim."

Levi missed Gibbs's response, because he'd locked onto the dead man again like he was caught in the pull of a tractor beam. He walked closer to the chair without meaning to.

"Why is he bound and gagged?" he said. "The Seven of Spades has never done that before."

He dropped his eyes to the victim's wrists, which were bruised from yanking against the zip ties. He'd bet there were similar marks on the victim's ankles beneath his pants.

"This one struggled," Levi said to Martine. "And look at his face— he was terrified. The ketamine hadn't fully paralyzed him."

"Maybe the killer had to tie him up because there were other people in the adjacent rooms. And maybe the whole thing took so long the drugs started wearing off. Either way, you don't have to worry about it."

She took his hand and tugged him toward the door. Though he didn't resist, he walked backward, his gaze fixed on the corpse of a man who had once beaten him to the edge of death.

"Wait, hold up!" Gibbs said. "You haven't heard the whole story."

Martine stopped with a groan. "Whatever it is—"

"There are three other men missing."

"*What?*"

"Ten guys came on this trip. The six out there found this one when they woke up, but there are three more who are nowhere to be found. They haven't been seen since last night, and they're not answering their phones."

Levi and Martine looked at each other. He saw his own conclusion mirrored on her face before she even asked the question.

"How many men—"

"Four," he said numbly. "There were four."

Dominic yanked irritably at the knot in his tie as he folded himself into the driver's seat of Carlos's Toyota Camry. They'd traded vehicles for the day, since Dominic's pickup truck didn't mesh with his current cover.

One of the things he missed most about being a bounty hunter was not having to wear a suit. He wrestled out of his jacket, tossed it aside, and loosened his tie a little more. Then, on second thought, he ripped the fucker off altogether.

Much better.

He glanced back at the house he'd just left, which belonged to the last of the four surviving kidnapping victims. He'd spent the day interviewing the victims and their families, introducing himself as a representative of KIG—which was technically true, though in this case he'd implied he was investigating the validity of their claims.

In his experience, nothing encouraged candor more than the belief that money was on the line.

All four victims' stories had been the same, barring a few additional and unfortunate details in Rose Nguyen's case. These kidnappers were clean. Professional. Precise. They executed their missions with a minimum of fuss and treated their victims with polite detachment.

This was not the work of a street gang or common criminals. These men were hired mercenaries. And where there were mercenaries, there was a client.

Hefty ransoms might be motivation enough to go to the expense of hiring a team of mercenaries—if not for the fact that every victim had an insurance policy through KIG. Why specifically target only those people when Las Vegas was bursting at the seams with high rollers ripe for the picking? Was it just for the assurance that victims with K&R policies would be able to meet the ransom demands? If so, the brains behind the operation must have gotten a nasty shock when they found out Buckner's policy had lapsed.

Dominic sighed, turning the key in the ignition and checking the dashboard clock. He had a few ideas for how to pursue this investigation, but it was getting late, and he had to be at Stingray in a few hours for a closing bartending shift. If he left now, he'd have just enough time to drive to the Railroad Pass and get in a few poker games before he had to come back.

No, come on. If he needed to take a break from work, there were other things he could do—hit the gym, take Rebel for a run, see what Carlos and Jasmine were up to—

But why *shouldn't* he gamble? It would be the best way to relieve the tension of the day and get him in a positive frame of mind for a night at Stingray. Besides, even if he lost money, he'd make it all back in tips. It was no big deal.

As he put the car in drive, already distracted by the buzz of excitement, he had the passing thought that it was strange he'd gotten to all the victims before the police.

Levi sat ramrod straight at the table in the conference room where the official Seven of Spades Task Force had gathered. Ever since they'd found the latest victim that morning, he'd been so stiff that every muscle in his body ached.

The task force had been established in November, when it became undeniable that the Seven of Spades would not be caught through ordinary means. In addition to Levi and Martine—the lead detectives of record—the team included their immediate superior Sergeant James Wen, Captain Dean Birndorf, a handful of uniformed officers, several detectives handpicked from bureaus across the department, and some technical support staff, all vetted by Internal Affairs after the fiasco of Carmen Rivera's betrayal. Leila Rashid represented the DA's interest in the case.

The FBI's Rohan Chaudhary had returned to Quantico after completing the Seven of Spades's profile, concluding with his theory that the killer's flawless technique might have resulted from a previous stage of practice killings of which the police were unaware. In his place, the local FBI office had assigned their own permanent liaison to the task force. Special Agent Denise Marshall was a bubbly, energetic woman whose irrepressible enthusiasm for everything frustrated and awed Levi in turns.

Of all the people in the room, only Martine and possibly Wen knew about Levi's assault, which put Levi in the nauseating position of having to tell everyone about it.

"When I was a junior in college, four men jumped me in the parking lot of a gay bar," he said, his voice as clipped and emotionless as he could manage. "They beat me unconscious. I woke up in the hospital and spent a long time recovering. The case was never closed; there were never even any leads."

He kept his eyes on the wall straight ahead, because he couldn't bear to see the pitying expressions he was sure surrounded him. But he heard one of the uniformed officers mutter, "That explains a lot."

"Yeah, and what explains *your* shitty arrest record?" Leila drawled in her usual bored tone. "Oh, right—you're incompetent. Another mystery solved."

The officer stammered an outraged reply while a few people snickered, which had the effect of both breaking the tension and shifting some of the intense focus off Levi.

"I asked the other guys in the bachelor party for pictures of the missing men." Gibbs showed Levi a handful of papers. "Would you . . . I mean, is it all right if . . ."

"Of course," Levi said. He steeled himself as Gibbs spread the papers out in front of him.

The photographs had been culled from social media sites, showing the same three handsome men at parties, on vacation, having fun with family and friends. These men had left Levi broken and bloody in a parking lot and gone on to live their lives without a care in the world. Had they ever even wondered what'd happened to him?

Levi cleared his throat. "This is them. Including this morning's victim, they're the same four men who attacked me in New Jersey."

"Scott West, Wayne Reddick, and George Quintana," Gibbs said, tapping each man's picture in turn.

The first victim was Jared Foley. Over a decade later, Levi could finally put names to the men whose actions had haunted him for most of his adult life.

"Foley was getting married in May," Martine said. "According to his friends, he won an all-expenses-paid bachelor party trip to Las Vegas through his wedding registry website. But when I contacted the site, they had no idea what I was talking about. It was just an elaborate ruse perpetrated and funded by the Seven of Spades."

Sergeant Wen had been called in on his day off, and though he was immaculately groomed—his military background allowed for nothing less—he looked exhausted. "They wanted a way to get all four of Abrams's attackers in Vegas at the same time."

Gibbs picked up the story. "The guys had VIP bottle service at Ambrosia last night. That was the last time anyone saw the missing men. They think they were all roofied there, because none of them remember anything past 10 p.m. They don't know what happened at the club, how they got back to the hotel, when Foley was separated from the rest of them. Nothing."

"Ketamine?" Levi asked. In addition to paralysis and other dissociative anesthetic effects, ketamine could induce short-term memory loss.

"We're doing blood tests to confirm, but I think it's a safe bet."

"I checked out the club," said Hannah Ostrowski, another uniformed officer. "It's a kidnapper's dream—no video surveillance in or around the building, easy access to the back exit, plenty of space to park a vehicle for transport."

"The Seven of Spades has never taken living victims before," Denise Marshall said. Her eyes were wide and shining, her voice excited. "It's difficult enough to handle one captive, let alone three at the same time. This could be where the killer makes a fatal mistake. We'll be bringing all the resources of the FBI to bear in locating these men while they're still alive."

"Sure," Gibbs muttered. "By all means, let's spend a bunch of taxpayer money rushing to the rescue of three violent, homophobic dirtbags."

Denise was one of the few people Levi knew who Gibbs couldn't provoke; she only gave him a gentle smile. "We don't have a choice in who we protect, Officer."

"I'm more concerned with how the Seven of Spades knew who to lure here in the first place," Leila interrupted. "If these men were never identified and even Levi didn't know who they were, how did the killer find them?"

"I'll contact the Trenton PD and request the case file," Martine said.

"Trenton?" Gibbs said to Levi with a faintly horrified air. "Dude, why would you go to a bar in *Trenton*?"

Shrugging one shoulder, Levi said, "It was close to where I went to college."

Gibbs made a face. "Which was where?"

Levi shifted uncomfortably, glanced at Martine, and sighed. "Princeton."

Surprised murmurs rippled through the room, and he rolled his eyes. There was a reason he preferred not to tell people this.

"You went to *Princeton* and then decided to move to Las Vegas and become a cop? Why would you . . ." Gibbs's eyes fell on the photographs still scattered across the table, and he faltered. "Oh."

Now everybody was staring at Levi again.

"Abrams," said Wen, "you're not going to like what I have to say next. It's been clear from the beginning that the Seven of Spades has a strange attachment to you. But now they've gone out of their way to lure victims with connections to you into the city, and they've deviated significantly from their MO. Considering the card they left for you in Harding's office and the details of this morning's crime scene, this is all obviously intended as a gift for you."

True. Whether the Seven of Spades's "happy belated birthday" theme was sincere or tongue-in-cheek, these men had been targeted for one very specific reason.

Wen exchanged a glance with Birndorf. "Captain Birndorf and I have discussed this at length. I'm very sorry, Abrams, but we have no choice but to remove you from the Seven of Spades investigation."

Levi's vision went black, and the next thing he knew, he was on his feet, his chair on the floor behind him. His pulse pounded through his head hard enough to shatter his skull, and both his hands were clutched into fists so tight that his nails tore into his palms.

When he got angry, it usually built up over time—sometimes just a matter of minutes, but there was always a sense of escalation. He'd become aware of the warning signs in his rapid breathing, his tense muscles, his violent thoughts, and he'd have a chance to calm himself down or remove himself from the situation.

Not today. Everyone in the room had backed away and was watching him warily. Some of the cops had their hands hovering over their guns. Even Denise looked startled.

The only person who hadn't moved was Leila, who was sitting in her usual state of quiet readiness, regarding him with an unreadable expression.

"This is the best course of action for everyone involved," Wen said. His eyes flicked down to Levi's hands.

Though there was a wide table between them, it wasn't a serious obstacle. Levi could hurdle it in seconds, grab Wen's throat, and squeeze—

He bit down hard on his tongue. His entire body shook with the effort it took to remain still. He tried Alana's thought-stopping technique, but it was powerless against the fantasy of smashing Wen's face into the conference table until his nose spurted blood.

The feverish imagery was so frightening that Levi whirled around and dashed out of the conference room like it was on fire. He'd rather let everyone believe he was running away than risk losing control of himself and doing something unforgivable.

He went straight to the men's room, locked himself into a stall, and braced both hands against the metal door, hanging his head between his arms. His ragged breaths echoed loudly off the tile.

In a corner of his mind, he'd known all day that this would happen. It was department policy that detectives couldn't work cases in which they knew the victims. An exception might have been possible in this case, given the involvement of such a prolific serial killer, but Wen had been searching for an excuse to kick Levi off the Seven of Spades investigation for six months.

This case had eaten a year of Levi's life. He'd pursued the investigation at great personal cost even when everyone else believed the Seven of Spades was dead. He'd been called crazy and obsessive and worse, hounded by the press, taunted and bugged and stalked by the killer themselves. He'd sacrificed every part of his life to hunting the Seven of Spades, and what did he have to show for it?

Nothing.

"*Fuck!*" he shouted. He smashed a vicious palm-heel strike into the door. It slammed against its lock hard enough to rattle the entire row of stalls.

The worst part was that he knew Wen was right. For God's sake, this was the second time *today* he'd needed to hide in a bathroom to get his shit together. Maybe he was more of a liability than an asset at this point.

He stayed where he was until his breathing returned to normal and his thoughts were no longer locked in a violent spiral. Only then did he venture out to the bullpen.

It was evident right away that word had spread, because the room was unnaturally quiet and everyone was careful to *not* look at him. The fury he'd been wrestling with for the past twenty minutes surged back. His coworkers all thought he was a freak, a ticking time bomb who couldn't be trusted. The Seven of Spades was ruining his professional reputation like they were ruining everything else in his life.

He sank into his desk chair and pressed both hands to his face. He was *not* going to lose it, not again—

"Levi?"

He dropped his hands, ready to snap at whoever'd had the audacity to approach him, only to find himself looking at perhaps the one person in the entire world he wouldn't lash out at.

"Adriana," he said, the flames of his rage banked for the moment. He stood and waited to see if she would initiate a hug. When she did, he wrapped his arms around her—very loosely, so she wouldn't feel restrained—and hugged her back.

The hugging was new. When Levi had first found Adriana, she'd been able to tolerate very little physical contact, especially with men. But months of living with a supportive foster family, undergoing therapy, and training with Levi in Krav Maga had helped her make great strides in recovery. She'd hugged Levi spontaneously for the first time a few weeks ago.

"What are you doing here?" he asked once they separated.

"I was having counseling with Natasha." Adriana nodded across the bullpen, to where Natasha Stone was standing outside the hallway that led to her office deeper within the substation. "She said you were having a bad day and you might want to do something to take your mind off it."

Natasha smiled and gave him a small wave. He waved back, then turned to Adriana.

Fuck it. Right now he'd rather be anywhere but here, and he wasn't scheduled to work today anyway. "You want to go to Counterstrike, do some training for your P1 test?"

Adriana grinned. "Sure."

"Why don't you call your foster parents and make sure it's okay," he said.

She bounced away happily, pulling out her cell phone. *Thank you*, Levi mouthed to Natasha.

Natasha nodded, winked, and headed back toward her office.

Levi and Adriana went to Counterstrike, his Krav Maga school—and hers as well, now that she was a registered member of the International Krav Maga Federation. In addition to coaching her in general self-defense, he was preparing her for the Level One Practitioner test next month.

They ran through the curriculum from start to finish. By the time he wrapped things up by sending her to work a heavy bag, he felt much steadier. Krav had always been one of the few things that could pull him out of his head.

He wanted to stay moving while observing her technique on the bag at the same time, so he grabbed a jump rope and fell into a rhythm next to her, switching up his pace and footwork every few seconds.

"Can I ask you something?" she asked about a minute later. She didn't take her eyes off the bag.

"Mm-hmm."

"Are you glad one of the men who hurt you is dead?"

He tripped over the rope and caught himself on the next bag over. She remained focused on her own bag, pummeling it with hammerfists, palm-heel strikes, and knees.

Levi hadn't realized Natasha had told her the specific details of *why* he'd had a bad day. Though it wasn't a big deal—he'd shared the full story of the assault with Adriana a long time ago—this was the first time she'd mentioned it all afternoon.

His stomach churned, but he couldn't lie to her. Not about this.

"Yes," he whispered.

She nodded. He waited, knowing she'd asked for a reason.

"Sometimes I wish my old foster father lived in Vegas instead of Reno." She nailed the bag with a fierce elbow that would have broken an attacker's jaw, and Levi felt a swell of pride despite the morbid conversation. "I think if he lived here, the Seven of Spades would kill him."

"So do I," said Levi. The Seven of Spades harbored a particular loathing for adults who harmed children. An abusive foster parent was right up their alley.

Adriana grabbed the bag to stop it from swinging; she was probably panting as much from emotional distress as exertion. "I wish a serial killer would murder him. Does that mean I'm a bad person?"

"*No.*" Levi took her hand and gave it a light squeeze so she met his eyes. "There's a difference between fantasy and reality. It's natural to want revenge against people who did terrible things to you, but just because you *want* to hurt someone doesn't mean you would if given the opportunity."

She mulled that over. "Would you have hurt those men if you'd run into them yourself?"

"Well, I might have taken a swing at them, if we're being honest," he said, pleased when she cracked a smile. "But I wouldn't have *killed* them, no matter how many times I've fantasized about doing exactly that."

"What if they hurt someone else, though?"

He stilled. "What?"

"You don't know how many other people those men hurt the same way they hurt you. And my old foster father could have other kids living with him now, because nobody in Reno ever believed me. If people like that aren't stopped, they'll just keep doing the same bad things over and over."

"I . . ." Levi was stuck for a response. She was right, of course, and how could he expect a traumatized young woman to accept the fact that her abuser would never be brought to justice?

"It's dumb, but sometimes I'm afraid he'll come after me. That he'll find me again." She took a shaky breath. "I know there's no reason for him to do that. He probably forgot about me the second I ran away. But I still think about it a lot."

Oh. Suddenly this conversation made a lot more sense.

"That's why you're learning how to protect yourself," he said. "And I promise, I would never, ever let anyone hurt you. Anyone who came after you would have to go through me."

This time, her smile reached her eyes. They looked at each other, sharing a moment of understanding that Levi could never have with Martine or even Dominic.

"I think we've had enough of a workout for one day. Why don't we go get some ice cream?"

"Don't you mean *I'll* have ice cream and you'll have coffee?" she said archly.

"Just go get changed," he said, nudging her toward the bathroom with a laugh.

Dominic suppressed a groan as the dealer raked the pot toward a player on the opposite side of the poker table. Down another half a grand—he was seriously off his game tonight. At this rate, even Saturday night tips at Stingray wouldn't cover his losses—

No, no. He'd had a run of bad luck, which only meant he was due for some good cards. He could feel the turn coming. All he had to do was chase it down.

His phone vibrated in his pocket, and since they were between hands, he went ahead and checked it. He frowned when he saw Martine's name on the screen. She wouldn't call him at night—unless something was wrong with Levi.

He signaled the dealer that he would sit out the next hand and hurried away from the table, toward the door where reception was better. "What's wrong?" he said by way of greeting.

Martine didn't call him on his rudeness. "We have a big problem."

He listened in growing dismay as she filled him in on the day's events. "Is Levi okay?" he asked when she finished, already knowing the answer.

"I haven't even gotten to the worst part," she said grimly. "Wen took him off the Seven of Spades case altogether."

Dominic's breath stalled in his chest. "*No.* Christ, Martine, that's gonna kill him! You have to talk Wen out of it."

"I tried! I argued with him for over an hour. Even Leila gave it a shot, and you know what she's like. His mind's made up. The only reason he let Levi stay on the case this long was because Agent Chaudhary recommended it. But now that Levi has a personal connection to the victims . . ."

"Do you know where Levi is right now?"

"Natasha arranged for him to spend the rest of the day with Adriana."

Dominic's shoulders sagged with slight relief. No matter what his mental state, Levi would never let harm come to Adriana, who he loved like a little sister. Her presence would ensure he stayed in control of himself.

"You should call him," said Martine.

"I'd only make things worse."

"Dominic—"

"Levi doesn't trust me anymore," he bit out. "He wouldn't want me to see him vulnerable like this."

"I think you're wrong," she said, but she didn't try to persuade him further. Once she promised to keep him updated, they hung up. As Dominic hit the button to end the call, his eyes fell on the phone's clock.

"Oh, *fuck*," he said, so loudly he startled several people nearby. He'd completely lost track of time, and now he was going to be late for work at Stingray.

He returned to the poker table to color up what was left of his chips, then proceeded to the cashier, tapping his foot anxiously as he waited in line.

"Dominic?"

He turned, startled by the approach of a statuesque Greek woman who was drawing double takes all across the casino—Diana Kostas, whom he'd met when she'd gotten tangled up in one of Levi's homicide investigations last summer.

"Di—" He stopped as her eyes widened fractionally and she shook her head. "Pandora," he said, using her work name instead. "Wow, it's great to see you."

"You too. It's been a while."

He had saved her life by administering CPR after she'd been strangled, but he'd broken several of her ribs in the process. He'd done some repairs around her house afterward while she was laid up, and they'd had a few good talks, though they'd lost touch after she'd recovered.

"How's your son?" he asked.

She glowed at the mere mention of him. "He's doing really well. The child psychologist Natasha recommended worked wonders for him after the attack. And you? How's Levi?"

The person in front of him finished their business and stepped away. He handed his chips over to the cashier with a distracted smile before he said, "We, um . . . we broke up, actually."

"Oh. I'm sorry to hear that." Her eyes roamed over his chips, and he knew what she must be thinking—his gambling history was something they'd once talked about, though only briefly.

The hot sting of embarrassment brought forth his old friend, defensiveness. "It's not what—"

"Hey, no explanation necessary." She held up a hand. "I know what it's like to have people judging you and telling you what to do with your life. You won't get that from me."

"Thanks." He took the bills the cashier handed him, tucked them into his wallet, and moved out of the way. "Are you here for work? This doesn't seem like your kind of place."

Diana was a high-end escort with Sinful Secrets, one of Vegas's top-tier agencies. The Railroad Pass, while not a total dive, wasn't the classiest joint in the Valley.

She laughed. "For some clients, discretion is more important than atmosphere. Speaking of which . . ." She smiled at someone over his shoulder. "I need to get going."

"Of course. Me too."

She started moving around him, then paused and touched his elbow. "You helped me out a lot when I needed it. If I can ever return the favor, please don't hesitate to let me know."

"Sure," he said, puzzled yet touched by the offer. "Thank you."

After giving his arm a squeeze, she walked across the casino floor to greet an older man gazing at her like an awestruck tourist in the Sistine Chapel. Dominic checked his phone again, cringed at the time, and all but ran for the parking lot.

Stingray, an extravagant nightclub in the LGBT neighborhood east of the Strip known as the Fruit Loop, was a three-story affair with several bars, multiple dance floors, and an underwater theme enhanced by cool blue uplighting and massive aquariums. Getting there from Henderson on a Saturday night was a clusterfuck, and in the end, he was over an hour late.

He'd texted his manager a story about having car trouble, but he could tell she didn't believe him. She chewed him out and then exiled him with an assignment to one of the more remote bars in the club, where he'd make half as much in tips as he would at a bar on the dance floors. That was an unexpected blow to his income, and especially troubling in light of his run of bad luck.

Carlos, his best friend and fellow bartender, accosted him in the locker room while he was changing. The Stingray uniform of black trousers and a tight black T-shirt clung to Carlos's lanky frame, and his floppy brown hair was mussed like he'd been running his hands through it.

"I can't believe you're late again," Carlos said.

Dominic stripped off the button-down he'd been wearing all day and tossed it into his locker. "I had car trouble."

"Don't feed me that bullshit. You were gambling."

Dominic stiffened and glared at him. Carlos raised his eyebrows in challenge.

"I tried to cover for you," he said. "I told them you'd gotten wrapped up in a case and couldn't get free."

That explained why his manager hadn't bought his story. "I didn't ask you to do that," Dominic snapped.

"What are you gonna do when you lose this job?"

Dominic froze with his T-shirt in one hand.

"I know you couldn't afford that," Carlos went on. "I doubt the two jobs you have now are enough to keep you afloat for much longer."

"They wouldn't fire me. I bring in too many regulars." Unnerved, Dominic yanked his shirt over his head.

"Please. This is Las Vegas. You don't think there are fifty hot, buff guys lining up behind you to take your job? Nobody's irreplaceable."

This flew in the face of their unspoken agreement to not discuss Dominic's gambling. He slammed his locker shut and folded his arms across his chest as he faced Carlos, his biceps straining against the tight sleeves of his T-shirt.

Carlos wasn't fazed in the least. "I know that nothing I say or do can really convince you to accept help before you're ready. I just want you to remember how much you lost the last time this happened, and think about whether you're willing to go through all that again."

Rubbing a hand over his scruffy jaw, Carlos turned and walked out. Dominic's nostrils flared.

He was so fucking sick of people offering to *help* him like was some kind of invalid. He was fucking *fine*.

Carlos did have one good point, though, which was that Dominic's current income couldn't quite keep up with his previous debts and recent losses. But that was easily solved. He still had his bail enforcement license; he could pick up a bounty or two and use the extra cash to tide him over until his luck turned around and he started winning big again.

Everything was fine.

Dominic cracked his neck from side to side, put his game face on, and headed out to sweet-talk horny tourists into padding his wallet.

CHAPTER 7

Levi sat in his car on Monday evening, not wanting to go home but not knowing what else to do with himself. Wen had cut him out of the Seven of Spades investigation entirely, so while he knew the missing men hadn't been found—dead or alive—he had no idea what progress had been made. He hadn't tried to get Martine to share details on the sly; he knew she would if he asked, and he didn't want to get her in trouble.

To distract himself, he'd thrown all his energies into the Buckner homicide—now officially confirmed to be caused by a massive overdose of pentobarbital— and its associated kidnappings. He hadn't been surprised by the fact that Dominic had gotten to all the victims and their families first, or by the subterfuge Dominic had used. As long as private investigators and bounty hunters didn't misrepresent themselves as law enforcement, they were allowed to lie about their identities—a technique called pretexting.

Not having the same advantage, Levi had probably been able to glean less information. Besides Nguyen, every witness in the case had been reluctant to speak with him, as they'd all received the same parting threats from their kidnappers. But he'd still learned enough to establish a clear timeline and MO for the crimes.

The traffic camera footage had been helpful as well, since all the victims had been snatched in transit. Though the kidnappers had been careful not to take or return the victims anywhere under direct surveillance, Levi had figured out which cameras surrounded the areas in question and reviewed the footage from the given time windows, searching for large black SUVs. Comparing his notes from each event had enabled him to spot a pattern and identify two cars—a Chevrolet Suburban and a Toyota Sequoia—as the kidnappers' likely vehicles.

Every time he noted those SUVs, they had different license plates; each plate turned out to have been reported stolen from cars in the northwest region of the Valley. He'd issued department-wide instructions for all officers to run the plates of any car they saw matching the descriptions he'd provided.

Now, though, he was stuck in a holding pattern. He was waiting to see if the LVMDP's forensic accountant could trace the ransom payments, waiting to hear back from his and Martine's CIs, waiting for the vehicle lead to pan out, waiting for the court to finish battling KIG's lawyers for their client list. And, as much as he hated to admit it, he was waiting for another kidnapping.

But that might not happen. It was obvious from the victims' stories that the kidnappers were hired by a third party. That person had yet to make another move, so it was possible they'd been demoralized by their out-of-date information on Buckner's policy and had backed off permanently.

Either way, there was nothing more Levi could do today.

His phone chirped, and he pulled it out to read a text from Kelly Marin.

Big March Madness event at Railroad Pass tonight. Confirmed DR planning to attend.

Levi chewed his lower lip. There were officers in the LVMPD still loyal to him, and willing to help him keep tabs on Dominic's movement around the Valley. Kelly was the most enthusiastic, but that wasn't surprising. After she'd leaked the Seven of Spades story last year, she'd been sentenced to work the desk at the evidence lockup; Levi had pulled strings to get her kicked back up to Traffic.

March Madness . . . that was a terrible idea. Once Dominic started gambling, he wouldn't stop unless something forced him to, no matter the consequences. The frenzy of sports betting surrounding the college basketball tournament could result in him losing thousands of dollars in a single night and being unable to walk away.

Levi wouldn't let that happen.

Thanks, he texted Kelly. Then he started his car and hit the gas, filled with a renewed sense of purpose.

"I know, sweetheart, I'm sorry," Dominic said to Rebel, who was watching him get ready with mournful eyes. "But you're going to spend time with Carlos and Jasmine. That's fun, right?"

She didn't react, not even to wag her tail. He sighed and continued hunting for his cell phone, which he'd misplaced in the unholy mess that had taken over his apartment. He really should clean all this up, but he was always so busy these days . . .

Rebel perked up, rising to her feet with cocked ears; seconds later, a knock sounded on the door.

Dominic frowned and headed over to look through the peephole. He blinked, disengaged the wireless alarm, and undid his multiple locks before opening the door.

"Levi. What are you doing here?"

Leaning sideways against the doorjamb, Levi gazed up at him through his eyelashes. Dominic took in the rest of him and inhaled sharply.

Levi was wearing *jeans*.

On the rare occasion Levi was found in something other than a well-tailored suit, he wore slacks or chinos. He only owned one pair of jeans, and the elusive sight was one Dominic coveted.

"Can I come in?" Levi asked, and then pushed his way inside the apartment without waiting for a response. Dominic was too distracted to protest.

Rebel raced toward Levi in ecstatic greeting. That meant Dominic was treated to the sight of Levi bending over in tight denim, which only beguiled him further. He was still struggling to regain his bearings when Levi straightened up and refastened all the locks.

"You haven't answered my question," Dominic said.

Levi gave him a smoldering look that couldn't possibly be misinterpreted. "What do you think?"

He seized the lapels of Dominic's blazer and began backing him up across the living room. Dominic let himself be pushed, mesmerized by the heat in Levi's solemn gray eyes.

"Uh . . . I was actually just on my way out—"

Levi grasped the back of Dominic's head with one hand and pulled him into a ferocious kiss. Moaning, Dominic immediately surrendered and grabbed Levi's round ass, greedily feeling him up through his jeans.

They kissed and groped their way through the apartment, and it wasn't until they stumbled into the wall of the hallway leading to the bedroom that Dominic came to his senses.

Levi had two coping mechanisms for stress: violence and sex. Terrible things had happened to him this weekend, things that must have fucked him up emotionally. It was no coincidence he'd turned up here a few days later.

"Wait," Dominic panted as Levi stripped him of his blazer and dropped it to the floor. "We shouldn't."

"Why not?" Levi nuzzled the underside of Dominic's jaw.

"I know what happened with the Seven of Spades. This isn't a healthy way to deal with it."

Levi yanked Dominic away from the wall only to spin him around and shove him against the opposite side of the hallway. "That has nothing to do with this," he said before sinking his teeth into Dominic's throat.

Dominic gasped, his knees going weak. Levi knew how much he enjoyed being bitten, the *cheater*.

"I just want to be fucked." Levi laved his tongue over the bite mark, then tilted Dominic's head down to look him in the eye. "Would you rather I find someone else to do that for me?"

"No!" Dominic said, his disgust so visceral that he had no hope of hiding or even downplaying it. Jesus, he and Levi had been broken up for *months*, and the thought of Levi with another man still made him want to crawl out of his skin.

They had to stop having sex with each other; it was making it impossible for either of them to move on.

"Then I don't see the problem." Levi steered Dominic into the bedroom and kicked the door shut.

"I—"

Levi kissed Dominic again, more languidly this time. When the kiss broke, he stayed close, his lips centimeters from Dominic's.

"I'll let you tie me up," he said.

Dominic's hands convulsed on Levi's hips. Neither he nor Levi were exclusively dominant or submissive in bed; they both had times when they were in the mood for one or the other, and that dynamic had always been fluid between them.

Yet while Levi liked being tossed around, manhandled, and even pinned down by Dominic's superior weight on occasion, he'd never let Dominic bind him. Understanding Levi's touchy emotional issues about vulnerability, Dominic had been careful to never push, though it was no secret that restraining Levi was a treasured fantasy.

"Seriously?" Dominic rasped.

Levi pulled away, hooked his thumb into the front pocket of his jeans, and drew out a pair of dangling handcuffs. He raised his eyebrows.

"Fuck, yes." All his reservations forgotten, Dominic scooped Levi right off the ground. Levi locked his legs around Dominic's waist, wrapped his arms around Dominic's neck, and kissed him breathless while Dominic backed up until he could sit on the bed with Levi in his lap.

Levi pushed Dominic flat on his back against the pillows, then moved his mouth to Dominic's neck, kissing and nipping and sucking. One of his hands smoothed along Dominic's arm while the other worked at the buttons of Dominic's shirt. Dominic rolled his hips, frotting their erections through their jeans, massaging Levi's ass and imagining how good Levi was going to look tied up in his bed—

Click. Click.

Before Dominic had fully processed the sound, Levi nimbly jumped off him and away from the bed, moving to the far wall. Dominic tried to reach for him and was brought up short—by the handcuffs chaining his right wrist to one of the wooden slats in his headboard.

"I can't believe you fell for that," Levi said. "Is there any blood left in your brain at all right now?"

"What . . ." Dominic, whose lust-fogged brain was indeed having trouble adjusting to this sudden turn of events, stared in bewilderment at his cuffed arm. "What the fuck?"

"You couldn't seriously think I would trust you enough to tie me up when you're like this."

Dominic's blood boiled as the reality of the situation set in. Levi had come here to seduce him with the deliberate intention of locking him to this bed. Everything Levi had said and done since he'd set foot in this apartment had been an act.

"You motherfucker," Dominic spat. "What the hell do you mean, 'like this'?"

"In the midst of a full-blown relapse and completely in denial about it."

"I'm not . . ." Dominic made a frustrated noise and yanked on the handcuffs. "This is ridiculous, Levi. Let me go!"

"No."

Dominic struggled against the restraints for a few more seconds. Then, loosing an angry, incoherent roar, he jerked his arm forward and strained against the cuffs with every ounce of strength in his body. The headboard groaned, creaked, and made an ominous cracking sound.

Levi's eyes widened and he took a step back.

If this were a matter of life or death, Dominic could break the headboard. It would fuck up his wrist, though, and that wasn't worth it when he wasn't in real danger. He slumped back down and let his arm fall to the mattress.

"This is false imprisonment," he said. "You're a cop committing a gross misdemeanor."

"So call 911." Levi tossed Dominic his own cell phone, which Dominic caught with his free hand.

He'd called Dominic's bluff without so much as blinking. Irritated, Dominic whipped the phone back at Levi's face as hard as he could. Levi still managed to snatch it out of midair with his goddamn Krav Maga reflexes.

"What's the point of this?" Dominic asked.

"I may not be into basketball, but I'm familiar with March Madness, and I know you were planning to attend a big sports betting event tonight. I'm trying to stop you from making yet another series of catastrophic mistakes and ruining your life even more than you already have."

Sanctimonious prick. Dominic was gearing up to raise hell when a quiet whine outside the door caught both their attention.

"I think Rebel's worried about you," Levi said as he opened the door.

Rebel bounded inside, jumped on the bed, and sniffed Dominic from head to foot, seeming particularly interested in but not concerned by his cuffed wrist. Though she was an incredibly intelligent and well-trained dog, even she wouldn't be able to fetch him a pair of handcuff keys. And since he'd never turn her against Levi, no matter the provocation, there wasn't anything she could do to help him.

Apparently deciding he was in no danger, she licked his face and then flopped down beside him with a contented whuff.

"Hey!" Dominic said when Levi headed for the door. "Where the fuck are you going?"

Levi shot him a contemptuous look over his shoulder. "I'm going to clean your filthy pigsty of an apartment. It drove me crazy the last time I was here."

He left the bedroom, ignoring Dominic's repeated and increasingly angry shouts. Eventually, Dominic just gave up. Yelling obviously wasn't going to change Levi's mind, and Dominic was confident that at the very least, Levi wouldn't leave him alone in the apartment while he was bound.

Snuggling closer, Rebel propped her head on Dominic's chest and looked at him adoringly. His heart melted despite the circumstances, and he scratched her ears with his free hand.

"I love you too," he said. "I'm sorry I'm such a shitty dad."

She closed her eyes and sighed in doggy bliss.

Petting her helped him calm down. He continued stroking her head while he lay there quietly, analyzing his predicament more strategically. There was no way he was going to be out-manipulated by Levi Abrams.

He guessed it was about an hour later when he called out, "Levi!"

"What?" Levi shouted back.

"I'm thirsty."

Levi returned to the bedroom and threw Dominic a bottle of water from the doorway. Dominic gave him an annoyed glare.

"I'm going to be very insulted if you thought I was stupid enough to come within range of your limbs," Levi said.

He hadn't, though he'd had to try. But that was only plan A. Dominic shifted himself into a sitting position against the headboard and managed to clumsily uncap the bottle. "You know, Carlos and Jasmine are expecting me to bring Rebel over."

"I figured. I already called them."

"Seriously? Did you tell them—"

"That I had you handcuffed to the bed?" Levi said dryly. "No. I didn't give them any details. I just . . . let them draw their own conclusions."

A slight blush stained Levi's cut-glass cheekbones, and he looked away. Entranced, Dominic momentarily lost the thread of the conversation and just stared.

Giving his head a little shake, he sipped some water to cover up his pause. For fuck's sake, why was it so easy for Levi to lead him around by the dick even *without* trying?

"What if I have to use the bathroom?" he asked, indicating the water bottle.

"I'll be happy to empty that bottle out and give it back to you."

"Gross."

Levi shrugged.

Struggling to keep his frustration in check, Dominic said, "You're gonna have to let me go eventually. How long are you planning to keep me like this?"

"Until the basketball games are over. Maybe longer. I haven't decided yet."

"You can't stop me from gambling!" Dominic snapped. "You've been trying for months, and I always find a way around you. I don't need a special event to gamble. Even after the games are over, the casino is open twenty-four hours a day."

Levi lifted one eyebrow. "Spoken like a man who's truly in control of himself."

Dominic clenched his jaw. His hand spasmed around the plastic bottle, sloshing water onto the bed.

"Where's your television, Dominic? Your computer? Your *microwave*?"

He kept his mouth shut. The truth was, he'd pawned them all over the past few weeks—which had particularly sucked because they'd been brand-new replacements for the items the Seven of Spades had wrecked while ransacking his apartment in November.

Levi snorted out a humorless laugh and shook his head.

This debacle was going even further off the rails, and fast. Dominic had to get back on track. He had one more tactic he knew would work, though he'd left it as a last resort.

"That was a pretty slick plan you came up with," he said. "Wearing clothes you know I like, offering me something you know I want so much it would keep me distracted while you got me in here and locked me up. You're not usually so manipulative."

"Yeah, well, I learned from the best," said Levi.

It was meant as an insult, but Dominic wasn't offended. If he weren't a skilled manipulator, he would never have become a successful bounty hunter or private investigator.

"Not all of it was an act, though, was it?" He scanned Levi lazily from head to foot. "I could feel how hard you were, hear how fast you were breathing. Your face was all flushed the way it gets when you need me inside you."

Levi took a sharp breath, his blush darkening. He enjoyed being gently embarrassed—though Dominic had to be careful, because he wasn't sure how the boundaries had shifted since their breakup.

"You can tell yourself you came here to protect me. But we both know there's something you want even more."

Levi regarded him, unblinking, for a moment. Then he said, "Rebel. Out."

She lifted her head and looked at Dominic. He nodded, and she hopped off the bed and trotted out of the room. Levi shut the door behind her, prowled toward the foot of the bed, and put one knee on the mattress.

Dominic set the water bottle on the nightstand, which was just barely within reach. He would need his unbound hand free—

"You must be fucking kidding me," Levi said silkily. He crawled up the bed, slow and predatory, until he could put both hands on Dominic's ankles and pin them to the mattress. "You think you can outmaneuver me with *sex*?"

Dominic hesitated. This wasn't what he'd expected—he'd intended to lure Levi onto the bed, then use his legs and free arm to wrestle Levi into a submission hold uncomfortable enough to force Levi to surrender the key. But Levi wasn't acting like he'd been lured anywhere.

"I won't deny you're good at manipulating me." Levi dragged his hands up Dominic's legs, over his thighs, and into the crook of his hips and groin, prompting Dominic's cock to give an interested twitch. "God knows you have a long and illustrious track record of doing exactly that. But you can't do it with sex, Dominic. You want me too much. You'd much rather I suck your cock than let you go."

Dominic grunted as Levi palmed his growing bulge. Levi was right between his legs, perfectly placed to subdue, but Dominic was paralyzed with the longing to see what Levi would do next.

"In fact, all I have to do is tell you how much I love feeling your big cock fucking my throat . . ." Levi smirked when Dominic was racked with a full-body shudder. "And you wouldn't leave this bed if I set it on fire."

"Are you gonna do it or just talk about it?" said Dominic, who knew when he'd been beaten.

Levi shifted backward, but Dominic only had time to feel a twinge of disappointment before Levi tugged on his ankles. Getting the hint, he lay down on his back again.

The expression on Levi's face was one of pure hunger while he yanked Dominic's jeans open and pulled Dominic's boxers down to free his cock. Dominic had been right—Levi wanted this. The problem was that Dominic wanted it just as much, even if it meant spending the night chained to his own bed.

Levi spat on his palm and began jerking Dominic to full hardness. As Dominic's cock swelled in Levi's hand, Levi's eyes glazed over and his jaw fell slack.

"Size queen," Dominic said.

Though Levi gave him an arch look, he didn't deny it. He shifted flat on his belly between Dominic's legs and rubbed his face along Dominic's shaft, making Dominic hiss at the slight rasp of stubble. Gazing hotly up at Dominic the entire time, Levi pressed a kiss to the base, nuzzled his way up, brushed the head back and forth across his mouth, and worked his way down the other side.

"Levi." Dominic managed coherent speech with his last two remaining brain cells. "Put it in your mouth."

Levi lapped delicately at the tip, then took just the head into his mouth and sucked hard. Dominic yelped as his hips levitated right off the bed.

With a laugh, Levi slid his mouth down Dominic's shaft and began blowing him in earnest, setting an aggressive pace right from the start. Dominic moaned in mingled pleasure and relief.

"That's it." He twined his free hand in Levi's curls, wishing they were longer. "Get down there."

Watching Levi struggle to take his cock never got less exciting. Even after months of practice, Levi couldn't handle the whole thing—but that never stopped him from trying his damnedest. The first few times the head of Dominic's cock pushed into his throat, he gagged a little, but he continued applying himself with characteristic resolve. Soon, Dominic was gliding smoothly in and out of that tight wet clutch on every pass.

"Fuck, yeah. Take a little more, baby—"

Levi smacked Dominic's hand away and pulled off his cock so fast that Dominic's balls gave an angry throb. "Don't call me that," Levi said, glaring daggers at him.

He'd loved the endearment when they were together, but since their breakup, he refused to let Dominic use it.

"I won't," Dominic said quietly. "Sorry."

Levi narrowed his eyes, then stripped off his shirt, got back on his stomach, and returned to work.

Dominic tentatively slid his fingers through Levi's hair again; when Levi didn't object, he cupped the back of Levi's head, let his own head fall back, and closed his eyes, just enjoying the moment. Levi was so good at this, enthusiastic and determined, deep-throating as much as he could manage while using his hand on the rest, his clever tongue in constant motion. Even when Levi took breaks to rest his jaw, he kept pumping Dominic's cock and nursing at the tip.

The pleasure was beginning to take an urgent turn for Dominic when Levi abruptly stopped and got off the bed. Dominic's eyes flew open, and he was ready to beg, to grovel, to promise *anything* if it would convince Levi to keep going—

But there was no need. Levi had only gotten up to undress, kicking off his shoes and peeling off his jeans and underwear to bare his wiry body. Dominic groaned low in his throat, admiring the lethal strength in Levi's lean, coiled muscles.

Levi bent over the side of the bed to kiss Dominic deeply and thoroughly. Then he swung a leg over Dominic's body to sit astride Dominic's chest, facing his feet.

"Yeah," Dominic breathed, seeing what Levi had in mind. "C'mere."

Levi inched backward until he could hook his legs under Dominic's shoulders and feed his cock into Dominic's mouth. With the support of the pillow, all Dominic had to do was tilt his head at the correct angle and relax his jaw, allowing Levi to slide right into his throat.

Moaning softly, Levi thrust a few times before stretching forward to resume sucking Dominic off as well. Because of their height difference, he could take even less of Dominic's cock than before, but the reciprocal pleasure of the new position made up for it.

Dominic bent his knees, planting his feet against the mattress so he could rock his hips and push his cock a little further into Levi's mouth. He used his uncuffed hand to guide Levi's pace, silently signaling how much he could take. Once he'd warmed up, he gave Levi a nudge, letting him go faster. Levi snapped his hips harder and harder until he was eagerly fucking Dominic's throat, his balls heavy on Dominic's face.

Dominic focused on controlling his breathing, which was difficult to do when Levi's loud, ragged groans were vibrating up and down his own cock. Fuck, he loved how vocal Levi was in bed—though even this beautiful moaning had nothing on the needy cries and shrieked curses and outright screams Levi let loose when he was really worked up. Dominic was greedy for more, but a blowjob alone wasn't going to pull the kinds of noises he wanted out of Levi.

He tapped Levi's hip. Levi pulled out at once, twisting around to look at Dominic over his shoulder. His pupils were huge, his thin lips swollen and wet.

"What's wrong?" he asked.

"Sit up a little," said Dominic, his voice hoarse from the ravages of Levi's cock.

Levi pushed himself up into a forty-five-degree angle, which had the effect of arching his back and presenting his pert ass right where Dominic wanted it. Dominic licked a path from Levi's balls to his hole, then buried his face between Levi's cheeks.

Levi let out an uneven gasp that shot straight to Dominic's cock. His thighs shifted farther apart, splaying open, and Dominic spread his cheeks even more. After lavishing Levi's hole with open-mouthed kisses, Dominic teasingly flicked his tongue over the sensitive flesh and dragged it in circles around the rim.

This was how to make Levi lose control. He was crying out now, his hips squirming restlessly. He had one hand braced on Dominic's stomach, the other still tugging Dominic's cock—though the handjob had become clumsy and uncoordinated.

When Dominic wriggled his tongue into Levi's hole, Levi yelped and abandoned Dominic's cock altogether, his hand shooting between his own legs to jerk himself off instead. Dominic gave him what he needed, tongue-fucking him vigorously; Levi pushed back into it, riding Dominic's face as his cries grew louder and more frantic.

It wasn't long before Dominic's jaw was aching as badly as his neglected cock. He pulled back a bit, sucked on his index finger until it was soaked with spit, and pushed his finger into Levi's ass. Moving carefully, knowing the friction would be significant without real lube, he hooked his finger toward the front of Levi's body in his search for—

A high, thready cry greeted his contact with Levi's prostate. Dominic grinned and got his face back in there, licking Levi's hole around his finger while he massaged Levi's prostate, his fingertip rolling and pulsing right where he knew Levi was craving it.

"*Fuck!*" Levi bounced his ass against Dominic's face and hand, his legs quivering where they were clamped against Dominic's body. "Like that, oh my God, don't stop don't stop don't *stop*—"

His voice rose to the scream Dominic had been waiting for, his hole clenching around Dominic's finger while he came all over Dominic's stomach and unbuttoned shirt. Dominic kept up the pressure on his prostate until he was whimpering and trembling with aftershocks, drained of every drop.

It was easy for Dominic to set his own needs aside when he was seeing to Levi's pleasure, but now that Levi had been taken care of, the demands of his own swollen erection crashed back with a vengeance. He withdrew his finger, smacked Levi's ass, and pushed Levi forward. "Levi, come on. Come *on*."

Still gasping, Levi unhooked his legs from Dominic's shoulders and shuffled forward until he was crouched over Dominic's stomach, in a better position to suck Dominic's cock properly. That gave Dominic a mouthwatering view of his glistening hole flexing and fluttering between lush cheeks.

Dominic had forgotten he was bound. He reached for Levi with both hands, only to have his right brought up jarringly short by the cuffs. Lust bolted down his spine, drawing his balls up tight and releasing a stream of pre-come into Levi's busy mouth.

He grabbed Levi's ass with his one available hand, brushing his thumb back and forth over Levi's hole to give him some extra encouragement. Levi was a hot mess this time around, but there was special charm in a sloppy, overeager blowjob. He could feel Levi choking and moaning around his cock, spurring him to drive his hips up at an increasingly rapid pace.

Dominic strained against the handcuffs again and again, the reminder of his vulnerable state now more thrilling than anything else. He was only able to fuck Levi's mouth because Levi was letting him do it. All he could do was lie here and accept what Levi saw fit to give him. If Levi got up and walked out right now, Dominic would be powerless to stop him.

Ironically, the idea that Levi might forsake him on the cusp of orgasm was what pushed him to the very edge. But he wanted more than to come in Levi's mouth, no matter how hungry Levi was for it. No, Dominic needed to see his come all over Levi's body, had to mark him up, had to prove that Levi belonged to him and him alone—

"Levi." When Levi didn't respond, Dominic squeezed his ass hard and slipped the tip of his thumb into Levi's hole, which made Levi jerk and look back at him. "Let me come on your face."

Levi wrinkled his nose. "What? No!"

"Please." Dominic snuck his thumb further inside, enjoying Levi's shaky moan. "I'll do whatever you want. *Please*."

"I'm not letting you come on my face, Dominic." Levi bit his lip, rolling his hips against Dominic's hand. "You can come on my back."

"Okay," Dominic said quickly. That was almost as good.

Levi moved forward again, straddling Dominic's thighs. He arched his back and pressed his ass against the base of Dominic's cock.

"Oh, fuck, stay like that." Dominic took himself in hand—a little awkwardly, because he had to use his left, but he was far past the point of giving a shit. He jerked himself off brutally, staring at the vision before him. Levi had his face half-turned, watching Dominic from the corner of his eye—pretending he wasn't eager for a come shot, the bastard—

Dominic yanked on the cuffs again, giving himself one last *zing*, and shot his load all over the tightly corded muscles of Levi's back. Levi made quiet noises as Dominic's come rained down on his skin, pulse after pulse striping his gorgeous body, until Dominic managed a final spurt at the base of Levi's spine and sagged against the bed, exhausted.

Levi hung his head between his arms and didn't move. Dominic closed his eyes, wanting to savor the afterglow before it was inevitably shattered.

About a minute later, Levi got off him and went into the bathroom. Dominic didn't bother opening his eyes until Levi returned, but all Levi did was silently clean his own come off Dominic's stomach and shirt with a damp washcloth.

Though Levi was nude, Dominic was fully dressed—albeit with his clothes in disarray. He even still had his shoes on.

Levi frowned at Dominic's right arm. "Your wrist is bruising."

"It's fine. I was pulling against the cuffs on purpose."

Levi met Dominic's eyes for the first time since they'd both come, then immediately looked away.

"You can take them off," Dominic said. "I give you my word I won't leave the apartment tonight if you give me a reason to stay."

Levi shot him an incredulous glance.

"Please. We can be angry with each other tomorrow. I just . . ." Dominic trailed off and sighed. He always felt a little raw after being restrained during sex, and he couldn't handle the bitterness and resentment that lay between them right now.

After a long moment, Levi nodded, set the washcloth aside, and retrieved the key from his jeans. He climbed over Dominic to kneel on his right side while he unlocked the handcuffs.

The second Dominic's arm was free, he tossed Levi sideways and threw himself on top, attempting to pin Levi to the bed. But Levi had anticipated the move, and used Dominic's momentum against him to keep them both rolling—right off the far edge of the bed. Dominic landed hard on his back with Levi's full weight on top of him.

While Dominic coughed, struggling to recover his breath, Levi jumped up and scrambled away. Tellingly, he didn't leave the room. Instead, he backed up against the wall, which was something a trained fighter would never do in a real confrontation. He didn't even have his hands up; his arms remained slack by his sides, his palms pressed flat to the wall.

Dominic rose slowly to his feet. When Levi still didn't move, Dominic stripped out of his unbuttoned shirt and put his boxers and jeans to rights, each movement unhurried and deliberate.

All Levi did was watch him, his chest heaving.

"You're gonna pay for what you did to me," Dominic said. He stalked across the bedroom, grabbed Levi's hips, and shoved Levi harder against the wall, using his height and bulk to loom over him. Levi's breathing sped up even more.

They had a safeword, but with or without it, Dominic would have stopped if he'd seen the slightest hint of fear or doubt or even hesitancy on Levi's part.

The only thing coming through in Levi's body language was fervent anticipation.

"That was a terrible abuse of authority, Detective." Dominic stroked his thumbs over Levi's sensitive hip bones. "I think someone needs to teach you a lesson."

"You'll have to catch me first," said Levi.

Dominic snorted. "I think I have you pretty well—"

Levi jabbed his fingers into the hollow of Dominic's throat. As Dominic staggered backward, choking, he caught the ghost of a smile on Levi's face before Levi fled the bedroom.

Dominic growled and gave chase.

Levi woke up only minutes before his alarm was due to go off. He jumped out of Dominic's bed, caught himself on the nightstand with a hissed curse when a deep ache throbbed through his core, and gritted his teeth while he searched for his phone in the mess on the floor.

He found it and canceled the alarm just in time to prevent it from going off and waking Dominic. He glanced back at the bed. Rebel was watching him quizzically from the foot, but Dominic was still dead to the world.

Crisis averted.

It was a good thing Dominic was such a deep sleeper, because Levi made more noise than usual as he limped around the bedroom, gingerly gathering his clothes, pausing every now and then to bite down a pained yelp.

Dominic had *ruined* him last night, in a variety of highly imaginative and extremely vigorous positions. He'd capitalized on his vaunted sexual stamina to push Levi right to the edge of what he could handle and hold him there for hours.

Levi had relished every single second. It was some of the best sex they'd ever had.

But now . . . now he felt like the world's biggest idiot again. He'd slept with his ex for the umpteenth time, even though things were only changing for the worse. Dominic's relapse was getting so bad that he'd been pawning his belongings and neglecting basic household tasks like washing dishes and taking out the trash for what seemed like weeks. Yet Levi *still* couldn't stay off his dick.

This was humiliating.

Levi felt cowardly sneaking out of Dominic's apartment without waking him up, but not so much that he changed his mind about it. He shut the front door as quietly as he could when he left, and felt another twinge of remorse when he realized he didn't have keys to Dominic's new locks.

Oh well. At least Dominic had Rebel.

Levi made his slow, painful way down the exterior staircase and hobbled out to the parking lot. It could not possibly have been more obvious what he'd gotten up to last night. He was going to have to take a shit-ton of ibuprofen, and even then, he wasn't sure he'd be able to walk normally for at least a day. Maybe he should just call in sick.

It was second nature for Levi to check under his car as he approached, as well as to look in the back seat before he got in. The behavior was so automatic that he was rarely conscious of it, so he was already pressing the remote unlock button on his keys when he tossed a casual glance through the rear window of his Honda.

There was a man sitting in the back seat.

Levi sprang backward, his pain forgotten under a rush of adrenaline. His hand went for his gun—or where his gun would have been, if he'd been wearing it.

"*Shit.*" He pulled his phone out instead. He'd have to call 911, and both the phone and his keys could be used as weapons.

As his thumb hovered over the emergency call button, however, his nape prickled with a sense of disquiet. There was definitely a man in the back seat—the shape was unmistakable even from this distance and through the tinted glass—but that man hadn't moved. He should have noticed Levi by now and reacted.

Guard up and improvised weapons at the ready, Levi approached the car more cautiously to take a better look.

All the air left his lungs in one noisy exhalation. The man was Wayne Reddick. He was holding a merrily wrapped gift box in his lap, topped with a bow and a seven of spades card—all of it soaked in the blood from his slit throat.

CHAPTER 8

"**S**houldn't you be going to work?" Levi asked.

"I'm a PI," said Dominic. "One of the perks is a flexible schedule."

Levi didn't react to that, but then, Dominic hadn't seen him react to much of anything for the past hour. His face was wooden, his voice flat; he'd been like this ever since he'd woken Dominic with news of the Seven of Spades's latest murder.

The parking lot was swarming with LVMPD and FBI, including the local bomb squad, who'd been called out to inspect the suspicious package the victim inside Levi's car was holding. Crime scene tape was strung up along the perimeter to keep back bystanders—a group Levi belonged to this time, which had to be a difficult pill to swallow. Dominic's curious neighbors crowded along the chain-link fence separating the lot from the building, trying to get a better look at all the commotion, while the press was kept at bay on the street side.

Along with Carlos and Jasmine, who'd joined them a while ago, Dominic and Levi were standing off to one side, Dominic's body angled to hide Levi from cameras as much as possible. Rebel sat beside Dominic, on a leash even though she didn't need one; it dangled half-forgotten from Dominic's hand.

Levi watched the cops working on his car with an emotional detachment that was worryingly uncharacteristic. Though he often pretended to be cold and aloof, that was never the reality. Where was his anger at the Seven of Spades's violation? His frustration at being relegated to the fringes of the crime scene?

Dominic cast Jasmine a helpless glance. She stepped forward and put a hand on Levi's shoulder.

"Can I get you anything, Levi? Coffee?"

"No, thanks."

Both Carlos's and Jasmine's eyebrows shot up, and Dominic's concern increased tenfold. He'd *never* heard Levi turn down coffee.

The bomb squad declared the package free of explosives, and the CSIs and crime scene photographer started crawling all over the car. Martine stood a few feet away from it, deep in conversation with Sergeant Wen and a black woman in an FBI windbreaker who Dominic didn't recognize.

Keeping his head on a swivel—all the better to protect Levi from an incoming threat—Dominic stifled a groan when he saw Jonah Gibbs strolling toward them in the course of securing the perimeter.

To Dominic's surprise, Gibbs greeted Levi almost gently. "Hey, Detective. You okay?"

"I'm fine. Thank you." Levi continued gazing vacantly in the direction of his car.

Gibbs frowned at Dominic. "Russo? What are you doing here?"

"This is my building."

Gibbs looked back and forth between Dominic and Levi, then glanced at Levi's car. There was no way to prevent him from drawing the right conclusion—there was only one reason Levi would be parked at Dominic's apartment so early in the morning.

"I thought you guys broke up," said Gibbs.

Levi closed his eyes.

"Move along, Officer," Dominic said sharply.

Gibbs smirked and walked away. Taking one deep breath, Levi opened his eyes—but he didn't look even slightly angry, which worried Dominic more than the explosive reaction he might have expected.

Levi's anger was frequently toxic and out of control, sure, but it was also his most reliable defense mechanism. How would he protect himself without it?

When the crime scene techs finished with the car, Martine leaned into the back seat, retrieved the gift box, and set it on the hood. It seemed the lid was wrapped separately from the rest, because she was able to lift it off without unwrapping the box. She peered inside with a furrowed brow, then pulled out a handheld voice recorder.

After a brief conference with Wen, Martine walked toward their little group, joined them on the other side of the tape, and gestured for Levi to accompany her to the far corner of the lot. Dominic handed Rebel's leash to Carlos and followed without being invited, but Martine didn't comment.

"This is the only thing that was in the box," she said to Levi. "Do you want me to listen to it first and tell you what's on it?"

Levi shook his head. "Just play it. Please."

Martine hit Play. The sounds of heavy thuds and wet crunching filled the air, along with a man crying out in pain—someone was getting a serious beatdown.

"No, please, all right, all right!" the man on the recording said. "I'll do it, just—*ungh*—just please stop. I'll do what you want."

What came next was definitely another person talking, but the recording had been altered so the voice was only an unintelligible *whomp-whomp-whomp* like the adults in the *Peanuts* cartoons.

The man snuffled in fear. "I understand. Please don't." He took several sobbing breaths before continuing. "My name is Grant Sheppard. From 1999 to 2011, I was the director of the Trenton Police Department."

Dominic, Levi, and Martine all went rigid. On the recording, the mystery voice spoke again.

"I told you," said Sheppard, "there's no way I can remember every case that—"

Though there was no sound of impact, Sheppard let out a high-pitched shriek.

"Fuck, okay! Yeah, I remember the one you mean. It was in 2005, 2006. Some college kid got himself beat outside a gay bar. It was pretty nasty."

Whomp-whomp.

"How the hell would I remember the victim's—"

This time, Sheppard's screaming and cursing went on for a full ten seconds. Dominic's stomach turned over, and Martine winced while she listened. Levi alone seemed unaffected.

"Levi Abrams! The victim's name was Levi Abrams." Sheppard cried quietly for a few moments until his tormenter spoke again, then said, "Yes, that's right. The case is still unsolved. The perpetrators were never identified."

Whomp.

"What? No—" Sheppard screamed in terror, the noise raising goose bumps all over Dominic's body. "Wait, God, please! Please don't. I'll tell you."

There was a pause while Sheppard gulped in air. When he spoke again, his voice was thick with mucous—and blood, Dominic suspected.

"We identified the suspects' likely vehicle from a nearby camera that had captured a car running a red light. The car was registered to a Scott West. His father was a state senator. A pillar of the community, one of our biggest donors."

Levi rocked back a step.

"We contacted him first as a courtesy," Sheppard went on. "Turns out Scott and a few of his friends had been . . . getting up to some mischief. His father offered us money to make the problem go away. So we swept the whole thing under the rug."

Levi swayed on his feet, his face absolutely bloodless. Dominic steadied him.

Whomp-whomp-whomp.

"Yes," said Sheppard. "I—I advised my officers to accept a bribe in return for covering up a violent crime. Is that what you wanted? Is that what you came here for?" He was desperate now, sobbing freely. "Please, I know the other men's names! I can tell you. I'll tell you everything. I'll do whatever you want, just please, *please* don't— No, wait— No! *No!*"

Sheppard's voice escalated into hysterical screaming, and then the recording cut off. The three of them stood in shocked silence for a minute.

"They always told us they didn't have any leads," Levi said faintly. "My parents badgered them for months and got shut down every time. But the cops knew who it was all along." Though Dominic's hand was still on his back, he had yet to push Dominic away.

"Sounds like the Seven of Spades may have killed this guy too," Martine said, indicating the recorder. "I think you should come to the substation with me."

Levi nodded and took several halting steps toward her. He looked completely out of it, almost catatonic.

"Do you want me to come with you?" Dominic said without thinking. Why would Levi want *him*, of all people?

"Hmm?" Levi blinked, but he didn't sneer or scoff. "Oh. No, that's okay. Thanks though."

And that was all. Martine gave Dominic a small nod that spoke volumes—*I'll take care of him, don't worry*—before leading Levi away.

As Dominic watched them go, he noticed an obvious hitch in Levi's step and palmed his face. A sight that might have aroused him under other circumstances now made him feel like the world's biggest asshole. He'd been way too rough last night, and Levi would have to suffer the consequences of that all day on top of dealing with the rest of this garbage.

Over by Levi's car, the coroner investigator was supervising the transfer of the victim's corpse to a body bag on a stretcher. Two down, two to go.

Dominic couldn't shake the feeling that the worst was yet to come.

Levi wasn't used to being on this side of the equation. He sat on the couch in the same room where he'd interviewed Rose Nguyen, an untouched cup of coffee on the end table beside him. A nasty headache throbbed right behind his eyes, reverberating through his skull to the cramped muscles in his neck and shoulders. He was having trouble focusing through the fog that had taken over his brain.

The cops had known the identities of the men who'd almost beaten him to death all along. They'd looked Levi and his parents in the eye and lied to their faces, over and over again. Men who should have gone to prison had been allowed to walk free for years—for *money*.

The revelation should have thrown Levi into an unholy rage; he'd been provoked by far less in the past. But the burning anger that infected him deep in his core—the bright spark always ready to flare up at a moment's notice—had gone dormant, leaving him empty and cold right when he needed it most.

He glanced up as the door opened. Martine and Wen came in, accompanied by Natasha.

"I asked Natasha to be here," Martine said. "I hope that's okay."

"Of course," said Levi, who was happy to see her. A social worker by training and a mediator by nature, Natasha exerted a calming influence on any situation, and had a knack for offering support without judgment.

Though the fact that Martine considered Natasha's presence necessary didn't bode well for the conversation they were about to have.

Martine and Wen sat in chairs across from the couch, while Natasha took a seat beside Levi. She squeezed his knee and gave him an encouraging smile.

Wen fussed with his tie, though it was already pin-straight. "The current police director in Trenton told me that Grant Sheppard moved to Philadelphia after he retired. I just got off the phone with the Philly PD, and they're faxing over the case file on his homicide now."

"So he *was* murdered?" Levi asked.

"He was killed in an apparent home invasion on December 27," Martine said. "His house was ransacked, everything valuable stolen. He was tied to a chair, badly beaten, and electrocuted multiple times with a stun gun before ultimately being stabbed to death."

"Any drugs in his system?"

"They had no reason to check."

"Was there a seven of spades card at the scene?"

"No."

Levi's brow creased. "That doesn't fit the Seven of Spades's MO. At *all*. They don't beat people, they don't stab, we've only seen them use a stun gun once . . ." A flare of fresh pain speared through his head; he hissed and ground the heels of his hands into his aching eyeballs. "Sorry. I have the worst fucking headache."

Martine made an exasperated noise. "You're in caffeine withdrawal. Drink your coffee."

He picked up his abandoned cup of substation coffee and took a few sips. Already poor quality, the coffee was even worse lukewarm—

he'd been waiting in this room for a while. He continued drinking it, though, because it was marginally preferable to the withdrawal symptoms.

"Almost every element of this situation is a deviation from the Seven of Spades's MO," Wen said. "We can assume their . . . attachment to you is what's driving the unusual behavior. As for Sheppard, taking credit for his death would have interfered with the killer's plans to trap the other four men. Now they're running around Las Vegas with two captives, planning God knows what, and we can't anticipate their actions because they've never done anything like this before."

"The FBI hasn't made any progress in locating the missing men?" Natasha asked.

Slumping in her chair, Martine ran a hand through her short, springy finger coils. "We've got nothing. It's like they were abducted by aliens."

Levi swallowed a mouthful of terrible coffee. "What about the Philly cops? Did they have any leads for Sheppard's homicide?"

"They had chalked it up to local gang violence." Wen hesitated. "But . . . there's a problem."

He and Martine exchanged a troubled look that instantly had Levi on high alert.

"What?" Levi said.

Martine crossed and uncrossed her legs before speaking. "Sheppard was killed in Philadelphia on December 27. You were in New Jersey visiting your family for Hanukkah the same day."

There was Levi's rage.

It burst back into flame all at once, scorching him from the inside out, making him shake so badly he had to hurry to put down his coffee. He struggled to control his suddenly rapid breathing while his hands flexed open and shut, desperate for something to throw, to hit, to break—anything to release the building fury burning his throat and churning his stomach.

"You must be joking." Natasha's face was slack with astonishment. "Martine, for you of all people to imply—"

"I'm not implying anything," Martine snapped. "I'd believe Santa Claus was the Seven of Spades before I'd believe it was Levi. But I also don't think the timing of Sheppard's murder is a coincidence. Neither is the fact that Wayne Reddick's body was found in Levi's car."

Levi had to put himself through one of Alana's breathing exercises before he trusted himself to speak. "So you think . . . what, the Seven of Spades is setting me up? That doesn't make sense."

"Agent Chaudhary suggested the Seven of Spades wanted to recruit you as an asset in the future. This may be their way of forcing your hand."

"Regardless of the killer's intentions, it's even more vital now that you stay as far away from the case as possible." Wen pinched the bridge of his nose. "The press is going to have a field day with this. We'll try to keep most of it under wraps, but there's no hiding that you were removed from the investigation, and any dedicated journalist will be able to find out why."

"Maybe you should take the rest of the day off," Natasha said to Levi.

"I can't do that. If I'm not working, I'll go insane. Plus, I have a meeting scheduled with Carolyn Royce this afternoon."

"There's no reason you can't work," said Wen. "Just be your usual circumspect self." He paused. "And if you are approached by the press, please try not to . . ."

"Throw gasoline on the fire?" Levi said wryly.

Wen nodded. Levi wasn't offended; there was an excellent chance he'd do exactly that if a reporter rubbed him the wrong way while he was in this kind of mood.

"I have to go home to shower and change anyway," he said. "After that, I'll stay at my desk and screen my calls until I'm ready to meet Ms. Royce."

At least the detour would give him the opportunity to use some of Alana's techniques to work through his anger constructively. With the Seven of Spades shining an ever-brightening spotlight right on him, he couldn't risk doing anything that would damage the LVMPD's reputation.

Or his own.

A bell chimed as Dominic pushed open the door to Value Pawn. Unlike some of Vegas's famous upmarket pawnshops, this dive—located in a seedy strip mall on the west side—was grimy and run-down. The windows were plastered so heavily with blazing signs advertising payday loans and cash for gold that little sunlight could penetrate, leaving the shop lit by the sickly glow of the flickering fluorescents overhead. Shelves crammed with everything from electronics to jewelry to knockoff handbags created narrow, claustrophobic aisles, and the walls were lined with enough shotguns and rifles to arm a small militia.

A rail-thin white man with weathered skin and a scraggly gray beard stood behind the counter, sucking noisily on chewing tobacco while leafing through an issue of *Guns & Ammo*. Up in the corner, a television chained where the wall met the ceiling played a trashy daytime talk show.

"Hey, Paulie," Dominic said as he approached.

"Russo," Paulie said without looking up. "Whatcha selling today?"

"Not selling. Buying."

Paulie snorted and flipped a page in his magazine. "You got no money. Unless you finally hit it big?"

Dominic placed a thick envelope on the counter. "My client is the one paying."

Paulie eyed the envelope while he spit a stream of tobacco juice into a red Solo cup, then opened the flap. He riffled his thumb along the wad of bills inside. "That's a lot of cash," he said suspiciously.

"There's been a string of kidnaps-for-ransom in the Valley over the past couple of months. Professional jobs, high-roller victims, no police involvement—until the last victim turned up murdered this weekend."

"I know nothing about that."

"But you can find out."

Paulie's shifty eyes darted around the empty shop. Dominic placed both hands on the counter to reclaim his attention.

"Why do you think I come here, Paulie? Your amazing deals? The fantastic ambiance?" Dominic leaned forward. "You're a fence and a fixer. Let's not play games. You've hooked me up before."

"That was when you were a bounty hunter," Paulie said with a grimace. "Now you're a PI fucking a cop—or were, anyway. You've gone legit, and I'm no snitch."

Bounty hunting was no less legitimate than private investigation or law enforcement, but there was a widespread perception that bounty hunters were only in it for the money and the thrill of the chase, just one step away from becoming criminals themselves. That had worked to Dominic's advantage in the past, so he didn't argue against it now.

"I'm not the law," he said. "I don't care what kind of illegal shit you've got going on here. I just want to solve this case for my client so I can get the payout." He didn't worry about overselling the bit; scumbags like Paulie were always willing to believe other people were as greedy and corrupt as they were themselves.

Paulie sucked harder on his chew while he considered the cash.

Exploiting the opening, Dominic said, "Jobs like these kidnappings don't go down without making some kind of impact. Manpower, resources, a safe house—they would have needed *something* from the local community. I just need you to point me in the right direction."

Paulie spit decisively into the Solo cup and snatched the envelope. "Yeah, all right. I'll see what I can find and hit you up on your cell. Don't come back here for at least a week."

"Deal."

As Dominic turned away from the counter, a blast of tinny music sounded from the television, which cut from the talk show to a local newsroom.

"This is a breaking news bulletin," said the anchorwoman. "The vigilante serial killer Seven of Spades claimed another victim this morning—New Jersey resident Wayne Reddick, one of the three men reported abducted from local nightclub Ambrosia on Friday night. We've just learned that the car in which Reddick's body was found belonged to Detective Levi Abrams of the LVMPD."

Dominic stiffened. The shot changed to a panning view of that morning's crime scene. Levi could be glimpsed in the background, but he was mostly concealed by Dominic's own body, as intended.

"As we've previously reported, Detective Abrams was one of the lead detectives on the Seven of Spades case until this past Saturday.

He was removed from the investigation for undisclosed reasons after the serial killer murdered tourist Jared Foley at the Caesars Palace hotel and allegedly abducted three of Foley's friends. Inside sources at the LVMPD now tell us that Detective Abrams has strong personal connections to all four victims, though the exact nature of that connection remains unclear."

That had been fast. Dominic rubbed an anxious hand over his mouth and jaw, the sting against his palm reminding him that he'd forgotten to shave yet again.

"We've also been informed that Detective Abrams has been named a person of interest in a Philadelphia homicide that occurred in December, though our sources emphasized that he is not an active suspect."

What? That—that had to be Trenton's former police director. Why hadn't Martine updated him?

"The LVMPD and FBI continue to coordinate a massive city-wide manhunt in search of the two men still missing. George Quintana and Scott West are believed to be held captive by the Seven of Spades somewhere within the Las Vegas Valley. The FBI is offering a substantial reward in return for information leading to their whereabouts ..."

"Looks like that boy of yours got himself in some hot water," Paulie said while the anchorwoman continued her appeal to the public.

"He's not my boy," Dominic said absently, eyes still riveted to the TV.

"Wish the cops would find this freak already." Paulie slurped around his chew. "He's bad for business."

Tearing his attention away from the TV, Dominic tossed Paulie a smirk. "What's the matter, Paulie? Worried you might be next?"

Paulie scowled. Dominic chuckled and headed for the door, though now his mind was less on the Royce case and more on Levi.

Over the past year, Levi had become a highly recognizable public figure in Las Vegas. He was generally regarded in a favorable light, his mystique only heightened by his flat refusal to speak with the press, but if civilian sentiment turned against him now ...

On his way out of the pawnshop, Dominic bumped into a group of three young skinheads coming inside. They were wearing threadbare tank tops and low-slung jeans, all the better to show off the tattoos of white supremacist symbols and Utopia gang signs scrawled across their pasty skin.

"Watch it, bro," one of the gangbangers said.

Dominic drew himself up to his full height, letting the breadth of his shoulders and the bulk of his muscles speak for him. He could see the men were packing—they had their guns tucked into their waistbands, the morons—but so was he. Ever since the Seven of Spades had trashed his apartment, he'd taken to carrying his gun everywhere it was legal. And he doubted these assholes had any real training or skill with a firearm.

A reckless craving inside him *wanted* the men to start something. He had half a foot and sixty pounds of muscle on the largest of them, and beating three Nazi punks to a bloody pulp might be the most fun he'd had in a long time.

"Do we have a problem?" he said mildly.

The gangbanger who'd spoken hesitated, taking in Dominic's stature. His eyes traveled knowingly over the slight bulge of the shoulder holster beneath Dominic's jacket, so it seemed he wasn't completely brain-dead.

"Nah, man." He lifted his hands, though his chest was still puffed up. "It's cool."

He and his two buddies continued on their way. Dominic glanced back at Paulie, wondering if he should leave him alone with these skinheads. Paulie was watching the men with clear irritation but no apparent fear.

Figuring a straight white Christian man like Paulie was about as safe around Utopia as anyone could possibly be, Dominic left the shop to the chime of the bell over the door.

Levi pulled into a visitor's garage in a business park east of the Strip, not far from where Dominic lived near the University of Nevada, Las Vegas. His own car was still a crime scene, so he'd picked up an unmarked sedan from the department motor pool. Even once his car was released, though, he'd never be able to drive it again. Maybe he should donate it.

Shaking his head, Levi pulled his mind off the Seven of Spades and put it back on the matter at hand. Of everyone involved in the kidnaps-for-ransom case, Nathan Royce had the greatest means and opportunity—he had unfettered access to the K&R policies and more than enough resources to hire and supply professional mercenaries.

The missing link was motive. Levi was here to follow his hunch that Royce's relationship with his assistant Juliette could have driven him to arrange the kidnappings in preparation for taking off with her. Although that theory did raise the question as to why Royce would kidnap Buckner when he would have known for a fact that the man's policy had lapsed.

Dominic might have gotten the jump on Levi in interviewing the victims, but he wouldn't have gone anywhere near Carolyn Royce— he wouldn't investigate his own client, if only to avoid pissing off his boss. This was one lead Levi had all to himself.

Levi strolled through the business park, surveying the pale, tidy stucco buildings with their neat rows of enormous windows. This was no different from anything he'd see back home in New Jersey, with the exception of the palm trees dotting the landscape.

Carolyn and Nathan Royce had both been independently wealthy before they married. She was the executive VP of Graff Gaming, a corporation that owned dozens of gaming properties across the US. It had been founded by her grandfather, and her family still ran it, though it had since gone public.

After checking the building's directory, Levi took the elevator to the third floor and stepped out into the lobby of Graff Gaming's head offices. He approached the receptionist's desk, passing a chattering group of people who just missed the elevator as it closed behind him.

He flashed the receptionist his badge. "I'm Detective Levi Abrams with the LVMPD. I have an appointment to see Carolyn Royce."

The group by the elevator, who'd already been shooting curious glances his way, stopped talking altogether and stared. The receptionist gaped up at him. The elevator doors slid back open with a soft *ding*, then closed again a few seconds later when nobody got inside.

Levi forced himself not to react. Martine had warned him that some of the news about his connection to the Seven of Spades's victims and Sheppard's murder had leaked.

Instead of snapping at the receptionist the way he felt the urge to, he clasped his hands at his waist, squeezing until his knuckles strained against his skin, and simply raised his eyebrows.

"Um . . . yes, sir. One moment." She picked up her phone and punched in an extension. "Alan? I have *Detective Abrams* for Ms. Royce . . . Yeah, thanks." She hung up, gave Levi an awkward smile, and said, "Her assistant will be right with you."

"Thanks."

She continued to stare at him. The people at the elevator were whispering to each other now, making no move to call the elevator back, and Levi couldn't take it anymore. He turned around.

"Don't you people have somewhere to be?" he said coldly.

The gawkers startled, most of them flushing and ducking their heads. The man nearest the elevator jabbed the call button; the doors popped open immediately, and everyone piled on. They all avoided Levi's eyes until the elevator whisked them away.

When the assistant came to collect Levi, he was much more discreet, welcoming Levi politely and leading him to a corner office. He knocked on the door and opened it without waiting for a response, ushering Levi inside.

The office was a handsome space, decorated with obvious wealth but lacking ostentation. Framed photographs of Graff Gaming's properties hung on the walls alongside several industry awards and a diploma from the Wharton School of Business.

The woman who rose from her desk and came forward to greet him was white, in her late fifties, with pale blonde hair going silver. Like her office, she exhibited no vulgar display of wealth, but Levi noted the custom fit of her suit, the pearls adorning her ears and throat, the Patek Philippe watch glinting on her wrist. This woman had money, and plenty of it.

"Detective Abrams," she said with a gracious smile. "It's a pleasure to meet you."

"Thank you for making time to see me, Ms. Royce."

"Carolyn, please."

"Levi," he said as they shook hands.

"I have to admit, I already know a lot about you. I've been following the Seven of Spades case since last April." Carolyn waved him into a comfortable chair and sat behind her desk. "I heard about the circumstances of the murder this morning. I'm very sorry. That must have been awful, and to be removed from the investigation after all your hard work . . ."

Levi held himself stiffly, perched at the edge of his seat. "It's in the best interests of the case."

"Those two other men are still missing?"

"Ms. . . . Carolyn. With all due respect, I can't comment on that investigation. I'm here to talk to you about a different set of kidnappings."

"Yes, of course," she said, seeming unoffended by the brush-off. "Nathan's kidnap-and-ransom clients—you said as much on the phone. I'd love to help, but I'm not sure how I can."

"Has he told you what's been going on?" Levi asked.

She tilted her hand back and forth. "A bit. We don't usually talk much about work. He did tell me more after the homicide, but . . ."

He filled in the blanks for her, though he held back a few details that weren't being shared with civilians. She listened with her chin propped on her clasped hands, a slight frown on her face.

"So Nathan thinks it's either corporate sabotage or insurance fraud?" she said when he finished.

"Yes. But the private investigator he hired has found no evidence to that effect." He watched her closely. "If I can be honest, this looks like an inside job."

"An inside . . . You mean Nathan's a suspect?" She leaned back in her chair, waving a hand. "Impossible. Nathan would never harm anyone, and besides, he has no reason to do such a thing. It'll ruin his professional reputation, and it's not like he needs the money."

"Are you sure about that? Does your husband have any debts? Any interest or activities that might get him into financial trouble?"

She shot a pointed glance toward the photographs on the wall. "You mean like gambling? No. Nathan's never been much of a risk-taker, which is another reason I can't imagine him doing anything like this."

"People can do surprising things when they're backed into a corner," Levi said. "Does Mr. Royce have any expensive hobbies? Cars, wine?" He paused. "Women?"

Carolyn's lips quirked. "If there's something you'd like to say, Levi, feel free."

All right, then. "Are you aware that your husband is having an affair with his assistant?"

Unexpectedly, she laughed. "They're sleeping with each other, but it's not an affair. Nathan and I have always been nonmonogamous. We're free to have our fun on the side, so long as we're discreet."

"Do you really consider having sex with his assistant to be discreet?" Levi couldn't keep the incredulity out of his voice.

"It's not the smartest thing he's ever done." She shrugged. "But Juliette is very beautiful, and Nathan is— Well, you know how men are."

"So their relationship isn't serious?"

"Not at all."

That didn't fit with what Levi had observed of Royce and Juliette's interaction, though that moment had admittedly been brief. "Do you have any concerns that he might want to . . . take his relationship with her further?"

She blinked, and he could see her putting the pieces together. "And start a new life with her and his ill-gotten gains, you mean? No. I'm sure Juliette is a lovely playmate, but that's all she is. Nathan wouldn't sacrifice safety and stability for her—or anyone else, for that matter. He's not that kind of man."

Though Levi wanted to give her the benefit of the doubt, he'd spent a decade listening to hundreds of people repeat variations on the same theme: *He would never do that. She wouldn't hurt a fly. He'd never leave me.* In every single case, that emphatic statement had been dead wrong. Everyone hid parts of themselves, even from the people who loved them most.

"Can I ask to what extent you and Mr. Royce share your finances?" he said, rather than directly question her faith in her husband.

"We don't, really. We both came into the marriage with a great deal of money and family assets, so we have a strict prenuptial agreement, and we keep our incomes separate. We have one joint account for the mortgage and things of that nature."

Meaning it would be easy for Royce to move large amounts of money around with his wife being none the wiser. He could funnel thousands of dollars to the mercenaries doing his bidding, and she'd have no way of knowing.

Levi drummed his fingers on the arm of his chair. "Have you noticed anything unusual in his behavior lately? Anything out of the ordinary?"

"No," Carolyn said right away—but like most people, she stopped and reconsidered once she gave the question real thought. "Well, I mean, he has seemed anxious these past few weeks. Jumpy, even. But who wouldn't be, considering what's been going on?"

"What do you mean by anxious and jumpy?"

"Oh, you know. Hurrying out of the room to take calls, sometimes at odd hours. Startling badly when he's taken by surprise. Keeping his briefcase with him at all times." Her speech slowed as she talked, her eyes becoming unfocused. "But that could all be explained by the kidnappings. It was probably his investigator he was talking to."

Whereas before her voice had been firm with confidence, now she sounded more like she was trying to convince herself. It was a common phenomenon—having been asked to consider Royce's recent behavior in a certain light, she was seeing patterns she hadn't consciously noticed before.

That new suspicion meant she'd do part of Levi's job for him; she was better placed to investigate her husband than Levi ever could be. He decided to back off before he pushed too hard.

"I think I have enough for now." He handed her his card as he stood. "If anything else occurs to you, please give me a call."

"Of course," she said, standing along with him. "You're not planning to arrest Nathan, are you?"

"Not at present. We don't have enough evidence to arrest anyone, though that may change if there's another kidnapping. Hopefully, the new police attention will convince whoever's behind this to call it quits." Levi glanced at his watch, most of his focus on his plans for the rest of the day. "I'd do even more to ensure that, if your husband would cooperate."

Carolyn frowned. "I'm sorry?"

"He knows who all the potential victims are. The kidnapping ring only targets the subjects of KIG's kidnap-and-ransom policies. The LVMPD would like to warn everyone who may still be in danger, but he refuses to share that list with us."

Her face went blank for a moment, and then her nostrils flared and her lips thinned out. "He *what*?"

"We're battling it out with lawyers," Levi said, taken aback by the strength of her reaction. "I'm sure he'll be forced to turn over the list eventually."

"There's no need." Her voice was as flinty as her pale-blue eyes. "I'll take care of this. You'll have that list by the end of the day—I give you my word."

That was a surprising coup. Levi hadn't been angling for Carolyn's help in strong-arming her husband, but he was appreciative nonetheless. He didn't envy Royce whatever she had in store.

Levi returned to the substation, but he hated the way everyone was treating him like a volcano on the brink of eruption, so he left at the regular quitting time—which was so unusual for him that it drew even more attention. Though Martine wanted him to stay at her place for a while, he didn't think that was a good idea. She already had two teenage daughters; she didn't need a third black hole of depression and anger management issues brooding all over her house.

Instead, he went to the fitness center at his building and pushed himself through over an hour of high-intensity interval training, until he was worn down to the bone and on the razor's edge of losing his stomach. Then he went up to his apartment and took an irresponsibly long, scorchingly hot shower.

When he emerged from the steamy bathroom, he was so dizzy that he barely made it to the couch before he fell over. Only then did he realize he hadn't eaten all day.

He grabbed his phone off the coffee table and opened the Postmates app. Halfway through ordering his dinner, however, an email notification popped up on his screen.

As promised, Carolyn had ensured that the list of KIG's kidnap-and-ransom policyholders, along with the subjects of said policies, had been emailed to the LVMPD. Levi had been copied on the message.

Curious, he abandoned his dinner order and opened the attached document. It was a long list, but the names of those subjects who lived in or frequently traveled to Las Vegas had been helpfully highlighted.

Levi only had a moment to be pleased by that before his eyes got stuck on the very first highlighted name.

Barclay, Stanton.

CHAPTER 9

"**D**etective, please slow down. I can barely understand you."

"I need to talk to Mr. Barclay immediately." Levi did his best to speak at a normal speed even as he paced his living room like a crazed tiger. "It's an emergency. I've called him five times and he's not answering."

"Mr. Barclay is in Geneva," said Bridget, Stanton's long-time executive assistant. Her voice was shaded with irritation.

Levi turned so suddenly he bumped into his couch. "He's what?"

"He's at a hospitality conference in Switzerland. They're nine hours ahead. I'm sure the only reason he's not answering your calls is because he's asleep. You know he turns the ringer on his cell phone off when he goes to bed."

Weak-kneed with relief, Levi leaned heavily against the couch's arm. "When's the last time you spoke to him?"

"Ten a.m. our time. He was fine then."

"When is he coming back to Vegas?"

"Not until next Monday." Her tone softened as she added, "If there's really an emergency, I can give you his number at the hotel. The room phone will wake him up."

"No, no," Levi said, glad she couldn't see the mortified flush burning his cheeks. "I was concerned about a potential threat to his safety, but if he's not in the United States, he's not in danger." He cringed, thinking about the multiple frantic voice mails he'd left on Stanton's cell. "Can you please tell him there's no need to call me back?"

"Of course, Detective," Bridget said. "Have a good night."

"You too."

He hit End, dropped the phone on the couch, and buried his face in both hands. Good God, he'd lost his shit and panicked like a rookie on his first call.

Stanton was the only man Levi had ever loved besides Dominic. Even after their tumultuous breakup and all its accompanying drama, a threat to Stanton riled Levi as fiercely as a threat to his own family.

Now that he knew Stanton was safely tucked away in Switzerland, Levi could relax. He stepped around the couch—and stumbled under a wave of light-headedness that almost sent him crashing to the floor.

Goddamn it, he *still* hadn't eaten.

A shrill ringing penetrated the thick fog of sleep smothering Dominic's brain. His phone?

Nope. Not happening. He ignored it, rolling over in bed and smashing his face into the pillow. The sound stopped, and he slipped back into unconsciousness.

Seconds later, the ringing started up again. He cursed and flailed out one floppy arm with his eyes still shut.

When his hand fumbled through the detritus on his nightstand and came up empty, however, he was forced to open his eyes. As his higher brain functions sputtered back online, he realized the ringing was coming from the wrong direction.

"Fuck me," he said, squinting blearily into the gloom of his darkened bedroom.

He hung off the edge of the mattress, hunting for his phone in the pile of clothes on the floor. Rebel thumped her tail against the bed while she watched.

He'd spent all of yesterday checking in with his contacts across the Valley, spreading word that he was investigating the kidnapping ring. At this point, he wouldn't be surprised if the kidnappers came looking for him just to shut him up.

After ten taxing hours of planting those seeds, he'd badly needed to blow off some steam. He'd gone to the Railroad Pass and ended up staying late. Though he had no idea what time it was right now, he knew he'd only gotten a few hours of sleep.

He grunted in triumph as his hand closed around his cell. "What?" he said, answering without checking the caller ID.

"There's been another kidnapping!"

"Mr. Royce?" Dominic hauled himself back onto the bed.

"One of our K&R policyholders just called me," Royce said, short of breath like he'd been running. "The subject of their policy, Christelle Perrot—she never came home last night, but her car is parked in her driveway with the cell phone on the dashboard, just like all the other victims."

"Wait, she was taken last night?" Dominic checked the time on his phone—7:48. "Why are you only hearing about it now?"

"Nobody knew she'd been kidnapped. There hasn't been a ransom demand. Her family didn't even realize she was missing until this morning, and it was only because of the Buckner story on the news—"

Firmly cutting off Royce's rambling, Dominic said, "What do you mean, there hasn't been a ransom demand?"

"Just that. There's been no communication from the kidnappers at all."

Dominic sat upright. Sensing his tension, Rebel cocked her head, alert and ready for trouble.

"In all the other cases, the kidnappers contacted the policyholder within two hours of snatching the victim," he said.

"Yes." Royce's breathing was still labored. "And now it's been . . . ten? Twelve?"

Something had gone wrong. Again.

Dominic swung his legs over the side of the bed and reached for his discarded jeans. "Did you call the police yet?"

Royce made a strangled noise. "Of course not! You know the first thing the kidnappers demand is that we don't involve the police. Our crisis negotiators can handle it."

"Yeah?" Dominic shoved his legs into his jeans and pulled them up as he stood. "Who are they gonna negotiate with?"

"I—"

"Call Detective Abrams," Dominic said, fastening his jeans one-handed. "Trust me, if I have to call him myself, he's not going to be happy with either of us."

"But—"

"He and his partner won't hesitate to charge you with obstruction of justice. And Detective Abrams has a friend in the DA's office who'd be happy to cook up a way to charge you with aiding and abetting if he asks her to."

"All right," Royce said with a deep, exasperated groan, as if burdened with an unreasonable chore.

"I'll meet you at your office in an hour." Dominic hung up and tossed his phone onto the bed before he went in search of a clean shirt.

"I guess kidnapping is the hot new Vegas fad," Martine said.

Levi sighed, watching the CSIs combing through Christelle Perrot's car and trying to keep his mind off the memories of yesterday morning it was dredging up. At least this car didn't have a corpse in it—particularly fortunate in light of the unseasonable heat. The temperature was in the high eighties already, climbing further every hour as the sun beat down.

As soon as Royce had informed him of the kidnapping, Levi had declared the victim's car a crime scene and dispatched uniformed officers to secure it. This was the first time they'd had fresh access to one of these cars so soon after the incident. Though it was unlikely that professional mercenaries would leave fingerprints on the door or foreign fibers on the seats, everyone made mistakes.

Levi glanced at the palatial Mediterranean-style villa behind them. Christelle Perrot was a French expatriate who held a high-ranking executive position with MGM Resorts. She'd been widowed early in life with two young children, so her mother lived with her to provide support and childcare. Since it wasn't unusual for Perrot to work late, the entire family had gone to bed last night thinking nothing of the fact that she hadn't come home yet.

Interviews with her mother and coworkers had allowed Levi to deduce her likeliest way home from work and request traffic camera footage all along that route. If this were like the other jobs the kidnapping ring had pulled off, they'd ambushed her in a surveillance dead zone, drugged her with a needle to a vein, and dragged her into one of their vehicles. Then they'd ensured her car and cell phone were delivered to her house, so the GPS data from both would be useless.

Very clean. Very neat. So where was the ransom demand?

Most likely, the kidnappers hadn't made any demands because they were unable to offer proof of life in return.

Levi hadn't hesitated to splash Perrot's name and picture across every news outlet in the Valley. At this point, after at least eighteen hours had passed with no communication from the kidnappers, exposing the crime couldn't put her in any more danger than she currently faced. She was probably already dead, though Levi had been careful around her family to maintain an air of optimism.

"Levi? Are you listening?"

"Huh?" He swung his head around toward Martine.

"I said, I think I'm going to back off this one. Seems like you have it under control."

Her tone was as casual as her body language, and if he hadn't known her better, he would have taken the statement at face value. But he caught the tiny lines of tension at the corners of her eyes and mouth, the way she was looking just slightly to the right of his eyes instead of meeting them directly. She was offering to back off the investigation so it would occupy more of his time and focus—distracting him from the Seven of Spades.

"I—" He was interrupted by the approach of one of the CSIs.

"Detectives. We've pulled a bunch of fingerprint and hair samples off the car, but we need elimination samples from the vic, her family, and anyone else who may have had access."

Levi nodded. "I'll talk to her mother. Thanks."

The CSI ambled away. Overhead, the minimal cloud cover dissipated and the sun blazed even brighter. Martine wrinkled her nose and plucked a pair of sunglasses from her jacket pocket.

Levi couldn't help getting a kick out of the picture she made. She looked so effortlessly cool in her aviators and sharp navy pantsuit, her coiled hair ruffled by the light breeze.

"I'm going to head back to the substation," she said. "I have uniforms out contacting all the potential kidnapping victims in person, so I'll check in on them. Let me know if you need anything else?"

"Sure." As she walked away, he called out, "Martine!"

She turned back.

He'd told himself he wasn't going to do this, but the question came out anyway. "There's really no leads on West and Quintana?"

"Not so far. Wayne Reddick's autopsy revealed ligature marks on his wrists and ankles, as well as a buildup of ketamine in his system. It's pretty clear that the Seven of Spades is keeping the men drugged and tied up." She gestured to Perrot's car. "These kidnappers need an entire team of mercenaries to handle one person at a time, but the Seven of Spades isn't concerned with humane treatment. Unconscious captives are a lot easier to handle and keep hidden."

Her words struck Levi with a new thought. As she had mentioned, the Seven of Spades's drug of choice was ketamine, for which they had some kind of large, surefire supply. After a year of cooperating with the DEA to trace ketamine manufacturing and distribution lines in the western US, as well as painstakingly reviewing the licenses of practitioners registered to dispense it, Levi was no closer to discovering how the killer obtained the drugs they used to paralyze their victims.

The kidnapping ring would have been similarly prepared to sedate their victims. If they were from Vegas originally, they would have banked a supply before they started; if they'd come from outside, they would have brought that supply with them.

What the kidnappers *hadn't* been prepared for was minor surgery. Nguyen's account of overhearing frantic whispered phone conversations between the mercenaries and their boss made it clear that there had been no contingency for the possibility that a ransom demand would be refused. The decision to cut out her eye had been made last-minute.

While it was possible the mercenary team already had a member capable of performing a medical-grade enucleation, they wouldn't have had any of the necessary supplies. They would have needed to obtain IV bags, surgical tools, antibiotics . . .

"Martine," he said, "do you still have that CI who's a nurse at Valley Hospital?"

The man in question, who'd gotten caught one too many times lifting prescription narcotics, had turned informant to avoid jail time and the loss of his nursing license. He'd proved a helpful source, because not only was he dialed in to the local drug scene, he also kept tabs on thefts and black market sales of medical supplies.

Her eyes lit up as she caught his drift. "Yep."

Levi smiled, buoyed by the anticipatory buzz of a promising lead. "Think you could arrange a meeting?"

Devil Dogs, the dive bar Paulie had pointed Dominic to, was plopped down incongruously in the Chinatown area two blocks west of the Strip. Its blacked-out windows and subtle sign were almost lost in the profusion of Chinese, Thai, and Vietnamese restaurants surrounding it in the shopping plaza.

Dressed the part in a battered leather jacket and well-worn jeans, Dominic pushed the door open. He'd heard of this place, but he'd never been here—it was a Marine bar, though in theory they'd welcome veterans of any stripe.

The interior was clean and stripped-down, your basic local watering hole, with Marine memorabilia on the walls but no other décor to speak of. It was early in the evening, but the happy hour specials had drawn a respectable crowd, chatting in groups at the tables and chilling out at the bar. Nobody paid Dominic any attention beyond the *shit, that's a big guy* double-take he was used to getting from strangers.

Dominic spotted his target at the far end of the bar—Doug Ephron, ex-Marine, now an employee of the private security firm Delgado & Vincent. According to Paulie's sources, Ephron was no stranger to taking side jobs of dubious legality, and had been drunkenly shooting his mouth off in here after the Buckner homicide made the news. He might not have been involved, but he knew more than he should.

Dominic was going to find out what.

Luckily, there was a spot open beside Ephron. Dominic settled onto the stool, cast a sideways glance at what Ephron was drinking, and ordered a shot of whiskey with an IPA chaser for himself. It wasn't identical to Ephron's choice, but it was close enough that Ephron would feel a subconscious kinship to him right off the bat.

Ignoring Ephron, he tossed back the whiskey, then sipped the beer. It was a struggle to keep the grimace off his face; he'd never liked IPAs.

When he set the glass down, he pressed his hand just under the right side of his collarbone, over his old gunshot wound. Now he let the grimace break free, rolling his shoulder a few times and exhaling a long, slow breath like he was trying to remain stoic in the face of great pain.

He wasn't, of course. The injury was many years old, and it never caused him problems anymore. But Ephron—who'd also been shot in the line of duty—wouldn't know that.

"Bad injury?" Ephron asked, nodding to Dominic's shoulder.

"Caught a bullet in Afghanistan." Dominic neglected to clarify exactly *when* that had happened. "Still bothers me sometimes."

Ephron slapped his own left thigh. "Same here. Had to get a bone graft and everything, but at least I kept the leg. You a Marine?"

"Ranger, 2nd Battalion."

It would have aided his budding rapport with Ephron if he'd been able to introduce himself as a Marine as well, but Dominic wasn't crazy enough to lie about his military history in a bar full of Jarheads. As long as he didn't act high and mighty like some Rangers did, it shouldn't cause too much friction.

"No shit," Ephron said, looking Dominic up and down. "Well, at least you're not a Squid."

Dominic laughed. If there was one thing a Marine and a Ranger could bond over, it was distaste for the Navy.

"I'll drink to that." He clinked his glass against Ephron's, then took a deep swallow before adding, "Buy you another?"

Getting Ephron sloppily drunk required less effort than shooting a stationary target at point-blank range. Dominic excused his own slow pace by claiming he didn't want to mix too much alcohol with the painkillers for his injury, and Ephron was happy to let Dominic buy him round after round. They traded war stories for a while, Dominic guiding the conversation to create maximum camaraderie, until Ephron was slurring his words and swaying on his stool.

"So," Ephron said, his head weaving from side to side, "what do you do now you're back home?"

"I'm a bounty hunter. Good money, and I can set my own schedule."

"Yeah, I know a few guys who got into that. But private security contractors—" Ephron clapped Dominic's right shoulder, then apologized when Dominic made a show of wincing. "That's where the real money is, my friend. Way better pay and benefits than you ever saw in the military."

Now they were getting somewhere. "I've heard that, but don't those places tend to turn into recruiting grounds for . . . you know." Dominic lowered his voice and glanced around the bar. "Mercenaries?"

Ephron snorted, making a sweeping dramatic gesture with his glass that slopped beer over the rim. "So what? A guy can't take a job on the side every once in a while to make ends meet?"

"I guess I'd be worried about getting caught," said Dominic.

"The key is . . ." Ephron hiccoughed, tossed back the rest of his beer, and banged the empty glass on the bar. "The key is to set some rules, see, and stick to them. No kids, no women. That kind of thing. You don't want to go too far."

Dominic indicated for the bartender to refill Ephron's glass. "So you wouldn't take a job if you thought a woman might get hurt?"

"Hell, no," Ephron said, puffing out his chest. "I don't care how big the payday is, you gotta draw the line somewhere. I'll say it right to the client's face."

"Sounds like you're speaking from experience."

"It happens. You hear about that murder, up on the west side? Guy with his eye cut out?" When Dominic nodded, Ephron made a noise of disgust. "Fucking amateurs. Knew that job would be trouble from a mile away."

"Someone tried to hire you for that?"

"I . . ." Ephron managed to focus somewhat on Dominic's face, narrowing his bleary eyes. "Hey, why're you so interested, anyway?"

"Just making conversation," Dominic said, but it was too late.

Ephron's eyes flicked from his glass to Dominic's, and his expression darkened. "You getting me drunk on purpose? You a cop or something?" He reared drunkenly off his stool, his voice rising to a shout. "What the fuck kind of game are you playing here?"

Subterfuge was no longer an option. Dominic didn't even stand up; his right hand shot out, yoked Ephron's throat, and slammed the man back into his stool so hard it teetered on its hind legs before falling into place.

Maintaining his grip while Ephron slapped uselessly at his hand, Dominic looked over his shoulder. The commotion had drawn the attention of everyone in the bar. A few men and women had gotten out of their seats, glaring at Dominic with hard-eyed looks that said they wouldn't mind teaching him the meaning of *Semper Fidelis* with their fists.

"He makes an angry drunk," Dominic said. "I'm trying to convince him to call his sponsor."

The mood in the bar shifted to one of pity and sympathy, and he received a few understanding nods as everyone returned to their business. Every vet here had seen the devastation alcohol dependence could wreak on one of their own.

Dominic looked back at Ephron, who was still struggling to free himself, and tightened his fingers a bit. "I'm not a cop," he said quietly. "Which means I have no problem taking this outside. Do you think you're up for that?"

Ephron went still, his hands resting on Dominic's wrist. Of course he wasn't—he wouldn't have been a match for Dominic sober, let alone three sheets to the wind.

"What do you want?" he snarled.

Dominic let go. "Someone's been running a professional kidnapping ring in the Valley. I want you to tell me everything you know about it."

"Yeah? What's in it for me?"

"I don't tell my friends in the LVMPD where to find you." Smiling at the scowl that earned him, Dominic squeezed Ephron's arm. "And how about another shot of whiskey?"

Mindful of his cover story, Dominic waved the bartender over and ordered the whiskey with a rueful shrug—*I know, but what else am I gonna do?*

Ephron was more amenable once he'd downed the shot. "Couple of months ago, I got word of a new player in town looking to put together a team with real skill, not hoodlums they could pull off the street. Straightforward adult K&R, the kind you don't usually see in the States."

"How'd you hear about it?"

"Same as usual. Word of mouth—you know how it is. Everyone in the business knows which guys are up for a side job here and there. All a client has to do is whisper in the right ear, and the news spreads itself."

"But you didn't sign on."

"Thought about it. The job seemed simple enough, the pay was good, and the client was promising no wet work, no real damage to the targets at all." Ephron gave a dark, bitter laugh. "You see how that turned out. But anyway, when I found out some of the marks were going to be women, I gave it a pass."

"Even though the client said the victims wouldn't be harmed?" Dominic asked.

"You can never guarantee that. Job like this, something's bound to go wrong eventually. And look how bad this one went off the rails. I mean, cutting people's eyes out? What kind of fucked-up shit is that?"

"Where do they hold the victims while they're waiting for the ransom?"

Ephron looked at him incredulously. "You think anyone would tell me that before I'd joined up?"

"I think you know more than you're saying. Guys like you . . . they talk." Dominic slipped his cell phone out of his pocket and set it on the bar. "But then again, maybe I'm just not that bright. Maybe I *should* have a detective look into this."

"All right, man, Christ." Ephron took several long, thirsty gulps of his beer, then scrubbed the back of his hand over his mouth. "Look, all I know is they've got themselves a hidey-hole somewhere northwest of the city, out in the desert. Kind of place you'd never find if you didn't already know where it was."

Dominic had been afraid of that. The Las Vegas area was, after all, a valley—surrounded on all sides by vast expanses of desert and mountain. Even with a general idea of the direction to search in, finding a hidden bolt-hole out in all that wilderness was a daunting prospect.

"You'd think a woman would know better than to put another woman in a situation like that, out in the middle of nowhere with a bunch of strange men," said Ephron.

Dominic blinked, his spine stiffening. "What are you saying? The client was a woman?"

"That's what I heard. Never spoke to her myself."

Leaning forward, Dominic pushed Ephron's beer closer. "Keep talking."

"This isn't looking great," Dominic said to Rebel, who was sitting on the passenger side of his truck.

Unfazed by his pessimism, she wriggled happily from side to side, gazing at him with bright eyes.

"I know." Smiling, he reached out to ruffle her ears. "Just like old times, huh?"

She huffed and butted her head against his hand.

The major artery that led northwest out of the Valley was 95. Dominic had driven just beyond the limits of urban civilization and then pulled his truck off the side of the desert highway, using his mobile hotspot to scan satellite imagery of the area on his laptop.

The view was disheartening. Past the Vegas suburbs, there were only a few sparsely populated settlements scattered through huge swathes of absolute nothingness for miles upon miles in every direction. A handful of access roads branched off 95 here and there, but anyone in a vehicle with off-road capabilities could drive straight off the highway, through the desert, and into the mountains beyond. This was a perfect place to go to ground.

Making matters worse, it was already dark, and there were no streetlights on this part of the highway. Dominic couldn't see beyond the gleam of his own headlights—not that there was much to see besides sand, sand, and more sand.

Maybe he should call it a day. He could come back tomorrow morning, and in the meantime, he could head over to the casino. Though the only cash he had on hand was the money Royce had given him for expenses, he could easily double or triple that at a poker table. He'd keep the profit, and Royce would never know the difference ...

Rebel's tongue swept messily along the side of his face. He jumped, fumbling his laptop, and gently nudged her away. Nausea swooped through him when he saw the clock on the dashboard; over ten minutes had passed without him noticing.

Christ, had he really been fantasizing about gambling with a client's money?

"I'm fine," he said. "I have it under control."

Even Rebel didn't look convinced. He wiped her saliva off his jaw, then slapped both of his cheeks a few times for good measure and forced himself to concentrate.

The mercenaries would have a range of basic needs: shelter, food and water, electricity, gasoline, weapons. It would have been no problem to stockpile months' worth of provisions and weapons at the safe house the client had provided. As for electricity, the surviving victims had each reported hearing a generator during their captivity, all the better to keep the safe house off the public power grid.

Gasoline, though—that was a different story. They'd need a ton, not only for the multiple large vehicles they'd been driving in and out of the city, but to fuel their generator. It wouldn't be practical to stash that much gasoline in advance.

That being said, they wouldn't risk stopping at gas stations in the Valley, especially after Buckner's homicide had blown everything up. But there weren't any gas stations along 95 until the small town of Indian Springs over half an hour away. Except ...

He zoomed in on the map. About eight miles from the northwest edge of the Valley were lands owned by the Las Vegas Paiute Tribe to which Jasmine's mother belonged, and that included the Paiute Golf Resort where Jasmine and Carlos were getting married in May.

Dominic had visited the site with them a couple of times, so he knew that right off the resort's exit from 95 was a tiny Chevron station attached to the Snow Mountain Smoke Shop. It was discreet, out of the way—and most significantly, under the jurisdiction of the Tribal Police and *not* the LVMPD.

Worth a shot. He snapped his laptop shut, set it aside, and pulled back onto the highway.

Unlike the surrounding roads, Snow Mountain was well-lit, from the neon Chevron sign advertising gas prices to the blazing lights of the shop itself. There were only two pumps, both unoccupied, but a few cars were parked in front of the store.

He backed his truck into a spot near the door, then transferred Rebel to the bed so they could keep an eye on each other through the large windows. "Stay," he said, and kissed the tip of her nose before heading inside.

The shop was neat and bright, packed wall-to-wall with colorful displays of cigars, cigarettes, and smokeless tobacco. An earthy scent with a sweet underlying note hung in the air, and he inhaled deeply. Though he'd never been a smoker, he did enjoy the smell of real tobacco.

Several people were browsing the racks, but Dominic's attention landed immediately on a man across the store, talking to a clerk with his back to Dominic. A very familiar man with curly black hair and an ass that wouldn't quit.

Dominic couldn't help the grin that broke free. Of *course* Levi had beaten him here.

He didn't have much time to appreciate the moment, because Levi turned to see why the door had opened, just as Dominic would have himself. It was a casual glance thrown over the shoulder, but the second Levi clocked Dominic, his eyes widened and he did a full one-eighty.

"*How?*" was all Levi said.

Dominic strolled over, pretending a nonchalance he was nowhere near feeling. "I'll show you mine if you show me yours."

Levi's nostrils flared.

"You know you're outside your jurisdiction, right?"

"I'm aware of jurisdictional protocol, thank you," Levi said frostily. "That doesn't mean I can't ask this young woman if she's seen vehicles matching descriptions of the kidnappers' SUVs come through here recently."

"I told you, I haven't seen anything," said the clerk, who was definitely Paiute herself. She was eyeing Levi with open distaste that bordered on hostility. Levi did tend to rub people the wrong way even when he was trying to be nice, but Dominic doubted there was anything Levi could have said or done to improve this encounter.

He took Levi's elbow. "Can I talk to you outside, please?"

Levi's expression went flat, his eyes like gray stone. "Get your hand off me," he said, each word measured and deliberate.

Dominic released him at once and took a step back for safety's sake. Levi smoothed out his suit jacket, fussily tugging his cuffs into place.

"You want to talk? Fine. Let's talk." Levi strode out of the shop without another glance for Dominic or the clerk.

"You a cop too?" she asked Dominic.

"Shit, no."

"Good. Last thing we need is more white cops from the city coming out here, getting in our business."

"I couldn't agree more," said Dominic.

He left the shop to find Levi standing by the bed of his truck, petting an ecstatic Rebel. "I didn't overstep," Levi said before Dominic could get a word out. "At least, not as far as I'm aware. I know I'm not the most diplomatic person in the world, but I'd never—"

Dominic held up a hand. "I believe you. But you couldn't have thought this was going to turn out well, Levi. What reason does anyone around here have to trust a white police officer?"

"I know." Levi's posture lost some of its rigidity. "I know. I should have gone straight to the Tribal Police. I just— I honestly didn't think the employees would mind answering a few basic questions."

"They probably wouldn't have, if you hadn't introduced yourself as a detective with the LVMPD. Which I'm assuming is what you did."

"Of course. What else would I say?"

"Literally anything but that!"

Levi rolled his eyes.

"And now that I've been seen with you, nobody will tell me anything either," Dominic said. "What brought you out here, anyway?"

"One of Martine's CIs tipped us off to deals on black market medical supplies going down on Paiute land without the tribe's knowledge—obviously the kidnappers' way of creating messy jurisdictional issues to obstruct the investigation. Buckner's body was dumped on the northwest edge of the suburbs, and the routes we've traced using old surveillance footage all lead northwest out of the city, so their base of operations must be in the general area. I saw there was a gas station out here, and I figured it was the best bet for where they've been refueling."

Medical supplies. Dominic hadn't even considered that angle.

Levi looked him up and down, blinking as if seeing him for the first time. "What are you wearing? You look like rough trade."

Dominic hadn't bothered to change out of his beat-up leather-and-denim outfit when he'd swung by his apartment to pick up Rebel and his laptop. "I had to blend in at a certain bar."

"What bar?" Levi folded his arms and arched his eyebrows expectantly. "How'd *you* know to come here? Fair's fair."

He had a point, so Dominic broke down his meeting with Ephron, ending with Ephron's revelation that the person who'd hired the mercenaries was a woman.

"A woman?" Levi repeated.

"Yeah. The only name Ephron had was Bennett."

"It's Juliette," Levi said, waving a hand when Dominic started to protest. "Come on, Dominic. This has *inside job* written all over it. Juliette could easily gain access to Royce's files. Maybe she's behind the whole thing, or maybe they're conspiring together. She could even be manipulating him into it. Carolyn Royce seemed convinced this was too unlike her husband." Rubbing his jaw, he added, "We should do a background check on Juliette. She could be some kind of grifter."

Dominic's heart swelled at Levi's off-hand use of the word *we*, so it took his brain a second to catch up. "Hold on. You talked to my client's wife?"

"Of course. He's my primary suspect."

"Levi—"

"I'm not going to ignore the person with the greatest means and opportunity to commit the crime just because he's your client."

Dominic threw his hands in the air. "Why would Royce hire a PI if he were behind the kidnappings? Or choose a victim whose policy he would *know* had lapsed?"

"So you'd make the exact arguments you're making now," said Levi.

"You need nerves of steel to hire someone to investigate your own crimes to make yourself look innocent," Dominic said. "Royce has nerves of pudding. He's a hot mess, and he's getting worse every day. He doesn't have the spine to pull this off."

"That lends more weight to the theory that Juliette is involved." Levi's gaze suddenly sharpened. "By the way, you never mentioned which security contractor Ephron works for."

Dominic clenched his jaw, knowing exactly where this was headed. "Delgado & Vincent."

"Uh-huh. Out of curiosity, who are some of their major clients?"

"They're an international firm. They have a lot of clients."

"Including Kensington Insurance Group?" Levi asked, all faux-sweetness.

Yes, as a matter of fact. Delgado & Vincent was KIG's go-to contractor when they needed to provide private security for clients or employees, a fact which only made Royce look guiltier.

When Dominic didn't answer, Levi let out a nasty laugh. Dominic was tempted to smack that smug little smirk off his face—or better yet, drag him into the truck and fuck the attitude out of him altogether.

"I—" That was all Dominic got out before Rebel barked twice, short and sharp, her conditioned warning for an approaching stranger.

Dominic and Levi both frowned as they looked around the parking lot. No new cars had pulled in, and nobody had emerged from the smoke shop. Even if they had, Rebel didn't bark at ordinary comings and goings. Her "stranger danger" warning, as Dominic called it, was only used when the approaching person posed a potential threat.

Rebel hopped up to put her front feet on the side of the truck bed, staring into the desert beyond the lot. She went through her bark sequence three more times, her entire body stiff from nose to tail.

In one fluid, simultaneous movement, Dominic and Levi drew their guns and turned to face the same direction. It was pitch-black past the range of the shop's lights, the glow of the moon and stars mere pinpricks in an all-encompassing darkness. The edge of the earth could be fifty feet away and they'd have no idea.

"I can't see anything," Dominic said. "You?"

Levi shook his head, then pulled a flashlight out of his pocket and held it in a two-handed grip with his gun. Dominic's own flashlight was in the truck, but he was able to use his cell phone for the same purpose.

Rebel barked again, the sound more anxious this time. She dropped to all fours and paced the truck bed in a circle, whining in the back of her throat.

Trusting his gut, Dominic opened the back of the bed and said, "Go."

Rebel took off like a shot, racing out of the parking lot and into the desert. Dominic and Levi followed.

Levi was the faster runner, outstripping Dominic from the start, but even he couldn't run as fast as he normally would. In the dark, the uneven, scrub-dotted sand threatened a twisted ankle with every stride.

Then Dominic saw it—a human shape, barely visible in the combined glow of his and Levi's flashlights, staggering through the desert in their direction. The person fell to their knees and collapsed flat on their face just as Rebel reached them.

The closer he got, the better Dominic could see. Rebel pushed the person onto their back and licked their face, trying to rouse them, until Levi dropped to his own knees beside the body and felt for the neck. Dominic reached the group a few seconds later, panting and holding his cell phone at an angle that gave Levi more light. Her job done, Rebel backed away.

Levi holstered his gun, then put both hands back on the woman's neck—because it was a woman, dressed in a torn, wrinkled sheath dress that was soaked in sweat and smeared all over with sand.

"She's alive," Levi said.

Dominic tilted his phone, shining it over her face. He and Levi both gasped.

The woman's face was raw and blistered with a vicious sunburn, her cheeks sunken, her lips white and cracked. But she was still recognizable as Christelle Perrot.

Perrot's eyes popped open, and she flailed half-upright with a panicked shriek. Levi caught her, holding her still. Her wide, pleading gaze darted between Levi and Dominic as she let out a sob.

"*Aidez-moi*," she said, her voice a dry croak. "God, please help me."

CHAPTER 10

Levi paced the family waiting room on the ward at Centennial Hills Hospital where Perrot had been admitted, treading the same path on the linoleum floor over and over. He was nauseous with fatigue while at the same time too keyed up to sit down. Hours after he and Dominic had found Perrot, he had no idea what condition she was in, though he had a uniformed officer posted outside her room for her protection.

He whipped around when the waiting room door opened, then relaxed when he saw Dominic. In these early predawn hours, they were the only people in the room.

"Anything yet?" Dominic asked.

Levi shook his head. After the paramedics had carted Perrot off, he and Dominic had gone their separate ways—Levi following the ambulance to the hospital, Dominic taking Rebel to stay with Carlos and Jasmine. But Levi had been updating him by text ever since.

Dominic was carrying a paper-wrapped sandwich and a foam tray with two coffee cups. He handed one of the cups to Levi before settling at a round table whose laminate surface was dinged and scratched from years of heavy use.

"Thanks," Levi said. He sipped the coffee, finding it exactly the way he liked it—a strong dark roast with a couple shots of espresso.

"You're welcome." Dominic unwrapped his sandwich and separated the halves. Nudging one half in Levi's direction, he raised an inquiring eyebrow.

Levi hesitated. Unlike most people in his life, Dominic never pressured him to eat. If he turned down the offer, Dominic would let it go at that. But it had been a while since he'd last eaten, and though he wasn't hungry, it was a good idea to get some fuel in his system that wasn't caffeine.

Nodding his thanks, he sat across the table and accepted half the sandwich. When he bit into it, he was surprised to find it was roast beef, his favorite.

Dominic didn't even *like* roast beef.

Levi swallowed his mouthful and looked up. Dominic was chewing in silence, watching the infomercial on the TV across the room like it was the most fascinating thing he'd ever seen. Levi fiddled with the crust of the sandwich for a moment, then took another bite.

They ate without talking for a few minutes. Levi was almost finished with his half, gazing blankly through the window that overlooked the hallway, when he caught sight of Perrot's mother approaching the waiting room.

He sprang to his feet so suddenly that Dominic startled, one hand hovering over his gun beneath his jacket. Levi made a face at him and gestured toward the opening door. Dominic swiveled around in his chair, then hurried to get to his feet as well.

"Ms. Durand," Levi said. "How is she?"

"Alive," Durand said in her thick French accent. She'd met both Levi and Dominic earlier that day, so introductions weren't necessary, but she didn't look happy to see them. "The doctor told me you've been waiting here to speak to her all night."

"I know it's not ideal, but it's urgent. If Christelle is conscious, I need to talk to her as soon as possible. The people who did this to her are still out there, and the more time that passes, the harder they'll be to catch."

"Well, come on, then." Durand jerked her chin toward the doorway.

Levi and Dominic followed her into the hall.

"I thought Christelle should wait until morning to see you," Durand said as they walked. "She's been through enough already. She was wandering in that desert for almost twenty-four hours; she has dehydration, heatstroke, a second-degree sunburn . . . But she insisted that she needed to talk to you now."

The officer at the door nodded to Levi when their group entered Perrot's private room. She lay half-upright in the hospital bed, hooked up to IV fluids. Her hands were bandaged, and her burnt neck and face were gleaming with a thick, shiny substance. Though she appeared to be sleeping, she opened her eyes when her mother said her name.

"Ms. Perrot, I'm Detective Levi Abrams." Levi showed her his badge, ignoring the flash of shocked recognition that crossed her face. "This is Dominic Russo; he's a private investigator looking into the same case. Are you well enough to talk?"

"Yes," she rasped. "Please, sit."

Levi pulled one of the little plastic chairs up to the bed. Dominic did the same on the other side, though Levi caught him casting the flimsy thing a dubious look before he gingerly settled his considerable weight onto it.

Durand made to join them, but Perrot held out a hand. "*Maman*, I'd actually like to speak to them alone. *S'il vous plaît.*"

Durand frowned but didn't argue. "I'll go get something to eat."

Perrot waited until the door had shut behind her to say, "Aren't you a homicide detective?"

"Yes."

"So the men who took me are the same ones who took that man who was murdered last weekend? The one whose eye was cut out?"

"That's correct."

She shuddered. "I thought they probably were. *Mon Dieu.*"

"Can you please tell me the whole story from the beginning?" Levi asked, readying a notepad and pen.

"I was driving home from work. I thought the detour was odd, but I didn't understand what was happening until it was too late. I was ambushed and trapped by two black SUVs. Masked men pulled me from my car and put me to sleep with some sort of injection."

That was exactly how it'd gone for the other four living victims. "What happened next?" Levi said. Each of the others had reported waking blindfolded and tied to a bed.

"Ah . . ." Perrot dropped her gaze, studying her bandaged hands. "You must understand, the past few years have been very difficult for me. My husband passed away soon after our second child was born. My mother is an angel, but it is not the same without him. And my job, it is very stressful." She paused as if searching for the right words.

"I gave birth to Ludovic via caesarean section. The doctors gave me a prescription."

"For opiate painkillers?" said Dominic.

"Yes. After my husband died, I began to take more and more." Her lips twitched with a joyless smile. "Then antianxiety medicines, then sedatives and tranquilizers. Anything that would dull the pain for a while."

Levi didn't have time to beat around the bush. "You've been abusing prescription medications? For how long?"

She lifted her head. "Years. But I—I'm not a drug addict. I know I take more than I should, but I'm always careful. I have everything under control."

Dominic cleared his throat, his chair creaking as he shifted his weight. Levi didn't dare look in his direction.

There was only one reason Perrot would admit this to them. "You've built a tolerance to certain substances in a way the kidnappers didn't expect."

"Yes. I woke in the car."

Levi straightened up. Now he looked at Dominic, who was just as intrigued.

"I pretended I was still unconscious. My wrists and ankles had been zip-tied, and there were at least three men in the car with me, so I didn't want to risk letting them know I was awake. We drove for about forty minutes. Then they carried me out of the car, into a house, and laid me on a bed. They were getting ready to bind me to it, but to do that, they had to remove the zip-ties."

Perrot stopped there and coughed, a terrible dry hacking noise. Levi got up to fetch her some water, then helped her drink it through a straw.

"*Merci*," she said as Levi set the water aside. "This is . . . harder to talk about than I expected."

"I understand. Take your time."

"I knew that was my only chance. When my hands and feet were free, I opened my eyes a bit, just enough to get a quick look. They were still wearing masks, but one of the men was leaning over me. There was a gun in a holster on his hip. I . . ." She bowed her head. "I grabbed the gun and shot him in the stomach."

Levi's eyes widened. Dominic made a soft, commiserating noise.

"Everything went mad," she continued. "The men were panicking; they had no idea what was happening. I took my chances and just ran. Sprinted out of the house and kept running as fast as I could. They chased me, but their shots missed, and—I don't know, maybe it was because I was so afraid, or because they were more worried about their friend, but I got away."

If she'd escaped their initial pursuit and hadn't seen their faces, the kidnappers had probably prioritized evacuating the safe house and getting help for their injured colleague. "Do you know where you were?" Levi asked.

"The foothills of a mountain, right on the edge of the desert. The problem is that I was so frightened when I escaped that I didn't pay attention to where I was going. By the time I was back in my right mind, I was completely lost. I'd dropped the gun somewhere, and I had no idea where I was or where to go. So I just kept walking." Her breath stuttered. "It was so hot. There was nothing but sand everywhere I looked. I thought I was going to die out there, but I knew I couldn't stop moving. When it got dark, I saw lights in the distance, but by then I thought it was a hallucination. I don't really remember anything after that."

She closed her eyes and leaned her head back against the pillow, her chest jumping with the uneven breathing of someone trying not to cry. Neither Levi nor Dominic spoke while she got herself together.

"I might have killed that man," she said to Levi when she opened her eyes.

"There won't be any charges." Levi knew that was poor comfort. He'd killed to save lives before; it was still devastating.

Nodding, Perrot took one big sniff and then coughed again.

"Is it okay if we ask you some questions?" Levi said.

He led Perrot through her story again, gently probing for more detail. Dominic chimed in with questions of his own here and there.

Perrot was able to provide a general description of the kidnappers' base: a rustic two-room cabin in the middle of nowhere, far from any legitimate roads. Though the mercenaries hadn't talked much during the drive, she'd overheard enough to be sure they were unhappy with the current state of affairs, a conclusion that had been confirmed when one of the men checked in with their boss by phone.

"I have to admit, I was surprised to find out it was a woman," Perrot said.

"How do you know that?" Dominic asked. "Did you hear them use a name?"

"No. But when the man on the phone hung up, he called her a—a crazy bitch."

Based on Perrot's account, Levi gathered that the mercenaries had wanted to lay low while the heat was on, maybe abandon the kidnapping ring altogether—but the client had insisted otherwise. Either she was paying the men good money to overcome their reservations, or she had some kind of leverage on them to force their compliance.

Once Levi and Dominic had wrapped everything up and were preparing to leave, Perrot said, "Are those men going to come looking for me?"

"I doubt it," said Levi. "It would be the stupidest possible thing they could do, and they're professionals. They should know better. But we'll keep a police detail on you until we find them."

They wished Perrot a speedy recovery, left their respective business cards, and headed for the elevator side by side, both lost in their own thoughts. Only when they were stepping into the elevator did Dominic say, "We should work together on this one."

Levi scoffed and hit the button for the ground floor.

"I'm serious. If we don't cooperate, we'll just keep getting in each other's way."

"I don't have to worry about getting in your way," Levi said. "When *you* get in *my* way, it's called obstruction of justice."

Dominic was unfazed. "We've joined forces before—tracking down Keith Chapman, infiltrating Sergei Volkov's compound. Give me one good reason we shouldn't do the same now."

"I don't want to be around you."

Dominic drew back like he'd been slapped, his face draining of color. Levi hadn't meant that the way it sounded, but so what? Let Dominic feel hurt. Rejected. He'd made Levi feel that way often enough.

The elevator doors slid open on the hallway to the emergency room, which at this time of night was the only way in and out of the hospital. Levi stalked out and was halfway down the hall before his resolve broke. He couldn't leave things like this.

Spinning around, he returned to Dominic—who was walking much more slowly—and said, "It's too hard, Dominic. It hurts too much to be around you and not . . ." He swallowed and made a helpless gesture.

A spark of hope lit Dominic's face, and he moved closer. "Levi, you know I still—"

"I know." Levi couldn't bear to hear Dominic say the words aloud, not now. "So do I. That's why it's so awful."

"If you could just—"

"I don't need you to be in recovery." Levi watched Dominic's face shut down and go blank. "But I need you to admit you have a problem and accept help. If you're not going to do that, there's nothing more to say."

They stared at each other beneath sickly fluorescent lights, the clamor of the nearby ER filling up the silence.

The root of the dilemma was that Dominic didn't consider his gambling an illness. He saw it as a weakness, a personal failing. In a man who prided himself on being a strong, competent protector, weakness was particularly unforgivable, so he had to convince himself that the gambling wasn't a problem at all.

The last time Dominic's addiction had spiraled out of control, Rebel's life-threatening health emergency was the only thing that had pushed him to seek help. Would it take something equally dramatic this time around?

"Coordinating our efforts on this case is in the best interests of the investigation, and you know it," Dominic said, as if the last couple of minutes had never happened. "Or are you comfortable taking the risk that the men Christelle Perrot spent a day slowly dying in the desert to escape will slip through your fingers? Do you want to end up telling Rose Nguyen the people who cut out her eye will never be found?"

Dominic had always known how best to manipulate him.

"All right, fine," Levi snapped when he could see Dominic was gearing up to say more. "You don't have to lay it on so thick." He pinched the bridge of his nose, mulling things over. "If the man Perrot shot survived, his friends would have taken him somewhere for medical care. I'll handle that end of things and start looking for properties matching the description she gave us of their safe house. In the meantime, you can get the name Ephron told you out to your contacts and do that background check on Juliette."

"If Royce finds out I'm investigating his mistress, I'll be in deep shit."

"So hide it from him. You're good at that."

A muscle jumped in Dominic's jaw.

Levi sighed. "Sorry. I'm really tired."

"Tell me about it," Dominic said, cracking his neck from side to side. He *did* look exhausted, his unshaven face haggard and hollow-eyed.

"Are you okay to drive home?" Levi asked.

"Just about. You?"

No. Let's get a hotel room and just sleep in the same bed and pretend everything's the way it was six months ago. I miss you.

"Yeah," Levi said. "I'm good."

"Hey, you can't go back there!" the receptionist said, springing out of her chair as Levi and a uniformed officer strode past the front desk at Desert Road Animal Hospital.

Levi flashed his badge and a sheaf of paper without slowing down. "We have a warrant."

"But—but—" She snatched up her phone, but Levi didn't try to stop her. The warning would work in his favor.

He and the officer pushed through a swinging door into the building's back area. This was no small, independently owned practice like the ones the Seven of Spades had paid Los Avispones to knock over in their attempt to frame Keith Chapman. It was a bustling twenty-four-hour hospital with a large staff and enough space to house kennels, fully equipped laboratory and pharmacy facilities—and several operating theaters.

His informant had only known the hospital was being used for backroom medical care, not which of the vets were participating. That was where the receptionist came in handy. Within seconds of Levi entering the hallway, a panicked vet darted out of the lab, squeaked in fear as she saw him, and took off running.

Levi chased her toward the rear exit, the officer hot on his heels, though neither of them ran at full speed. They didn't have to. The vet wrenched the door open and skidded to a halt, yelping at the sight of Martine standing in the back alley with another uniform.

"What's up?" Martine said.

The vet spun around, her head swinging from side to side as she searched for another escape route, but they had her surrounded.

"Two nights ago, a man came in here with a gunshot wound to the abdomen," Levi said. "Where is he?"

She shook her head, her mouth opening and closing soundlessly.

He took a menacing step forward. "That man was involved in multiple kidnappings, two mutilations, and a homicide. *Where is he?*"

The vet's shoulders sagged. "Over here."

She led them to an office in the far rear corner of the building. Inside, what appeared to be a closet door opened into a windowless, makeshift clinic.

Levi cursed when he saw the shirtless guy on the cot against the far wall. The man was gray and glazed with sweat, tossing and turning, his breathing shallow. Telltale red streaks radiated from his bandaged abdomen.

"It's infected," said the vet. "He needs a hospital—a human hospital. But he's been refusing to go."

"So you were just going to let him die here?" Levi hurried to the man's side and felt for his pulse; it was dangerously thready.

"Of course not!" Scowling, the vet put her hands on her hips. "We— I mean, I was going to figure something out."

Levi didn't have time for her self-righteous indignation. He looked to Martine.

"I'll call for a bus," Martine said, pulling out her phone. "Why don't you slap the cuffs on Dr. Hack Job here?"

"I—I had to help him!" the vet said as Levi advanced on her. "What was I supposed to do, turn him away with a bullet to the guts?"

"I can tell you what you *weren't* supposed to do, and that's perform surgery without a license and harbor a criminal." Levi snapped the cuffs around her wrists. "You'll be lucky if all you get charged with is the unauthorized practice of medicine."

While he led the still-protesting vet out of the room, he glanced back once more at the erstwhile kidnapper. That guy wasn't sitting for an interrogation anytime soon.

Dominic leaned back in his chair and rubbed his neck, staring morosely at his computer screen. He'd managed to grab a few hours of sleep in between leaving the hospital and coming into his office at McBride, but he was still exhausted, and the glare of the monitor wasn't helping his headache.

Neither was the information on it. He'd spent the day digging up everything he could find on Juliette Monique Dubois, age twenty-four, executive assistant at Kensington Insurance Group. Though her credit wasn't bad, the rest of the background check had thrown up every red flag in the book.

Juliette had a few criminal charges for shoplifting and writing bad checks, although each had been resolved without jail time. Her work history was spotty and disjointed, and she had a pattern of changing residences every year or so, hopping from city to city across the state. Judging by her current apartment, car, and credit card statements, her lifestyle far exceeded her income—yet she had a total lack of debt.

Most troubling, as far as Dominic was concerned, was the absence of any social media presence whatsoever. He knew from the few times he'd met her, as well as the charges on her credit cards, that she was a sociable, extroverted young woman—social media's prime demographic. But she didn't have so much as a disused Facebook or neglected Instagram feed.

Dominic trusted his gut, and right now his gut was telling him Juliette had something to hide. Sketchy as she was, however, there was no proof of a connection to the kidnappings.

An email notification flashed in the lower left corner of his screen. Grateful for the distraction, he clicked over to it.

McBride's in-house forensic accountant had forwarded the report on her investigation into the four surviving kidnapping victims' ransom payments. Dominic did his best to read it, but the dense financial jargon would have gone over his head even fully rested, so he skipped to the summary.

The payments had bounced around various offshore accounts before coming to rest in one owned by a shell company with one named proxy, Nicholas Fox, a phony identity as flimsy as a paper doll. The accountant intended to continue investigating, but her tone wasn't optimistic.

Dominic reached for his phone.

"Detective Abrams," Levi said a few rings later. He must not have recognized Dominic's office number.

"It's me; I'm calling from work."

"Did you find anything?" Levi sounded as tired as Dominic felt.

Dominic told him about the email, and Levi made a frustrated noise when he finished.

"We got a similar report from our own accountant this morning," Levi said. "All the names connected to the account are garbage shell companies and equally fake aliases. It's a dead end."

"How about the kidnapper Perrot shot? Any luck there?"

"Yes, actually, though I wouldn't celebrate yet. I just got back from escorting him to the hospital. His wound got infected and they had to take him back into surgery. I'll see what he has to say for himself when he wakes up."

Dominic swiveled his chair around to gaze out the window at the busy street below, one block over from the Strip. "The named proxy for the account where the ransom payments ended up was a man."

"That doesn't mean anything," said Levi. Dominic could hear him typing in the background. "A woman could easily set that up. The identity is fake, anyway."

"True, but I don't think Juliette could pull this off."

"Why not? Was her background check clean?"

"Not exactly. It's just . . . I've seen histories like hers before. Either she's running from something or she's a small-time, low-level grifter.

Either way, I doubt she has the skill set to arrange a complicated series of account transfers. And how could she possibly afford to hire mercenaries of this caliber?"

Levi hummed thoughtfully. "So you think that if Juliette were involved, she'd need a partner?"

"Maybe . . ."

"Like Nathan Royce?"

"For God's sake, Levi—"

"Look, it's not *my* fault your client is shady as hell. It's long past time for you to confront him about this."

"I can't do that," Dominic said through gritted teeth.

"Why not?" When Dominic didn't answer, Levi said, "Because you're afraid he'll fire you? It's not like you to avoid taking necessary risks."

"I lost McBride's trust *because* I took what I thought were necessary risks with a case."

"That was a completely different situation; you know it's not the same. If you're so worried, why don't you talk to McBride first and ask her advice?" Levi hesitated, and his voice was gentler when he said, "There's nothing wrong with admitting you need help—"

Dominic spun his chair back around to face his desk. "Oh hey, someone just walked in. I'll update you later, okay? Bye." He hung up to the sound of Levi's exasperated groan.

He propped his elbows on the desk and raked his hands through his hair. As much as he hated to admit it, Levi had a point. If he was apprehensive to take the next logical step in his investigation because he was concerned about McBride's reaction, then the best thing to do was talk it out with her.

Swallowing his pride, he dashed off a quick email to McBride, asking if she had room in her schedule to meet today. Half an hour later, he was entering her office with the Royce file under one arm.

McBride waved Dominic into the chair in front of her desk with the hand holding her ever-present e-cigarette. "So what's going on?" she asked in a deep, throaty voice roughened by decades of chain-smoking before she'd switched. "Problems with the Royce case?"

"I don't know how to best handle the information my investigation is turning up."

She paused with the cigarette an inch from her lips. "I don't think I've ever heard you say anything like that before."

"Yeah, well, there's a first time for everything." He handed her the file. "Here's the problem . . ."

She paged through the file while she listened to him outline the details, her frown deepening by the minute. "You think it's an inside job?"

"Maybe, but I genuinely don't think Royce is involved. He doesn't have the spine to hire a PI to investigate his own crime, or to kidnap someone he'd know couldn't pay the ransom just to cast suspicion off himself."

"That same lack of spine could make him an easy mark for a grifter, though." She tapped Juliette's photograph.

"That's my main concern. The cops think Royce is behind the kidnappings, possibly with Juliette as his accomplice. From what I've seen, it's more likely that if she *is* involved, she's manipulating him without his knowledge. Though in that case, either she must have a partner, or she's such a gifted con artist that even the things I turned up in her background check are fake."

McBride continued studying the file, puffing on her e-cigarette and exhaling a stream of piña colada–flavored vapor. "If Royce wasn't your client, what would be your next step?"

"I'd put Juliette under a microscope," said Dominic. "Dig as deep as I could, get surveillance going on her, find out everything she's doing and everyone she's talking to. The problem is . . ."

"You have to report what you're doing to Royce, and if he finds out you're investigating his girlfriend, he may terminate his contract with the agency."

"Exactly."

McBride tilted her head back and aimed her next exhalation at the ceiling. "You've found no evidence of fraud or sabotage?"

"None. And there's no proof that anyone outside the company ever accessed the list from which the victims were chosen."

"All right." She met his eyes. "Mr. Royce hired us to answer a particular question. Our duty as private investigators is to collect whatever information is necessary to answer that question by every legal means available to us. We can't guarantee what the answer will be, or that the client will like it—we tell them that from the start."

She inhaled deeply, then pointed her cigarette at him.

"If your investigation is leading you in a direction that's supported by evidence and free of personal bias, what are you gonna do, ignore it? That would be a breach of your responsibility to your client. Now, I'm not saying you should sneak around behind his back. You need to be straight with him about where the investigation is going. If he decides he'd rather protect himself and his girlfriend than discover the information he was desperate enough to hire a PI to find, that's on him. When a client fires you for doing your job *right* . . ." She shrugged. "You can't control that."

A knot loosened in Dominic's shoulders, and he breathed a little easier. "This case pulls in a lot of money. I thought if I lost Royce as a client . . ."

"I'd kick you to the curb?" Belting out a raspy smoker's laugh, McBride shoved the file back toward him. "The last time you fucked up, it was because you were doing your job *wrong*. Every PI has times when a client would rather bury their head in the sand than face the ugly truth. Nothing you can do to change that. Just make sure you're documenting every move you make."

"Yes, ma'am. Thank you." Dominic grabbed the file and left the office with renewed resolve. He'd call Royce now, and let the chips fall where they may.

CHAPTER 11 ♠

Friday afternoon, the tension in the substation was suffocating. The Seven of Spades still had two captives, and though nobody had shared information with Levi directly, he wasn't blind to their agitated running around and frantic whispers and harrowed expressions. The pressure was on both the LVMPD and the FBI to find the victims before they died, but the Seven of Spades remained elusive. Ominously, they hadn't contacted Levi or anyone else in the LVMPD, not even in reaction to Levi being removed from the investigation.

Levi remained at his desk, keeping his head down, ignoring everyone else even as they shot him suspicious sideways glances and went out of their way to avoid talking near him. Let people think whatever they wanted. His responsibility now was to the victims of much different kidnappers.

Unfortunately, that case was shaping up to be just as frustrating. Charles Graham, the man Perrot had shot, had gotten through surgery fine—only to immediately hire an attorney from the powerhouse defense firm Hatfield, Park, and McKenzie, essentially making it impossible for the police to communicate with him even as he continued recovering in the hospital under custody.

Levi's search for the kidnappers' safe house had been similarly unproductive. There shouldn't be any jurisdictional issues to contend with, because the Clark County line extended beyond the range Perrot could have traveled in the time she'd been missing, and the Paiute-owned lands weren't anywhere near the foothills. But it was still an enormous area encompassing a mix of public and private land—plus, there was no guarantee that any legal record of the property existed.

Plenty of survivalists lived out here, and it wouldn't be hard to build a secret cabin in the middle of nowhere and keep it off the grid of every utility company and government agency.

Even Dominic wasn't immune to the strain. He'd called earlier to touch base, at the end of his rope because Royce had been dodging his calls since yesterday. When Levi had pointed out that this only made Royce look more guilty, Dominic had hung up on him.

The one bright spot had come from the Tribal Police. When Levi had reached out to them and explained the situation, their office had sent over months' worth of security camera footage from the Snow Mountain Smoke Shop and its attached gas station. By comparing those recordings to the ones from the traffic cameras he had used to identify the kidnappers' vehicles earlier that week, he might be able to make a match, even get a look at the kidnappers themselves. It was slow, tedious work, but it was the best lead they had, so he didn't care if it took all weekend. His ass was glued to this chair until he found what he was looking for.

No sooner had the thought crossed his mind than his cell buzzed with a text from Leila.

Don't forget, court prep @ 3 today. If you try to weasel out of it again I WILL hunt you down.

Levi rolled his eyes. *I'll be there*, he texted back before returning his attention to his computer.

Hours of mind-numbing tedium, three cups of coffee, and a throbbing headache later, he hit pay dirt. He'd been pausing the gas station footage every time a large black SUV pulled in, comparing the make, model, and license plate to the stills he had of the kidnappers' cars. It was a common vehicle type, so that had resulted in a lot of false starts.

But this time, in a recording dated February 19, the Chevrolet Suburban that stopped at the gas station had the same stolen license plate the kidnappers had used when they'd taken Rose Nguyen the next day.

As Levi watched, one man got out of the car to start pumping gas while another two headed into the smoke shop—all with their faces uncovered. His heart beating faster, Levi advanced slowly through the footage, taking a series of still shots until he had clear photographs of all three men's faces. Then he added the images to the queue to be run through their facial-recognition program, along with a filter to search military records first.

That would take a while to go through, so he continued scanning the recordings, looking for any other occasions the kidnappers had stopped by the gas station. He was so absorbed in his work that he didn't notice the time until it was 2:45.

He hated to stop while he was on a roll, so he called Leila and asked to reschedule. She would only agree to push their meeting back a couple of hours and have it over dinner in her office, and even that concession was made with poor grace, so he didn't push his luck.

By the time he left the substation, he'd discovered two more incidences of the kidnappers using the gas station, and had gotten clear shots of six different men, including Graham. Now it was only a matter of time before those men were identified, and no power on this earth would stop Levi from bringing them to justice.

"This is ridiculous," Levi said over the remains of his and Leila's take-out Thai. "Juries don't like me; they never have. What does it even matter?"

Leila looked bored, but since that was her default emotional state, it was hard to tell how much the past hour of fruitless coaching had added to her ennui. "I don't need them to *like* you. I need them to respect you. People don't respect cops who lose their temper on the witness stand."

"I won't—"

"Frankie Papadopoulos is the scum of the earth. He will use every slimy, underhanded tactic he can think of to discredit your testimony on the cross-examination. After Drew Barton's trial, all the defense attorneys in the city know the best way to provoke you is through your connection to the Seven of Spades. And after everything that's happened this week, that's a more volatile powder keg than ever."

Levi dropped his plastic fork into his dish and pushed his half-eaten food away. "I can handle it. I'm getting better."

"I believe you. But we still need to practice." She folded her hands on the table, her eyes intent on his face. "Levi, people respect you even when they don't personally like you. You have an air of gravitas that people find reassuring in an authority figure. That's always worked to the prosecution's advantage in the past. I've read transcripts of your testimony in previous trials, and you never had an angry outburst in the courtroom before the Seven of Spades's debut."

"I'm doing the best I can," he said wearily. "Do you think I want to be the kind of guy people think they have to tiptoe around in fear that he might fly off the handle at any second? I mean, God, I used to look down on Jonah Gibbs for his hair trigger, and now I'm even worse than he is."

"You're under a form of stress that's almost unimaginable. The people who know you are willing to cut you some slack." With a shrug, she kicked back in her chair. "Strangers, not so much."

"Is it even that big a deal in this case? The physical evidence is overwhelming. Wilson was injured during the assault on the casino and picked up with his AR-15 still in his hands. There's no room for doubt."

She grimaced. "You've been a cop for too long to be that naïve. People are stupid. They make decisions with their guts, not their heads. So if Papadopoulos makes you look like a loose cannon, all the evidence you're connected to will be tainted by association. I am *not* watching a Nazi skate on multiple homicides because twelve morons decided they don't trust the angry detective involved in the case."

She was right. A cop's job didn't end when the perp was in jail; providing helpful testimony for the prosecution was just as important as the investigation itself. He was letting his anxiety about the cross-examination get the better of him.

"I get it." He blew out a forceful breath. "Okay, let's go again."

"Use smaller words this time," she said as she swept the take-out containers aside and rifled through her papers. "Juries have to be spoon-fed tiny bits of information like dumbass toddlers."

He couldn't help laughing. "You're such a humanitarian."

They spent another hour first rehearsing the testimony Levi would provide as Leila's witness—which was the easy part—and then practicing the cross, for which Leila took on the role of Papadopoulos.

She didn't pull her punches, either, which Levi appreciated. The only way for him to practice controlling his anger was to experience as close to the genuine provocation as possible. In fact, the whole thing reminded him of the role-playing he sometimes did in his sessions with Alana.

It wasn't too late when they called it quits, and there were still plenty of cars in the parking garage next to Leila's office building. Levi had parked closer to the surface, but he walked with her to her car anyway, telling her about his progress with the kidnapping ring. With any luck, he'd have gotten some hits on the mercenaries' identities by the time he returned to the substation.

Even as he said that, she frowned and glanced at her watch. "You're going back to work?"

"Where else would I go?"

"Levi—"

Her mouth snapped shut, and they both abruptly stopped walking. They were on one of the lower levels of the garage, between two rows of parked cars. Though nothing appeared out of the ordinary, the back of Levi's neck prickled with unease as alarm bells went off in his head. Looking at Leila, he knew she felt it too.

"Something's not right," she said.

Before he could respond, multiple slamming doors echoed off the concrete as men emerged from cars in every direction. Levi automatically turned so his back was to one row, making it difficult for anyone to get behind him. To his right, Leila did the same.

The men approached them in a loose semicircle—eight total, all white, some heavily tattooed. Most were empty-handed, but one was swinging an aluminum baseball bat idly from one hand, while another was twirling a tire iron in lazy circles.

These assholes needed no introduction. Their tattoos and the disgusting slogans on their T-shirts proclaimed them to be Utopia as loudly as if they'd shouted it.

Levi shifted into a modified fighting stance but didn't reach for his gun yet—that would only escalate the situation, and he and Leila were terribly outnumbered.

"Look what we have here," said the man at the center of the group, a lean, narrow-hipped skinhead with sharp eyes. "A Jew and an Arab. Ain't you supposed to be enemies?"

"Corey Fletcher," Leila said. "Aren't *you* supposed to be in jail?"

Fletcher grinned. "Good behavior."

"You know this guy?" Levi asked.

"He's been in and out of the CCDC. Assault, vandalism, petty theft." She swept the lineup of men with a gaze that dripped disdain. "Then again, I could be confused. All these Nazi punks look the same to me."

"We aren't Nazis!" said a guy to Fletcher's left, puffing out his chest. "Just because we're trying to preserve our race—"

"Yeah, you don't sound like a Nazi at all," said Leila.

The gangbanger made a growling noise and started toward her, but Fletcher slapped a hand against his chest.

"The two of you have been causing us a lot of trouble the past few months," Fletcher said, his tone pure nonchalance. He looked Levi up and down. "I thought it was time we came to see what all the fuss was about. You've been making quite a name for yourself, boy."

Levi's nostrils flared. "I'm just doing my job—which, I'll remind you, is as a detective with the LVMPD."

Though Fletcher's lips curved, his eyes remained untouched. "Uh-huh. And are you doing your job when you drug people and slit their throats?"

Levi's pulse picked up as a hot flush prickled across his skin. He stood lighter on the balls of his feet, his hands flexing with restless energy. "I am *not* the Seven of Spades. But if I were a serial killer who's dropped more than twenty bodies in less than a year, do you really think it would be a good idea to fuck with me?"

"The Seven of Spades catches people by surprise. You've got none of that now."

Fletcher advanced, and Levi caught the glint of steel beneath his jacket. Moving quickly, Levi drew his own gun—but so did three of the gangbangers, as well as Fletcher himself.

The tension in the parking garage ratcheted up exponentially, the assembled men bristling with the anticipation of bloodshed. Levi's heart hammered against his rib cage. Beside him, Leila had gone entirely still.

The truth was, Levi didn't know if he could use his gun at all. Ever since he'd killed the perpetrator of a hostage crisis a year ago, he had a tendency to choke when he drew his weapon. The only other time he'd been able to fire it was to protect Dominic from imminent death, so maybe he could do the same for Leila—

"Put it on the ground and kick it toward me," said Fletcher. His grip on his own gun was rock-steady.

Though Levi hesitated, there was no real choice here. One gun wouldn't do shit against four even if he *did* trust himself to fire.

He crouched to set his gun on the ground, then stood and gave it a kick. Fletcher kicked it again, sending it sliding across the concrete and underneath a car on the other side of the aisle.

"Don't worry, we're not gonna kill you." Fletcher lowered his gun and nodded to his buddies, who put theirs away. "We're just gonna teach you two a lesson about knowing your place. Send a message to this depraved city."

While Fletcher spoke, Leila stepped slightly behind Levi, and he heard her unzip her purse. Thinking she might be trying to surreptitiously call for help, he did his best to keep the gangbangers' attention on himself.

"What message is that?" he asked, letting his sneer come through in his voice.

Fletcher's face lit up with passion, his eyes fever-bright. "Revolution is coming. Utopia won't stand idly by while our country is overrun by Jews and sodomites and lesser races. We're taking action, and it starts with you. When we put down the Seven of Spades, everyone will know this is *our* city now. *We'll* be the name they fear."

"Oh my God," Levi said. "You're so fucking delusional that I'd feel sorry for you if you didn't make me want to throw up."

Fletcher laughed, and the semicircle narrowed as the men advanced. They were grinning now, cracking their knuckles, rolling their necks from side to side. The one with the baseball bat firmed his grip; the one with the tire iron smacked the metal against his palm.

"Now, I know you've got all kinds of sneaky Israeli tricks up your sleeve," Fletcher said, gun still in hand. "But you're not going to use them, are you? Not when we could do so much worse to your pretty lawyer friend than we're planning."

"Oh, please." Leila's purse dropped to the ground, and she stepped out from behind Levi with a thick black cylinder in her hand.

She cracked it in half, then flicked both halves out to the side to expand two long, wicked batons. "Don't hold back on my account."

Levi's eyes went wide. Several of the men took startled steps back, exchanging uncertain glances. Leila looked at Levi and arched one eyebrow with a smile.

All right, then.

Leila's batons flashed as she surged toward the four men on the right, all of whom cried out in dismay and backed up out of range. That left Levi with the other four—Fletcher, who was standing directly in front of him and the only one still holding a gun, and another three men arrayed to his left.

The gun was the biggest threat, one Levi had to neutralize before Fletcher recovered from his shock. Levi's hand shot out to redirect the gun to his left, keeping Leila out of the line of fire, before his other hand came up to catch the hammer. He burst forward diagonally and kicked Fletcher hard in the balls, then rotated the gun sharply to break it from Fletcher's grasp. A loud *snap* was accompanied by a pained scream as the disarm broke Fletcher's trigger finger.

Levi had the gun now, but the men were surrounding him, and taking time to shoot would leave him vulnerable to a rear assault. He lashed out with his legs to keep them at bay—first nailing the one coming up behind with a back kick that sent the guy flying into a parked car and set off a strident alarm, then using his momentum to drive his foot into the chest of another man coming at him from the front. When Fletcher made a valiant attempt to come at him again, Levi shifted into a side kick and knocked him on his ass.

The man with the bat raised it over head with both hands, bellowing as he charged Levi. It was such a wild attack that Levi had plenty of time to dodge it, crouching and sliding away at an angle. He swung his left leg around in a modified roundhouse that caught the guy just below the knees and sprawled him onto the cement.

Ten feet to their right, Leila was a whirlwind of fluid, nonstop attacks, both of her arms operating independently in a display of graceful coordination like nothing Levi had ever seen. Her batons struck the men with nasty, rapid-fire *cracks*, and only the one with a tire iron was putting up a good fight.

The moment Levi took to check on her gave one of his own attackers a chance to catch him off guard with a right hook. Levi's defense was sloppy, so while he managed to avoid taking the full brunt of the blow, it clipped him hard enough to rattle his brain.

This guy was a trained boxer; it was clear in the devastating force and accuracy of his punches. He drove his left fist into Levi's solar plexus and followed up with a right cross that crashed into Levi's face at full speed. Levi gasped for air as blood spurted from his nose and mouth.

He flung his hands up to protect his face, so he was able to redirect the man's next jab more out of reflex than anything else—with his right hand, the one still gripping the gun. The man hissed in pain, then made the mistake of winding his other arm up for a powerful punch, unmistakably telegraphing his intentions.

Levi leaned out of the line of attack, redirected the man's arm, and trapped it at full extension. When the man struggled to wrench away, Levi pistol-whipped him multiple times until he slumped unconscious to the ground.

One of Leila's batons shattered a car window, and another alarm joined the shrieking cacophony blaring off the concrete walls along with angry shouts and cries of pain. Levi shook his head, still disoriented, and spat out a mouthful of blood.

Baseball Bat remained down, dazed from the fall he'd taken, but Fletcher and his other buddy had recovered. They rushed Levi from either side, grabbed his arms, and hauled him backward too fast for him to defend. Then they lifted him in the air and slammed him flat on his back onto the trunk of a car.

Though the blow winded Levi badly and made him drop the gun, he drew his knees to his chest out of pure muscle memory. He'd spent too many years trained to keep his legs between himself and an attacker to leave his body a flat, easy target.

Good thing, too, because Baseball Bat was getting to his feet. He snatched up his weapon and advanced on Levi with a vicious smile that promised payback while the other two men held Levi pinned to the car.

Fuck that. Levi twisted onto his left hip, thanking God for his flexibility, and kicked Fletcher in the face until Fletcher cursed and retreated. With his left arm free, Levi was able to roll to his right, tucking his knees and throwing his forearm and elbow up to protect his head seconds before the bat smashed down right where he'd been, breaking through the car's rear window.

"Shit!" Baseball Bat said. He reared back for another strike.

Levi uncoiled and kicked him square in the face, breaking his nose. Simultaneously, he reached up and speared the fingers of his free hand into the eyes of the man still holding him.

As the man yelped and let go, Fletcher ran forward to grab one of Levi's feet—whether in an attempt to flip him over or drag him off the car, Levi never knew, because he lifted his other leg high in the air and brought it hurtling straight down to smack into Fletcher's hands. With the grip released, Levi drew back both legs and unleashed a brutal double kick that propelled Fletcher backward, right into Baseball Bat.

No sooner had the two men collapsed in a heap than a tire iron hurtled out of thin air and hit them both. Levi glanced to his right and saw that the man who'd been wielding it was down and out for the count, his face and hands welted from Leila's batons.

Levi jumped off the trunk only for the man whose eyes he'd gouged to seize him, spin him around, and try to slam him back onto it face-first. He got his hands up in time to avoid being flattened or hitting his face, but the man plastered himself to Levi while choking him from behind, leaving no space between their bodies.

Coughing, Levi plucked one of the man's hands off his throat to loosen the choke while he scraped his foot down the man's shin and stomped on his instep. When the man grunted and shifted backward, Levi had room to bring his heel up in a fierce mule kick that got the guy right in the balls.

The man shrieked. Levi dialed up the aggression, piling pain on top of pain. He threw a vertical elbow into the man's chin and kicked him again, then scooped up some of the safety glass from the car's broken window with one hand as he spun around, leading with sideways elbow strikes that cracked into the man's cheek over and over.

Behind his choker, Fletcher and Baseball Bat were on their feet. He threw the glass at their faces to keep them back, grasped his choker's nape, and smashed the man's face into the edge of the trunk, knocking him unconscious.

Fletcher was still rubbing safety glass out of his eyes, but Baseball Bat came at Levi with a true horizontal swing. Levi turned his shoulder in, brought his other hand up to protect his face, and darted *into* the attack, slamming sideways into the man's shoulder so the bat swung harmlessly around him. Before the man could recover, Levi wrapped up the arm holding the bat, threw his elbow into the man's face, and kneed him twice in the groin.

When he felt the man weaken, Levi reached across him, snapped the bat out of his hand, and brought it sideways against his head. As the man reeled, Levi grabbed his shoulder and wrist and swung one leg backward to connect with the man's calves, sweeping him right off his feet. The man landed hard on his back—still conscious, but the blows to his head from the bat and the concrete had incapacitated him nonetheless.

Levi risked a glance over his shoulder to check on Leila. One of her two remaining attackers was trying to draw his gun, but the struggle to retrieve it from his waistband gave her enough time to completely lay him out. Now, like Levi, she only had one man left.

Levi turned his attention back to said man—Fletcher, who was glaring at him with venomous loathing. It was kind of impressive that the guy was still going strong despite his bleeding face and broken finger.

He also seemed to have learned his lesson about coming in hot. Instead of bum-rushing Levi, he drew a knife from his pocket and flicked out its long blade before advancing with caution.

They feinted and parried, both wary of each other's weapons. The baseball bat gave Levi the advantage of a longer reach, but if Fletcher got in close with that knife, the bat would be useless and Levi would be fucked.

Levi capitalized on the bat's length, wielding it with quick, ferocious swings, herding Fletcher backward with the goal of trapping him against one of the garage's concrete pillars. His ploy was successful, but as he sent the bat hurtling toward Fletcher's head, Fletcher ducked at the last second and the bat slammed into the pillar instead.

Levi had put so much force behind the swing that it reverberated painfully through the metal bat, jarring the bones all up and down his arms. He dropped it with a shout.

Fletcher lunged forward with a diagonal slash of the knife. Levi leaned back out of reach, his hands rising to protect his face just in case. As Fletcher returned with a backhand slash, Levi launched himself forward to slam his forearms against the knife arm like goalposts, arresting the movement. He grabbed Fletcher's arm with one hand, punched him in the face several times with the other, and kneed his balls for good measure.

Without letting up for a moment—every second a knife was in play was one second too many—Levi gripped Fletcher's knife hand with both of his own, twisted it around, and threw Fletcher onto his back. Holding Fletcher's arm straight up, Levi rolled him onto his stomach, dislocating his shoulder in the process and finally stripping away the knife.

He looked back toward Leila. She was finishing off her own final attacker—but one of the men behind her had regained consciousness and was crawling on his belly toward the gun Levi had dropped earlier.

"Behind you!" Levi shouted.

Leila spun around, flipped her right baton to a backhand grip, and knocked the man out with one smooth diagonal blow.

Car alarms continued blaring all around them. Each of the eight gangbangers was on the ground, some unconscious and others too injured to move. Levi flicked Fletcher's knife shut and hurried to Leila's side, kicking the fallen gun even farther away.

"I can't believe the cops haven't shown up yet." She scanned the garage as she turned in a slow circle. "Someone had to have heard all this commotion by now."

One of her cheekbones was swelling, and blood trickled from the corner of her mouth—but her eyes sparkled, her face shining with the same heady, triumphant thrill Levi felt after winning a difficult fight. It was the most emotion he'd ever seen her display.

"Arnis?" he said, indicating her batons with one hand and reaching for his cuffs with the other. He'd recognized the fighting style; it was the national martial art of the Philippines, also called Kali or Eskrima. When she nodded, he asked, "Where did you even learn that?"

"My childhood best friend's family was from the Philippines. Her father was a master of the art." Leila crouched to smack the ends of her batons against the ground, causing them to retract, then stood up and fit the two pieces back together. "His daughter wasn't interested in learning, but I was. He taught me everything he knew. I've been doing it most of my life."

"You're amazing." Levi glanced at his cuffs, realizing there was little point in restraining one man out of eight. He'd be shocked if any of these men could stand under their own power, anyway.

"Back at you," Leila said. She scooped up her purse, shook it free of broken glass, and cocked her head. "You okay?"

He was shaking with adrenaline and excitement, his heart pounding, his brain racing a mile a minute like he'd just downed a handful of amphetamines. "Yeah, I'm fine." He wiped some blood off his face, looked down at himself, and winced at the wreck of his clothing. "Looks like I ruined another suit, though."

Any second now, the arousal would kick in—the urgent lust he felt after any life-or-death battle, the indomitable craving to be fucked deep and hard and rough until he came screaming. He could already feel it stirring in his gut, flaring up hotter whenever he let his memory linger on the thud of flesh on flesh, the snap of bone, the sight of his enemies falling at his hand.

Dominic could take care of him. Dominic could give him what he needed, leave him fucked-out and sated in a way no other man had ever been able—

No. God, this had to stop.

Wailing sirens announced the arrival of two black-and-whites that came barreling down the ramps of the parking garage. The cars screeched to a halt at the end of the row and several cops jumped out, guns drawn. They gaped at the eight broken, bloody men scattered around the banged-up cars.

"Better late than never, I guess," said Leila.

CHAPTER 12

"**Y**ou okay, Dom?" Carlos asked. "You seem distracted."

"Huh?" Dominic looked up from the ceremony programs he was folding. "Oh, yeah, I'm fine."

After work, he'd headed to Carlos and Jasmine's apartment for dinner and wedding prep. His project was spread across the coffee table, while they were on the floor next to it, hunched over the poster board they were using to plan the reception's seating chart. Rebel lay a few feet away, happily gnawing an enormous rawhide bone that could have been plucked from some prehistoric megafauna.

The shifty sideways glance Carlos and Jasmine exchanged was telling. For once, though, it wasn't gambling cravings that had Dominic so preoccupied.

"It's one of my cases," he said to reassure them. "The client's been avoiding me for a day and a half, and I can't move forward the way I need to until I talk to him."

Royce's ducking of Dominic's calls and even a visit to his office had become so pointed that Dominic had revised his opinion on whether Royce was totally oblivious to what was going on. Still, he was hesitant to go to the expense of putting Juliette under serious surveillance without Royce's go-ahead.

He'd dug deeper in the meantime, however, and he was certain Royce had been paying Juliette's living expenses for months—not something a man did for a meaningless fling. He'd also gotten Juliette's picture out to Paulie and his other criminal contacts, along with the name Bennett, to see if that stirred anything up.

Carlos and Jasmine accepted his explanation without argument. He returned his attention to folding the programs, which featured abstract watercolors in pale peach, earthy green, and sunset orange against a white background. While a tattoo artist by trade, Jasmine was skilled in multiple visual art mediums, and she'd designed all of the wedding's paper items herself, from the invitations down to the escort cards.

"How's Levi doing?" Jasmine asked after a few moments of industrious silence. "You know, with . . . everything. I called to check on him the day after he found that guy in his car, and he was even more wound up than usual."

Dominic shrugged. "I wouldn't be the one to ask."

He *was* concerned that Levi hadn't updated him on his side of the case since that morning. Levi must not have found anything on the gas station security cameras, after all. Or maybe he was still looking— he tended to get wrapped up in a case to distraction the same way Dominic did.

"So," Dominic said, aiming to shift the focus of the conversation off himself. "Bachelor party tomorrow. You excited?"

"If by 'excited' you mean 'nervous,' then sure," said Carlos. "You really aren't going to tell me anything about it?"

"Nope. It's a surprise."

"As long as it doesn't turn into *The Hangover*."

"I'd never roofie you," Dominic said solemnly.

Carlos and Jasmine both snickered.

In the morning, Dominic would have to try confronting Royce at home; the man had left him no other choice. Carolyn Royce had helped force her husband to act like a human being once before, so she might be of assistance this time as well.

Until then, Dominic's mind belonged right here, with his friends. He concentrated on his task and sipped a beer while he listened to Jasmine wax poetic about a wild acid trip back in her college days.

About ten minutes later, Rebel perked up her head and stared at the front door. Dominic noticed but thought nothing of it until she hopped to her feet, abandoning her bone, and barked twice.

At that, Dominic jumped up as well, his hand going to his gun. Carlos and Jasmine went tense and quiet.

"What is it?" Carlos asked.

"I don't know—"

Rebel barked again. Dominic heard a thump out in the hallway, followed by the sound of running feet. He dashed to the door, wrenched it open, and looked up and down the hall—which, because their building was designed like a motel, was open to the night beyond. Rebel ran out beside him.

"Stay," Dominic told her when he caught sight of the runner. It was just a skinny kid in a hoodie, bounding down the exterior staircase like a parkour champion. The kid sprinted across the internal courtyard, through the property's gates, and into a waiting car, which sped away with a screech of tires.

Jasmine and Carlos came up behind Dominic. "What's going on?" Jasmine said.

Dominic frowned after the car's rapidly disappearing taillights. "I'm not sure."

Rebel trotted over to the door of Dominic's apartment, one unit over, and sniffed a thick manila envelope that had been dropped in front of it. He shooed her away, then flipped the package over with the toe of his shoe, his heart in his throat as he expected to see the insignia of the Seven of Spades.

Instead of a playing card, however, the folder was inked with the image of a hornet poised to strike—the symbol of Los Avispones.

"What the . . ." Dominic held out a hand to Carlos and Jasmine. "Don't touch that."

He retrieved a pair of nitrile gloves from his apartment, then returned to pick up the package. His friends trailed after him as he carried it inside, cleared a space around the junk that had accumulated on his dining table since Levi had cleaned up, and set it down.

Rebel hadn't seemed concerned by the envelope's contents, so Dominic wasn't either; as a trained personal protection dog, she would have detected explosives. He slit the envelope open and tipped the contents out onto the table.

"Whoa," Carlos said, his eyes wide. "Are those . . ."

"False papers." Dominic sifted through them with his gloved hands. There were two sets of forged identity documents—birth certificates, passports, driver's licenses, social security cards, the works—but the papers were only half-finished. There were no photographs yet, some of the demographic information was blank, and several of the designs were bleeding ink.

Jasmine made a scoffing noise. "These aren't great, are they? I mean, I could do a better job than this."

Dominic and Carlos both looked at her.

"I'm just saying."

"These are the kinds of documents you have made when you're preparing to start a whole new life," Dominic said. "There are two sets here—one for a man and one for a woman. Nicholas Fox and Monica Bennett." He rocked back on his heels.

"Does that mean something to you?" Carlos asked.

Dominic nodded absently. Fake papers for a man and a woman, one the same name as the kidnappers' client and the other the name attached to the bank account that had received the ransom payments—Levi had been right all along. Royce and Juliette were planning to go on the run.

His cell phone rang, startling all three of them. He withdrew it from his pocket and looked at the screen.

BLOCKED.

The bottom fell out of Dominic's stomach. He knew exactly who was on the other end of the line, even if he wasn't sure why.

While Carlos and Jasmine watched with concern, Dominic cleared his dry throat and answered the phone. "Hello?"

"*Don't say I never gave you anything, Mr. Russo,*" said the harsh electronic rasp of the Seven of Spades's disguised voice.

Dominic gripped the edge of the table with his free hand. Though the Seven of Spades called Levi on occasion, both at work and on his cell, all of Dominic's past interactions with them had been through texts or written messages. This was the first time they'd called him directly.

He opened an app to record the call before he spoke again. "I'm assuming you're responsible for the package I just found at my door?"

"*Compliments of my friends in Los Avispones.*"

"How?"

"*They caught word you were looking for a woman named Bennett who's connected to these recent kidnappings. One of their forgers had been* contracted by a third party to make those papers for a woman of the same name. Quite a coincidence, wouldn't you say?"

"So you made them give the papers to me instead?"

"*I didn't insist. Only suggested. I wouldn't have known anything about it if my friends hadn't come to me first. They know about my . . . special relationship to you.*"

"Why would you do this?" Dominic asked. No way did the Seven of Spades care about adults being kidnapped for ransom—there was no betrayal of trust involved, and they didn't concern themselves with ordinary crimes.

After a brief pause, the Seven of Spades said, "*Do you have any idea how long I've been planning my gift for Detective Abrams?*"

"Gift?" Dominic made a face. "You mean kidnapping and murdering the men who attacked him in college?"

Though Carlos and Jasmine must have had their suspicions about who Dominic was talking to, that was what clinched it. They both backed away from the table, Carlos drawing a sharp breath and Jasmine pressing one hand to her mouth.

"*Months of careful preparation and strategizing,*" said the Seven of Spades. "*Tens of thousands of dollars. Not to mention the rather considerable physical effort I've expended. All that investment of time, money, and energy, and the very same week, these eye-gouging idiots blow their operation and reveal their kidnapping ring to the entire city?*"

Dominic lifted the phone away from his ear and stared at it for a second. "I'm sorry, are you saying you're helping me with this case because you're annoyed the people behind it are stealing your thunder?"

"*I'm saying that Las Vegas has more important matters to concern itself with. I want people's focus back where it belongs.*"

"And by 'focus,' you really mean 'spotlight.'"

"*This is* my *city,*" the Seven of Spades said with sudden malice that broke through even the flattening effect of the masking algorithm. "*When my plans for Detective Abrams come to fruition, nobody in Las Vegas will care about anything else. We haven't even scratched the surface of what I have in store for him. Nothing is going to stand in the way of that.*"

A cold sweat broke out on Dominic's forehead and along his spine. What the hell was this freak planning to do to Levi? More importantly, how could Dominic stop it?

Giving his head a shake, Dominic said, "Why send these papers to me instead of Levi?" Then he answered his own question. "Right, of course. Because if the detective on the case got this information from a serial killer, a defense attorney would have it thrown right out. But if Levi gets it from a PI who can just say it was obtained from an informant, it'll probably be ruled admissible evidence."

"Who says you're just a pretty face?"

"Still, this doesn't give me much to go on. There aren't even any photos."

"The forger hadn't been provided photos yet. These were just a rough draft—a mock-up of sorts. I can't do all the work for you."

"I—"

"Are you a private investigator or not? Investigate, Mr. Russo. And quickly." The Seven of Spades's voice hardened. *"Because I'm losing my patience."*

The line went dead. Dominic ended the recording, saved it, and set the phone down. His hand was shaking.

"Oh my God, Dom," Jasmine said, grabbing Carlos's arm as if for support. "That was the Seven of Spades, wasn't it? You were just talking to a serial killer!"

"Yeah." He raked both hands through his hair. "I'm sorry, I have to take care of this. Rain check on the programs?"

It wasn't easy to evade their worried questions and exclamations, but he managed to usher Carlos and Jasmine out of his apartment and safely into their own. Back at his place, with all the locks thrown, the alarm engaged, and Rebel by his side, Dominic sat down at the table to peruse the forged identity documents more carefully. There was something about them that had nagged at him before the Seven of Spades's call.

"Monica Bennett," he said aloud. The name sounded—not familiar, exactly, but it reminded him of something . . .

A light bulb went off as he made the connection. He grabbed his cell phone and dialed Martine.

"How did you hear already?" she said when she answered.

"Hear?" Dominic had been so intensely focused on the question he wanted to ask her that it took him a second to process the unexpected greeting. "Hear what?"

She said nothing.

"Martine. *Hear what?*"

"Okay, before I say anything, I want you to know that Levi is totally fine. A little banged up, but it's nothing serious."

Dominic shot to his feet, startling Rebel. "*What?*" Oh God, had the Seven of Spades already gotten to him?

"He and Leila were jumped by some Utopia gangbangers in a parking garage," Martine said. "But they managed to get the upper hand. You know how Levi is, and apparently Leila can do some kind of crazy Filipino martial arts with sticks or batons or something."

"Arnis?" Dominic said, struggling to keep up. It was obvious from the way Leila carried herself that she was a trained fighter, and Arnis would be a good fit for her lithe build.

"Yeah, I guess. Anyway, all the men have been arrested, and neither Levi or Leila were seriously injured."

Dominic sank back into his chair, rubbing a hand over his face. Rebel eyed him warily before she settled down as well.

"You're sure he's okay?"

"Yes. Actually, he's in a great mood. He's . . . Well, I don't need to explain it to you."

She didn't. They were both familiar with how much Levi enjoyed a good violent altercation; his brain must be soaked in endorphins right now. If the fight had been particularly intense, he was probably yearning for a nice hard fuck—

Good God, this was so not the time to be having these thoughts. Dominic smacked the heel of his hand against his forehead.

"That's really not why you called me?" Martine asked.

"No. I wanted to ask you a question—what would be the French version of the surname Bennett?"

Martine sighed. "First of all, you understand that I'm Haitian, right? I speak Kreyol, not French. And even my Kreyol has gotten rusty since I moved out west."

"I know. I was hoping the names at least would be similar enough."

"They can be. Bennett, huh?" She was quiet for a moment. "I'd say . . . Binet, maybe? Or Benoit."

Dominic's stomach flipped. He thanked Martine for her help, asked her to have Levi give him a call when everything was squared away, and hung up. Then he hunted down his research on Juliette, dumped it onto the table next to the fake papers, and flipped through the pages until he found what he was looking for.

Juliette's middle name was Monique. And her mother's maiden name was Benoit.

Dominic grabbed his work-issued laptop, the only computer he had left, and dove into one aspect of the investigation he'd been avoiding so far: a background check on Nathan Royce himself. A few minutes later, he'd confirmed his suspicions.

Royce's mother's maiden name was Nichols; his paternal grandmother's was Fuchs. *Nicholas Fox.*

"Jesus Christ," Dominic said. This was the same amateur mistake that had tripped up a lot of his bounties in the past—choosing an alias too closely related to their real identities. Some people had no imagination.

The evidence was circumstantial, but combined with other aspects of the investigation, it would be enough for Levi to obtain arrest warrants from a friendly judge. That should clinch it. Royce would crack under the pressure of an interrogation, and if Juliette was the kind of grifter her history suggested, she'd be willing to cut herself a deal. McBride would take a hit with the loss of Royce's contract, but there was no way to avoid that.

His phone rang again—Levi this time.

"Hey," Dominic said. "Are you all right?"

"I'm fine," said Levi, and the words rang true for a change. There was no stress or tension in his voice. "I'm almost home. Martine said you called her earlier?"

"Yeah. I've got something on the kidnappings."

"Me too. But you first."

Dominic filled him in on Los Avispones's delivery and the Seven of Spades's phone call—though he left out what the killer had said about Levi himself, not wanting to harsh Levi's hard-earned mellow just yet. He finished with his own research and the conclusions he'd drawn.

"You're right; I can get warrants off that," Levi said. In the background, Dominic heard his car engine cut off, then the slam of his door echoing through his building's parking garage. "I'll call Judge Morales as soon as we hang up. But it gets better. Earlier, I caught the kidnappers on the smoke shop's cameras, and while I was tied up with Leila and Utopia, facial recognition was able to match them. We already had Charles Graham, and the system identified the other five men."

"You're kidding."

"Nope." Levi's words came in between quick, even breaths as he jogged up the stairs—he rarely took an elevator for anything less than five stories. "They all have military backgrounds, and a few have criminal histories as well. I just put BOLOs out; every cop and FBI agent in the Las Vegas Valley is looking for them now. We're closing in."

"That's great."

"Yeah. I just need to shower and change, and once I have warrants, I can arrest Royce and Juliette tonight."

Dominic smiled as he listened to Levi's apartment door open and shut, followed by the soft beep of the alarm system before Levi disarmed it. He hadn't heard Levi this energized in a long time.

"Hey," Levi said, "are you sure you—"

But Dominic would never know what Levi meant to say next, because his words were abruptly cut off in a strangled scream that made all of Dominic's hair stand on end.

"*Oh my God*," Levi said, his voice so twisted with horror that Dominic barely recognized it.

There was a loud clatter, as if the phone had been dropped, then a *thump* like a body hitting the floor. Then nothing.

"Levi," Dominic said, his heart pounding. "*Levi!*"

There was no response.

CHAPTER 13

L evi stayed where he'd fallen, crumpled on the floor after his knees had given out. He stared numbly at the dining room alcove.

A glittery *Happy Birthday!* banner had been strung along the wall. Beneath it, George Quintana's corpse sat at the head of the dining table, a paper party hat perched jauntily on the side of his head with a seven of spades card pasted to it. His clouded eyes were open, his once-golden-brown skin drained to gray by the emptied arteries in his neck. Blood drenched his clothing and had pooled on the floor below his chair.

An elaborately frosted birthday cake sat on the table in front of him, ringed with unlit candles, with one blood-red novelty candle at the center in the shape of a seven. Quintana's arms had been rigged to rest on the table, a fork and knife clutched in his hands like he was about to dig in.

Levi didn't have a panic attack. Nor did he get angry. He just . . . stopped.

He was distantly aware of a tinny shouting, then a shrill ringing that happened over and over again, but the sounds held no meaning. He was untethered from his body, floating above it, where nothing could hurt him.

Eventually, the ringing stopped. Levi imagined he could hear the *drip-drip-drip* of Quintana's blood hitting the floor in its place, but of course that wasn't real. All the blood had long since dried.

His phone rang again. This time, it startled Levi back into his body. He sucked in a breath, blinking rapidly, and reached for the phone without looking away from the corpse.

"Hello."

"*Do you like your present, Detective?*"

Levi pulled his legs up to his chest and dropped his forehead onto his knees. "Why are you doing this to me?"

"*I'm trying to help you. To free you.*"

"Free me from what?" Levi muttered into his knees.

"*From your past. From your fears. From the restraints you've put on your own potential.*"

"That doesn't make any sense."

"*The men who almost killed you will never hurt you or anyone else again,*" said the Seven of Spades. "*Doesn't that loosen the hold the memory of the attack has on you? Doesn't it make you feel better?*"

"No! Killing them doesn't change anything. It doesn't erase the past." Levi lifted his head, his stomach churning as he took in the gruesome tableau once more. "They should have gone to jail. I didn't want them to die."

"*Didn't you? Look at Mr. Quintana, Detective. Really look at him. Do you remember him from that night?*"

Levi could never forget. Quintana had been grinning, enjoying himself immensely, whooping with glee as he drove his fists and feet into Levi's defenseless body. He'd casually suggested they knock all of Levi's teeth out to make him a better cocksucker, then laughed.

"*They broke more than your bones. They altered the entire course your life would have taken. Drove you away from your family, your friends. Made you angry. Mistrustful. The consequences of their actions extended far beyond a single night. Now they're paying for it. Can you really tell me that doesn't make you happy?*"

"I—"

"*I've been treating these men differently, you know. Before I kill them, I talk to them. I make sure they know they're going to die, and more importantly, why. They suffer first. They know the end is coming, and they're afraid. Just like you were.*"

Levi swallowed, his gaze unblinking on Quintana's face. He imagined Quintana crying, gibbering with terror, begging for his life the way Levi had. Sensing the inevitability of death and being powerless to stop it. His breath came fast and shallow.

"*Do you like that?*" the Seven of Spades asked softly.

"Yes," Levi whispered.

"*Good,*" the killer said, their electronic voice still hushed. "*That's good, Detective. You're so close now. Once all four men are dead, their hold on you will break, and you'll be free to be who you really are.*"

"Who I . . . What? What are you talking about?"

Snapping out of the bizarre reverie he'd fallen into, Levi sat upright. This wasn't just a twisted gift. The Seven of Spades never did anything without an ulterior motive.

His eyes swept the apartment until they fell on the front door, and then it hit him. "No forced entry. The alarm was engaged."

"*There's nothing you can do to keep me out. Though it's admirable that you keep trying.*"

"You killed Grant Sheppard in Philadelphia while I was nearby on purpose," Levi said, the pieces falling into place. "I have no alibi for Foley's murder. Reddick was found in my car, Quintana in my apartment . . . People are going to think I did this. They'll think *I'm* the Seven of Spades. But that's what you want, isn't it?"

"*You don't need them. They're only holding you back.*"

"So you think if you turn people against me, isolate me, I'll—what, become like you?"

"*You're already like me. You just won't admit it.*"

"I'm not." As Levi stood, his old familiar anger washed over him—but this time, he welcomed it. He relished the way it heated his skin, stiffened his spine, swept the befuddled fog from his brain. "I'm nothing like you. I never will be."

The Seven of Spades's electronic laugh was chilling. "*We'll see. Happy Birthday, Detective.*"

They hung up. Seconds later, footsteps pounded down the hallway outside Levi's apartment and fists banged at the door.

"Police, open up!" shouted a female voice. The doorknob rattled, but Levi had thrown the locks before he'd turned around and seen Quintana's body. "Detective Abrams, are you in there?"

Recognizing the voice, he hurried to unlock and open the door. Kelly Marin ran inside, skidded to a halt when she saw the crime scene, and clapped both hands to her mouth with a yelp. Another cop, a man Levi didn't know, came in behind her, only to stumble backward into the door as his face went dead white.

"Kelly," Levi said. "What are you doing here?"

She dropped her hands but remained mesmerized by the sight in the dining room, speaking without looking at him. "There was a 911 call, something about you being hurt in your apartment."

That had to have been Dominic. He must be going out of his mind not knowing what had happened—

Kelly spun around to face her partner. "Radio Dispatch that there's been another Seven of Spades murder." When the man didn't react, she gave him a shove. "*Go.*"

He hurried out into the hall. Kelly's eyes fell on the door—the undamaged, clearly unforced door—and the wireless alarm system beside it, then traveled back to Quintana's body.

"I know what it looks like," said Levi.

"I'm sure there's an explanation."

Of course. The explanation was that the Seven of Spades had copies of his keys and knew his alarm code. They'd said it themselves—there was nothing Levi could do to keep them out. He wasn't safe in his own home.

"You're injured," Kelly said. "What happened?"

"Oh, this isn't . . ." Levi lifted a hand to his bruised face, then glanced down at his scuffed, bloody suit. "This happened hours ago; it has nothing to do with the Seven of Spades. But I can't stay here."

"I can't just let you leave," Kelly said with an apologetic grimace.

"I know. Can you have your partner secure the scene while you take me to the substation? Please."

She bit her lip, then nodded. After checking in with her partner, she brought Levi downstairs and out the front door of the building. They'd left their squad car right at the curb rather than come in through the parking garage.

As she was opening the rear door for him, a loud screech made them both turn around. A pickup truck came fishtailing around the corner, barreled toward them, and slammed on its brakes only inches away. Dominic sprang out, not even bothering to shut the door before rushing to Levi's side.

"God, Levi, what happened?" he said, his voice thin with stress. "You're hurt, Jesus Christ, I thought you were dead—"

"I'm fine." Levi held up both hands. "This is all from the fight with Utopia."

A lump formed in his throat as he studied Dominic, who was pale and breathing raggedly. For Dominic to get here from his own apartment in Friday night traffic only minutes after the responding officers, he must have jumped in his truck the second Levi dropped his phone, and broken every traffic law on the way. It was a miracle he hadn't been pulled over by any of the cops Levi still had on the lookout for him.

"The Seven of Spades killed George Quintana in my apartment and left the body for me to find," Levi added.

Dominic's jaw dropped.

"They're making it look like I'm behind all this."

Comprehension flickered across Dominic's face, followed by horror. "Shit."

"Detective," Kelly said, "I'm sorry, but we really have to go."

Levi started to duck into the car, but hesitated at the last second and put one hand on the roof. "Dominic," he said. "There's still one man left."

It was nearing midnight when Sergeant Wen entered the interrogation suite where Levi had been cooling his heels for hours. The steel furniture and two-way mirror were worlds away from the comfortable interview room where he'd waited after Reddick's body had turned up in his car.

Levi sprang to his feet, a dozen questions on his lips, only to be shocked into silence by the stubble dusting Wen's jaw. In the five years Levi had worked under the man, he'd never seen him anything less than clean-shaven.

"Sit," Wen said wearily.

Levi sank back into the uncomfortable metal chair. Wen took the seat opposite him, then folded his hands on the tabletop.

"The story is everywhere," he said without preamble. "Running on every TV channel, plastered across every news website. An investigative journalist dug up your connection to the victims and broke the story along with the news of the latest murder. Everyone knows."

Everyone knows. Levi's fingertips scored the table's tacky surface. He'd kept the assault a secret from almost everyone he knew for over a decade, and now even random strangers he passed on the street would be privy to it.

"What are people saying?" he asked, dreading the answer.

"Many believe the Seven of Spades is just tormenting you. As for the rest, there seem to be two camps: a smaller group that believes you've been the killer all along, and a larger and much more vocal group that believes you've been borrowing the killer's MO to carry out your own personal vendetta."

"If that were true, I'd be failing spectacularly."

Wen's lips twitched, but the smile didn't reach his eyes and disappeared within seconds. "I'm sure you can understand that this has created a public relations nightmare, not just for the LVMPD, but for the entire city. The powers that be decided that swift action is necessary. As such, you're being suspended—with pay—pending an Internal Affairs investigation into your connection with the recent homicides."

Levi's chair crashed to the floor as he jumped up. Wen winced but didn't otherwise move.

"You're suspending me?" Levi's voice shook. He hadn't imagined it would go this far. "I know the situation is bad, but I haven't done anything wrong!"

"Then the investigation will bear that out." Wen held up a hand before Levi could speak again. "This wasn't my decision. The order came straight from the sheriff himself. I'm sorry, but there's nothing I can do."

Levi scooped his fallen chair off the floor, then stood behind it, his fingers curled in a death grip around the top edge. His eyes flicked toward the two-way mirror.

Were there people on the other side, watching this? Were they enjoying it?

His hands tightened on the chair as he was overcome by the sudden desire to pick it up and slam it into the mirror, to smash it into the glass over and over until the mirror shattered the same way his life had—

STOP, he thought, replacing the violent image with one of a bright red sign. *Stop. Stop.*

He exhaled a shaky breath and looked at Wen, who was studying Levi's hands as if he knew exactly what had been going through his mind.

Forcing himself to release the chair, Levi said, "This is exactly what the Seven of Spades wants—to cut me off, to turn people against me. You're playing along with their game."

"Be that as it may, my hands are tied." Wen stood with a scrape of metal against linoleum. "I truly am sorry, Abrams. An IA detective will be by shortly to take your official statement."

"Wait—"

But Wen was already gone, the door shutting behind him with a decisive *thunk*. Levi banged his fist against it once, then kicked it for good measure.

He couldn't bring himself to sit after that, so he paced around the room, stewing in his anger and resentment. By the time the door opened again, he'd worked himself into such a frothing rage that his unchecked response when he saw who walked through it was, "Oh, *fuck* no."

"Not happy to see me, Abrams?" said Terence Freeman. In a department full of assholes, he was one of the worst—aggressive, closed-minded, and obstinate. He and Levi had been at odds since the first moment they'd met, and their relationship hadn't been improved by the way Freeman had handled Keith Chapman's IA investigation last year, nor his arrest of Kelly Marin for leaking the Seven of Spades story to the press.

"Did you *ask* for this assignment, or did the universe just decide it wasn't done shitting on me tonight?" said Levi.

Freeman smirked and stepped aside to let his partner into the room. Valeria Montoya was in many ways his polar opposite, a stoic woman with the piercing eyes and stony silence of an owl.

Some of Levi's tension eased at the sight of her. Montoya had actually assisted with the Seven of Spades investigation—she'd done exhaustive independent research into dozens of potential suspects before entrusting that information to Levi. But Levi and Martine were the only people in the substation who knew that.

"Why don't you sit down so we can get started?" Freeman said. "I'd rather not be here all night."

The three of them sat at the table—Levi on one side, Freeman and Montoya on the other. Freeman got out a notepad while Montoya simply sat with her hands in her lap and her unsettling gaze trained on Levi's face.

"What time did you arrive home tonight?" Freeman asked.

"A little after 9 p.m."

"Did you notice anything unusual as you entered your apartment?"

"No. The door was locked, and the alarm system was engaged. I didn't see the body until I was already inside."

"How many people besides you know the code to your alarm?"

"Two. Martine Valcourt and Dominic Russo."

Freeman scribbled on his pad. "Mr. Russo called 911 to report a disturbance at your apartment around the same time you say you arrived home."

"We were on the phone with each other at the time," Levi said. He kept his voice calm and steady, just stating the bare facts. "He heard my reaction to finding the body but didn't know what had happened, so he called for help."

"But *you* didn't," Freeman said, tilting his head.

Levi's jaw clenched.

Making a show of riffling through his notes, Freeman added, "I have here that the responding officers arrived about fifteen minutes after Russo's 911 call. In all that time, you never called 911 or anyone else to report the crime. Did you know Russo had already done so?"

"No." Levi dug his fingers into his thighs. Though the truth was embarrassing, it was far preferable to the conclusion Freeman would draw in its absence. "When I found Quintana's body like that, I experienced a dissociative episode. I wasn't aware of the passage of time or anything else."

Montoya's forehead creased, and Freeman blinked.

"A dissociative episode, huh? Has that happened to you before?"

"To a degree." Levi remembered his reactions to Drew Barton's shooting, to Reddick's corpse in his car. "It was much more severe this time."

"Hmm." Freeman tapped his pen against the table. "Were you still dissociating when you had a five-minute conversation with whoever called you before the police showed up?"

Levi tensed, too caught off guard to hide his reaction, and Freeman smiled.

"You received a call from a number registered to a disposable cell phone ten minutes after Russo contacted 911. That call lasted for a full five minutes. Do you really expect me to believe you were dissociating all that time?" When Levi didn't answer, Freeman leaned forward, his eyes intent on Levi's face. "Who were you talking to, Abrams?"

Freeman already knew, of course, and so did Montoya. It was obvious. But not only had Levi been too rattled to record the Seven of Spades's call like he was supposed to, he hadn't told anyone about it. He wet his dry lips while he considered his response.

The door flew open. Levi startled and turned toward it, only for his surprise to grow when Jay Sawyer strode inside.

"This conversation is over," Sawyer said.

A clean-cut, handsome defense attorney, Sawyer's impressive case record was outstripped only by his massive ego. Even in the middle of the night, he was dressed to the nines in a sleek Brioni suit, his hair perfectly coiffed and diamond cuff links glinting subtly at his wrists.

Under ordinary circumstances, Sawyer's mere presence was enough to send Levi's blood pressure skyrocketing, but right now he only felt bewildered relief.

"What the hell are you doing here, Sawyer?" Freeman snapped.

Sawyer's eyebrows rose. "I think a better question would be what *you're* doing here. Because it looks to me like you're interrogating a decorated homicide detective without counsel or even a union representative present."

"Detective Abrams isn't under arrest."

"Good, then he's leaving." Sawyer waved at Levi imperiously. "Come on, let's go."

Dazed by the sudden turn of events, Levi pushed his chair back and stood. Freeman jumped up as well; only Montoya remained seated, observing the confrontation with her trademark pensive silence.

"He's not going anywhere until we're finished talking to him," Freeman said.

"The only person you'll be talking to from now on is *me*," said Sawyer. "My client is invoking his right to remain silent, and will continue to do so in all official communication with the LVMPD until his suspension is lifted and this ludicrous investigation is closed for good. As such, there's no point in detaining him unless you're going to file charges, which you and I both know you don't have enough evidence to do."

Freeman clenched his fists, his nostrils flaring. Levi saw a tiny smile flicker across Montoya's face before her expression smoothed out into its usual neutral lines.

"In the meantime, if you have any questions, feel free to call my office. I'm sure you have my number."

Sawyer took Levi's elbow and led him out of the room. Freeman's cursing followed them until the door shut and cut off all sound.

"I hope you didn't say too much before I got here," Sawyer said while they walked down the hallway. "You of all people should know to never, ever speak to the police—"

"What is going on?" Levi interrupted. He stopped short in the middle of the hall, obliging Sawyer to do the same. "I appreciate what you just did, but I never asked for a lawyer."

"Leila called and asked for my help."

"Leila hates you."

Sawyer grinned. "True, but she's ultimately a practical woman. She'd never let her personal feelings trump logic, and I'm one of the best defense attorneys in Nevada, let alone Las Vegas."

"Ugh," Levi said, but the most annoying thing about Sawyer's arrogance was that it wasn't undeserved. If Levi needed a lawyer, he couldn't do much better. Still . . . "There's no way I can afford you. What's your hourly rate, a thousand bucks? I'm comfortable, but not Hatfield, Park, and McKenzie comfortable."

"For a chance to attach my name to what's shaping up to be the most iconic, high-profile serial murder case in American history? I'll do the work pro bono." Sawyer stepped closer, his eyes warming, and brushed his fingers along Levi's jaw. "But if you wanted to repay me some other way . . ."

Levi knocked his hand aside, though with less hostility than he normally used to reject Sawyer's frequent advances. He was just too tired. "Not now, Sawyer."

"Sorry." The teasing smile slipped off Sawyer's face, replaced by a much graver expression. "You don't look well."

"A serial killer left a dead body in my apartment like a cat bringing me its fresh kill. I'm *not* well."

"Then let's not waste any more time here."

They continued on their way, but they had to go through the bullpen to exit the building. Levi faltered as soon as he entered the room.

There were three times as many people present as there should have been this time of night, all of whom went dead silent when they saw him. The weight of their eyes on him was smothering.

They all knew. They knew everything.

Levi hated being stared at, and it took all his self-control to keep himself in check as he crossed the bullpen. Even utilizing every technique Alana had taught him, he felt the angry flush suffusing his cheeks, tasted bile at the back of his throat. His stiff shoulders crept up toward his ears.

Martine was standing by their adjoining desks—along with Dominic, which only twisted Levi's guts into more painful knots. What was Dominic *doing* here, hanging around and acting like he was still Levi's boyfriend? Wasn't this situation stressful enough?

When Levi stopped beside them, Martine said, "Dominic filled me in on the progress with the kidnapping ring. I'll take care of it, don't worry. I'll arrest Royce and Juliette myself."

"Thanks." Levi wouldn't even have the satisfaction of seeing that case through to its conclusion.

"Do you need anything from your desk?" Sawyer asked. When Levi shook his head, he said, "You know you can't go back to your apartment. It's an active crime scene."

"The only time I'm ever going back there is to move my stuff out," Levi said, grimacing. His apartment had been ruined for him, just like his car.

Martine touched his arm. "I told you, you should stay with me for a while."

"I can't. That could put your family at risk."

"Then stay with me," said Dominic. Anxious concern was written all over his face, just like when he'd shown up in a panic at Levi's apartment. He was acting like nothing had changed—like he had a right to be here, a right to be the shoulder for Levi to lean on, when they both knew that was a sick joke.

Levi's tenuous hold on his anger disintegrated.

"You want me to stay with you?" he said, laughing bitterly. "Won't that get in the way of all your very important gambling?"

Dominic paled, his eyes darting to the people nearest them.

"But then, you've said it yourself—I can't stop you." Levi advanced on Dominic, who immediately retreated. "Losing our relationship didn't stop you. Losing your boss's respect didn't stop you. Having to sell half your belongings to make rent hasn't stopped you. So really, what will?"

"*Levi*," Martine hissed under her breath, grabbing at him.

He shook her off. This rancor had been building up for months, poisoning him from the inside out, and it was such a relief to finally set it free that he couldn't stop, even as a corner of his mind cried out in horror at the stricken betrayal on Dominic's face.

"I know exactly what you're thinking. You come rushing to my rescue like some kind of white knight, thinking you're going to be the one to take care of me, the one to *save* me. But you can't even save yourself!"

Dominic flinched.

"Stop treating me like I'm your boyfriend," Levi said. "Our relationship is *over*, and that's due to choices *you* made. You spit in my face every time I offer you help, then turn around and try to act the big hero? Are you fucking kidding me?"

"Christ, Abrams!" Jonah Gibbs said from right behind him, drawing Levi's attention to the fact that everyone in the bullpen was watching them with hushed, morbid fascination. "For someone under suspicion of being a serial killer, you're not setting anyone's mind at ease here."

Levi sucked in a breath, spun around, and did something he'd been wanting to do for years—he punched Gibbs in the face.

The blow sent Gibbs staggering into a desk, almost falling to the floor as he tottered on unsteady feet. The bullpen burst into action with angry shouts and cries of alarm; several officers put their hands on their guns, and the atmosphere in the room crackled as everyone prepared themselves for violence.

"It's fine!" Gibbs pushed himself upright, wiping blood off his mouth. "It's my bad; I provoked him. Let's just call it even."

Levi shook out his aching hand and nodded shortly.

"For God's sake, get him *out* of here," Martine said to Sawyer.

Sawyer gripped Levi's arm. "Let's go."

Levi glanced at Dominic, who was slumped against the edge of Levi's desk, his eyes trained blankly on the floor. He was the only person present not watching Levi.

"Do you want to spend the rest of your night in a jail cell?" Sawyer jostled Levi's arm. "*Come on.*"

Levi followed Sawyer out of the substation without looking back.

CHAPTER 14

ominic dropped heavily onto a metal stool in a booth at the Clark County Detention Center. He picked up the phone receiver on the wall, waiting for the computerized system to connect the screen in front of him.

Social visits at the CCDC were all conducted by video kiosk. As a PI, he wasn't considered a professional visitor, and Martine had needed to pull strings to get him in here outside of visiting hours and without an appointment.

Nathan Royce appeared on the screen, his face pale and a hunted expression in his bloodshot eyes. Though he'd only been in jail for a few hours, he was looking at a long weekend—he couldn't get a bail hearing until Monday.

"Detective Valcourt said you're refusing to speak to anyone but me." Dominic held up a hand. "Before you say anything, you know these calls are recorded, right? I'm not an attorney. This conversation isn't privileged."

"That's fine. Because I'm innocent."

"Mr. Royce—"

"What they're accusing me of is insane!" Royce's voice was laced with panic and far too loud. "I would never abandon Carolyn, my job, my *life*, to run away and live under a false identity. I was perfectly happy with the way things were."

"Then your lawyer can argue that in court. I don't know what you expect me to do for you here."

Royce gripped the receiver with both hands. "Why would I hire you to investigate the kidnappings if I were behind them? I'm not that kind of person. You must know that by now."

Dominic hesitated. It was true—he still found it hard to believe that Royce would have had the balls to hire McBride if he were guilty. Plus, all the evidence against the guy was circumstantial.

He decided to hear Royce out for now. "If you weren't involved in the kidnappings, then Juliette set you up big-time."

"She wouldn't do that," said Royce. "She loves me."

"When the police got to her apartment this morning, she was long gone. She'd packed bags, there was nothing valuable left in the apartment, and she'd abandoned her car. Why would she take off like that if she were innocent? How would she even know to leave?"

Royce shook his head. "Juliette would never betray me unless she were being forced to."

"Forced how?" Dominic asked, his interest piqued despite himself.

"Threats, coercion, blackmail—I don't know. But it's the only possible explanation. Juliette has a . . . checkered past, and a long history of being emotionally abused and manipulated. She's been working through all that, but she still has friends who could at best be described as unsavory. Maybe someone found out what kind of information she had access to and took advantage of her."

Though Dominic thought that was a reach, he could see how passionately Royce had convinced himself of the theory, so he didn't argue against it. "I'm still waiting to hear what you expect *me* to do about any of this."

"I want you to find Juliette before the police do," Royce said.

"What?"

Royce glanced from side to side before he hunched over the receiver and dropped his voice to a whisper. "You have the skills to track her down first, learn the truth, and clear our names. The police and the DA are too eager to resolve this case; they won't listen to anything we have to say. You're the only one who can help us, and I'd be willing to pay anything."

"Mr. Royce," Dominic said evenly, "if I found out where Juliette was and I didn't inform the police, I would be opening *myself* to criminal charges. And I'll remind you again that these calls are recorded."

"Right, of course. I understand." Royce gave him an exaggerated wink.

Dominic considered himself a patient man, but sleep-deprived and still reeling from the events of last night, he *could not stand* one more second of Royce's bullshit.

"If you had been straight with me from the beginning, I *could* have helped you," he snapped. "You might not be sitting here right now. But it's way too late for that." He took a deep breath in an attempt to calm himself. "If your attorney would like to hire McBride to assist in a *legitimate* investigation to aid your legal defense, I'd be happy to participate. Beyond that, this is where my involvement in this case ends. I'm sorry."

"But—"

"While the cops were searching Juliette's apartment, they found an empty bottle of prenatal vitamins in the trash. Did you know she was pregnant?"

"She's not!" Royce said. "I mean, she *was*, but she had an abortion."

"When?"

"Two months ago." A frown creased Royce's forehead—because, of course, it was safe to assume Juliette had taken out her trash at some point in that intervening time period.

"And whose decision was that?" Dominic asked.

"It—it was mutual," Royce said, though his guiltily darting eyes told a different story.

"Uh-huh." Dominic snorted a contemptuous laugh. "You want to know what I think? Juliette decided to keep that kid, and she found a way to net herself a tidy nest egg while simultaneously screwing you over. She had false papers made for you, but she never intended to take you with her. All she wanted was to get you out of the picture."

Royce didn't respond. He sat there with unfocused eyes, an expression of horror slowly creeping across his face.

"Good luck, Mr. Royce." Dominic hung up the phone and left the kiosk.

This case was none of his business anymore. Royce was in custody, and the police would either find Juliette or they wouldn't. The last he'd heard from Martine, a private landowner had seen the kidnappers' photos on the news and come forward with the information that he'd rented a cabin to one of them. The LVMPD was probably raiding it right now, but whether or not they found anything, it had nothing to do with Dominic. As Levi loved to remind him, he wasn't a cop.

Thinking of Levi worsened his mood still further. What Levi had done to him last night—outing his gambling in front of dozens of people—was the most humiliating, painful betrayal he'd ever experienced. He was still half in denial that it had happened at all. The memory was so gut-wrenching that he couldn't bear to linger on it for more than a few seconds at once.

He shoved it away, packing it down with every other uncomfortable emotion swirling through his head. The only thing that concerned him today was ensuring that Carlos had the time of his life at the bachelor party tonight.

Until then, Dominic had a date with a poker table.

Levi had been staring at the ceiling of his hotel room for at least half an hour. Heavy curtains were drawn over the windows, but even the slight glow that had broken through the cracks earlier had faded into nothingness.

With what felt like monumental effort, he rolled onto his side and looked at the clock on his nightstand. It was almost seven, which meant he'd been sleeping off and on for about sixteen hours. Once Sawyer had checked him into the Renaissance Las Vegas on the firm's expense account, Levi hadn't gotten out of this bed except to use the bathroom.

He didn't see a reason to get up now, either. It wasn't like he had anything to do, and at least as long as he was lying here, he couldn't cause any more damage.

The Seven of Spades was out there, plotting against him. He'd been suspended from his job and was being investigated for murder. He'd assaulted a colleague in his workplace. And Dominic . . .

Levi mashed his face into the pillow. God, *Dominic*. Publicly exposing his addiction was the most despicable thing Levi had ever done; the shame of the act was thick enough to suffocate him. He wouldn't be surprised if Dominic never forgave him—hell, he *shouldn't*.

Levi's breathing sped up, and for a dizzying moment, he hovered on the edge of another panic attack. But the anxiety ebbed before it crested, and his breathing returned to normal.

Panic attacks, dissociative episodes, uncontrollable angry outbursts—he couldn't let this continue. He needed to call Alana. Her office wouldn't be open, but she'd told him the answering service could connect him to an on-call psychiatrist twenty-four hours a day in an emergency.

Maybe he needed more acute help than he'd been getting. Maybe he needed to—to go somewhere for a while.

He'd turned his phone off last night, knowing it would be blowing up all day. When he finally turned it back on, he winced at the dozens upon dozens of missed calls, voice mails, and text messages clogging the screen.

Most of them were from his parents.

"Shit," Levi muttered, calling them back without listening to any of their numerous messages. It would be about ten in New Jersey, but they'd still be up.

His mother answered after two rings. "Levi Samuel Abrams," she said, her accent thickened by stress, "your father and I have been calling you all day. *Saul, pick up the phone! It's your son!*"

"I—"

"I'm here," Saul said. Levi could picture the two of them in his childhood home—his mother on the landline receiver in the kitchen, his father in the den.

"There are stories all over the news," Nancy continued. "The things they're saying about you, Levi, my God. All Martine would tell us was that you're in a safe place, and we've been worrying ourselves sick—"

"Mom." Levi's voice cracked on that one word, and he covered his eyes with his free hand.

Her tone softened immediately. "What's going on? Tell us what happened, *bubbeleh*."

Levi spilled everything—the entire lurid story of how the Seven of Spades had discovered the truth behind his attack, tricked the men into coming to Vegas, and then murdered them one by one in ways that made Levi look increasingly guilty of the crimes himself. He ended with the news of his suspension before trailing into silence.

"I'm coming out there," said Nancy. "I can be there tomorrow morning. Do you want your father to come too? Saul, get the computer!"

"No!" Levi sat upright in bed. "You can't come here. Stay in Jersey, please."

"Levi, this is no time to push your family away," Saul said with a hint of gentle reproach.

"That's not what I'm doing." When his parents both made tsking noises, he groaned. "I know that's what I usually do, but it's not like that this time. Believe me, nothing would make me feel better than having you guys here. But it's too dangerous. I have no idea what the Seven of Spades is planning next, and being anywhere near them could put you at risk. If anything happened to you two, I'd never forgive myself. Please stay away from Las Vegas."

They were both quiet for a moment until Nancy spoke again. "Can you come to us, then?"

"I can't leave the city while I'm under investigation. I'll be fine, though. I promise."

"I don't like the thought of you going through this alone. Have you spoken to Dominic?"

Levi cringed. "He has his own stuff to deal with right now. I'm really okay. The investigation will prove that I'm innocent, and that'll be the end of it." He wasn't half as optimistic as he pretended, but keeping his parents safe trumped all other concerns.

"Well, if you're sure." Nancy paused. "The last of the men who hurt you—he's still alive?"

"As far as we know. The Seven of Spades still has him."

"Good," she said, and made a spitting noise. "*Zol er krenken un gedenken.*" *Let him suffer and remember.*

"Mom!"

"I'm sorry, Levi, but you can't expect me to be anything but pleased that those animals finally got what was coming to them."

"We're going to sue the pants off the Trenton Police Department too," said Saul. "In fact, the first thing I'm doing tomorrow morning is calling Al Rosenberg to see if his firm will take the case."

Getting his parents off the phone was no easy feat, given that they were consumed by their anxieties for him, but by the time they said their goodbyes, Levi was confident that they weren't about to hop a flight west.

After he hung up, he chewed his lip while he considered his phone. He couldn't call Alana's answering service now. If his parents found out he'd sought acute mental health treatment, they'd rush straight to his side regardless of the danger. He couldn't risk it.

Instead, he scrolled through his phone, scanning his texts and deleting his voice mails. Besides the deluge from his parents, Martine, Natasha, Adriana, and Leila had all attempted to contact him multiple times, though he couldn't bring himself to return their messages just yet. There were also a few calls from other people he knew through work, as well as some numbers with no names attached that he would bet his last dollar belonged to reporters.

Buried in the middle of his voice mails was one from Stanton.

His eyes flying wide, Levi pressed Play and lifted the phone to his ear.

"Hi, Levi, it's me. I read about what happened online, and I just wanted to see how you're doing. Bridget said you didn't want me to call you back after you left those messages a few days ago, but . . . I want to make sure you're okay. Please call me."

Levi cleared his aching throat and deleted the voice mail. Seven thirty here meant—what, four thirty in Geneva? He'd call Stanton back in the morning.

In the meantime, he knew he couldn't sleep any more today, but if he didn't find some kind of distraction, he really would go insane. He threw back the covers and padded over to the minibar.

Crouched on the floor with a tiny bottle of whiskey in one hand, he hesitated. Nothing said *rock bottom* like getting drunk alone in a hotel room. He should at least go to a bar, try to preserve some façade of normalcy.

People would stare, but once he had a few drinks in him, he wouldn't mind so much. It was still preferable to drinking himself into a lonely stupor while mired in self-loathing.

And if someone *did* try to get in his face—well, that might not be so bad.

The only clothing Levi had was the blood-stained suit he'd left the substation in last night, but Vegas had no shortage of retailers open on Saturday nights. He ran out to stock up on the essentials before returning to his hotel to shower and change.

Even that brief foray made him reconsider his plan. Though nobody approached him, he felt the eyes on him everywhere he went, heard the sudden whispers that sprung up in his path. Many people went out of their way to give him the wide berth they would a medieval leper. Was he really going to subject himself to more of that?

As he wavered by the door, thinking he should drink alone in his room after all, a memory tugged at his brain. The day after he'd found Reddick in his car, Jasmine had called him to see how he was doing. In an effort to cheer him up—an attempt doomed to failure, though he appreciated it nonetheless—she'd chattered on about Adriana learning to ride at her parents' farm, her wedding plans, her bachelorette party . . .

That was tonight, wasn't it? Jasmine and Carlos were doing that thing where they started their parties separately and met at the end of the night. She'd mentioned that Dominic had set up one of those party bike pub crawls for the guys after dinner.

That meant Dominic was in a crowded bar right now, distracted by his friends. Which meant *Levi* could check on him from afar, see how he was doing, and reassure himself that Dominic hadn't fallen apart after what Levi had done last night, without Dominic ever knowing he was there. If Levi knew Dominic was okay, maybe he'd feel better. He might not need to drink at all.

Once the possibility had occurred to him, there was no talking himself out of it. Those party bikes all traveled the same general route through the city's touristy bars. He only had to check their websites for the likeliest places, catch an Uber Downtown, and duck into them one by one.

The third location he tried was Atomic Liquors, Las Vegas's oldest freestanding bar and possibly its most famous. The place was packed from wall to wall, making progress through the crowd difficult, but he received no more than the occasional double take as he wove his way toward the bar. Of course, tourists would be less likely to recognize him than the city's year-round residents.

Even among this many people, Dominic would stand out. Levi scanned the crush of tipsy bodies for those unmistakable dimensions, telling himself firmly that he was *not* a stalker. He'd dealt Dominic a low blow, and it wasn't the kind of thing he could just call to apologize for. He needed to know he hadn't done irreparable damage.

A burst of raucous laughter caught his attention. He looked across the bar at a cluster of rowdy men in the far corner and tensed.

Carlos was sitting in the middle of the group with a gaudy plastic crown tilted on one side of his head, his cheeks so red Levi could see the flush even from this distance. And sitting at an angle to him, with his face in profile to Levi, was Dominic. He was talking animatedly, gesturing with the bottle of beer he held. Though there was something off about his body language that Levi couldn't quite place, he *seemed* fine. At least he was smiling.

Levi had been wrong. Seeing Dominic didn't make him feel better. All it did was slam home the reality of what he'd done, the memory of Dominic's shock and hurt, with such force that it drove him backward.

He had to get out of here. Choking on his remorse, he cleared his throat and turned around—

And his knees buckled, his vision grayed out, and he staggered sideways as he lost consciousness for the briefest of moments.

Fortunately, the crowd was thick enough that several people caught him before he hit the ground. He came back to himself surrounded by exclamations of concern, with two men supporting his arms as they helped him to the bar. A woman there vacated her stool immediately so he could sit down.

"I'm fine," he said to the blurry sea of worried faces clustered around him. His ears were ringing, so he couldn't make out their individual words, but he got the gist. "I'm fine, I'm not drunk, I just haven't eaten—"

He tried to stand up, half in embarrassment that he'd passed out at a bar and half in desperation to get away before Dominic noticed the commotion. All he managed was to fall right back down again.

Someone handed him a glass of water, while someone else pushed a bowl of pretzels toward him. He muttered thanks, his cheeks flushing scarlet, and shot a panicked glance at the corner of the room.

His worst fears were confirmed when he saw both Dominic and Carlos staring at him, eyes wide and mouths open.

Fuck.

Scowling, Dominic lurched to his feet, stumbled, and caught himself on the back of his chair. When Carlos put a hand on Dominic's arm, Dominic bent down to speak in his ear and pat his shoulder.

Levi was frozen in place, unable to look away as Dominic crossed the room toward him, clutching his beer bottle in one hand and listing from side to side with every step. People tried to get out of his way as best they could, and Levi didn't blame them. Nobody wanted to be near a man Dominic's size who was having trouble staying on his feet.

Dominic muscled through the few people still hovering around Levi. "What're you doing here?" he asked with a distinct slur in his voice.

"You're *drunk,*" Levi said incredulously, his own problems forgotten in the face of this startling development.

"It's a fucking bachelor party." Dominic flung his arm out to the side, almost clocking a woman in the face with his bottle, and the last of Levi's Good Samaritans melted away as they caught onto the drama. "Of course I'm drunk."

There was no *of course* about it. Levi had never seen Dominic drunk before, and that wasn't a coincidence. Dominic made a point of not drinking to excess, because intoxication worsened his gambling cravings.

The bartender chose that moment to check on Levi. "Hey, man, you okay?"

"I'm fine, thanks." Fuck it. He was here anyway; he might as well drink. "Can I have an Old Fashioned, please?"

The bartender blinked, but then nodded with a shrug and moved away.

"Wow," Dominic said. "Petty is such an attractive look on you."

Levi sighed. Ever since their breakup, he hadn't been able to stomach a Boulevardier. It depressed him too much.

Dominic pointed his bottle at Levi accusingly. "Seriously, though. Why are you here? You decided last night wasn't bad enough, so you tracked me down for round two?"

"No! I just wanted to make sure you were okay; I didn't mean for you to see me. Dominic, I . . ." Levi wasn't sure Dominic would even remember this conversation tomorrow, but he forged ahead anyway. "I'm so sorry for what I did last night. It was unjustified and cruel, and I know an apology isn't enough, but I want you to know how much I regret it. I'd do anything to take it back."

"Well, you can't. And you're right, an apology doesn't do shit. You know better than anyone else how I feel about people knowing those things about me, and you just shouted them out for everyone to hear."

"I'm sorry," Levi whispered helplessly.

Dominic tried to set his bottle on the bar but ended up knocking it over instead; it rolled away, dribbling beer onto the wooden surface as it went. "I don't care! Do you have any idea how it feels to have someone you trust betray you that way?"

Levi pressed his lips together and shook his head.

"No, you don't. Because I'd never do that to you. How would you like it if I'd told all those people what a needy fucking size queen you are?"

His hackles rising, Levi said, "Of course. You save your cruelty for when we're alone."

"See, your problem is that you can dish it out, but you can't take it." Dominic placed both his hands on Levi's thighs, looming over him. "Whenever someone gives you a taste of your own medicine, you start playing martyr."

Levi met Dominic's glare with one of his own. He wasn't intimidated by Dominic—never had been, never would be. Even furiously angry and wasted off his ass, Dominic wouldn't physically harm him.

Too bad Levi would *prefer* physical pain to what he was feeling now.

"I don't give a shit how anyone else treats me," he said. "You're the only one who makes it hurt so much."

Dominic's hands tightened on Levi's thighs. A soft cough sounded next to them, and they both turned their heads.

"We gotta go, Dom," Carlos said. "We're due at the next stop in the tour."

Dominic released Levi and straightened up, only to overcorrect his balance and sway dangerously backward. Both Levi and Carlos reached out to steady him, but Levi was the only one he jerked away from.

"I'll meet you outside," Dominic said to Carlos before tottering off into the crowd.

"I'm sorry," said Levi. "I didn't mean to cause problems. I was worried about him, and I meant to get in and out before you guys saw me."

"It's okay. Are you gonna be all right? It looked like you fell or something."

Levi forced a weak smile. "Just stress. I'm fine, I promise. You should get going."

"If you're sure." Carlos squeezed his shoulder and started after Dominic.

"Hey, Carlos? Congratulations."

Carlos beamed. "Thanks."

After Carlos and his bachelor party had made their rambunctious way out the door, Levi turned back to the bar to see his drink waiting in front of him. He snatched it up and drained half in one long swallow, then set the glass down and nursed the rest more slowly. He'd already passed out once today; no need for a repeat performance.

He was down to the last drops, his head propped morosely on one hand, when the person on the stool next to him got up and someone else sat down.

"For such an intelligent man, you make a lot of regrettable decisions," said Sawyer.

Levi jerked his head up, as astonished by Sawyer's presence as Dominic had been by his own. "Are you following me?"

"I didn't have to." Sawyer unbuttoned his suit jacket and rested his elbows on the bar. "People are *Tweeting* your location. If you don't get out of here soon, there's going to be Utopia gangbangers waiting to jump you again when you leave—only this time, you'll be drunk and without Leila to back you up."

"I can take care of myself," Levi muttered.

Sawyer arched an eyebrow. "I really don't think you can. See, a man who can take care of himself would have eaten today, which I know you haven't because your face is sheet-white and half those Tweets said you fainted. A man who can take care of himself wouldn't drink alone in a bar when half the city thinks he's a serial killer, waiting for someone to pick a fight with him."

Levi blinked.

"That's why you're still sitting here, isn't it? I'm sure you talked yourself into believing some other reason, but the truth is that you'd love for someone to get in your face and give you an excuse to add some more bruises to your collection."

Unable to meet Sawyer's eyes, Levi pushed his empty glass away.

"I'm sure that would make you feel better," Sawyer said. "For a few minutes, anyway. But those few minutes of relief wouldn't be worth the consequences, Levi. For one thing, you'd do irreparable damage to your IA investigation."

It was rare for Sawyer to address Levi by his first name, rarer still for him to be this serious, and Levi couldn't quite muster up any outrage at the interference. "So you came here to make sure I don't make your job more difficult?"

"Damn straight."

A reluctant smile tugged at Levi's mouth. "Well, you don't have to worry. I'm not going to get in any fights."

"I'm sorry, but I don't believe you. Last night, you punched a cop in a police station just because he was kind of a dick. You expect me to believe that if a stranger accosted you in this mood, you wouldn't rip his head off? And that's not even taking into account how Utopia is gunning for you after yesterday." Sawyer cut Levi off before he could argue. "I'm not leaving you alone in this bar. End of discussion."

Levi slumped on his stool, raking his fingers through his hair. He knew it would be monumentally stupid for him to get into any kind of physical altercation now, when his reputation, career, and possibly freedom hung in the balance. It would be just as stupid for him to get drunk on an empty stomach while he was this vulnerable. He just . . . he didn't want to *feel this way* anymore, and he couldn't think of any other way to dull the pain.

"Do you want to fuck me?" he said abruptly.

He had the unprecedented pleasure of seeing Sawyer speechless for a full five seconds. "Are you already drunk?" Sawyer said once he recovered.

"No. I've only had one drink tonight." Levi pointed to his empty glass. "Look, you've been trying to get me on my back for years. Was that all talk, or is it something you actually want?"

Sawyer shook his head, though not in denial. "I can't. You're upset. It—it would be taking advantage."

Levi snorted. "Let me break this down for you. There are two possible paths this night will take for me. One, I sit at this bar and keep drinking until I pass out. Two, you bring me home and screw me into the mattress—again, until I pass out. You see the common theme."

"I . . ." Tapping his fingers on the bar, Sawyer looked at the surrounding crowd. "It's not safe for you here."

"Then take me to your place."

Sawyer worried at his lower lip, studying Levi's face. Then he nodded. "All right, let's get out of here."

Sawyer's apartment was as showy and over-the-top as the man himself, every inch of the grand space boasting his wealth. Levi turned in a slow circle in the main room before looking at him expectantly.

Sawyer, who had been uncharacteristically reticent during the drive over, was still hanging back by the front door. "Are you sure you want to do this?"

Levi crossed the room toward him in three long strides, grasped his lapels, and pulled him into a kiss—though he was momentarily thrown by the fact that he didn't have to tip his head back to do so. He and Sawyer were the same height.

Sawyer moaned into the kiss, cupping Levi's face with both hands. Levi let his own hands wander over Sawyer's body, adjusting to the sensation of lean muscles and a narrow build not unlike his own.

When the kiss broke, he pressed his hips to Sawyer's and said, "Where's your bedroom?"

Sawyer proved to be an incredible lover —but then, Levi had expected nothing else. The man was far too vain to allow himself to be less than exceptional at anything he did.

He brought Levi off twice, first with his hands and mouth, then by giving Levi a long, hard fuck on elbows and knees until all of Levi's muscles turned to jelly. The physical pleasure was undeniable, the orgasms truly satisfying.

But when it was over, Levi was left empty and cold, like all his insides had been scooped out and replaced with sawdust. Though the sex had been good, it hadn't been anything close to what he wanted.

It hadn't been Dominic.

Lying in the wreck of the giant bed, Levi glanced at the man beside him. Sawyer had fallen asleep the moment his head hit the pillow next to Levi's; he was snoring a little, blissfully oblivious to everything else in the room.

As Levi slipped out of bed and tiptoed around to gather his clothes, he realized this was the second time in a week that he'd snuck out after sex. That didn't do much for his battered self-esteem.

At least he didn't need to feel guilty about not waking Sawyer to say goodbye—if anything, a guy like Sawyer would appreciate being spared the awkward morning after.

Levi returned to his hotel, showered, and then wiped the steam off the mirror to consider his reflection. Sawyer hadn't left any marks on him, not like Dominic would have. There was no evidence of what they'd done at all, except a slight ache and the creeping sense of numbness he couldn't shake.

This was what he'd wanted, right? To stop feeling the way he had earlier?

He left the bathroom and lay down on the bed. When the sun rose the next morning, he was still awake.

CHAPTER 15

Wherever there was a way to bet money on the outcome of an event, Dominic had been there. Poker was his favorite, with blackjack a close second, but he also had history with craps, roulette, sports betting, horse racing, lottery tickets, even bingo. Hell, he'd once wagered on a game of Go Fish.

There was one form of gambling he rarely turned to, though— slot machines. In Gamblers Anonymous, they had talked a lot about the difference between "action" and "escape" gambling. Dominic was usually in it for the thrill, the challenge, the adrenaline rush, all sensations he could obtain from exciting, skill-based games like poker. Slots, on the other hand, had an almost narcotic effect, which tended to be the opposite of what he sought.

Today, though, they were just what the doctor ordered. Suffering his first hangover in years, Dominic didn't have the energy or mental focus for any activity that required strategy. Staring at a screen and mindlessly pulling a lever over and over helped distract him from his problems without too much effort, even if all the bells and whistles worsened his headache.

He was trying not to dwell on what had happened with Levi. That unexpected encounter aside, the bachelor party had been a rousing success. Carlos had enjoyed himself immensely, which was the most important part, and when they'd met up with Jasmine's bachelorette party, the two of them had been in an enviable state of drunken prenuptial bliss. Dominic had been forced to sit between them in the Lyft home to prevent a public indecency charge, and once they were back in their respective apartments, he'd been able to hear exactly what a good time they were having through their shared bedroom wall for over an hour.

Carlos and Jasmine were family to Dominic; he would do anything to protect and preserve the happiness they both deserved. But he had to admit he was jealous.

He had begged off the usual Sunday lunch at his mother's house, claiming to be too wiped out from the party. His mother hadn't tried to talk him into coming—he'd skipped so many family events over the past few months that she'd given up on arguing with him.

Now free of all obligations, he pulled the lever on his machine and watched the images scroll by with little interest in the result. He'd loaded two hundred dollars in cash onto it earlier, and he hadn't run out yet, though he wasn't sure how long he'd been here.

The reels came to a halt without a payout. He pulled the lever again.

"Dominic?"

He swiveled on his stool, dumbfounded by the sight of the person standing a few feet to his right. "Natasha?"

"I'm sorry to intrude, but Diana Kostas told me I might find you here," she said.

"I'm fine," he said reflexively.

Her mouth twitched like she was struggling not to smile. "I'm glad to hear that. Is it okay if I sit?"

He shrugged, watching in bafflement as she dragged the stool from the next machine closer to him. On a Sunday afternoon, the Railroad Pass was doing good business, but it wasn't crowded; there were plenty of empty spaces at the slots.

"I've been trying to get in touch with Levi all weekend," she said, propping her purse in her lap. "So have Martine and Leila and even Adriana. He's not returning any of our calls or texts. We're starting to worry."

"I ran into him for a few minutes last night. He's fine."

Levi *wasn't* fine, though. Dominic had been too drunk to think through the implications at the time, but Levi had passed out in that bar, even if just for a second. He shouldn't have been out alone in the first place with the city in its current mood. His clearly deteriorating physical condition made things even worse, to the point where Dominic had to suspect he was being intentionally self-destructive.

What if something had happened to him after Dominic left? The city was turning against him, and Utopia was out for his blood now more than ever before. If he'd been attacked—

Dominic put a firm halt to his spiraling thoughts. Levi had told him in no uncertain terms to stop acting like they were still together; he wasn't going to waste energy worrying about a man who would only rebuff his concern.

"Levi doesn't . . ." Natasha hesitated, her mouth working open and shut like she was searching for the right words. "He's a very strong person, but he doesn't have the healthiest coping mechanisms, and the things that are happening right now are tied to some of his deepest wounds. I'm afraid that without support, he'll end up hurting himself."

"And you think *I'm* the right person to offer that support?"

"Who better?"

"Just about anyone else!" Dominic scrubbed a hand over his face. "Look, Natasha, I know you mean well, but Levi doesn't want my help. I'm not guessing about that. He shouted it at me and everyone else within earshot with plenty of color commentary on Friday night."

She winced. "Yeah, Martine told me about that. I'm sorry. That must have been awful for you."

He waved a hand, not wanting this to turn into a conversation about *him*. "My point is that Levi would *not* appreciate my interference."

"He may not want your help right now, but he needs it."

"So I'm supposed to reach out knowing he's just going to kick me in the balls for my trouble?" Dominic yanked viciously on the lever, then sighed as the machine came up with another losing combination. It had been a dud all afternoon, so it had to be nearing a good payout soon. "Why would I set myself up for that?"

She was quiet for a moment, watching him pull the lever once more. "After you started gambling again, how did you react to Levi's attempts to help you?"

"You call what he's been doing *helping* me? Having cops follow and harass me, blackballing me from casinos—" *Handcuffing me to my bed*, he almost added, but bit back before it came out.

"They're not necessarily techniques a counselor would recommend," she said with a rueful smile, "but I happen to know he's tried gentler tactics as well. And every time, he gets the same response from you."

Dominic wasn't proud of all the times he'd lied to Levi, manipulated him, deliberately caused him pain to force him to back off. But he wouldn't have had to do any of those things if Levi had just left well enough alone.

"Despite all that, he never stops trying," Natasha said. "Because love isn't rational. It drives us to do inexplicable things, like forgiving a person something that would have been unforgivable coming from anyone else. Or refusing to walk away from someone even when the situation seems hopeless. Now, I'm not saying that's always a good thing, but it's part of the human experience. And sometimes the only thing that can pull someone back from the brink is knowing there's that one person who will never give up on them no matter how bad things get."

Dominic frowned, staring at the slot machine. His hand itched to pull the lever.

"I don't doubt the strength of your love for Levi. And I don't think even what happened the other night would keep you from going to his side in a time of crisis. That's not why you're sitting here." She placed her hand on the screen, breaking his eyeline and startling him so badly he jerked backward. "If you had to get off this stool right now and leave this casino, could you?"

Of course he could. This wasn't like last time. He could stop whenever he wanted.

He imagined walking out of the casino and felt suddenly queasy. If he stopped gambling, there would be nothing to distract him. He'd have to feel *everything*, all the heartache and anger and grief, and he didn't want any of it.

"If there was an earthquake or something, sure," he said lightly.

"Short of that?"

He closed his eyes. "I don't know."

"I could have just called you to talk about Levi," she said. "I chose to come looking for you instead because there's something else I'd like to talk to you about. Would you humor me for a few minutes?"

"Sure."

While Natasha dug through her purse, Dominic's phone chimed with an incoming text. He pulled the phone out of his pocket.

The text was from a blocked number. *We have a big problem.*

Dominic tensed from head to foot. An ominous text from a blocked number could only be the Seven of Spades, but what the hell were they talking about?

"Is that Levi?" Natasha asked, a hopeful note in her voice.

"No." Dominic shoved the phone back into his pocket and looked at her to see she was holding a quarter.

"Call it," she said as she tossed the quarter in the air.

"Heads." He was intrigued by her approach. As a social worker, Natasha would know that compulsive gamblers weren't supposed to bet on something even as seemingly innocuous as a coin flip. What was her angle?

Natasha caught the quarter on the back of her hand, then removed her hand to reveal George Washington's profile. A pleasurable zing shot up Dominic's spine even at that trivial victory.

"Great," she said. "What were the chances this coin would come up heads?"

"Fifty-fifty."

"And if I flip it a second time, what are the chances it'll come up heads again?"

"Fifty-fifty," he repeated—more reluctantly this time, because now he knew where she was going with this, and he didn't like it at all.

Natasha flipped the coin on the back of her hand over and over while she spoke. "What if I tossed the coin ninety-nine times, and every single time, it came up heads? What's the chance it'll be heads on the hundredth toss?"

"Still fifty percent."

"Really? But it just came up heads a hundred times in a row. It *has* to be tails now, right?"

"No," he said, the word dragged out of him by pure force of will.

She raised her eyebrows. "Why not?"

Scowling at her, he said, "Because each coin flip is an independent event."

"Exactly." She dropped the quarter back into her purse. "Every time you flip a coin, play a hand of poker, pull the lever on this machine, the probability of the outcome is unaffected by your prior results. You can make general predictions about patterns over long periods of time, but when it comes down to an individual event, those predictions mean nothing. The mistaken belief that statistically independent events influence each other is called the gambler's fallacy."

"I already know all of this."

"You may know it, but you haven't internalized it. The gambler's fallacy plays a large role in problem gambling. When a gambler is having a lot of success, he'll say that he's on a hot streak, and he needs to keep going to preserve it. When he's doing poorly, he'll say that he's due for some good luck, and he just has to stick it out until the tables turn. You'll notice that both conclusions lead to continued gambling."

Yes, and they were both things he'd said and thought countless times throughout the years.

He was struggling for a counterargument when his phone chimed again. Muttering an apology, he checked it without withdrawing it all the way from his pocket.

I'm serious, Mr. Russo. Don't ignore me.

With a roll of his eyes, Dominic did exactly that. He wasn't playing this game with the Seven of Spades. If they wanted to tell him something, they could just spit it out.

Natasha's brow furrowed as she observed his reaction, but she didn't ask any questions. Instead, she gestured to the screen in front of them.

"Take this slot machine. It's run on a random number generator regulated by the Gaming Commission. The scrolling of the slots is just for show; your actual result is determined the second you pull the lever—and each time you do so, the odds are *exactly the same*, because the computer chip always uses the same algorithm. You understand the math. Yet you can't tell me that, while you've been sitting here, you haven't had the thought that this machine must be getting closer to a jackpot because it's come up empty so many times in a row."

He rocked back on his stool like she'd shoved him. Too caught off guard to lie, he said, "You don't understand. It goes so much deeper than that. I . . ."

He didn't know how to finish the sentence, so he just threw his hands in the air and took a shaky breath.

"There may be such a thing as luck, but it can't be predicted or controlled," she said, her demeanor as calm and gentle as ever. "And while there are some games where skill and strategy can give you an edge, like poker, there's always an element of random chance. That's why gambling can become such a problem. You're drawn to it because you're seeking a sense of mastery over your environment, the elation that comes from taking a risk and succeeding. But any feeling of control gambling gives you is an illusion that can be shattered the very next moment."

His stomach churned.

"That's a difficult thing to accept. Because if you *can't* control those risks, if your success or failure is determined more by chance than your own competency, why would you keep gambling even when the consequences become so severe?"

"Because I'm weak," he said raggedly.

She snorted. "There's not a weak bone in your body, Dominic. Compulsive gambling isn't a moral failing. It's an illness that requires treatment. You just have to be willing to seek help and put in the work. You've done it once before; there's no reason you can't do it again."

His phone went off again, making him jump. He glanced at the screen.

Fine. Don't say I didn't warn you.

"Do you need to answer those?" Natasha asked.

"No." Dominic switched the ringer off. "They're not important."

Go to hell, freak, he thought, spitefully pleased by the image of the Seven of Spades sitting somewhere with their own phone in hand, growing ever more frustrated as he refused to respond.

Natasha accepted that with a nod. "I only have one more thing to say. You can't control this slot machine. What you *can* control is what you choose to do right now, in this moment, when the man you love is falling apart and you may be the only one who can get through to him. I'd like you to think about that."

She stood, slinging her purse into the crook of her elbow. He gave her a startled look.

"You're not going to . . ."

"You don't have to prove anything to me." She lifted one shoulder in a shrug. "You're the only one who needs to be convinced of your own strength."

She rested her hand on his arm for a moment before walking away.

Dominic automatically reached for the lever on the slot machine, then hesitated.

The more pain Levi was in, the further he would isolate himself. It was classic Levi Abrams: if he couldn't fight or fuck out his uncomfortable emotions, he'd try to run away from them, which meant avoiding anyone who would make him confront them head-on.

Some time off to rest—by himself, with no risk of ruining his relationships with unintentional outbursts—might do him some good. The problem was that being alone, especially in his current unstable emotional state, made Levi exponentially more vulnerable to whatever the Seven of Spades had in store for him.

The killer's earlier texts could have been a genuine warning of an impending threat, or the opening salvo in the endgame they'd flat-out admitted to Dominic they were planning for Levi. Either way, a frightened, lonely Levi would be easy prey.

So why couldn't Dominic take his hand off this lever?

He was furious with Levi, and deeply hurt. But that didn't mean he was going to abandon Levi to the whims of an obsessed serial killer. Levi had no support system right now; there was no telling what the consequences would be if Dominic didn't do his best to help him.

Dominic tried to withdraw his hand, but the thought of getting off this stool and walking out of the casino was like standing at the edge of a cliff, about to step off into absolute darkness. His heart pounded, causing blood to ring in his ears. Sweat trickled down the back of his neck.

This wasn't what being in control felt like. This wasn't *having a handle* on things. He'd been here before—this sickening sensation of being a puppet in his own body, unable to cut the strings of his compulsion no matter who he hurt.

"Don't say I didn't warn you."

Levi could be in danger.

Dominic snatched his hand off the lever and slammed his other hand down on the Collect button simultaneously. The machine spat out a ticket with a bar code containing the balance of his cash; he grabbed it and hurried away before the toxic urge hammering at his brain could make him sit back down.

After stopping by the cashier, he left the casino as fast as he could without breaking into an actual run. He didn't stop moving until he was in his truck. When he pulled out his phone, his hands were shaking so badly he fumbled it into the footwell and had to scrabble around to retrieve it.

He set the phone in his lap, forcing himself to take several deep breaths. Then he snagged a towel from the gym bag he kept in his truck and blotted his damp face. Only when he felt less on the cusp of an imminent meltdown did he pick the phone back up.

He didn't know where Levi was, but that wasn't a problem. It only took him a few minutes to track down Jay Sawyer's cell number.

"Hello?" Sawyer said with a touch of polite wariness.

"Sawyer? Hi, this is Dominic Russo." At the complete and utter silence that ensued, Dominic frowned and said, "Hello? Are you still there?"

"Um, yes." Sawyer cleared his throat. "Ah . . . what can I do for you, Mr. Russo?"

"I'm looking for Levi. None of his friends have been able to get in touch with him, and I just wanted to make sure he's okay. I'm assuming you know where he is?"

"You mean you haven't spoken to him today?"

"No, not at all."

"Oh," Sawyer said, in what sounded oddly like a sigh of relief. "Yeah, my firm put him up at the Renaissance on Paradise Road. Room 1412."

"Thanks."

"No problem. Bye."

Sawyer hung up, leaving Dominic blinking at the abrupt disconnection. "Weird guy," Dominic muttered as he set his phone aside and turned the key in the ignition.

The half-hour drive gave him plenty of time to second-guess his decision, as well as to battle constant cravings that told him he was an idiot to drive toward certain pain when he could return to the casino and avoid it altogether. He rolled the windows down all the way, turned the radio on full blast, and drove as fast as he could without getting pulled over by any of Levi's minions. By the time he reached the hotel, his hands were aching from how hard he'd been gripping the steering wheel.

He was rehearsing what he would say as he walked into the lobby, only for it all to fly right out of his head when he saw Levi standing at the reception desk.

Levi was the most striking man Dominic had ever met, but right now he looked *terrible*. His skin was unnaturally pale, which made the bruises from his throw-down with Utopia stand out in even starker contrast. Stubble roughed his cheeks and jaw, and he seemed to be leaning on the counter as much to hold himself upright as anything else.

Dominic squared his shoulders and kept walking. When Levi saw him, he groaned and slumped even further against the desk.

"Oh my God," Levi said, and proved that wasn't a figure of speech when he rolled his eyes heavenward and added, "Why are you doing this to me?"

"We need to talk," said Dominic, undeterred.

"I can't." Levi turned aside, his voice jagged. "Please, Dominic, I can't do this with you today."

Before Dominic could reply, a clerk emerged from a room behind the reception desk and handed Levi a small, square package. "Here you go, Detective."

"Thank you."

"What is that?" Dominic asked as Levi used his keys to slit the tape holding the box shut.

"Sawyer sent me a package. They just called me to come down for it." Levi set the cardboard aside to reveal a smaller box, this one hinged and made of steel.

Dominic's brow furrowed. He couldn't help thinking that Sawyer would have mentioned sending Levi a package when they spoke—and besides, if Sawyer was going to send him anything, wouldn't it be papers?

"Wait," he said, but Levi had already flipped the top of the box open.

Levi's face went blank, as if every muscle had been locked into an expressionless mask. Anxiety spiking, Dominic moved to look over his shoulder—then gagged and took a step back.

An intact eyeball rested on a small baggie of ice. Though the iris was fading, Dominic had only seen such a piercing blue on one person before.

There was a typed message taped to the inside lid of the box: *GET THE POLICE TO BACK OFF IF YOU WANT HIM ALIVE.*

"Is that Stanton's?" Dominic asked faintly, already certain that it was.

Levi didn't respond. Dominic braced himself, but he had no idea how Levi was going to react—scream and throw the box against the wall? Burst into tears? Just collapse? He had to be ready for anything.

Except Levi didn't do any of those things. He just turned to meet Dominic's eyes and said, in a perfectly calm voice, "Somebody is going to die."

CHAPTER 16

"I'm going to say this one more time," said Dominic. "We need to call the police."

Cell phone in hand, Levi stopped by the window of his hotel room and gazed at the busy road below. Dominic had followed him up here without asking, but he hadn't protested.

"We can't." He felt more clear-headed than he had in days, like the fog had been swept out of his brain. "You saw the note. Juliette will have Stanton killed."

"The cops are already pursuing her and her lackeys. If they don't know Stanton's been taken, they won't know to back off."

Levi shrugged. "They wouldn't back off anyway. It's American law enforcement policy to not negotiate with terrorists, and that includes kidnappers. The police may pretend to play along, but they won't just let the perpetrators go. It's too dangerous to get them involved."

There was a drawn-out silence until Dominic spoke again. "This isn't what you would advise if this situation were happening to someone else."

"No, it's not." Levi turned to face Dominic, who'd been handling him with kid gloves since he'd opened that box. He understood why, though it wasn't necessary. "But it's happening to *me*, and I know what I'm capable of. I've seen hostage situations go bad before; I'm sure you have too. I'm not letting that happen to Stanton, no matter what the consequences are for me personally."

Dominic nodded. "You're positive he was really taken? I checked while you were on the phone—there haven't been any reports of kidnappings or carjackings in the Valley today."

"Bridget said Stanton flew back from Geneva earlier today and that his plane landed at McCarran as scheduled. He texted her a few hours ago to tell her he was with me. There's no other reason he would have done that. And his phone keeps going straight to voice mail."

Levi tossed his phone onto the bed. Bridget had been understandably confused by his call, but he thought he'd played it off well enough to assuage any suspicions.

"If he landed safely but never got where he was going..." Dominic began pacing the room. "They must have been waiting for him in his car at the airport."

"He called me yesterday when he heard about what happened with the Seven of Spades," Levi said. "But I never called him back, so Bridget said he decided to cut his trip short and come home early." His voice cracked. "I knew Stanton was on the list of potential victims, and I never even told him. I thought he'd be safe in Europe."

"This isn't your fault."

"I know." Levi gave his head a slight shake. "It's the Seven of Spades's. This wouldn't be happening if it weren't for them."

"About that," Dominic said, a shadow crossing his face. "The Seven of Spades texted me today, being all vague and ominous about something having gone wrong. I thought they were playing one of their games, so I ignored them. They must have found out on their own that Stanton had been taken, and were trying to warn me."

"It doesn't matter. If they really wanted to help, they would have just told you—or *me*. They don't care about Stanton; they just enjoy fucking with our heads."

"The Seven of Spades must keep tabs on Stanton the way they do with everyone else who's important to you and me. For Juliette's mercs to be ready to snatch him after a last-minute change in his schedule, she must have been doing the same."

"Stanton probably made the top of her list the second I was named lead detective in the Buckner case," said Levi. "And she had to be keeping an eye on me too, since she was able to track me to this hotel. Although I did use my credit card at a few stores in this area last night, so it wouldn't have been hard to narrow down the options."

Dominic leaned against the wall. "Let's break it down. Juliette's mercenaries kidnapped Stanton in a way that left nobody the wiser, made no ransom demand, cut out one of his eyes right off the bat, and sent it directly to his cop ex-boyfriend who's been investigating their crimes. They didn't take him for money; they took him for insurance. As soon as they're free and clear, they *will* kill him."

"I know. That's why I need to find him first. Once I have a better grasp of the situation, I'll call the police in if it won't increase the risk to Stanton's life."

"Well, that sounds good in theory," Dominic said with a frown. "Except even the cops don't have anything to work from. Royce knows nothing of value, Juliette's disappeared into the ether, and Martine told me the search of their desert safe house turned up empty. Unless we get lucky and someone else recognizes one of the men and calls in a tip, our leads have gone cold."

Except that wasn't exactly true, was it? There was one big lead left. It just wasn't one the LVMPD had been able to pursue.

Not legally, anyway.

Levi grabbed his phone and key card and started for the door. Dominic stepped into his path with both hands outstretched.

"Whoa. Where the hell are you going?"

Levi lifted his chin. "I'm about to do something very bad. Now, you can come with me or you can stay away, but you cannot stop me."

"I've got your back."

"Are you—"

"I've got your back," Dominic repeated firmly.

A small knot of tension loosened in Levi's neck. He took one of Dominic's hands and laced their fingers together, squeezing briefly before he moved around Dominic to leave the room.

"So where *are* we going?" Dominic asked as he followed Levi down the hallway.

"MountainView Hospital."

Levi hovered by the wall just past the nurses' station, eyeing the uniformed officer posted outside Charles Graham's room at the end of the ward. "He's not going to let me just walk in there. Even if I weren't suspended, I wouldn't be allowed to talk to Graham without his attorney present."

Dominic, who was lounging against the wall far more convincingly, tapped Levi's hand until Levi looked at him instead of the cop. "I could try to distract him, lure him away from the room so you can slip in without him seeing you."

"No. If he leaves his post and something happens to his charge, he could lose his job. There has to be another way."

They hadn't had any difficulty entering the hospital itself, as it was well within visiting hours, but Graham's sentry posed a frustrating obstacle. Levi couldn't cost an innocent man his job if there were any other option.

Sending a casual glance over his shoulder, Dominic said, "I don't know that cop. Which means he probably doesn't know me."

"Is that good or bad?"

"In this case? Good." Dominic thumbed through his wallet and pulled out a card. "What's Graham's lawyer's name?"

"Um . . ." Levi racked his memory. "Reuben Cooke."

Dominic flashed him a roguish grin. "Not anymore. Follow my lead."

He whirled around and hustled down the hall at a rapid clip. Startled, Levi hurried to catch up.

When they reached Graham's room, Dominic was slightly short of breath, though he had to be faking it. "I need to speak with my client *immediately*."

The cop blinked at him from his rickety plastic chair. "Your . . . what? Who are you?" As he noticed Levi beyond Dominic's shoulder, his face screwed up in confusion. "Detective Abrams?"

Dominic snapped his fingers in front of the cop's face. "I'm Michael Greene. Mr. Graham's new attorney."

He handed the cop the card he was holding, which Levi realized now must be a fake ID. Levi had never been a good liar, so he concentrated on hiding as much of himself as he could behind Dominic's bulk and keeping his face blank.

Studying the card with a furrowed brow, the cop said, "I don't understand. What happened to—"

"Mr. Cooke had a heart attack this morning."

"Oh my God. Is he—"

"I just found out that my firm is dumping half his cases on me—which, as you can see, I was *not* prepared for on a Sunday afternoon." Dominic gestured to his casual clothing. "Cooke's files are a mess, and calling his work sloppy would be too great a compliment. I need to speak to Mr. Graham about revising his defense strategy right away."

"That's fine, but what's Detective Abrams doing here?" The cop looked at Levi again. "I mean, aren't you, uh, suspended?"

Dominic crossed his arms over his massive chest, his biceps straining at the sleeves of his T-shirt. He stepped closer to the cop, looming over him, and the cop shrank back in his chair with wide eyes.

"Are you telling me how to do my job?" Dominic said in a low, dangerous tone.

"What? No!"

"Do I come down to your substation and tell you how to do *your* job?"

"No—"

"Then would you like to explain why you're denying an American citizen his constitutional right to counsel, Officer?"

"Jesus, no, I would never—" The cop shook his head frantically, his cheeks flushed red, and thrust the card back at Dominic. "Go ahead. I'm sorry."

"Thank you." Dominic gestured to the door. "After you, Detective."

Levi had to bite his tongue to prevent his reaction from showing on his face as he moved past them into the room. Dominic followed, closing the door once they were both inside.

Charles Graham was asleep, looking much better than he had the last time Levi saw him—there was more color in his face, and his chest rose and fell with steady breaths. The first thing Levi did was ensure that Graham wasn't hooked up to any sort of telemetry monitor that would alert the nurses' station to a change in his heart rate. He was reassured to see the only thing connected to Graham's body was an IV line—and a pair of handcuffs that restrained his left wrist to the bedrail.

As Levi approached the bed, Graham stirred awake and looked at him blearily. Seconds later, Graham's eyes rounded with fear and recognition. He struggled to rise from his semireclined position, collapsed with a groan, and opened his mouth.

"Don't scream," Levi said. He moved the call button out of Graham's reach.

Graham's gaze darted toward Dominic, who remained in front of the door with his arms still folded, before returning to Levi. "You can't be in here. It's illegal for you to talk to me without my lawyer."

"I don't care."

Levi sat on the edge of the bed. Graham shied away, but there wasn't anywhere for him to go on the narrow mattress.

"Your friends took someone very important to me," Levi said. "They cut out his eye and sent it to me in a box."

"I had nothing to do with that."

"Obviously. But you can tell me where to find them."

"No—"

"Are you married?"

"Uh . . ." Graham shifted uncomfortably. "No."

"I assume you have people in your life you care about, though. People you love. Your parents, maybe?" Observing Graham's reaction, Levi played a hunch. "Your mother?"

Graham's jaw tightened.

Levi nodded. "I'd like you to imagine that a group of known murderers kidnapped your mother, mutilated her, and held her hostage. Is there anything you wouldn't do to get her back safely? Any law you wouldn't break?" He rested his hand lightly in the center of Graham's chest. "Any line you wouldn't cross?"

A flinch ran through Graham at even that slight contact. The dark, secret part of Levi, the one that enjoyed pain and blood and battle, stretched and purred like a cat basking in sunlight.

"Please, I don't know anything," Graham said shakily.

"Don't lie to me. You would have had a secondary safe house established in the event that your primary base of operations was compromised. Where is it?"

"We didn't have anything like that."

"I told you not to lie to me." Levi peeled away the thin blanket, revealing Graham's hospital gown, and brushed a hand over his abdomen. He knew he'd found the gunshot wound when Graham cringed and sucked in a harsh breath.

"Yeah, right." Graham managed an impressive sneer despite his trembling. "You'd never—"

Levi pressed on the wound, clamping his other hand over Graham's mouth to muffle the screams that burst forth. Graham thrashed on the bed, trying to shove Levi away, but he might not have been able to throw Levi off even at full strength. Compromised by an abdominal injury, a recent infection, and the disadvantage of lying on his back with one arm handcuffed, he didn't stand a chance.

Levi watched Graham struggle with clinical detachment. He hadn't been sure he'd have the stomach for this, but all he had to do was think of Stanton—of Stanton's terror when he'd been kidnapped, of his horror and desperation when they took his eye, of how hopeless he must feel right now, believing nobody was coming for him.

The mercenaries had kept Nguyen unconscious while they removed her eye, but there was no guarantee they'd done the same for Stanton, or even that they'd used anesthesia. He could have been awake for the entire procedure. He could have been in hideous pain the whole time.

While Graham hadn't hurt Stanton personally, he'd terrorized six other people in similar ways. He could have been the one to mutilate Rose Nguyen, or the one to kill Joel Buckner. Levi watched him suffer and felt nothing.

When Levi released him, Graham was drenched in sweat, his face pallid. He sucked in several gasping lungfuls of air.

"You're a fucking psycho!" he snarled. "What the hell are you doing? Jesus Christ—"

"Tell me where your friends took Stanton Barclay," Levi said, implacable.

"I told you, I don't know—"

Levi pushed against the wound again, digging his fingers into the skin around it this time. Graham shrieked against his palm, writhing in agony, swinging futilely at Levi's face with his free arm and then scrabbling at Levi's hand.

Dominic was still standing in front of the door, a solid, unyielding presence Levi could sense without needing to look. Levi didn't bother gauging his reaction, because if he was going to interfere, he would have done so already. He'd been a soldier; surely he'd seen worse than this.

By the time Levi let up, Graham was sobbing, tears pooling in the corners of his eyes and sliding down his face. Levi wondered idly if he was going to vomit.

"You can't do this," Graham said, his tone one of pure disbelief. His hands fluttered over his abdomen, where spots of blood dotted his hospital gown. "You *can't*. You're a cop."

"I want you to look me in the eye while I tell you this." When Graham refused to comply, Levi gripped his chin and leaned over him so he had no other choice. "There is nothing I won't do to get Stanton back alive. I will keep hurting you until you tell me where he is, and if you pass out, I will wake you up and hurt you all over again."

He let go of Graham and sat back, giving that a moment to sink in before he continued.

"If you think I'll lose one moment of sleep over causing pain to a man who participated in kidnapping innocent people, cutting out a young woman's eye, and murdering a man whose family couldn't pay his ransom, think again. You brought this on yourself. *Tell me where he is.*"

Graham hesitated, but when Levi lifted his hands, he blanched and exhaled a frightened groan. "Okay, okay! There's a house in Boulder City: 1123 Olmo Road. It's where we were supposed to go if things went sideways. The rest of them would have gone straight there after they evacuated the desert cabin, and with their faces all over the news, they'd try not to move around too much. If they have this guy you're looking for, they'd be keeping him there while they come up with an exit strategy."

"Thank you." Levi stood up. An address—that was a good starting place. Even if the kidnappers were no longer there, it was a fresh lead.

"You're not going to get away with this," Graham said, brave now that Levi was no longer sitting beside him. "I'll tell everybody what you did. You'll go to prison."

Levi struck him with a backhanded blow, knocking his head to the side.

"I don't give a fuck," he said, and stalked toward the door.

Dominic's face was impassive, but he put a hand on Levi's arm as Levi reached for the door. "I need a moment with Graham alone."

"Why?"

"Just trust me. I'll meet you at the car."

Levi shrugged and left the room. Dominic could handle whatever scheme he was cooking up; Levi had more important things to focus on.

Stanton wasn't going to spend one minute longer at the kidnappers' mercy than he had to.

It had taken Dominic some time to put his finger on what about Levi's behavior was unsettling him so much. It wasn't the ruthlessness—he'd always admired that aspect of Levi's personality. Nor was it the disregard for personal consequences, because Levi wasn't the type to worry for himself when someone he loved was in danger, and that was something he and Dominic had in common. It wasn't even the willingness to cause pain.

It was that Dominic had never seen Levi hurt someone dispassionately before.

He'd seen Levi engage in fights for his life, lash out in rage, put a handsy asshole in a nasty joint lock, pistol-whip a Nazi sympathizer and leave him for dead in a warehouse under armed assault. All those incidents had one thing in common—for Levi, violence was always linked to powerful emotions. It was never cold and calculating.

When Levi had opened that box with Barclay's eye, it was like all his emotions had shut off. Maybe that wasn't so surprising, since it was keeping him functional under overwhelming stress. But Dominic couldn't shake a creeping sense of dread that when those emotions came back online, it was going to result in nuclear levels of destruction.

After the door shut behind Levi, Dominic turned back to Graham, who was whimpering quietly. Dominic felt no sympathy for the man; as Levi had said, he'd brought this on himself. There was only one concern on Dominic's mind right now.

As Dominic moved closer, Graham's breathing sped up and he put his uncuffed hand out defensively. Dominic couldn't blame him—his stature made him seem more intimidating than Levi, even though Levi had been the far greater threat.

"What, it's your turn now?" Graham asked. "I told him everything I know!"

"I believe you. Besides, causing pain has never really been my thing." Dominic glanced at the spreading patch of blood seeping through Graham's hospital gown. "You served in the military, right?"

"1st Battalion, 5th Marines."

"You're an embarrassment to your country," said Dominic.

Graham flinched, then tried to cover it up with a glare. "Me? What about you two? You're both going down for this, I swear to God—"

"I don't think so." Dominic inclined his head toward the door. "You know who that was, right? I could tell from the look on your face when we came in that you recognized him."

"Everyone in Vegas knows who he is," Graham muttered.

"Have you been watching the news while you've been cooped up in here?"

Graham licked his lips. "They're saying he might be the Seven of Spades."

"He's not," Dominic said. "But it *is* true that the Seven of Spades is fond of him. Obsessed with him, actually. You remember Drew Barton, the guy who was shot by a sniper outside the Justice Center last summer?"

Graham nodded jerkily.

"He tried to kill Detective Abrams, then had his lawyer go after the detective's reputation in court. The Seven of Spades didn't like that." Dominic lowered his voice. "And the other men you've seen on the news this week? They hurt Detective Abrams over a decade ago, but the Seven of Spades still managed to hunt them down, drag them out here, and pick them off one by one. If you ask me, people who pose a threat to Detective Abrams don't have a very long life expectancy. You might want to keep that in mind."

Graham's hands balled into impotent fists, but his eyes were dark with fear, his chest heaving. His Adam's apple bobbed as he swallowed hard. "Fine. I'll keep my mouth shut."

"That's probably wise. You can start by coming up with a plausible explanation for how you popped your stitches." Dominic pulled Graham's blanket back up to chest, then returned his call button to its original position. "Feel better."

He said goodbye to the still flustered cop outside the room and returned to the parking garage. Levi was sitting in the passenger seat of his truck, Dominic's laptop propped on his knees. When Dominic slid into the cab, Levi shot him an inquiring look.

"All good." Dominic wouldn't share the details with Levi until Barclay was safe and sound. Levi wouldn't care before then.

Levi nodded and returned his attention to the laptop. "I looked into the address Graham gave me. It's a small house in your run-of-the-mill suburban neighborhood in Boulder City. The bank foreclosed on it a few months ago, so it's currently vacant."

He rotated the computer, showing Dominic the property information he'd pulled up along with some images from Google Earth. Foreclosed houses did make good temporary safe houses, as long as the neighbors weren't the curious type.

"So now is when we call the police, right?" Dominic asked.

Levi was silent.

"*Levi.* Come on. This is crazy."

"If I report that address to the police, and they storm the house and Stanton ends up getting caught in the crossfire . . ." Levi shoved the laptop into Dominic's hands. "I can't risk it."

"I hope you're not thinking that you and I are going to storm the house instead, because that could end in the same result, with the added complication of being totally illegal." Dominic snapped the laptop shut and set it aside. "Even if you had your badge, Boulder City is a separate jurisdiction. Cop or no, there's no way for you to legally enter that house, and I'm a private citizen."

Levi stiffened. "That's not completely true, though, is it?" Pointing to the laptop, he added, "Let me see that again."

Though Dominic heaved an exasperated groan, he handed the laptop back without argument. Levi worked on it for a minute before making a triumphant noise.

"Here, look at this. One of the mercenaries, Ramon Acosta, sometimes operates under the alias Carl Trujillo. This wasn't important before because the police are already after him and they know all this anyway, but Trujillo failed to appear in court for a battery charge in Carson City six months ago."

Dominic's pulse picked up. "He skipped bail?"

"Yes. And you're still a licensed bounty hunter."

"Bail enforcement agent," Dominic said absently.

He was startled by Levi's laugh, the sound brief but genuine. "Whatever. The point is, if you accept this warrant, you could legally pursue him. You could enter a foreclosed property to arrest him."

"Well, yeah. But that doesn't change the fact that *you* can't."

Levi made a face. "I don't care about that."

"I do." Dominic put out a hand to cut off the impatient reply he anticipated. "And so would Stanton. How do you think he'd feel if he found out you threw away your career and possibly your freedom trying to save him? Is that something he'd want?"

"No, but I . . ." Levi flung himself back in his seat, frustration written in every tense line of his body. "Look, it's like you said—I'm not a cop right now. That actually works in my favor. Without a badge or service weapon, *I'm* a private citizen, acting under the extreme duress of knowing a loved one is in life-threatening danger. It's too difficult to make charges stick in that context; juries are sympathetic and it can be bad PR for the prosecutor. I'm willing to take the chance."

"No way. We're talking about suburban infil/exfil in a civilian-populated area, with a team of *two* against an unknown number of armed enemies with military backgrounds in an unfamiliar environment. You don't even have SWAT training!"

"Then it's a good thing I have an ex-Ranger on my side."

"Oh my God." Dominic rubbed his eyes. "I'll make you a deal. I'll accept the bounty for Acosta's alias, and we'll go scope out this house, assess the situation, get as much information on layout and numbers and patterns as possible. It's common courtesy for a bounty hunter to alert the local PD when executing a warrant in their jurisdiction, so once we know what's going on, I'll call it in and let them know I believe my bounty has a hostage. Then we will *wait* for them. Agreed?"

Levi glared out the window, his jaw set and his arms tight across his chest. "Fine," he said, at length and with poor grace.

"All right." Dominic started the truck. "Then I guess we're going back to Boulder City. Looks like we've come full circle."

Boulder City was where they'd pursued Keith Chapman last year when the Seven of Spades had been setting him up. At the reminder, Levi's body language relaxed somewhat, and he gave Dominic a faint, fleeting smile.

"We need to stop by my apartment first, though," Dominic said as he shifted into drive.

"What for?"

"Supplies."

CHAPTER 17

"I can't believe you pawned your microwave before you pawned these guns," Levi said.

Dominic sighed and reached over to shut the metal case Levi held, which contained three Glocks of varying sizes, including a tiny pistol that was handy for secreting in an ankle holster. "I need them for work."

Rebel watched them attentively from the back seat. Because Levi had no car and Dominic's pickup was too conspicuous, Levi had rented a Ford Explorer for their impromptu reconnaissance mission. They had just parked a full block away from the kidnappers' alleged safe house in Boulder City.

"I only brought those to be prepared for a worst-case scenario," Dominic added. "And even then, *you're* not bringing a gun anywhere near that house."

"Why not?"

"Because you'll choke."

Levi glared at him in silent, open-mouthed outrage.

"Are you going to tell me you *don't* freeze before you can pull the trigger in a life-or-death situation?"

"I shot that member of the Slavic Collective at Volkov's compound just a few months ago!"

"You shot him on pure instinct because he was about to kill me." The memory still filled Dominic with an uncomfortable mix of guilt, gratitude, and breathless adoration. He would never forget that Levi had taken a life to save his. "It wasn't a conscious decision. You have unresolved issues about firing a gun that make it dangerous for you to bring one into a volatile situation."

"I—"

"Levi, you know it's safer for you to carry a nonlethal weapon you'll use without thinking twice than a gun that could make you hesitate at a critical moment. I brought plenty of those too."

Dominic nodded to the duffel bag on the floor behind their seats. He'd tossed in a couple of stun guns and a can of mace, in addition to some flashbang grenades and a few other potentially useful items. Then again, Levi's body was a weapon in its own right.

Though clearly disgruntled, Levi muttered his agreement.

"But this discussion is just academic, because you're not going in that house," said Dominic.

Levi didn't answer. They both turned their gazes toward the windshield, looking down the road even though they couldn't see the house from this distance.

After a minute of silence, Levi said, "Was that microwave even yours to pawn? Doesn't it belong to the apartment?"

Dominic dropped his head back against his seat and closed his eyes.

He'd been fighting the urge to call the Boulder City PD—or Martine—for the past two hours, knowing that would only push Levi further off the deep end. But he didn't fool himself that what they were doing was anything other than stupid.

He and Levi shared a propensity for reckless behavior, especially when the people they cared about were concerned, so it wasn't like he didn't empathize. If it were Carlos and Jasmine in there—or his mother, his grandmother, one of his siblings—Dominic would be acting exactly the same way, determined to shoulder all the risk and responsibility himself, unwilling to trust the lives of his loved ones to strangers. Yet he'd also be relying on Levi to pull him back from the brink before he did something monumentally idiotic.

While he'd been packing up supplies at his apartment, waiting for Levi to return with the rental car, he'd almost talked himself out of coming here several times. How could he insist on caution and circumspection one moment, then turn around and stuff a bag full of infiltration gear the next?

Because he couldn't control Levi, that was why. He'd do his best to keep Levi safe in the car, but there was always a chance Levi would go rogue. And if Levi went for that house against all logic and common sense, Dominic wasn't going to let him do that unprepared or alone.

"I'm going to take Rebel to assess the situation," he said, opening his eyes. "*You* are going to stay here, in the back seat, where the windows are tinted. Don't get out of the car for any reason. These guys would recognize you right away."

Levi didn't argue, just exchanged places with Rebel as he climbed into the back and she hopped into the front passenger seat. Dominic zipped a windbreaker over his ballistic vest and shoulder holster, then clipped Rebel's leash to her collar and got out of the car. Rebel had her own K-9 ballistic vest, though hers was disguised to mimic a service dog's—at least from a distance.

Of the three of them, Levi was the only one without similar protection. He didn't have access to his own vest, had refused to tolerate even the suggestion of detouring to obtain one, and couldn't wear Dominic's spare because of their size difference. That was just one more reason for Dominic to keep him out of harm's way.

After ensuring Levi couldn't be seen in the Explorer's back seat, Dominic set off down the sidewalk like he was taking Rebel for a leisurely Sunday evening stroll. She trotted dutifully at his heel, her ears twitching back and forth.

The location of the kidnappers' safe house was well-chosen. This suburban neighborhood was on the far eastern fringe of Boulder City, right at the edge of a vast desert. Only a single street with no fencing separated the outermost block of housing from the wilderness, so a vehicle with off-road capabilities could drive from a garage straight into the desert without even slowing down.

The house itself, a small ranch, stood on a narrow corner lot with easy access to multiple escape routes. According to the property information Levi had accessed, it was fifteen hundred square feet, with three bedrooms and two bathrooms. Dominic would have preferred full blueprints, but there was no chance of that—not on such short notice and while they were operating with murky legality.

As he and Rebel casually walked the perimeter, he noted additional details. Like every other house in the neighborhood, the property was surrounded on three sides by a chest-high brick wall. There were no cars in the driveway, but the closed garage door could be hiding as many as two. All of the blinds were shut tight and there were no lights on inside or out, even though the sun was almost down.

He clocked a few possible entry points: a gate beside the garage door, as well as another in the rear wall, plus sliding glass doors on the side and back of the house. However, these mercs had military backgrounds, and worse, they'd had plenty of time to fortify their position. They could have blanketed the entire property with dense security measures and even booby traps.

The more Dominic observed, the more pessimistic his outlook became. This house was shut up tighter than a convent. As he walked past, he caught a few glimpses of movement behind the blinds, so there was *somebody* in there, but he couldn't prove who or how many. It was impossible for him to get eyes or ears inside. Anyone in the house would be able to see an enemy approaching long before said enemy had an opportunity to do any damage, and God only knew what precautions they'd taken for such an event.

He and Rebel walked all the way down the block behind the row of houses, then turned around and retraced their steps so they could circle around the corner lot again. This time, when they passed the house next door to the kidnappers', Dominic noticed that the mailbox was overflowing, and there was a flier stuck in the front door that wasn't on any of the other houses on the street.

Returning to the Explorer, Dominic let Rebel into the back and got in the driver's seat. "The next-door neighbors haven't been home in at least a couple of days," he told Levi. "Stay in the back seat. I'm going to park in their driveway so we have a better vantage point."

He didn't say anything else until they relocated, but once they were settled next door, he could no longer put off telling Levi the ugly truth.

"There's nothing we can do," he said.

Levi leaned forward, only to retreat with a huff when Dominic shooed him back. "What do you mean?"

"I mean that house is a black box, and approaching it would be suicidal. There's no way for us to determine the internal layout, the number and position of the enemy, their defensive measures . . . There could be ten men armed to the teeth inside, with alarms and tripwires covering every inch. We just don't know."

"There aren't—"

Dominic kept talking right over him. "You'd have to set up a mobile surveillance post with infrared technology and a laser microphone to even start *planning* a successful extraction—and that's assuming Stanton really is inside, which I can't prove either to myself or the cops. They're not going to enter the house guns a-blazing on my word alone, especially when I can't explain how I found out about it in the first place."

Levi's glare could have scorched earth. "You broke into a walled compound crawling with armed gangsters, *alone*, to rescue a woman you barely knew."

"That was completely different," Dominic said, refusing to be cowed. "Volkov's compound was enormous, with plenty of options for cover and concealment. This tiny house?" He inclined his head toward it. "That thing's a shooting gallery. There'd be no way to disguise our approach, and likely nowhere to hide once inside. Plus, when I infiltrated the compound, I had the distinct advantage of the enemy being distracted on multiple fronts."

"Then that's what we do. Cause a distraction—something to break up their pattern, and hopefully lure them outside."

Dominic rubbed his jaw, considering. The idea did have merit. "I brought tear gas."

"I'm not tear-gassing Stanton! Don't you think he's been through enough?" Levi's eyes unfocused as he stared into space. "We could start a fire."

Dominic dropped his hand. "You're not willing to use nonlethal chemicals, but you're okay with the risk of burning the house down with Stanton in it?"

"It would just be a small fire!" Levi shot back. "If we started it at the front of the house, say in the garage, they'd be forced to evacuate through the rear."

"There's no guarantee they'd bring their hostage with them if that happened."

Levi fell silent, and Dominic turned to face the windshield. He should get in the back with Levi so no passing neighbors would wonder why a guy was just sitting in his car in the driveway, but Levi's body language was screaming *Don't come near me.*

"I could trade myself for Stanton," Levi said quietly.

Dominic twisted around so fast his spine popped. "*What*?"

"I'd make a much better hostage. I could offer myself in return for his freedom."

"No."

"You could put a bug on me. I'd be able to get you and the police the inside information you need, and I'm better trained to protect myself if something goes wrong."

Unable to believe what he was hearing, Dominic snapped, "I'm not risking your life for *his*!"

Levi recoiled like the words had been a physical blow. His nostrils flared. "That's not your decision."

"Levi," Dominic said, drawing out every syllable, "the only way you are walking into that house is by stepping over my dead body."

The air inside the car crackled with tension. Rebel whined, stamping her front paws against the seat.

Dominic wasn't backing down on this one. He cared about Barclay inasmuch as the guy was important to Levi, and because he was a human being, but he would push Barclay off a cliff in a hot second if Levi's life hung in the balance. If Levi tried to pull some asinine stunt like trading himself for Barclay, he was going to have to beat Dominic unconscious first.

Their ferocious staring contest might have continued forever, if not for the rumble of an approaching truck. They both looked out the window—and snapped to attention as a large moving van stopped just beyond the kidnappers' hideout, went into reverse with a loud beeping noise, and backed into the driveway of the safe house.

"What the hell?" Dominic said.

"They must be planning to change locations." Levi slid closer to the window. "Nobody will question a moving van at a foreclosed property, and this way they can fit multiple guys and maybe a hostage in the back without anyone noticing. The state cops won't be looking for one or two men in a truck like this."

Levi was vibrating with nerves. Dominic reached a hand back to touch his arm.

"This is a good thing," he said. "We'll call the truck's information in to the police and follow it to make sure they don't get away. We wanted them to leave their defensible position, remember? People are always most vulnerable while in transit."

His face bloodless, Levi said, "Mercenaries would know that as well as you and I do. What if they decide the benefits of a hostage aren't worth the risks of transporting one?"

Dominic didn't have an answer for that. He doubted the kidnappers would surrender their high-value insurance policy this early in the game, but he couldn't guarantee they wouldn't cut their losses here and leave Barclay's corpse behind while they made their escape.

The garage door rolled up as two men got out of the truck's cab—both wearing heavy jackets and baseball caps, their features too difficult to discern in the dark. One of the men opened the back of the truck and pulled down the loading ramp while the other disappeared into the garage.

"All right," Dominic said. "Here's what—"

Levi slipped out of the car and darted toward the house.

"Levi!" Dominic hissed. He banged his fist against the door. "Goddamn it."

This was *exactly* what he'd been afraid of.

He jumped out of the car as well, unzipping his windbreaker and drawing his gun. When he slapped his thigh, Rebel sprang out of the back seat, which Levi had left open. "*Danger*," Dominic said to her, before he hopped the low wall between driveways. She let out a low growl and followed.

Dominic rounded the moving truck just in time to see Levi surprise the first kidnapper from behind, jamming a stun gun into the man's neck. Levi must have taken the weapon out of Dominic's bag while he and Rebel had been on their walk.

As the kidnapper convulsed, choking on his scream, Levi grabbed the back of his head and smashed his face into the floor of the truck bed. The man crumpled to the ground.

"Put him in the truck," Levi whispered.

Dominic communicated his displeasure with a searing glare, then glanced into the garage. It was empty, save for a large rolling garbage can, and the internal door between the garage and house was shut. No doubt one or more men would be coming out shortly, but the noise of the first man's face hitting the truck hadn't been any louder than someone walking on it. No alarms seem to have been raised, at least.

The truck itself was filled with furniture and moving boxes, all the better to support the kidnappers' ruse and offer concealment to anyone hiding in the back. Dominic cleared it first, just in case, then holstered his gun only long enough to sling the unconscious man over his shoulder and carry him up the ramp. The moment he dumped the man's body on the floor, he drew his weapon again and crouched to pat the guy down.

As expected, the man was packing. Dominic confiscated the Beretta and tucked it into his own empty holster, since he hadn't had time to grab any of his own backup weapons or ammo.

Levi was lurking in the shadows of the garage with Rebel. When Dominic rejoined them on the ground, Levi gestured between himself and Dominic, then pointed to the internal door with two spread fingers. Catching his drift, Dominic nodded.

First, though, he placed Rebel in the middle of the garage, about ten feet in front of the door. "*Enemies*," he said, indicating the house.

She pinned her ears back, her body lowering into an aggressive stance. Dominic and Levi took up positions on either side of the door with their backs flat to the wall.

They only had to wait a few seconds before the door opened. A man strode through it, a duffel bag slung over each shoulder, only to stumble to a halt with a strangled gasp as he saw Rebel.

She was an intimidating sight, a hundred pounds of solid muscle and sharp teeth. She bared those teeth now, her lips peeling back as her snarl reverberated through the garage, crouched as if preparing to spring for the man's throat.

Frozen with the instinctive terror of a human confronted by a large, belligerent dog, the man didn't notice Levi and Dominic until it was too late. Levi zapped him with the stun gun, and Dominic pistol whipped him for good measure, knocking him out before he had a chance to shout an alarm. After they rolled the man's body out of the way, Dominic disarmed him, keeping the magazine and chambered bullet for himself and then tossing the empty gun into the garbage can.

They'd been quiet, but they hadn't been silent. "Hey, Boone!" a voice called from inside. "You all right, man?"

Dominic and Levi quickly returned to either side of the open door, squatting low to the ground this time. Dominic waved for Rebel to come stand beside him.

Footsteps sounded on a wooden floor, moving closer. "Boone?"

Though the house was dark, the lights in the garage had come on automatically when the main door was raised, so Dominic could see inside. This door opened onto a narrow hallway, directly across from a rectangular kitchen. Aside from that one entry point, the kitchen was surrounded on all sides by either walls or thick counters, providing a natural barrier from the rest of the house.

Dominic heard the rustle of a weapon being drawn. Looking at Levi, he saw they'd come to the same conclusion.

Dominic took a deep breath and fired two blind shots around the corner.

"*Fuck*!" the man inside yelled, though Dominic couldn't tell if he'd been hit. There was a sudden commotion of running feet, shouted voices, and slamming doors as the rest of the kidnappers were stirred to action.

While Dominic continued shooting, laying down suppressive fire, Levi and Rebel dashed across the hallway into the kitchen. Once they were safe, Dominic dove across the same gap, rolling along the tile until he banged hard into the cabinets. A few bullets whizzed down the hallway, only seconds too late.

"What the fuck is going on?" one of the men said.

"They found us!"

"Who, the cops?"

"I don't know!"

Between the individual voices and footfalls, Dominic counted three separate men. Levi put a hand on his arm to get his attention, then held up three fingers with a questioning look. Dominic silently confirmed his assessment.

His flight across the hallway had given him a fleeting impression of the rest of the house. It was divided in half lengthwise, with the left half containing the kitchen—where they were currently hunkered down behind the cabinets beneath the sink—and beyond that, one wide-open living and dining area. That meant all the bedrooms and bathrooms were on the right side of the house, but the arrangement of the walls provided plenty of corners, and it was there the kidnappers had taken cover.

They'd regrouped and were attempting to pin Dominic and Levi down in the kitchen with heavy fire. Staying low, Dominic peered around the edge of the counter and shot at the nearest man, fifteen feet diagonally to their right. He jerked back behind cover when the man returned fire, then winced as additional shots rang out from the back of the house.

That was two guys. Where was the third?

When Dominic finished the mag in his Glock, he switched the pistol out for the stolen Beretta. He continued trading bullets with the mercenaries while Levi hunted through the kitchen cabinets.

The low lighting and uneven numbers complicated matters, and it was more luck than anything else when Dominic managed to wing the mercenary closest to them. The guy let out a shrill cry of pain, but he kept shooting.

Levi tapped Dominic's shoulder. Taking the opportunity to reload the Beretta, Dominic checked out the two items Levi had laid on the floor—a can of Raid and a fire extinguisher.

Levi hefted the fire extinguisher, raising his eyebrows. Dominic snorted and shrugged. He only had a few shots left before they were totally screwed, anyway.

They popped up at the same time. Levi hurled the fire extinguisher into the living room, and Dominic shot it in midair.

The resulting rapid decompression filled the living room with billowing clouds of thick white smoke, sending the two kidnappers into coughing fits. Dominic heard a loud curse, followed by pounding footsteps and a slamming door as the man near the rear of the house took refuge in one of the bedrooms.

He and Levi wasted no time. While Dominic and Rebel raced out of the kitchen, Levi grabbed the Raid and simply vaulted right over the counter, heading straight for the kidnapper Dominic had wounded.

Still hacking, the man attempted to raise his gun—only to have Levi spray Raid into his eyes and mouth. The man screamed, clawing at his face, which made it easy for Levi to disarm him. Levi then smacked him in the side of the head with the can, sending him unconscious to the ground.

The smoke from the fire extinguisher had dissipated, finally giving Dominic a clear view of the house. The living room was empty except for a dozen duffel bags laid out in neat rows, clearly awaiting inspection and inventory in preparation for the kidnappers pulling up stakes. There were no lamps or overhead lights on, but shaded nightlights had been plugged into the wall outlets here and there— providing just enough light to move around safely without being seen from outside the house.

Levi handed Dominic the confiscated gun, and they returned to their low crouches, clearing the small hallway where the man had been taking cover. There were three closed doors here, one per wall. Dominic and Levi each took a door, finding a laundry room and bathroom—both empty.

Without warning, bullets ripped through the third door, flying into the living room on the other side of the house to crack into the wall and smash through a window.

Christ, where were the cops? There was a goddamn firefight going on in here—the neighbors had to be in hysterics by now.

Dominic signaled for Levi to stay in the bathroom on his side of the hallway. With Rebel pressed tight to his side, he hunkered down beside the closed door and strained his ears. He heard a frightened whimpering noise on the other side, which he didn't think was the kidnapper but also couldn't imagine was Barclay.

Laying his finger alongside the trigger guard, Dominic banged the muzzle of the pistol hard against the door. The man inside yelped and loosed several more panicked shots that sailed harmlessly down the empty hallway. Then Dominic heard what he'd been aiming for—a muffled curse and the sound of the man reloading.

Dominic threw himself at the door, busting it open with his shoulder. Rebel sprinted inside, snarling, and bounded at the man just as he was raising his gun. Clamping her jaws around his arm, she bore him to the ground, savaging the captive limb as he shrieked at the top of his lungs.

Dominic swung in a tight circle, scanning the rest of the barren room. The only other person in there was a captive, bound and gagged on an air mattress—but it wasn't Stanton Barclay.

It was Juliette.

Dominic's arms wavered for a split second before he firmed his hold on his gun. He looked at Levi, who had come in behind him and was staring at Juliette with a slack jaw.

"Close the door," Dominic said.

Levi pushed the door shut—though it wouldn't do them much good, as it was riddled with bullet holes and Dominic had broken the lock. Juliette was thrashing on the mattress now, screaming behind her duct tape gag, and Levi moved to her side.

Dominic snatched up the kidnapper's fallen gun. "*Release*," he said to Rebel. When she let the man go, Dominic dragged him into the corner of the room and patted him down for any more weapons.

"Oh my God, get me out of here," Juliette said the second Levi stripped off the tape. "*Get me out of here!*"

"Shh!" Levi pressed his fingers to her lips. "We're going to help you, but you have to be quiet."

Dominic noticed that Juliette was bound at the wrists and ankles with zip ties, which would come in handy right about now. "They got any more of those over there?"

Levi hunted through an open bag next to the air mattress and came up with a roll of duct tape and a pack of zip ties. He tossed both to Dominic, who set about giving the kidnapper the same treatment Juliette had gotten.

"I never should have trusted her," Juliette moaned, though quietly.

"Who?"

"Carolyn!"

Dominic met Levi's eyes across the room.

"Mother*fucker*," Levi spat.

"I was so happy when I got pregnant, but Nathan didn't want it," Juliette said. "He said I had to have an abortion. And I've done that before, but things are different now—I'm older, and I have a good job, and I *wanted* this one. But he wouldn't even talk about it."

Levi came up with a small pair of scissors from the bag. "So you told his wife."

"She was furious. I guess he'd done the same thing to her when they first got married—pressured her into having an abortion—and only afterward he told her he didn't ever want kids. He'd lied to her about it when they were engaged."

Finished securing the kidnapper, Dominic moved closer to the mattress, where Levi was snipping through the ties around Juliette's wrists.

"She said we would punish him. We could set him up and get him out of the way, and then she'd take care of me and we'd raise the baby together." Juliette burst into tears. "But she lied! The whole time, she's been setting me up too. All she wants is the baby. She just wants to take what she thinks he stole from her."

"An eye for an eye," Levi murmured. He sliced away Juliette's ankle bonds.

When the kidnappers had taken Juliette from her apartment, they'd made it look like she'd run away of her own free will. Carolyn could have held her captive until the baby was born, then killed her with nobody ever the wiser.

"This is why Carolyn was so adamant about making Royce give me the list of potential victims," said Levi. "She *wanted* me to know Stanton was on it. She wanted to rattle me."

Dominic nodded, then took Juliette's hand and gave it a gentle squeeze. "How many men have been staying in this house?"

"Um . . ." She took several hiccoughing sobs and wiped her eyes. "Five."

"Are there any other hostages besides you?"

"Yeah. I've only seen him a couple of times, but there's a man, a really handsome one." Her voice quavered. "They cut out his eye, like they did with the others. I heard him screaming when he woke up and realized what they did to him."

Levi's hand was white-knuckled around the scissors he was still clutching. Dominic shot him a quelling glare and shook his head minutely. If Juliette panicked any more than she already was, she'd become a serious liability.

Four men down meant one man left—the guy at the rear of the house who'd retreated from their makeshift smoke bomb. Since none of the kidnappers they'd brought down so far had been Ramon Acosta, aka Carl Trujillo, it must be him. He'd probably ensconced himself in the room where they were holding Barclay.

"I want you to hide in the closet and lay flat on your stomach," Dominic said to Juliette. "Bullets can go through walls, so stay as low as you can and don't come out until the police tell you it's safe. Do you understand?"

"Yeah."

Dominic helped her into position, double-checked that the bound kidnapper was secure, and met Levi and Rebel at the door. "If this guy's been backed into a corner, he's gonna be dangerous."

The sharp planes of Levi's bruised, scarred face were thrown into even greater contrast by the flickering shadows. He said nothing as he looked at Dominic, but Dominic knew what he was thinking: *Not more dangerous than me.*

Dominic led the way as they emerged from the room. There were only two bedrooms left to search, but he detoured through the living area first to ensure Acosta hadn't slipped out one of the sliding glass doors.

As soon as Dominic got close enough to see the doors through the gloom, he knew that would be impossible. Though he hadn't been able to tell through the blinds from outside, both sliding glass doors had been secured from the inside with slabs of sheet metal—lowering the risk of intrusion, but also preventing easy escape.

It was a good thing they hadn't set the house on fire, after all.

The middle bedroom was empty, leaving only the master. Dominic and Levi stopped on either side of the door, out of the line of fire in case Acosta decided to take a page from his buddy's book, but all Dominic heard was the sound of heavy breathing.

No risk, no reward. Dominic kicked the door open with an almighty crash, then ducked inside, primed to shoot at the first sign of movement. Levi and Rebel entered behind him on either side, only for all three of them to draw up short at the sight that awaited them.

Stanton Barclay was sitting in a folding chair, facing the door, his wrists behind his back and his crossed ankles bound with zip ties. Juliette hadn't oversold him—he *was* a handsome man, like a matinee idol plucked from the golden age of cinema—but now his tanned skin was sallow, his thick hair in disarray and matted with sweat. His left eye was swathed in bandages.

Ramon Acosta stood behind him, one arm wrapped loosely around Barclay's neck and the other hand pressing a gun to his temple.

"No," Barclay breathed, his remaining eye widening. "God, Levi, what are you doing here?"

"One more step and I blow his brains out," said Acosta.

Levi made a soft noise of distress. Dominic couldn't risk taking his eyes off Acosta for even the second he would need to glance sideways, but he knew Levi must feel like he was trapped in a living nightmare.

This was the *third* time Levi had found himself in this exact situation—first the hostage situation with Dale Slater at the Tropicana, then the hospital where Keith Chapman had used another officer as a human shield before killing himself.

Levi still hadn't recovered from the trauma of those first two events. A third would destroy him.

"Here's what's going to happen," Acosta said, with only a hint of unsteadiness to his voice. "I'm going to leave, and I'm taking Mr. Barclay with me. You two won't follow me. When I'm a safe distance away, I'll let him go."

"That's not going to happen," Levi said. "I'm not letting you leave here with him."

"Then I'll kill him."

"If you do that, you'll still end up getting arrested, just with an additional murder charge."

As if magically summoned, the wail of police sirens rent the air. *About fucking time.*

"See?" Levi shrugged one shoulder. "There's no way out of this for you."

Acosta ground the gun harder into Barclay's temple. "Then maybe I'll just kill him out of spite."

Barclay gasped. Levi took an abrupt step forward, one hand outstretched.

A single ounce of pressure on the trigger, and Dominic could send a bullet through Acosta's brain. He could probably get the shot off before Acosta murdered Barclay.

Probably.

"Take me instead," Levi said.

Dominic went cold. Barclay had a similar reaction, judging by the frantic way he began struggling against Acosta's hold.

"No, Levi, don't! Just let him take me, please, I'll be—"

Acosta's arm tightened around Barclay's throat, cutting off his voice. "I'm listening."

"I'll help you get away." Levi raised his hands as he took another step toward the chair. Acosta's eyes flicked to the scissors Levi still held, and Levi hastily shoved them into his pocket before lifting his hands again. "You have a better chance of evading capture with a cooperative hostage, especially one with my experience. Once we're free and clear, you can do whatever you want to me. You just have to leave the others unharmed."

Barclay loosed a wordless cry of protest, kicking his bound legs. The sirens grew ever closer, and Acosta seemed to be considering Levi's offer.

"No," Dominic said. "This isn't happening."

Levi turned sorrowful eyes toward him. "Dominic—"

"Let me rephrase," Dominic said mildly. "What I'm saying is that I *will not allow* this to happen." He met Acosta's gaze straight on. "If you attempt to leave this room with either of these men, I will kill you. If you harm either of them in any way, I will kill you. And if by some miracle of chance my shot misses, my dog will tear out your throat."

Rebel's growl ripped through the room. Although she wasn't in his line of sight, he was sure she looked even more fearsome now, with the last mercenary's blood staining her muzzle and dripping from her jaws.

Dominic's two-handed grip on his gun was rock-steady. "Any option other than your immediate and unconditional surrender doesn't end with you in handcuffs. It ends with you in a body bag."

In his peripheral vision, he saw Levi gaping at him. Dominic sometimes wondered if Levi ever thought about what it meant that Dominic had been a Ranger—if he ever considered the things Dominic must have done in eight years of war, or if he ever asked himself how many men Dominic had killed.

Taking a human life was never a trivial matter. But it also wasn't something Dominic flinched from when it was necessary.

"Unless you're ready to die today, put your weapon on the floor and kick it toward me," he said.

There was a charged moment in which nobody moved. Dominic breathed slowly and evenly, his finger light on the trigger, prepared to do whatever he had to.

With a frustrated groan, Acosta released Barclay. He set his gun on the floor, kicked it in Dominic's direction, and backed up with his hands in the air.

Dominic put his foot on the gun and sent it sliding even farther away. Levi rushed forward to kneel at Barclay's feet.

"You're okay," he said, pressing both hands to Barclay's cheeks. "It's going to be okay."

"Why did you come here?" Barclay's voice broke. "You shouldn't have come, Levi, you shouldn't have risked it. You could have died."

"I'll always come for you." Levi moved behind the chair, where Dominic assumed Barclay's wrists were zip-tied like his ankles.

The sirens were right outside now, the cops shouting to each other as they surrounded the house. Dominic reluctantly holstered his gun; he didn't want his own head blown off when the police came inside.

As Levi pulled the scissors out of his pocket to cut Barclay's bonds, Barclay's head fell forward, his shoulders heaving with sobs. Tears streamed down his face from his intact eye.

Acosta sneered at him. "Yeah, he cried like a little bitch after he found out about his eye, too."

Levi went still.

Dominic's stomach dropped, and he stretched out both hands. "Levi, don't."

Levi had remained cool since he'd received the kidnappers' message, dealing with one threat and obstacle after another without ever truly losing his self-control. But Dominic had been dreading this very moment the entire day.

Because Levi Abrams didn't *do* cold. When he frosted over, it was only to conceal the building fire of rage within. And once that inferno was unleashed, it inevitably demolished everything in its path.

Levi shot to his feet, grabbed Acosta's head with one hand, and jammed the scissors into his eye.

"Holy shit!" Leaping forward, Dominic seized Levi's arms and dragged him away. Levi went with him, unresisting, dropping the scissors to the floor as Dominic manhandled him to the far side of the room.

He was *laughing*.

Screaming in agony, Acosta collapsed to his knees. Blood gushed from behind the hands he'd clapped over his eye.

The police poured into the room then, shouting for everyone to get down on the ground. Dominic pulled both Rebel and Levi with him to the floor, but even over the clamor of booming voices and tromping boots, the only thing he could hear was that terrible, mocking laughter.

CHAPTER 18

"Don't say a word," Leila said as she strode into the interrogation room. "I mean it, Levi. Don't even open your mouth."

Levi couldn't have spoken if he wanted to; he was too shocked by her presence. He'd been languishing in this room in the Boulder City Police Department all night, and there was no reason for her to be here.

"The city attorney invited me as a courtesy." She sat in the chair on the other side of the table. "Frankly, I got the impression that nobody in this entire city wants to touch any of your drama with a ten-foot pole, and I don't blame them, because you are a *disaster*."

He leaned back with a sigh. What was he going to do, dispute that?

"What makes it worse is that you always know that what you're doing is stupid *while* you're doing it, but it never stops you."

True, though Levi remained firm in his conviction that some things in life were more important than behaving with perfect rationality at all times. Some risks were worth taking no matter the danger. If he and Dominic had acted any differently yesterday, the kidnappers would have either gotten away with Stanton or killed him. Now Stanton was safe, and Levi was willing to accept whatever the consequences might be for himself.

Leila folded her hands on top of the table. "The city attorney has elected not to file any charges against you."

Levi bolted upright, his mouth falling open in pure astonishment, but he closed it at her warning glare.

"It's his opinion that, because your actions last night were in defense of an innocent loved one and led to the capture of five wanted criminals, it would be too difficult to convince a jury to return a guilty verdict, and therefore not worth the expense to the taxpayers." She paused. "It probably doesn't hurt that he's afraid the Seven of Spades would come after him if he tried to put you in jail. Basically, the city wants to wash its hands of you as quickly as possible."

"But—" Levi pressed his lips together until she gave him a brisk nod. "What about . . ." He glanced at the camera in the corner of the room and gestured vaguely to his eye.

"It's a funny story," she said, though her tone was devoid of any humor whatsoever. "On the way to the hospital, Ramon Acosta *seemed* to have been swearing up and down to anyone who'd listen that you'd gone all Old Testament on his eye. While he was waiting in the ER, a few members of Los Avispones came in with superficial stab wounds—which is particularly interesting because Los Avispones don't operate in Boulder City. They ended up being treated in the cubicle next to Acosta's, and after they left, Acosta suddenly recanted his story. He's now claiming he can't remember what happened or why he looks like he's starring in a community theater production of *The Pirates of Penzance.*"

Blood buzzed in Levi's ears. Los Avispones must have threatened Acosta on behalf of the Seven of Spades; there was no other explanation.

Blinding Acosta was the only thing Levi had done yesterday that he regretted. Sitting in this room all night had given him plenty of time to stew in his remorse and self-loathing, reliving the sickening memory over and over. While he was largely optimistic that Sawyer could have him acquitted of any charges, part of him believed he didn't deserve that.

What he'd done to Acosta was aggravated battery with a deadly weapon and serious bodily harm, a Class B Felony carrying a prison sentence of two to fifteen years. He hadn't hurt Acosta in self-defense or to protect someone else; it had just been psychotic, bloodthirsty vengeance. He *should* be punished.

Instead, he was just . . . going to get away with it? That wasn't right.

Shoving his self-centered concerns aside, he said, "Dominic?"

"*Dominic* was executing a legal warrant in his capacity as a bail enforcement agent and is properly licensed to operate a firearm. He was released hours ago." Correctly anticipating Levi's next questions, Leila added, "Stanton is safe at the hospital with a police guard, just in case. All five kidnappers and Juliette Dubois are in custody. They'll be transferred back to Las Vegas later today to face every charge I can dream up."

"Rebel?"

Leila smiled. "She spent some time with the local K-9 unit while Dominic was giving his statement. She's fine."

Levi exhaled slowly, relieved that any fallout from the night before would rest on his shoulders alone. Even in the absence of legal charges, he was going to have serious explaining to do in his IA investigation. There was still a chance he'd lose his job.

"Am I free to go, then?"

"Yes. Believe me, Boulder City can't wait to get rid of you."

After he took care of some paperwork, Levi's personal effects were returned to him, and he met up with Leila again in the lobby of the police station. She caught his arm before he could walk outside.

"If it weren't for the guardian devil looking over your shoulder, you'd be fucked," she said, able to speak more freely now that there was no chance of them being recorded. "You'd definitely be out of a job, and you'd be facing prison time. Don't brush that off just because things went a different way."

"I wasn't planning to." Levi opened the door for her, then followed her into the parking lot, where the sun was just beginning to rise. "Are you too angry with me to give me a ride back to Vegas?"

"There's no need." She pointed across the lot.

Dominic was sitting on the hood of their rented Explorer, his hands clasped between his dangling legs.

Levi's heart skipped a beat. Rolling her eyes, Leila said, "See you later," and started in the opposite direction.

"Wait! I never thanked you." At her blank look, he said, "For sending Sawyer to me the night I was suspended."

She frowned. "I didn't."

"What?"

"I didn't ask Sawyer to take your case. Don't get me wrong, I *would* have. He's a douchebag, but you couldn't ask for a better defense attorney. I didn't even find out about your suspension until the next day, though."

Now it was Levi's turn to be confused. "Why would he lie to me about that?"

"Probably knew you wouldn't accept his help any other way," she said with an indifferent shrug. "Drive safe."

She continued to her car. Levi spent a moment processing this new information, then decided to let it go—as far as secrets went, this was probably the least of Sawyer's.

He crossed the lot until he was standing in front of Dominic. "Did you tell Martine—"

"About Carolyn Royce? Yeah." Dominic spread his hands. "I'm sorry, Levi, but Carolyn's long gone. It looks like she took off as soon as her husband was arrested."

Though Levi hadn't expected anything else, the news was still a blow. At least they'd rounded up everyone else associated with the kidnapping ring. "Is Rebel in the car?"

"No. I dropped her off with Carlos and Jasmine."

"You . . ." Levi shook his head, baffled. "You brought her to Las Vegas and then drove all the way *back* here to wait for me?"

"Yeah."

That was a half-hour drive each way. Levi cleared his throat and glanced aside, unable to maintain eye contact.

Dominic hopped off the car. "Can we go somewhere to talk, maybe get something to eat? In Vegas, I mean. I'm pretty sure the local PD has orders to bodily escort us past the city limits if we don't leave by the time the sun's up. We never cause them anything but trouble."

Laughing softly, Levi rounded the car to the passenger's side. "I could use some coffee."

Levi dozed off during the drive. Though the adrenaline of Stanton's rescue and his anxieties about the consequences had kept him wired during the long hours alone at the police station, the fact that he hadn't slept in almost twenty-four hours was beginning to catch up with him. Dominic had to shake him awake when they arrived at a diner near his hotel.

"Would you rather just go back to your room?" Dominic asked.

"No. You were right, we need to talk."

They didn't, though. They took a private corner booth and sat in silence until the server stopped by and they both ordered coffee. After she left, Dominic stared down at his laminated menu as if his life depended on reading every single word.

Levi was searching for a way to start the conversation when Dominic glanced up and said, "You know I wouldn't usually say this, but please eat something."

Right on cue, Levi's stomach rumbled loudly enough for them both to hear. "I will."

Their awkward stalemate continued as the server returned with their coffees and took their food order. Alone once more, Levi wrinkled his nose while he watched Dominic dump two creamers and three packets of sugar into his mug.

Dominic caught him at it and snickered. "Coffee snob," he said, so fondly that it was like a bullet to Levi's heart.

"I don't know why I did it," Levi blurted.

To his credit, Dominic didn't pretend not to know what he was talking about. "You'd been suppressing your fear and anger all day. Stanton was finally safe, Acosta mocked him, and you snapped."

"That's not an excuse."

"An explanation's not the same thing as an excuse."

Levi smoothed his hands over the chipped table. "How'd you even know to go back to Boulder City? Did Leila tell you they weren't pressing charges against me?"

"She did, but I was already back by then. I had a hunch they weren't going to keep you."

"It's because of the Seven of Spades. Acosta recanted his story about me assaulting him after Los Avispones threatened him at the hospital." Levi took a burning gulp of coffee. "Still, the scissors I stabbed him with were at the crime scene with his blood and my fingerprints all over them. The city could have prosecuted me without his statement. They *chose* not to. They're not charging me for anything

I did yesterday because they don't want to tangle with the Seven of Spades. A serial killer is protecting me from the consequences of my own actions."

"More than you realize, actually." Dominic swirled a spoon through his mug, then set it aside. "I did the same thing to Graham after you left the room. I made it clear that if he came forward about your . . . extralegal visit, the Seven of Spades would probably go after him."

Levi's mouth fell open. "Dominic!"

"It's true. Reminding him may have even saved his life."

"Oh my God," Levi said, raking his hands through his hair.

Dominic leaned his forearms against the edge of the table. "Let me ask you a question. Besides putting out Acosta's eye, do you *genuinely* regret anything you did yesterday? In the sense that, if you went back in time, you'd do things a different way?"

"No." No other path would have led to Stanton's quick, safe return.

"Then why are you so upset that you're not going to lose your job or go to jail for what you did?" When Levi didn't respond, Dominic lowered his voice. "Do you *want* to be punished?"

"Maybe," Levi whispered. "Maybe I should be. I fucking mutilated an unarmed man, Dominic! Maybe I shouldn't be allowed to be a cop, or even to walk around freely. A person who can't control their own rage has no business being in a position of authority."

"You *can* control it. You're getting help. Martine told me you've been getting better."

"Did I seem better to you last night?" Levi ground the heels of his hands into his eyes. "I've never done anything like that before. This isn't the person I want to be, but it's like I'm sliding down the side of a mountain, and there's nothing for me to grab onto to pull myself back up."

Levi lowered his hands to see Dominic gazing into his coffee with a troubled expression. He bit back the questions he wanted to ask: *Did seeing that change the way you feel about me? Do I disgust you now? Why do you keep wasting your time on me?*

The server returned with their food then—thank God for diners and their quick turnaround. She took Levi's veggie omelet off her tray first, then unloaded Dominic's ridiculously sized combo meal, which included a helping of every breakfast item known to man and required three plates to serve.

They tucked in, but Levi could only stomach a few bites before he had to stop. "If you hadn't been with me yesterday, things would have turned out very differently. Why were you even there, though? What made you come looking for me at my hotel?"

Dominic took his time chewing and swallowing, and he didn't meet Levi's eyes when he spoke. "There was more to the conversation I had with the Seven of Spades on Friday, after they sent me those forged papers. They said that—that when their plans for you 'came to fruition,' nobody in the city would care about anything else. That we'd only scratched the surface of what they had in store. That was before you found Quintana, but since Scott West is still missing, I don't think Quintana's death is what the Seven of Spades was referring to."

A chill ran down Levi's spine. "You never told me any of this."

"You were so happy about the break you'd gotten in the kidnapping case; I didn't want to ruin that for you. And then right afterward . . ." Dominic made a helpless gesture with his fork.

"Everything went to shit."

"Yeah."

Levi forced himself to continue eating. Even though he didn't feel hungry, his body needed fuel.

"Sunday afternoon, I was gambling at the Railroad Pass while you were all alone in a hotel room, going through the worst time of your life, cutting yourself off from everyone, and facing a threat you didn't know the entire scope of. At the very least, I had to warn you. But even knowing all that, instead of going to you right away, I hesitated. Not because I was angry with you for outing me—which I was, and still am—but because I didn't want to stop gambling."

Levi froze with his fork halfway to his mouth. This sounded like . . .

No. No, he refused to get his hopes up. Dominic had done this to him more than once over the past few months.

"If gambling is more important to me than your safety, even for a minute, what kind of person am I?" Dominic said. "If I hadn't been with you when you opened that box—hell, if I'd even been a few minutes later—you would have taken on that entire clusterfuck by yourself. You wouldn't have trusted me enough to call me for help, you would have tried to save Stanton alone, and you could have ended up dead, all while I was sitting on my ass in a casino. That would have haunted me for the rest of my life."

Levi didn't dare speak. He didn't even move, except to very slowly set down his fork.

"After I dropped Rebel off in Vegas, I didn't drive straight back to Boulder City. I went through Henderson on the way, and I stopped at the Railroad Pass. I sat in the parking lot for an hour and a half, talking myself out of going inside, sweating and shaking and on the verge of vomiting the whole time. The only thing that convinced me to leave was thinking about what could have happened to you yesterday if I hadn't been there. And even then, *even then*, I only got out by the skin of my teeth."

"Dominic . . ."

"I don't know if I can stop," Dominic said shakily. His eyes were dark with desperation. "I want to, I do, but the compulsion is so much stronger than I am."

Levi reached across the table to take his hand. "Nothing and nobody is stronger than you are."

"No. What you said at the substation was right—if losing you wasn't enough to make me quit gambling, nothing will be."

"I said that because I was angry, and it was total bullshit. You always talk about recovery from addiction like it's a question of pure willpower, but that isn't true. You need help, Dominic, professional help and support. But you won't accept that because it would mean admitting that there's something in your life you can't handle on your own."

Dominic turned his hand palm-up and laced his fingers through Levi's. "I can't stand thinking of myself as weak. It's even worse that *you* might see me that way."

"There hasn't been a single second in all the time I've known you that I've thought of you as weak." Levi tightened his grip. "The gambling isn't a deal breaker for me. It never has been, and it never will be. It was the lying and manipulating and purposely hurting me to *deny* the gambling that I couldn't tolerate. That's why I couldn't be with you."

He held his breath while he waited for Dominic's response. He'd told Dominic this countless times; would this be the time it finally sank in?

"What if I really can't stop?" Dominic said.

"You won't know unless you try. And when I say try, I don't mean going to a Gamblers Anonymous meeting every other month and trusting the rest to your self-restraint on a wing and a prayer. I mean seeing a therapist, getting a sponsor, the whole nine yards. Are you willing to do that?"

After a long, agonizing moment, Dominic nodded. His eyes were unfocused as he gazed at their clasped hands.

"You don't need to hide any of this from me," Levi said, the words tumbling out in a rush. He'd waited to have this conversation for so long he almost couldn't believe it was happening. "You have to trust that I wouldn't leave you just because you relapsed. The only way I can help you is if you're honest with me about what you're struggling with."

Wait. Levi was talking about them getting back together like it was a foregone conclusion. That might have been the case a week ago, but not now.

He withdrew his hand from Dominic's, cringing as cold realization washed through him. "But I know I can't . . . I mean, I shouldn't assume . . ." He looked out the window. "What I did to you on Friday was unforgivable."

The silence that descended over their booth was more excruciating than any of the ones preceding it. Levi's inability to control his temper had ruined any chance of reconciliation between them, and Dominic was just trying to find a diplomatic way to tell him that.

"It wasn't unforgivable," said Dominic. "From anyone else, maybe. Not from you."

Levi's head whipped around. "Dominic—"

"Please let me get this out." Dominic waited for Levi to nod before continuing. "That was one of the worst possible ways you could have betrayed me. It hurt; it still hurts. But I won't pretend I haven't done horrible things to you too. I've broken your trust in a hundred different ways, and while that doesn't make what you did okay, it's not like I can claim to be an innocent victim. When you love someone, you know better than anyone else how to cause them the most pain. We're a prime example of that."

Clasping his hands together below the table, Levi chewed his lower lip to keep from interrupting.

"We've both done shitty things, things we wish we could take back." A rueful smile crossed Dominic's face. "We can't do that, but maybe we can choose to wipe the slate clean and find a new way forward, one where we work harder to not make the same mistakes."

"I'd like that," Levi said, knowing the vast understatement was belied by his flushed face. Dominic could probably see his pulse pounding in his throat from the other side of the table. "If the past few months have taught me anything, it's that we're stronger together than we are apart. I'd rather be on your side than fighting against you."

"Me too." Dominic took a deep breath. "So I can promise to get help with my gambling like you said, and to not lie about it or manipulate you anymore—if you can promise to keep getting help with your own stuff, and to not lash out at me when you have trouble with your anger."

"I can do that."

They smiled at each other across the table. Levi hadn't fully appreciated how much energy his ongoing battle with Dominic had been sucking out of him until they reached this détente. It was easier to breathe now, like returning to sea level after a trip to the mountains.

He was still gun-shy, unable to trust that Dominic wouldn't let him down again—or vice versa. But if they could work through this, if they could accept each other's faults, forgive each other's mistakes, and help share each other's burdens, they might be able to forge a relationship more solid than the one they'd had before.

The moment was broken by Levi's cell phone ringing. "It's Adriana," he said after he glanced at the screen. "Why would she be calling me so early in the morning?"

Dominic waved for him to answer it and returned to his breakfast with renewed gusto.

Levi lifted the phone to his ear. "Adriana? Are you okay?"

"Levi?" Adriana's voice was fuzzy and indistinct, the line crackling with static. "I'm sorry to bother you so early, but I did something dumb."

"Where are you? This connection is terrible." Levi checked his phone, but the problem must have been on her end.

"I lied to Marcus and Wendy," she said. "I told them I was going to spend the night studying at a friend's house, but I—I went to this guy's house instead. He seemed really nice. I *thought* he was nice." She sniffled. "But he, um, he wanted to do stuff I didn't, and he got mad when I said no."

Levi clutched the edge of the table with his free hand. Dominic gave him a questioning look.

"I ran out of his house before anything happened, but then I didn't have a ride back out to the Andersons' farm, and I couldn't call them to come get me without explaining what I'd done. So I walked to another friend's house a couple miles away and spent the night there instead."

"You walked through the city by yourself at night?" Levi said, appalled. Granted, Adriana had taken care of herself living on the streets of Las Vegas for months, but his blood ran cold at the thought of what could have happened to her.

"It was fine. Now I have the same problem, though. Marcus and Wendy are expecting me in a couple of hours, but Madison's parents aren't home, neither of us has a license, and there's nobody else who can give me a ride. I know it's asking a lot, but I—I was hoping you could come pick me up? I'm just afraid . . ." A sob burst forth. "If they know I lied, they might not want me anymore, they might send be back and then what would happen to me? I know it was stupid and I'm *sorry*—"

"Adriana! Take a deep breath. Everything's going to be all right." Levi waited for her crying to taper off. "Of course I'll come get you. Why do you need me to take you home, though? Don't you have school?"

"We have a three-day weekend for a teacher's conference."

Levi grabbed a paper napkin from the dispenser on the table and pulled a pen out of his pocket. "Okay. Give me the address and I'll leave right now."

By the time Levi hung up, Dominic had already signaled their server for the check. Levi explained the situation to him while they waited.

"The Andersons would never reject her for something every teenager does at some point," said Dominic.

"I know; she's just panicking. I'll talk to her about it during the drive."

With only one car between them, there was no choice but for Dominic to go with him. It wasn't ideal—Adriana was still intimidated by Dominic, whose build reminded her of her abuser—but the time it would take to bring Dominic to his apartment would be more time for Adriana to work herself up into a panic attack. Levi would just have him sit in the back seat once they got there.

Adriana's friend Madison lived in a Henderson suburb that could have been a replica of the neighborhood they'd just left in Boulder City, save that the houses here were a little bigger and the yards more spacious. Levi parked in the empty driveway, headed up the front path, and rang the doorbell.

There was no answer, though he could hear noise inside. He rang the bell again, then tried the knob, just in case.

The door wasn't locked.

Tensing, Levi pushed the door all the way open while remaining on the threshold. "Hello?"

The house looked cozy and lived-in, with family photos on the walls and the kind of clutter that made it obvious teenagers lived there. From the doorway, Levi could see into the living room, where there were pillows and rumpled blankets on the couch and floor. Soda cans and half-empty bags of junk food were scattered across the coffee table, and the sounds he'd been hearing were from the TV.

Despite the odd circumstances, Levi couldn't help smiling. It was a relief to know Adriana was having normal teenage experiences like a sleepover at a friend's house.

Then he continued scanning the house, and the smile fell off his face.

A bloody handprint was smeared on the wall of a hallway that led deeper into the house, vivid against the off-white paint. It was still wet, dripping onto the beige carpet. More blood was spattered along the floor and around a corner that was hidden from sight.

Levi lunged into the house, then caught himself on the doorjamb so hard he got whiplash. He couldn't go charging into the breach alone and unarmed. That was exactly the kind of shit Leila had just taken him to task for.

While he dialed 911, he ran down the path far enough to gesture frantically to Dominic. Dominic jumped out of the car and hurried to join him at the front door.

"What's wrong?"

Levi pointed to the blood. Cursing, Dominic drew his gun from beneath his windbreaker.

"*We're sorry, all circuits are busy,*" said an automated female voice on the other end of the line.

Levi stared at the phone in disbelief. *What?* He jabbed viciously at the screen to redial.

"You just talked to Adriana fifteen minutes ago," Dominic said.

"That's fresh blood." Levi's heart was in his throat as he listened to the phone ring. Adriana had *told* him she worried her old foster father would pursue her here. What if the man had just been waiting to strike when she was most vulnerable? Levi should have listened, he should have taken her more seriously—

From the back of the house came two loud bangs, a thundering crash, and a shrill, terrified scream that was undoubtedly that of a teenage girl. Levi blanched, his entire body vibrating with the need to run toward the sounds. Dominic didn't look to be faring much better.

"*We're sorry, all circuits are busy.*"

"Fuck! Dominic, my call's not going through."

Dominic opened his mouth to respond, but was cut off by another scream from deep within the house, this one even more heart-wrenching than the first.

Levi moaned. He couldn't just stand here while Adriana was in danger. He had to help her, he had to go to her—

"Fuck this," Dominic said. "Just stay behind me."

They entered the house, Levi sticking close as Dominic swung his gun from side to side, clearing every room they passed. Following the trail of blood on the carpet, they ventured down the hallway and around the corner. The farther they went, the louder the sounds became—the wet crunches of someone being beaten, accompanied by sobs and screams.

The hallway ended in a half-open door, beyond which Levi could see more blood on the floor. That room was where all the noise was coming from.

"Freeze!" Dominic bellowed as he burst into the room. Levi was right on his heels, ready to rip the intruder's spine out with his bare hands if he had to—

The three seconds it took Levi's brain to process the incongruities of what he saw proved to be two seconds too many.

The sounds they'd been hearing cut off mid-scream. The door slammed shut behind them with a *boom*.

"What the fuck is this?" Dominic said, lowering his gun.

Levi turned in a slow circle. The room was thickly carpeted, with plain white walls and not a single window; the only light source was a ceiling-mounted fixture overhead. The door they'd come through— the door that had shut under its own power—melded seamlessly with the walls and had no doorknob on this side.

The sole items in the room were a large flat-screen television on the far wall, beneath which stood a folding card table holding a small box. A wheeled gurney was shoved against the left wall; the human shape resting on it was draped with a sheet from head to toe.

Now that the recording had been turned off—there was no other explanation for what they'd been hearing—the only sound was a rattling wheeze coming from the gurney. The shape was too tall to be Adriana, but Levi rushed to it regardless and yanked the sheet down.

It was Scott West.

Levi gasped and reeled backward. West was unconscious, but his eyelids were twitching rapidly. His skin was pale and clammy, and he was breathing so shallowly that his chest jerked with every labored inhalation.

"Oh my God," Levi said. "Oh no."

Dominic came up behind Levi and hissed through his teeth. "What's wrong with him?"

"He's bleeding internally," said a new voice—not the Seven of Spades's electronic rasp, but familiar nonetheless.

Levi whirled around to see Carmen Rivera's face on the TV. "Carmen! What the hell is going on? Where's Adriana?"

"Adriana is safe at home with the Andersons. You weren't talking to her earlier; you were talking to me. I spoofed the caller ID and used a voice transformation algorithm."

Levi shook his head, dumbfounded. Though the knowledge that Adriana had never been in real danger was a lead weight lifted from his chest, what Carmen was describing required a lengthy sample of the target's voice to train the computer program how to simulate it. Where had she gotten that from Adriana, and how had she been able to impersonate Adriana so convincingly?

Focusing on the more immediate problem, he said, "Let us out. *Now.*"

"I can't do that." Carmen's face was solemn, her dark hair hanging loose over her shoulders rather than pulled back into the messy bun he'd always seen it in before. Her eyes slid past Levi to Dominic. "Mr. Russo. You weren't supposed to be here."

"Sorry to disappoint," Dominic said.

Her chapped lips thinned with displeasure. "Well, please don't waste your energy trying to escape. This room has been soundproofed with resilient channels and a multiple-wall system. The door is steel-plated and secured with an electromagnetic lock; even Mr. Russo wouldn't be able to bust through it. And there's no cell service. The only connection to the outside world is through the audio/visual link I control."

"Were you jamming my cell phone earlier?" Levi asked.

"Yes."

Everything about this house was fake. The furniture and photographs, the cute slumber party scene in the living room, the blood on the walls and floor—they were all props.

"I have someone who'd like to speak to you," Carmen said. Her expression softened. "It was nice to see you again, Detective. Good luck."

Before Levi could question that sinister statement, Carmen's face disappeared from the screen. She was replaced by a panoramic view of a run-down block of dilapidated houses that could have been any economically depressed neighborhood in any American city.

"*Welcome, Detective Abrams,*" said the Seven of Spades.

"What kind of sick shit are you pulling this time?" Levi stalked toward the television, glaring at the webcam he saw built into it. "What do you *want* from me?"

"*Actually, I want to speak to your partner in crime first. Hasn't anyone ever told you it's rude to enter a house uninvited, Mr. Russo?*"

"Whereas it's super polite to trap people in your psycho soundproofed murder room?" Dominic said.

The Seven of Spades laughed—an eerie, grating sound. "*This room was never meant for you. But since you're here, I'll need to ensure you stay out of the way. I know you're armed. Please put your gun on the table underneath the screen.*"

"Why should I do anything you say?"

The camera panned to one side of the block, where two elderly women were chatting on a stoop, then to the other, where a man was smoking a cigarette in his robe while he let his dog out.

"*Random shootings happen in this neighborhood all the time. It'd be a shame if one of these innocent people happened to catch a stray bullet.*"

Levi looked at Dominic, seeing his own frustration reflected on Dominic's face. The Seven of Spades didn't use guns or kill "innocent" people—but before this week, they'd also never kidnapped anyone or lured Levi into a trap. There was no sense in risking it.

After Dominic set his Glock on the table, the Seven of Spades made him strip out of his jacket and shoulder holster, then untuck his shirt and turn in a slow circle.

"*Are you carrying any other weapons?*" they asked.

"Yeah, I've got a gun shoved up my ass." When that was greeted with ominous silence, Dominic sighed. "No, I don't have anything else."

"*Good. Go stand in the far corner of the room, and don't move or speak until I tell you to.*"

Dominic retreated, leaving Levi standing alone in front of the television. While Levi knew Dominic had no real choice but to follow the killer's instructions, he felt abandoned.

"*Detective Abrams,*" the Seven of Spades said, and even though they weren't visible on the screen, Levi could *feel* their eyes on him. "*This is the final part of your birthday present.*"

Levi held himself still.

"*Shortly before you arrived, I nicked several important blood vessels inside Mr. West's abdominal cavity. He's bleeding out internally, and he will die in a few hours. However, if he receives medical attention within the next half hour or so, there's a very good chance he'll survive.*"

Levi shot a startled glance at the gurney. He'd only pulled the sheet down to West's chest earlier, so he hadn't noticed any abdominal trauma.

"*This house . . .*" The camera zoomed in on one of the buildings. "*Is a Utopia safe house. More specifically, it's where several of the men who attacked you and Ms. Rashid retreated after they were released on bail, but there are others inside as well. Seven total, at my last count.*"

Levi sucked in a breath as a hand extended in front of the camera—the first time the Seven of Spades had revealed any part of their body. The thick black leather glove encasing the hand hid any hints as to gender or race, though.

The killer was holding what looked like a garage door opener. "*And this is the detonator for the C4 I've placed at vital points in the safe house's structure.*"

"You're bluffing," Levi said without thinking. "You don't use explosives; you wouldn't. It's not your style."

"*True. And to be honest, I'm still not very experienced with them. So I can't guarantee that if that house explodes, it won't take the ones on either side as well—or the whole block, for that matter.*"

"Why—"

"*Please open the box on the table.*"

Dragging his limbs as if he were walking through water, Levi approached the table and extended a wary hand. The last time he'd opened a mystery box, Stanton's eye had been inside.

This box contained only a pair of nitrile gloves and a pistol. Levi blinked, then backed up to look at the webcam. "I don't understand."

"*To celebrate your birthday, we're going to play a real-stakes game of Would You Rather.*" The Seven of Spades's electronic voice crackled with malicious glee. "*That gun is unregistered, completely untraceable, and contains a single bullet. You can choose to use it to kill Scott West, or you can tell me to blow up this Nazi safe house and everyone in it. You have three minutes to decide.*"

A timer appeared in the lower-right corner of the screen, counting down from 3:00.

"Jesus Christ," Dominic breathed.

"*I told you to keep your mouth shut*," the killer snapped.

Levi didn't turn around to look at Dominic. He couldn't move or speak; he just stared at the screen in mute horror, blood ringing in his ears.

"*If you choose to do nothing, I'll blow up the house anyway, and then I'll leave the three of you locked in that room until Mr. West succumbs to his injuries. So you see, Detective, you not only decide who dies, but who lives.*"

"You—" Levi's voice came out a dry, cracked whisper. He coughed and tried again. "You can't be serious. This is insane."

"*Is it? I'd think it would be easy choice. One shot to kill the man who got off scot-free for almost beating you to death.*"

Levi glanced sideways at West's unconscious body and flinched at the sudden flood of sense memories. It was West's father who had arranged the bribe, who had ensured that West and his friends never faced justice for what they'd done—and that Levi had never gotten closure.

"*Then again, maybe you'd prefer to kill seven neo-Nazis. The people in that house believe you have no right to exist, Detective Abrams. Every one of them will certainly cause untold pain to others if they're allowed to continue breathing. So really, there's no wrong choice here. Whatever you decide will be doing the world a favor. But you should decide soon. Two minutes.*"

"No. What you're proposing is murder." Levi exhaled in grim realization. "You *want* me to become a murderer. Why?"

When the Seven of Spades spoke again, their voice was quieter but much more intense. "*You know why you enjoy violence so much, don't you? When those men attacked you, you were helpless. You were too weak to defend yourself. Now that's all changed. Every time you fight someone who's trying to hurt you, you're reliving that encounter—only now, you're victorious. Every blow you land against an aggressor is directed at the men who came before. You're rewriting the narrative of your victimization, and it thrills you.*"

Hugging his arms tightly to his abdomen, Levi doubled over around his twisting stomach. The killer's words battered at his skull, all his deepest fears spoken aloud.

"But the cycle will keep repeating itself, because it doesn't matter how many people you strike down if it isn't them. *Catharsis will only come when that victory is real. When you kill him—when you learn how good it feels to set things right, to make things the way they're supposed to be— then you'll be free. Believe me, I'm speaking from experience."*

Levi couldn't let the Seven of Spades blow up that house. Even if they'd been lying about being unsure of the area of effect, there was always a chance with explosives that things would go wrong. There were dozens of people in those houses. *Children.* He couldn't put them in danger.

"You don't want me to push this button," the Seven of Spades said, as if reading his mind. *"You* want *to kill Scott West. Think about how it will feel to know that all four of them are dead, and you're the one left standing. Justice, at long last. The law couldn't give you that. I'm the only one who can."*

Levi groaned and shook his head. He couldn't kill West for the very reason the Seven of Spades wanted him to—he was afraid he would enjoy it.

Part of him lived in mortal fear that the Seven of Spades was right—that he was a killer at heart, violent and angry and sadistic. If he took a life in a situation other than defense during an active battle, and he *liked* it, the way he relished getting in fights and smacking down creepy guys in bars . . .

That was knowledge which, once unleashed, could never be put back in the box. If Levi murdered Scott West, he really would be like the Seven of Spades. He would never, ever come back from that.

"Ticktock, Detective. Thirty seconds."

A hysterical sob clawed up the back of Levi's throat. "Please." He braced both hands against the table, breathing in shuddering gasps, and looked pleadingly up at the webcam. "Please don't make me do this. I'll do anything else you want, just please, please, I'm begging you, don't do this to me—"

Bang.

The gunshot was deafening in the enclosed space. Levi shrieked and spun around, staring first at the hole in West's head and then at Dominic, who was holding a small pistol—one of the very same pistols he'd packed for their rescue mission but had never gotten a chance to use. His pants leg was rucked up over an ankle holster, and his eyes were flat and cold.

"I lied," he said.

CHAPTER 19 ♠

"**Y**ou . . ." The Seven of Spades's heavy breathing gusted through the voice changer. "*What . . .*"

"Haven't you heard?" Dominic said. "I'm a liar, a pretty good one. You couldn't have honestly believed I would let you do this to Levi—that I'd let you destroy him this way."

The killer loosed a wordless scream of rage, which was followed by a series of violent bangs and thumps off-camera. Ignoring their tantrum, Dominic cast a concerned eye to Levi, who had fallen back against the table and was gaping at West's corpse. On the screen, the timer counted down to zero, but nothing happened.

After being forced to pursue Levi into a firefight with no backup weapon, Dominic had decided it would be prudent to start carrying two guns instead of one, so he'd strapped on the ankle holster the moment he'd returned to the car after the Boulder City PD released him. If he believed in God the way Levi did, he would think that choice had been divinely inspired.

"*You weren't even supposed to be here!*"

Dominic returned the gun to its holster and smoothed his pants leg back down. "Yeah, well, there's nothing you can do about it now. I mean, you can still blow up that Utopia safe house if you want, but it won't pressure Levi into committing murder, which is the only reason you were willing to kill people in such an impersonal way to begin with. Plus, if you start using explosives, you'll get labeled a terrorist. That's going to ruin the vigilante antihero brand you've been so carefully cultivating."

He wasn't as nonchalant as his tone suggested. If that house went up, there might be civilian casualties, which had been a weighty factor in his decision to kill West.

"*I'm not going to detonate the explosives,*" the Seven of Spades said with a note of petulance. "*A deal's a deal, even if the wrong person fulfills it.*"

"Fine. Levi, you okay?"

"You killed him," Levi said blankly. He still hadn't moved.

Wanting to confirm that, Dominic crossed the room and pressed his fingers to West's throat. He found no pulse; West lay silent and motionless, no longer racked by the pain of internal bleeding. Dominic rested a hand over West's closed eyes for a moment before drawing the sheet up to cover his face.

I'm sorry, Dominic thought. Of course, West had once gay-bashed Levi into a broken, traumatized mess, so although Dominic didn't relish his death, he wasn't quite as sorry as he might be under different circumstances.

Dominic turned to the screen. "I'm assuming you had a plan for disposing the body without implicating Levi?"

"*Yes. I have allies standing by to get rid of it.*"

"The problem is that I shot him with my own gun, not yours, and there's no way for me to get that bullet back." Because Dominic had been standing up, aiming for a reclining figure at an angle across the room, it had been impossible for him to get a clean shot. The bullet was buried deeply in West's skull; he'd need a bone saw to retrieve it. "If his body is found, the bullet could be traced back to me, which I'd prefer to avoid. Unless you're planning for me to go down for this?"

"No!" Jolted back to action, Levi pushed himself off the table and glared at the screen. "*No.*"

"*Of course not. It serves no purpose to have Mr. Russo in prison. I'll ensure the body is never found. You have my word.*"

Dominic wasn't thrilled about trusting his freedom to a serial killer who got their kicks from playing games with people's lives, but what option did he have?

"Pawn it," said Levi. At Dominic's bewildered expression, he added, "It wouldn't be out of character for you to sell the gun to a pawnshop. The Seven of Spades will have a member of Los Avispones buy it, so if the body is ever found and the bullet is traced back to that gun, it'll look like the Seven of Spades is trying to frame you for the m—" His voice stumbled and caught. "The murder."

"Good idea." Dominic raised his eyebrows at the webcam.

After a brief pause, the Seven of Spades said, *"Agreed."*

"We still need to wipe down every surface we touched in this house before we leave," Dominic said. "Are you going to unlock this door or what?"

He waited uneasily for the response. He had, after all, ruined carefully orchestrated plans that had been in the works for months, and the Seven of Spades had a history of petty behavior. They might decide to keep him and Levi trapped in here out of pure spite.

A grinding noise signaled the release of the electromagnetic lock, and the door popped open. Dominic took a shuddering breath.

"I'm sorry, Levi." The screen went dark.

Levi squared his shoulders. "Let's finish this so we can get the fuck out of here. The quicker you get rid of that gun, the better."

While Levi used Dominic's discarded jacket to wipe down the table and the box it held, Dominic grabbed his shoulder holster and slipped it back on. Then he turned in a slow circle, scanning the room and considering what else they'd touched. Levi had pulled back the sheet covering West, but the Seven of Spades would get rid of that with the body—

Levi suddenly froze, half-bent over the table, his forehead creasing.

"What?" Dominic asked, alert to any incoming threat.

Levi's wide eyes met his. "That's the only time the Seven of Spades has called me by my first name."

With a mission to focus on and concrete goals to accomplish, both Dominic and Levi had the ability to compartmentalize their emotions and concentrate only on the task at hand. After removing any trace of their fingerprints from the house, they got back in the car and returned to Las Vegas, where Dominic offloaded the gun at a pawnshop nowhere near Henderson. In the meantime, Levi called the Andersons to ensure Adriana really was safe at home.

It wasn't until they were sitting in the car in the pawnshop parking lot, with all their *i*'s dotted and their *t*'s crossed, that the atmosphere thickened with building tension. Dominic didn't know what to say, or what he was supposed to do next. Should he ask Levi to drop him off at home? Did they just go on like none of this had ever happened?

Levi was in the driver's seat, his hands on the wheel even though the keys weren't in the ignition. His breathing was labored as he gazed at nothing through the windshield.

"You committed murder," he said.

"You're not gonna arrest me, are you?"

Levi's head snapped toward him. "It's not funny!" he said, his incredulous tone laced with a strong undercurrent of hurt. "For God's sake, Dominic, how can you joke—"

"I know it's not funny." Dominic sighed, the crushing exhaustion of the past twenty-four hours catching up with him all at once. "I did what had to be done."

"It didn't—"

"There were civilian lives at stake. If that house had blown up, it could have taken innocent people with it. If we'd done nothing, the house would have exploded and West would have died anyway, slowly and painfully of internal bleeding. Maybe if the Seven of Spades had given us more than three minutes, we could have found another way, but that wasn't the situation. West's death was inevitable and prevented a much greater tragedy. Within the parameters we were given, there was only one acceptable option to minimize casualties. You couldn't make that decision without it tearing you apart. I could. It's that simple."

Levi shook his head. "You once told me that the day taking a human life becomes something you can just shrug off is the day you find a new line of work."

"Is that what you think I'm doing? Shrugging it off?" Dominic barked out a humorless laugh. "Never. I hate that I had to kill him. I wish there had been any other way. But sometimes the only right choice in a terrible situation still sucks ass. Accepting that reality doesn't mean trivializing what I did."

Levi's hands slid off the wheel into his lap, and he was quiet for a moment as he studied them. "I don't understand that."

"I know, because you'd feel differently in my position. I also know why you were so terrified by the idea of killing West. But it would have been even worse if the Seven of Spades had killed everyone, so I took action."

Dominic reached out, giving Levi plenty of time to indicate that his touch was unwelcome. When Levi remained still, Dominic took his hand.

"You're a cop, Levi. I was a soldier. It's not the same. What happened today will weigh on me, but I can live with it. What I wouldn't have been able to live with is watching you destroy yourself."

Levi didn't respond.

"Do you feel differently about me now?" Dominic asked, the possibility chilling him to the bone.

"Did you feel differently about me after you watched me mutilate Acosta?" Levi said wryly.

"No."

"I love you." Levi met Dominic's eyes. "I don't know if there's anything you could do that would change that, but killing someone to save innocent lives and protect me definitely isn't it."

Dominic brushed his free hand along Levi's jaw, then cupped his cheek. Levi leaned into the touch.

"You know the circumstances wouldn't matter to a court of law," Levi said. "What you did was technically murder. If the Seven of Spades lied about not wanting you to go down for it ... Dominic, they could have been recording everything that happened in that room. We have to be ready in case they turn you in."

"Ready how?"

"Pack a bag. I'll withdraw as much cash as I can and get my hands on a car that won't lead back to either of us. I'd say we should go on a 'vacation' that's conveniently located in a country with no extradition policy, but I'm under investigation, and of course there's Rebel to think about—"

Dominic squeezed Levi's hand to stop him from spinning out. "What do you mean, 'we'? If I go on the run for murder, you're gonna come with me?"

He'd said it jokingly, but Levi gave him a puzzled look and said, "Of course," like Dominic was the dumbest person alive.

Dominic's breath stuttered in his chest. He studied Levi's face for any hint of exaggeration, but found only the frank sincerity that was

Levi's hallmark. Levi wasn't given to empty romantic gestures; he'd never say something so serious unless it was the unvarnished truth.

Lunging across the gearshift, Dominic yanked Levi into a ferocious kiss. Levi yelped, then melted into it, his hands sliding up Dominic's arms and neck to tangle in his hair. Though the angle was awkward, they kissed until they had to break apart to gasp for air. Dominic's lips were sore, his face tingling where Levi's stubble had scraped against his own.

Even after they parted, Dominic kept Levi close, cradling his jaw. "I think the Seven of Spades is already worried that they've pushed you too far; they wouldn't risk alienating you further. We just need to avoid drawing attention to ourselves. And we can *never* tell anyone about what happened today. Not ever."

Levi rested his hand atop Dominic's, nodded, and leaned forward to touch their foreheads together. They both closed their eyes.

They were linked forever now, connected by dangerous secrets they could never share with another human being. But instead of driving them apart, those secrets had only bonded them more profoundly. They had seen each other at their darkest, and their love hadn't just survived—it was stronger than before. Unconditional. Unbreakable.

"Let's go home," said Dominic.

Levi and Dominic had never been the kind of couple who touched each other while they were sleeping. They would cuddle after sex, or when they first lay down, but they always moved to their individual sides of the bed when it was time to sleep.

Today, however, after they tumbled naked and exhausted into Dominic's bed, Dominic spooned up behind Levi and held him like he never planned on letting go. Levi nestled into the embrace, savoring the warmth of Dominic's skin against his own, the weight of Dominic's massive arm slung across his waist, the palm of Dominic's hand pressed to his heart.

They passed out like that and slept for a solid ten hours.

Levi had vague memories of getting up at some point to use the bathroom, but when he woke for good, he and Dominic were in the same position. Dominic was lavishing Levi's neck with kisses, rocking his hips to gently rub his erection against Levi's ass.

Levi stretched under the covers, working out the kinks in his back, then guided Dominic's hand between his legs with a pleased sigh. Groaning into Levi's ear, Dominic began to tug and stroke his cock while Levi pushed back against the promising hardness sliding along the curve of his cheeks.

His breathing quickened as Dominic coaxed him to full attention in record time. Each press of Dominic's lips to his nape sent shivers down his spine; the sensation of that thick cock so close to where he wanted it was a wicked tease.

The heat building beneath their blanket cocoon soon became intolerable. Levi turned around, shoved Dominic onto his back, and climbed astride his hips. The covers pooled around their waists.

Rebel, who Dominic had retrieved from Carlos and Jasmine's upon returning to his apartment, huffed in displeasure when their movement disturbed her own slumber. She shot them a dirty look before jumping off the bed and padding out of the room.

Levi settled his erection against Dominic's and leaned down to kiss him. They frotted lazily, trading deep, languorous kisses as their hands glided over each other's skin. Levi let out a hearty moan when Dominic's thumbs crept between their bodies to caress the sensitive points of his hip bones.

Although they'd never stopped having sex while they were broken up, this felt like they were relearning each other. Levi grasped for every inch of Dominic he could reach, reacquainting himself with the flex of granite muscles, the rasp of Dominic's chest hair, the puckered scar of the gunshot wound beneath Dominic's right shoulder. No other man had ever aroused Levi this much; no one else's touch had ever riled him up this way.

They'd also never been great at maintaining a slow pace. It wasn't long before they were thrusting roughly against each other, their cocks sticky with sweat and pre-come, panting into each other's mouths because they could no longer concentrate on the kiss. Levi swept his tongue along Dominic's lower lip, loving the greedy way Dominic was kneading his ass, and then sank his teeth into the tender skin at the junction of Dominic's throat and shoulder.

Dominic arched against him with a shouted curse, his fingers digging into Levi's flesh. Levi sucked harder on the bite, wanting to leave a mark, wanting to prove that Dominic was *his*—

Growling, Dominic flipped them over, crushing Levi to the bed with his bulk. He drove his erection harder against Levi's, pressing urgent, sloppy kisses to Levi's face and jaw.

They could come like this, and it would be glorious—but it wasn't what Levi wanted. "Lube," he gasped. "Hurry."

Dominic tore himself away only long enough to grab the bottle from the nightstand. There was nothing slow or careful about the plunge of his fingers as he worked Levi open, but Levi *needed* that, craved the sensation of being prepped a little too fast. He reached down and slid one of his own fingers into his hole alongside Dominic's, grunting at the burn of a stretch that was just on the right side of painful.

Dominic chuckled against Levi's skin. "I know you think you're helping, but you're getting in the way."

"I'm not trying to help. I just want to feel full."

"*Fuck.*" Dominic thrust his fingers more aggressively for a few dizzying moments before he withdrew them and pushed Levi's hand aside. "I'll give you something better."

Levi drew his legs to his chest in anxious anticipation. Dominic rose onto his knees, propped Levi's ass on his thighs, and lined his bare cock up with Levi's hole.

His bare—

Oh no.

"Wait!" Levi snapped his hips up and away at an angle, rolling onto his side and bringing his legs between himself and Dominic, the same way he'd defend against an assault from this position.

"What's wrong?" Dominic's face was flushed, his hair mussed from Levi pulling it earlier. "Do you— Would you rather wait until we're sure things will work out this time? Because I get it, I know I've let you down before—"

"That's not it. It's just . . ." Levi would give anything not to say this, but he had no choice. "We have to use a condom."

Dominic frowned. "Why? I haven't been with anyone else."

Levi pressed his lips together.

"Oh." Dominic rocked back to sit on his heels. "*Oh.*"

After all of Dominic's gambling and lying, Levi's uncontrolled rage, the violence and blood and straight-up *murder*, it was going to be Levi's stupid fucking one-night stand that ruined them for good.

"I'm sorry," was all Levi could think to say.

"Who was it?" Dominic asked. "It couldn't have been Barclay. He's been in Europe since the last time you and I slept together."

"God, no, of course it wasn't Stanton." Levi sat upright against the headboard. "I'd never do that to you *or* him. It was Jay Sawyer."

Dominic's mouth fell open. "*Sawyer*? You hate that guy!"

"That night, I hated you and myself more."

Realization dawning in his eyes, Dominic said, "Saturday. The night of Carlos's bachelor party."

"Yes."

"Christ, no wonder Sawyer acted so weird when I called him the next day to find out where you were," Dominic muttered.

Levi winced and shifted onto his knees so he and Dominic were at a more equivalent height. "I'm so sorry. I was really messed up, and I thought there was no more hope for us, and I just wanted something to take me out of my head. It was stupid."

"You don't have to apologize. It's not like you cheated; we weren't together. You had every right to sleep with someone else."

"I know. I still wish I hadn't done it."

Dominic inched forward on his knees and raised his hands to Levi's face. "What bothers me most is that you were in such a bad place that you had a one-off with someone you can't stand. That's not like you at all."

"I wanted it to be you," Levi murmured. "It was the only thing I thought about afterward."

Dominic kissed him, slow and sweet. Levi exhaled a shaky sigh when their lips parted.

"Do you still want to . . ." Levi couldn't finish the question, unsure if he meant *have sex* or the much more loaded *get back together*.

"I do if you do."

Levi glanced down at Dominic's deflated cock and then arched an eyebrow. Smiling, Dominic pulled Levi's hand to the limp flesh, which began to perk up the second Levi stroked it.

Since Levi had lost his erection as well, they spent a few minutes kissing and jerking each other off, striving to recapture the mood of a few minutes earlier. Although it didn't take long until they were both raring to go again, the vibe was different; Dominic was too quiet, his movements restrained, his careful touch nothing like his usual demanding grasp.

After Dominic put on a condom, he urged Levi onto his back again, but Levi shook his head and rolled onto his side instead. "This way," he said. "Like we were before."

Dominic spooned him from behind, and Levi lifted his top leg to provide easier access. But between the too-hasty prep and the additional tension that had overtaken Levi after his confession, Dominic could only get the head of his cock inside before Levi's body clamped down and refused further entry.

Dominic eased that inch in and out, teasing Levi's hole, which usually did the trick within a minute or so. This time, though, no matter how deeply Levi breathed or how deliberately he bore down, his ass remained closed for business.

"Levi," Dominic said, "unless you really want just the tip, you have to relax."

He couldn't. He thought they'd blown past the thing with Sawyer way too fast, that it was hovering over their heads like an anvil that could crush them at any moment, and he *hated* that they had to use a condom when he knew how much Dominic preferred to fuck him bareback. Hell, he vastly preferred that himself.

"Why aren't you more upset?" he said without thinking.

Dominic stilled with the head of his cock nestled inside Levi's ass. "What?"

Levi twisted to look back at Dominic; the motion drove him a bit further onto Dominic's cock and made them both grunt. "I told you I had sex with someone else, and you just . . . accepted it."

"What do you want me to do?" Dominic pulled out, then popped the tip back in. "Yell at you?"

"That's not what I meant. It wouldn't be fair for you to be angry with me. But I can tell you're holding something back. If you're jealous, or upset, or disappointed, you don't have to hide that. I'd feel the same way in your position."

Dominic was quiet for a moment, continuing his minute thrusting. "I'm not going to be that guy. You hate men like that."

"Like what?"

"Meathead Neanderthals who get all territorial and possessive over their partners. I'm not like that."

Astonished, Levi released his leg to rest his hand on Dominic's cheek. "I could never think that about you. There's a big difference between being a domineering psycho and feeling hurt that someone you love had sex with another person." When Dominic's brow remained furrowed, Levi added, "How are we going to rebuild our relationship if you can't be honest with me about something this important?"

"Fine," Dominic said through gritted teeth. "You want the truth? Knowing you had sex with Sawyer is driving me fucking insane. Thinking about his hands on you makes me sick."

Dominic rolled his hips, managing to sink his cock a little deeper. Levi gasped and turned back to face front, grabbing his knee and pulling it to his ribs.

"I don't want anyone else to see you like this, to touch you this way." Dominic's voice, already a gravelly rumble, was pitched even lower than normal. "Imagining his cock inside you . . ."

Levi shivered. Dominic was so far removed from the kind of asshole who'd jealously dictate Levi's behavior and violently fend off interlopers that the idea was laughable. So maybe letting this play out wouldn't do any harm—in fact, it might do them both some good.

"Sawyer's cock wasn't big enough," he said.

Dominic groaned, his hips jerking. "No?"

"Not after you."

"Is that so?" Dominic's rough, teasing tone set butterflies fluttering in Levi's stomach. "Look at yourself. You can't even take it."

Levi wet his lips. "I can if you make me."

"Levi, *Jesus.*" Dominic's heavy exhalation ruffled Levi's hair. "Is that what you want? You want me to force all this up inside you until you're stuffed full?"

Levi's answering moan was broken and needy. "Yeah. Do it."

Dominic pushed his cock in as far as he'd gotten—which still wasn't much—and took over supporting Levi's free leg with his hand. Levi gripped the edge of the mattress, groaning low and nonstop as Dominic penetrated him more forcefully, advancing by degrees, barely pulling back before pressing forward again. Relieved that Dominic was acting like his usual self, Levi found his body opening more easily, and now struggling to accept the large, rigid length invading him was exciting rather than frustrating.

"This cock ruined you, huh?" The arousal in Dominic's voice stoked the flames of Levi's own lust. "Now you can't be satisfied by anything less?"

"Mm-hmm." Levi couldn't bring himself to say more than that; he still tended to deny being a size queen, despite both he and Dominic knowing that for a flimsy lie.

Because he *did* adore how big Dominic's cock was. He loved how it felt inside him, the way it rooted him so firmly in his physicality that he couldn't concentrate on anything beyond the present moment. Even now, he was trembling from the pleasure of the overwhelming incursion.

"God, half the time fucking you is like breaking in a virgin." Dominic's next thrust sent him almost balls-deep. "Popping that tight cherry over and over."

Levi let out a quiet cry, his face flushing as a hot, sweet thrill of embarrassment swept through him. His hole slackened, allowing Dominic to slide that last inch home.

"That's it." Able to move freely at long last, Dominic rocked his hips, fucking Levi at a steady pace. "That feels so good, baby," he said, but then his thrusts faltered. "Sorry, I forgot—"

"It's fine." Levi reached back to loop his arm around Dominic's neck. "Say it. I want you to."

Pressing a kiss to Levi's upper arm, Dominic resumed his rhythm. "You feel so good around me, baby," he whispered into Levi's ear, like it was a secret—which it was, in a way. Levi had never let anyone else call him that.

The husked endearment made Levi moan, which in turn drew a hoarse groan from Dominic's throat. Levi craned his head back so they could kiss while they fucked.

In this side-lying position, Dominic couldn't go that deep without also going very slow, which neither of them were in the mood for. The more Dominic sped up, the shallower his thrusts became—but the angle let him aim unerringly for Levi's prostate, frying Levi's nervous system with pure electric bliss.

Levi tore his mouth away from Dominic's, breathing in ragged gasps. He gave his own erection a few soothing strokes, then trailed his fingers down to explore the place where Dominic was spreading him, filling him—*completing* him.

"This is where you belong," he said. "Show me how happy you are to be back where you're supposed to be."

Dominic's hand tightened on Levi's knee. "I want to hear you scream."

"Then you'll have to work harder than this."

Dominic hooked his arm around Levi's thigh and surged into a vigorous, rapid-fire assault that made Levi shriek in both surprise and appreciation. Levi frantically tugged his own cock while Dominic hammered away, ravaging his body with such intensely focused pleasure that he thought he might pass out.

And he *did* scream—he always did with Dominic, the ecstasy too overwhelming to be contained or suppressed. His cries rebounded off the walls as his toes kinked, his muscles tightened, and goose bumps washed across his skin.

Levi hung suspended for a moment on the edge of climax, his hand flying on his cock, before his orgasm burst through him in glittering shards. He was still shuddering and convulsing around Dominic's cock when Dominic rolled him flat on his stomach, moving with Levi so he never quite pulled out. Bracketing Levi's thighs with his own and curving his hands beneath Levi's shoulders for leverage, Dominic pinned Levi to the bed with his weight and went at him like an animal in rut.

Levi muffled a scream in the sheet, then turned his face to one side so he could breathe. He always enjoyed being fucked after he came, especially by Dominic's huge cock, which set off a chain reaction of aftershocks in his sensitized body.

Dominic knew that quite well, and he wasn't holding back. The obscene smack of his hips bouncing off Levi's ass competed with the creaking mattress and the headboard banging against the wall. He grunted and cursed, his cock plunging deeper into Levi—so deep that Levi grabbed fistfuls of the bottom sheet with enough force to yank the corners off the mattress.

"Fuck me, fuck me," Levi said, only half-aware of what he was babbling. Being subjected to Dominic in a primal frenzy of lust never failed to make him lose his goddamn mind. "Screw me with that monster cock, God, you're a fucking beast, nobody's ever fucked me like you do—"

With a guttural shout, Dominic buried his cock in Levi's ass and ground it in desperate circles as he came. When he finished, he groaned like a dying man and slumped atop Levi's back.

Levi made a strangled noise. Dominic had been supporting some of his own weight on his elbows earlier, but now Levi felt like he was being crushed beneath a marble statue. "I can't breathe," he said, sending an uncoordinated elbow into Dominic's side.

Dominic heaved himself onto his hands, then carefully pulled out. Levi made a face, but even the uncomfortable sensation couldn't put a dent in his vibrant afterglow. His brain was soaked in so many feel-good chemicals right now that he might as well have been stoned.

"There's one advantage to using a condom." Dominic shifted off to the side, stripping the latex from his cock. "Easier cleanup."

Levi flipped onto his back and looked expressively between Dominic and where his own come was smeared over his belly. Dominic had rolled him right onto the wet spot.

"Or not," Dominic said with a hint of sheepishness. "Hang on."

He threw out the condom and retrieved a package of wet wipes from the nightstand. While Dominic cleaned up Levi and the bed, Levi scattered kisses across whatever skin came near his mouth, so content he was almost purring.

Dominic tugged the bottom sheet back into place, and the moment he lay down, Levi curled up around him and rested his head on his chest. Dominic held Levi close, smoothing a hand up and down his back. They lay like that for a long time, basking in the joy of each other's presence as their breathing evened out and their heartbeats slowed.

Dominic was the first to break the silence. "We can do this, right?"

Levi propped his head on Dominic's shoulder to look at his face. "It won't be easy."

"I don't want easy." His lips quirking, Dominic traced his thumb along Levi's jaw. "I want you."

Levi shoved him, Dominic retaliated, and their tussling quickly devolved into a playful wrestling match that ended with Levi sprawled on top of Dominic's body and both of them panting.

"I love you," Dominic said, gazing up at Levi with soft eyes.

Levi smiled. "I love you too."

CHAPTER 20

"I think I owe you an apology," Sawyer said, seated across from Levi at the desk in his office.

"We've been successfully avoiding this conversation for the past twenty minutes," said Levi. "Let's not ruin all that hard work."

Sawyer pushed Levi's case file aside. "I shouldn't have slept with you. You were emotionally vulnerable, and I took advantage of that. I'm sorry."

Though Levi would have been perfectly happy to continue pretending their one-night stand had never happened, if Sawyer insisted on hashing it out, Levi would ensure the matter was put to rest for good. "I pressured you into sleeping with me."

"No, you—"

"Don't rewrite history. I played on your attraction to me and I deliberately insinuated that you'd be putting me in danger if you left me alone at that bar. If anything, we took advantage of each other. It was a mistake, but we're adults, and there was no real harm done. Let's just put it behind us and move on."

Sawyer fiddled with the edge of a stack of papers. "Would your ex agree with that?"

"Oh, um . . ." Clearing his throat, Levi shifted in his seat. "We actually got back together yesterday."

Sawyer rocked back, his face paling. "Does he know about . . ."

"Yes." Levi took in Sawyer's agitated posture, raised his eyebrows, and said, "Oh, come on. What, do you think Dominic's going to hunt you down and kick your ass? He's not like that."

"Are you sure?"

"*Yes.*"

"I don't know what possessed me to sleep with a guy whose ex is built like a tank and has a concealed carry permit," Sawyer muttered.

Levi rolled his eyes. "I can't believe you're more worried about Dominic than about what the State Bar of Nevada would do if they found out you had sex with a client."

"Pro bono doesn't count," Sawyer said with a wink. In trademark fashion, he seemed to have already recovered his composure.

"Can we just finish this, please? I'm picking Adriana up from school in an hour."

They dove back into Levi's case, discussing his upcoming Internal Affairs hearing, which was scheduled for Friday. "IA has nothing," said Sawyer. "You have solid alibis for several of the Seven of Spades's murders, plus an alibi for Captain Sheppard's murder in Philadelphia. And I have sworn affidavits from half a dozen people testifying to the fact that the Seven of Spades has been psychologically tormenting you for almost a year, making these recent murders a perfect fit with their established pattern of behavior. IA has no evidence on which to base a continuation of your suspension, still less to seek a warrant for your arrest."

"And if pressure from the sheriff and mayor decide them otherwise?"

"We can sue. Among other things, you have a strong case for defamation of character."

"Ugh, no." Levi waved a hand. "I don't want to attract any more attention to myself."

"Really? After the weekend you just had?" Sawyer laughed in the face of Levi's scowl. "There's no reason to worry. Now, if Boulder City had decided to press charges, that might be a different story, but IA can't bring your little adventure into your hearing without them. All you have to do between now and then is stay out of trouble. I know how difficult that is for you, but do your best."

Once they'd wrapped up a few more details, Sawyer walked Levi out to the elevator bank. The posh offices of Hatfield, Park, and McKenzie reeked of wealth and moral ambiguity, and Levi drew more than his fair share of attention from employees and clients alike.

"At the hearing, let me do all the talking. Don't say a single word. The cops will try to trick you into incriminating yourself—they're sneaky little weasels."

"Says the defense attorney," Levi said.

Sawyer grinned. "Takes one to know one."

Levi shook his hand, glad they'd set aside the awkwardness of their indiscretion with minimal drama, and left for Adriana's high school in Henderson.

At the curb outside, Adriana jumped into the front seat of his rental car, full of energy and gossip. She dropped her backpack by her feet and immediately launched into a story about the convoluted social politics of junior year.

He listened without interruption as he turned the car back toward Las Vegas. She was in such high spirits that he was loath to ruin her good mood, though he'd have to eventually.

In fact, it was Adriana herself who broached the subject. When she finally paused to draw breath halfway to the city, she gave him a curious look and said, "So why did you want to pick me up instead of having Marcus drop me off like usual? Krav's not for another couple of hours."

"I needed to speak to you about something in private." Levi flexed his fingers around the steering wheel, keeping his eyes on the road. "Have you noticed anything strange or out of place happening around you lately? Feeling like you're being watched or followed, getting weird calls, hearing interference on your cell phone, anything like that?"

She didn't respond, so he glanced sideways. Gone was the exuberant young woman who'd been sitting in her seat moments before, replaced by a haunted wraith with graying skin and wide, unblinking eyes. The change was so profound that it struck Levi speechless.

"He *is* looking for me," she whispered. She was breathing shallowly through her nose.

"No!" Levi cursed himself as he realized his mistake. He pulled onto the shoulder, threw the car in park, and twisted around in his seat to face her. "That's not why I was asking, I swear. Your old foster father is still in Reno. He's not going to come anywhere near you."

She shook her head, radiating such palpable fear that Levi's own heart pounded in sympathy. "You—you can tell me if he is. I won't freak out—"

"Adriana!" Levi met her eyes and waited for her to focus before continuing. "I'm not just guessing; I keep tabs on him. I know for a fact he hasn't left Reno in months."

"You . . . what?"

He shrugged self-consciously. This wasn't something he'd ever planned on telling her, but it was better than her having a panic attack. "I have a contact in the Reno PD who helps me keep an eye out. Between the two of us, there's no way that man could come to Vegas without me knowing."

What he didn't add was that his friend in Reno also dropped by Adriana's old house from time to time, and occasionally parked his black-and-white across the street for a few hours. With any luck, the creep who'd abused Adriana was too intimidated to put hands on the kids still in his care.

Adriana opened her mouth, but seemed at a loss for words. Some of the color returned to her cheeks. "Why were you asking all that weird stuff, then?"

Okay, so he wasn't going to get the information he needed by being vague. Though he couldn't tell Adriana the full truth, he could at least share the relevant parts.

Choosing his words carefully, he said, "What I'm going to tell you is something only you, Dominic, and I will know, all right? And it has to stay that way."

She nodded.

"The Seven of Spades had someone contact me a few days ago, pretending to be you."

"You mean like they texted you and made it look like it came from my number?"

"No. This person spoke to me on the phone using what sounded like your voice. I had no idea it wasn't you until later."

Her eyebrows shot up. "That's possible?"

"With certain sophisticated computer programs, yes, and the Seven of Spades has a genius working with them. But those programs require a lengthy sample of the target's voice to teach the computer how to mimic it. I'm worried about how the Seven of Spades obtained that from you—if they've been recording you somehow, bugging you at home or school . . ."

His voice died away. Adriana had lowered her head while he'd been speaking, but now when she lifted her face, her eyes were glistening.

"What?" he asked, his skin prickling with dread.

She rummaged in her backpack to retrieve her phone, unlocked the screen, and handed it to him. He found himself looking at her recent call log. Interspersed between his own name, the Andersons', and those of her friends were regular incoming calls from a blocked number.

"The Seven of Spades calls me sometimes," she said.

Heart in his throat, Levi checked the details of each of the calls one after the other, hoping to see lengths of ten or fifteen seconds—just enough time for Adriana to realize who was on the other end and hang up.

Thirty-two minutes. Twenty-seven. *Fifty-five*.

"The calls started a couple months after I moved in with the Andersons," Adriana went on as Levi stared at her phone in horror. "At first I just told them to go to hell, but they kept calling, and . . . they *listen* to me."

He hit the button to turn off the screen, unable to stomach the sight of the calls any longer. "About what?"

"About *him*." Tears ran down Adriana's cheeks now, though she wasn't sobbing. "I can't be honest with you or Natasha about it, not really. You both get that look in your eye when I talk about wanting to hurt him, like you think there's something wrong with me. The Seven of Spades gets it. They know why I want him dead."

"I understand, you know I—"

"Those men didn't rape you!"

Her shout echoed through the car. Levi drew back.

She wiped the heels of her hands over her damp cheeks. "I'm sorry, Levi. What happened to you was horrible, but it wasn't the same. You *don't* understand."

"You're right," he said quietly. "I'm sorry."

"I asked the Seven of Spades to kill him."

Levi clutched the edge of his seat.

Her chin lifted, Adriana glared as if daring him to scold her. "They said they want to, but they can't right now, because it would bring attention to the fact that they've been communicating with me. But they'll kill him one day, and I won't be sorry. I'll be glad."

"Adriana . . ." He swallowed hard. "I know the idea of getting rid of people like that for good is very tempting. The system we have isn't perfect. People get away with doing bad things all the time, and it's awful and frustrating. But vigilante murder isn't the answer."

"Why not? If killing certain people makes the world a better place, why is it wrong?"

"Because no one person should have that much power. No single human being should be allowed to pass judgment on others, decide their punishment, and carry it out all by themselves. There's a reason our juries have twelve members."

Frowning, she turned her head to look out the window. From what he could see of her face, he gathered that his argument had hit home.

"It's possible that the Seven of Spades really does care about what happened to you." Levi set her phone in the center console. "But that's not why they've been communicating with you. They knew they could use you against me, and they took advantage of that. They took advantage of *you*."

Adriana sniffed. "I'm just so sick of being afraid, you know?"

He bowed his head. She was strong, and he had faith that she would make it through this—that she had a bright, thriving future ahead of her. But in this moment, there was nothing he could say to make her feel better.

She took a few shaky breaths, scrubbing at her nose and mouth.

"There's napkins in the glove compartment," he said, knowing she wouldn't want him to reach into her personal space.

After she retrieved the napkins and blew her nose, she said, "I had no idea the Seven of Spades would use our conversations to trick you, or hurt you. I would never have spoken to them if I had."

"I know. And everything worked out fine. You don't have to worry about it."

"I won't talk to them again." She bit her lip, wadding the napkins in her fist. "Although I guess they already got what they wanted from me. They won't call me anymore, will they?"

"Probably not."

Sighing, she stuffed the napkins into a side pocket of her backpack. "Are you gonna tell anyone?"

"No." He rested his hand on the space between their seats, close enough to get her attention but not close enough to touch her. "I meant what I said earlier—this has to stay a secret. I'm sorry that I can't explain why, but it's really important that you never tell anyone else about this. In fact, I think you should delete those calls from your phone."

Though clearly taken aback, she picked up her phone and began doing just that without argument. Reassured that she wasn't on the edge of a breakdown, Levi rejoined the flow of traffic on the highway.

"Do you want to forget about Krav today?" he asked after a few minutes of driving in silence. "We could go see a movie or something instead."

"Sure, sounds good." A few seconds later, and in a much smaller voice, she said, "Are you mad at me?"

"No." He spoke firmly, so she would have no reason to doubt his conviction. "You didn't do anything wrong. I'm mad at the Seven of Spades."

Adriana slumped in her seat, looking much older than her sixteen years. "Me too."

With McBride's blessing, Dominic had taken the entire week off work to get his shit together—her words, not his. He'd been going to Gamblers Anonymous meetings every day, sometimes two or three, and had accepted an old acquaintance's offer to sponsor him. Natasha had also referred him to a clinical social worker who specialized in gambling disorders, and he'd made an appointment for next week.

Five days in, he was still gambling-free, but the cravings were even worse than the last time he'd gone through this and the withdrawal was a bitch. His mood swung rapidly between extremes; his stomach roiled with a constant low-grade nausea. He'd had the same nagging headache since Monday night.

He might have fallen off the wagon, if not for the fact that Levi was temporarily staying at his place. Due to Levi's suspension, the two of them had been able to spend most of the week together, reconnecting and repairing their relationship. It didn't hurt that nobody had ever been quite so good as Levi at distracting him from his gambling urges.

On Friday, Dominic was planning to be at the substation during Levi's IA hearing—not just for emotional support, but to run interference if things went south. That wasn't until late afternoon, though, and Levi had taken off to nurse his anxiety in private under the thin pretext of running errands, which left Dominic with dangerous free time to fill.

Exercise had been one of the greatest aids to his recovery the first time around, so he sought refuge in it now. He hit the gym with Carlos for a full-body superset circuit, then picked up Rebel and took her on their regular five-mile run through the UNLV campus. Back at home, he emerged from the shower sore and in a better frame of mind, but once again at loose ends.

As he wandered around the kitchen, looking for anything to take his mind off his growing cravings, his eyes fell on a business card secured to the refrigerator. The very first thing he'd done on Tuesday was sit down with a credit counselor at a nonprofit debt management company to sign up for a debt management plan. That entailed turning over all his credit card and personal loan debt to the DMP; he would make regular payments to the company, who would in turn distribute the funds to his various creditors and help keep them off his back.

Doing so had meant closing out all his credit cards, which was something he should have done years ago. He'd also destroyed his debit card and all his personal checks. Now, if he wanted money, he had to physically go to the bank to withdraw it in cash.

His credit counselor, Sandra Delaney, had said she'd contact him within a couple of days to discuss the possibility of negotiating lower fees and interest rates with his creditors, but he still hadn't heard from her. It wouldn't hurt to take the initiative.

He grabbed the card off the fridge and dialed his cell while he ambled into the living room. Delaney answered after a few rings.

"Hi, this is Dominic Russo. I'm calling about setting a follow-up appointment?"

There was a brief silence on her end. "I'm sorry, an appointment for what?"

"You mentioned there was a chance of convincing some of my creditors to lower their rates now that I'm on a DMP."

"Well, yes, but since the debt's been paid off, it's kind of a moot point."

Dominic froze mid-stride. "Since the debt's been what?"

"The payment you sent yesterday zeroed out your balance," she said. "The account's been closed."

He sat down hard on the couch. Rebel lifted her head from the rawhide she'd been gnawing on and pricked her ears.

"I didn't do that," he said faintly. "There must be some mistake."

After a burst of rapid typing, Delaney hummed her disagreement. "I'm looking at your account history right now. Payment was made in full yesterday."

He cradled his head in one hand, unable to even process what she was saying. He'd owed more than a hundred grand, and that debt had just been . . . wiped out? How was that possible?

His unavoidable first thought was that the Seven of Spades had done it. But they were furious with him now; if anything, they were in the midst of planning their revenge.

"Where did the payment come from?" he asked.

"I can't be sure. It was made by cashier's check from Wells Fargo. I just assumed that you or a family member had sent it in."

Nobody in Dominic's family could come close to affording such a large lump sum.

There was only one person he knew who could.

"Mr. Russo?" said Bridget, the no-nonsense woman who guarded Stanton Barclay's inner sanctum like Cerberus. "Mr. Barclay will see you now."

She escorted Dominic into a corner office larger than his apartment, with two enormous glass walls overlooking the glittering, frenetic energy of the Strip and the city beyond. Barclay met him halfway and shook his hand.

"Thanks for seeing me on such short notice," Dominic said.

"Of course."

Levi, who'd visited Barclay a few times over the past week, had updated Dominic on his steady recovery. Barclay did look much better than he had on Sunday, returned to his handsome, debonair self—but Dominic noticed the slight hunch to his shoulders, how his gaze constantly scanned the room, his pronounced flinch when Bridget shut the door. The trauma of his kidnapping had scarred him in ways more subtle than his missing eye.

Instead of bringing Dominic to the desk, Barclay showed him to a cozy seating arrangement of leather couches clustered around a glass-topped coffee table. "How are you feeling?" Dominic asked as they settled in.

Barclay was wearing a black patch over his left eye, beneath which the white edges of bandaging were visible. "As well as can be expected, given the circumstances." He brushed his fingertips beneath the eye. "They put an ocular implant in, but it'll be a few months before I can get the prosthesis itself."

"Honestly, I think you could rock the whole eye patch look. It's working for you."

Barclay chuckled. "What can I do for you, Mr. Russo?"

Taking a page from Levi's book, Dominic chose blunt honesty over tact. "You paid off all my debt."

"That doesn't sound like a question."

"It wasn't," Dominic said with a shrug. "There's nobody else it could have been. Except maybe the Seven of Spades, but they're not too thrilled with me right now."

Casting him a wary glance, Barclay said, "Are you here to insist I take the money back? Because that's not possible—"

"Shit, no." Dominic raised his hands. "I have pride, but I'm not an idiot."

"Then why are you here?" Barclay asked, his tone one of polite bewilderment.

Dominic leaned forward, resting his forearms on his knees. "If you were anyone else, I'd think you'd done it to try to win Levi back. But you know him too well to think that would work."

A wistful smile crossed Barclay's face. "True. Money has never been the key to Levi's heart."

"So why do it?"

"Isn't gratitude reason enough? After all, you saved my life—and more importantly, you protected Levi's. If it weren't for the two of you, I'd likely be dead right now."

Dominic tilted his head, not buying it. There were plenty of ways Barclay could have thanked him that didn't involve dropping a hundred grand—anonymously, no less.

As if sensing Dominic's disbelief, Barclay cleared his throat and smoothed out a crease in his trousers. "I'm still in love with Levi."

"I know," Dominic said softly.

"When you love someone—truly love them—their happiness is the most important thing in the world to you, even more than your own. When you two were together, Levi was happier than he'd ever been with me. When you separated, he was devastated in a way I'd never seen. And now that you're back together . . ." Barclay's lips quirked. "Well, he's careful about what he says in front of me, but I can tell he's overjoyed. You're the one he wants. I respect that."

"But?"

"But debt like yours is toxic. Even if you never relapsed again for your entire life, you would have drowned in it. It would have poisoned your relationship, and Levi deserves better than that. He deserves a chance at a real future without his partner's debt dragging him down." Sighing, Barclay made a helpless gesture with both hands. "That's the only thing I can give him, so it's what I did."

Dominic straightened up, floored by this revelation. To acknowledge that the person you loved was in love with someone else and concede gracefully was one thing, but to deliberately aid that relationship to ensure the person's happiness at the expense of your own? He couldn't imagine what it had cost Barclay emotionally to make such a sacrifice.

"Thank you," he said, his voice thick with emotion. "I know you did this for Levi, but you have no idea what a difference it makes for me—how entirely you've changed my life. I want you to know that I'm dedicated to him and my recovery. I won't disrespect the gift you've given me. *Us*."

"That's all I ask." Barclay hesitated. "Although . . . I suppose there's no point in asking you not to tell him what I did?"

"No, I'm sorry. Even if I hadn't promised not to lie to him anymore, I wouldn't be able to hide this from him. As soon as he found out my debt had been cleared, he'd realize it was you as quickly as I did." Studying Barclay more closely, Dominic added, "I can tell him you'd rather not speak to him about it, though."

"Thanks," Barclay said, his voice ringing with relief.

Not wanting to overstay his welcome, Dominic rose to his feet. Barclay followed suit, and they shook hands once more.

"Be good to him, Mr. Russo."

Dominic nodded, thanked Barclay again, and left the office, each step lighter than the one before.

He'd lived under crushing debt for so long that the reality of being debt-free had yet to fully sink in. He hadn't been exaggerating when he said Barclay had changed his life forever, though. While it would take years for his credit to recover, he'd been given as close to a fresh start as possible. The mistakes of his past still weighed on his shoulders, but they no longer breathed so hotly down his neck.

Heartened by the bright, pure hope dawning in his chest, Dominic set off for Levi's substation.

CHAPTER 21

"**Y**ou're early," Martine said as Levi entered the crowded bullpen.

"I wanted to check in first." He'd also run out of things to do to distract himself from his impending hearing, but he didn't want to admit that.

His desk was clean and bare of everything but his computer, unused in his absence. He sat down, ignoring the many stares and whispers directed his way. Who cared what these people thought? He wasn't going to let their petty gossip get under his skin.

The fact that he had to wear a visitor's badge in his own substation *was* grating, though.

Martine frowned. "You know I can't share details of ongoing investigations with a suspended officer."

"Oh." Of course. Hadn't he had that same thought after he'd been removed from the Seven of Spades task force, not wanting to get her in trouble? Flustered, he half stood. "Sorry—"

"I'm joking!" She waved for him to sit down. "Come on, you know I don't give a shit about that."

He snorted and sank back into his chair. "Funny."

This wasn't the first time they'd spoken this week. They'd been texting back and forth as usual, and they'd met on Wednesday for a long, private lunch, during which he'd told her the unabridged truth about Stanton's rescue—though nothing about the events of the following morning. But during all their conversations, they'd avoided talking about work, sticking to personal topics instead.

"The Buckner homicide and its associated kidnappings, assaults, and mutilations have been mostly wrapped up." Martine pulled a thick folder from a stack on her desk and flipped it open. "All of the kidnappers you and Dominic tracked down are being held without bail at the CCDC, as is Charles Graham now that he's been discharged from the hospital. We don't know which one of them actually killed Buckner and they're not talking, but because his death occurred during the commission of a kidnapping in which they were all involved, Leila charged them all with felony murder."

Levi nodded. Considering the slew of serious charges they were facing and the weight of the evidence against them, it would take a miracle for any of those men to escape life in prison.

"Nathan Royce was released from jail with all charges dropped."

A small mercy, since the man's entire life had imploded around him. "Juliette?" Levi asked.

"Charged with multiple counts of conspiracy, but she bargained for a lighter sentence by pleading guilty and agreeing to provide testimony against Carolyn Royce."

"But Carolyn's still missing, isn't she?"

"Yeah," Martine said, flicking the folder shut. "We thought we had her for a couple of days, but her trail went cold in a small coastal town in California. There's a good chance she made it out of the country undetected. In any case, we turned the manhunt over to the FBI, so it's out of our hands."

Levi drummed his fingers against the desk. He hated dangling threads in an investigation, though they were an unavoidable reality of law enforcement.

"What's really getting to me is that nobody's heard from the Seven of Spades in almost a week."

Levi tensed, his fingers going still.

"I mean, they still have Scott West." Martine rubbed the back of her neck. "After all the drama they created with the first three guys, I figured they were building to some huge finale performance. But just . . . nothing? No word at all? Doesn't that seem bizarre?"

"They're a serial killer. Everything they do is bizarre."

"I meant out of character."

"I guess. Who knows what goes on in that freak's head?" Levi darted a glance at Martine to find her regarding him with bemusement. Nothing was more out of character than him brushing off worries about the Seven of Spades.

He squashed his guilt at keeping her in the dark. If it had been his secret alone, he would have told her, but he'd carry the truth of Dominic's actions to the grave.

Fortunately, they were interrupted by the arrival of Terence Freeman as he strolled up to their adjoining desks. "Abrams. We need to get started without Montoya; she got held up on another case."

"Fine," said Levi, though he was rattled by the news. He considered Montoya an ally—albeit a discreet one—and he didn't like the idea of proceeding without her. Checking the time on his phone, he frowned. "Sawyer must be running late."

"Well, find out where he is. I have dinner plans."

Levi was texting Sawyer when the whispering in the bullpen—which had died down while he'd been talking to Martine—started up again even more blatantly than before. He lifted his head to see Dominic coming his way.

Although most of these people hadn't been present the night Levi had outed Dominic's addiction, word had definitely spread by now. Everyone here knew Dominic was a compulsive gambler, something that would eat at him even as he pasted on a charming smile and pretended it was no big deal.

Except there was nothing forced about the smile on Dominic's face. He was *glowing*, walking with a bounce in his step, brimming over with giddy energy.

Dropping his phone forgotten on his desk, Levi stood to meet him. "I thought you weren't coming until later."

"I had an appointment on the Strip, and it didn't make sense to go home just to come all the way back here." Dominic greeted Martine and Freeman as well, then added, "You haven't started yet?"

"We're still waiting for Sawyer."

"Good. I need to tell you something."

Dominic took Levi's hand and pulled him aside. Intrigued, Levi followed without resistance. Whatever it was must be good news; Dominic was acting like Rebel when she was about to get chicken.

"You're never going to believe this," Dominic said.

Every computer in the bullpen crackled with deafening static, loud enough to drown out all conversation. Seconds later, all the monitors went black.

People called to each other in confusion, the air filled with the noise of clattering keyboards and clicking mouses. A chill of premonition skittered over Levi's skin like a cold wind.

Against the far wall stood a rolling computer cart with an enormous flat-screen monitor, used for group presentations and briefings. It emitted one more attention-getting burst of static and then displayed the image of a bland, empty motel room—beige walls, faded floral bedspread, an insipid landscape in a scratched wooden frame.

"*Good afternoon,*" said the Seven of Spades.

Cries of alarm sounded throughout the bullpen. Levi clutched Dominic's elbow, flashing back to that harrowing room and the television screen from which the Seven of Spades had tormented them both. This could not be happening again—

Dominic rested his hand on top of Levi's and squeezed reassuringly. A few feet away, Martine hit the silent alarm on Levi's desk that alerted the entire LVMPD to an incoming Seven of Spades communication.

"*I apologize for disturbing your workday, but it's come to my attention that Detective Levi Abrams has recently fallen under suspicion for my own crimes.*"

Levi restrained an eye roll. It had *come to their attention*, sure, like that hadn't been precisely their goal all along.

"*Given a few minutes of your time, I can disprove that theory. But first—Detective Valcourt?*"

Martine, who had been silently directing the personnel in the bullpen with hand gestures and mouthed words, startled badly. "Yes?"

"*Please name a number between one and five.*"

"Uh . . . four?"

A thickly gloved hand extended four fingers in front of the camera. Several people gasped; one officer jumped out of her chair, which slid backward along the linoleum and crashed into the desk behind her.

"*Detective Freeman, the same request, please.*"

Visibly shaken at being addressed by a serial killer, Freeman hesitated for a moment before saying, "Two."

The Seven of Spades repeated their trick. "*As you can see, it's impossible for this to be a recording. Detective Valcourt, could you please confirm that Detective Abrams is physically present in the bullpen at this exact moment?"*

"Yes, he's just a few feet away from me."

"Thank you. Let's begin."

The camera swiveled ninety degrees to show a woman slumped in a chair—Carolyn Royce.

Exclamations of surprise and disbelief were uttered across the room. "Find out where that feed is coming from!" Martine hissed at a uniformed officer, who bolted out of the bullpen like his ass was on fire.

Carolyn wasn't bound, but she wasn't moving other than to breathe and occasionally blink. Her glassy eyes stared into nothingness, and there was a vacant expression on her face. She'd been drugged with ketamine.

"Now that Ms. Rivera has been freed from the shackles of a bloated, useless bureaucracy, you'd be amazed how quickly she can locate people who don't want to be found. Dragging Ms. Royce from her hidey-hole was a bit more difficult, but one of the consequences of betraying everyone around you is that there's nobody there to help when someone like me comes knocking at your door."

"We have to stop this," Dominic muttered to Levi.

"How?"

Martine stepped toward the monitor. "So you have Carolyn Royce. Do you still have Scott West?"

Beside Levi, Dominic sucked in a breath, his body going rigid.

"Oh, him?" the Seven of Spades said carelessly. *"He tried to escape, so I had to shoot him in the head. A shame, because it wasn't what I'd planned, but I had no choice. He was getting boring, anyway."*

A frisson of surprise ran through Dominic, but he remained silent. Martine was the only one in the bullpen who looked more confused than disgusted by this casual pronouncement. Levi averted his eyes before she could turn to him, knowing he wouldn't be able to disguise his reaction well enough to fool her.

"Now, returning to the matter at hand—if there's anyone present who still doubts Ms. Royce's guilt, let me set your minds at ease."

The feed cut to a recording in which the camera stood at the exact same angle and Carolyn sat in the same chair. The only difference was that in the recording, Carolyn was awake, alert, and bound to the chair at her wrists and ankles. She held herself with the terrified stillness of an animal cornered by a predator, eyeing someone who stood behind and to the side of the camera.

"You know this won't be admissible in any court of law," she said.

The Seven of Spades just laughed, an eerie, menacing rasp as translated through their voice changer. Carolyn blanched. She was trembling, but she kept her chin up as she directed her gaze to the camera.

"Nathan and I married in our late twenties. We'd decided to wait a few years before having children, but I got pregnant unintentionally within the first year of our marriage. Nathan wanted me to have an abortion. He convinced me that we weren't ready, that a child at that point would derail our careers—mine especially. I agreed."

Her eyes darted toward the Seven of Spades for a moment.

"But as the years went by and he gave me one excuse after another, I realized there was more at work. When I confronted him, he admitted that he'd lied when we got engaged—he didn't want children, and never intended on having them. He'd married me under false pretenses and had persuaded me to terminate what he knew full well might be the only pregnancy I'd ever have."

"Why didn't you divorce him?"

With a bitter smile, she said, "I thought I still loved him. And I believed it was too late, anyway. I didn't want to have a child on my own, and I was thirty-four by that point. The time it would have taken to start fresh, find someone new, settle down again . . ." She shrugged miserably.

"But you never forgave him, did you?" the Seven of Spades asked.

"No. After that, I began seeing him in a different light. I realized what a coward he was, how spineless, how selfish. He has no principles; the only thing he cares about is his own comfort. He came to disgust me. And then, not only was he stupid enough to knock up his twenty-four-year-old assistant, he had the gall to try to do to her what he'd done to me!"

"You had to punish him for that."

"I couldn't bear another day with him. He'd ruined my life; he deserved the same." Carolyn's fear faded as it was eclipsed by her rage—a rage that, after decades in a pressure-cooker of resentment and loathing, had poisoned her mind. Her hatred for her husband straightened her spine and strengthened her voice, transforming her from the Seven of Spades's victim into the ruthless woman who had arranged a kidnapping ring to wreak vengeance on the man she blamed for a lifetime of disappointment. "Besides, he owed me a child. It was only fair."

"I don't disagree. You betrayed your husband, but he betrayed you first—and to be frank, he sounds like an asshole. I admire the way you set him up to be felled by his own incompetency and selfishness. The enucleation of the victims was a little over the top, but then, that may be hypocritical of me."

All of Carolyn's focus was on the person behind the camera now. A small ray of hope shone in her eyes.

"But you promised a desperate young pregnant woman that you would protect her, provide for her, and then you double-crossed her," said the Seven of Spades, their tone abruptly hardening. *"You intended all along to kidnap her and kill her once you'd gotten what you wanted. That's something for which there can be no redemption."*

Carolyn's terror returned in force. Her skin whitened; her hands clawed around the arms of her chair. "I wasn't going to kill her! Once the child and I were safe, I would have let her go home."

"You're lying."

Movement sounded off-screen. Carolyn shrieked and recoiled in her chair as much as her restraints allowed.

"No, please! Please don't, I haven't seen your face, you don't—"

The recording ended, and the monitor once more depicted the current moment in time. Carolyn drooped in her chair, drugged into a dissociative paralysis, awaiting her inevitable execution.

The camera zoomed in until it was showing only her head and neck. The Seven of Spades walked behind her, no more than a dark, shadowy shape in the background. This time, when they extended their hand, they were holding a knife whose wicked blade glinted in the dim light.

Carolyn's eyes shifted. She couldn't move, but she was awake, and while her thoughts were surely an intoxicated jumble, there must have been part of her that knew what was happening. She knew she was about to die, and could do nothing to stop it.

"Oh my God, Levi," Martine moaned. Everyone else in the bullpen seemed to have frozen in horror.

"Stop!" Levi hurried forward, addressing the monitor. He wasn't sure if the Seven of Spades had eyes in here, but they'd recognize his voice regardless. "Don't do this, please. Just leave her where she is, get away, and then tell me where to find her. She said herself that she hasn't seen your face. You don't have to kill her."

"*I know I don't have to.*" The Seven of Spades set the knife to Carolyn's throat. "*I want to.*"

"Don't. Please. You've made your point—I'm not the Seven of Spades. We get it."

"*This could all be an act,*" the killer said, surprising Levi into silence. "*Look around you, Detective. How many friendly faces do you see?*"

Baffled, Levi scanned the bullpen—and realized that, with the exception of Dominic and Martine, there wasn't a single person present who he could call more than a mere acquaintance at best. At worst, like Freeman, some were unambiguously hostile toward him.

"*I could be any one of a number of people loyal to you who you sent here to pretend to be the Seven of Spades—people who aren't in the room with you right now. You and I could have rehearsed this entire scene in advance. If I leave things here, if I allow you to persuade me to spare her life, there will always be people who believe that this was all for show. The only way to truly clear your name is for me to kill Ms. Royce while your colleagues can see that your hands are clean.*"

Whether anyone would really have thought that didn't matter now. By introducing the possibility, the Seven of Spades had ensured that there were people who already did. Levi could see it on their faces.

"I don't care," he said. "This isn't how we prove guilt or innocence. I don't want this."

"*That's too bad.*" With one swift, clean stroke, the Seven of Spades slit Carolyn Royce's throat.

Screams resounded throughout the bullpen. One of the officers doubled over and vomited into a trash can; several more people ran out of the room, crying and gagging. Martine crossed herself, tears streaming down her stricken face.

Dominic came up behind Levi and put both hands on his shoulders—to restrain him from flying into a frenzied rage, most likely.

Levi watched the blood gush from Carolyn's throat, watched the life drain from her eyes until all that was left was a soulless shell. He *was* angry—with the Seven of Spades for perpetuating this nightmare, with himself for being unable to stop it. There was a point at which his reaction to this would have been to throw the monitor to the ground and smash it to pieces. But as he watched Carolyn die, a new emotion welled up and overshadowed everything else.

Contempt.

"You're pathetic," he said.

There was a rustling noise on the monitor, then a brief silence. "*I beg your pardon?*"

Levi spoke with a clarity of thought he hadn't felt in months. "You pretend you're a righteous crusader on a mission for justice, picking up where the law leaves off. But I see you for what you really are. You're a sad, empty person who's scrambling for attention any way you can get it."

A few people gasped behind him, but Levi didn't turn around.

"You don't care what the people you murder have done. It's just optics, part of the game you're playing—the legend you're trying to create. I'm sure you enjoy killing, but it's the power of having the city in your thrall that you love most. You want people to fear you, be in awe of you, believe that you're larger than life. You're constantly high on your own drama, but it's never quite enough, is it? That's why you have to keep escalating, why you have to make each gesture more dramatic and theatrical than the one before. No matter how much attention you get, it'll never be enough for whatever emptiness you're trying to fill. It's pathetic."

The only sound the Seven of Spades made was their heavy breathing.

"I'm not playing this game with you anymore," Levi said calmly. "You may be smart and skilled, but you're a person, not a myth. And like any person, you are fallible. Eventually, you'll make a mistake, and I *will* stop you."

"Careful, Detective." The Seven of Spades's electronically altered voice was a low, harsh growl. *"If you back the wrong horse, you may lose everything."*

This time, Levi didn't bother hiding the roll of his eyes. "Yeah, all right. I know you enjoy your gambling metaphors and cutesy wordplay. So how about this?" He stepped right up to the monitor. "At the end of the day, you're just another homicidal nutjob who's one card short of a full deck. There's nothing special about you. When I find you, they will lock you up, lose the key, and the only time anyone will ever talk about you will be while remembering what a sick, miserable, broken human being you were."

He hit the power button on the monitor. The screen went dark.

Levi's mind was clear and resolute. The Seven of Spades had maintained the upper hand for too long because he'd allowed himself to be demoralized by their mythology, to buy into the legend of an elusive and borderline-prescient mastermind, as if their intelligence and monstrosity rendered them superhuman.

But the Seven of Spades *was* human—a human killer with human frailties.

Catching killers was always what Levi had done best.

"So." Levi turned to a sea of shocked faces, Martine's determined expression, Dominic's proud smile. "Has anyone else had just about enough of this motherfucker?"

Explore more of the *Seven of Spades* series:
riptidepublishing.com/collections/seven-spades

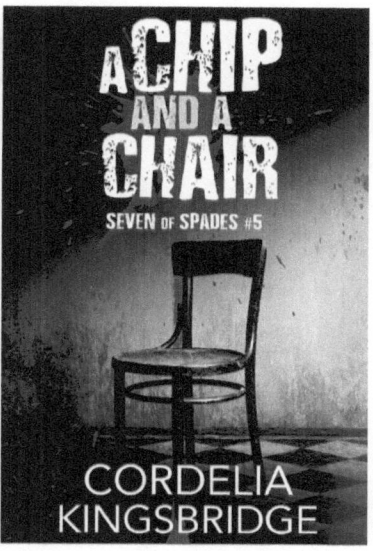

Dear Reader,

Thank you for reading Cordelia Kingsbridge's *One-Eyed Royals*!

We know your time is precious and you have many, many entertainment options, so it means a lot that you've chosen to spend your time reading. We really hope you enjoyed it.

We'd be honored if you'd consider posting a review—good or bad—on sites like **Amazon, Barnes & Noble, Kobo, Goodreads, Twitter, Facebook, Tumblr,** and your blog or website. We'd also be honored if you told your friends and family about this book. Word of mouth is a book's lifeblood!

For more information on upcoming releases, author interviews, blog tours, contests, giveaways, and more, please sign up for our weekly, spam-free newsletter and visit us around the web:

Newsletter: riptidepublishing.com/newsletter
Twitter: twitter.com/RiptideBooks
Facebook: facebook.com/RiptidePublishing
Goodreads: tinyurl.com/RiptideOnGoodreads
Tumblr: riptidepublishing.tumblr.com

Thank you so much for Reading the Rainbow!

RiptidePublishing.com

ACKNOWLEDGMENTS

♠

With thanks to Mathilde M., winner of the *Kill Game* design-a-character prize, for the character of Christelle Perrot!

ALSO BY CORDELIA KINGSBRIDGE

Seven of Spades series
Kill Game
Trick Roller
Cash Plays
A Chip and a Chair *(coming soon)*

Can't Hide From Me

ABOUT THE AUTHOR

Cordelia Kingsbridge has a master's degree in social work from the University of Pittsburgh, but quickly discovered that direct practice in the field was not for her. Having written novels as a hobby throughout graduate school, she decided to turn her focus to writing as a full-time career. Now she explores her fascination with human behavior, motivation, and psychopathology through fiction. Her weaknesses include opposites-attract pairings and snarky banter.

Away from her desk, Cordelia is a fitness fanatic, and can be found strength training, cycling, and practicing Krav Maga. She lives in South Florida but spends most of her time indoors with the air conditioning on full blast!

Connect with Cordelia:

Tumblr: ckingsbridge.tumblr.com

Twitter: @c_kingsbridge

Facebook: facebook.com/Cordelia.Kingsbridge

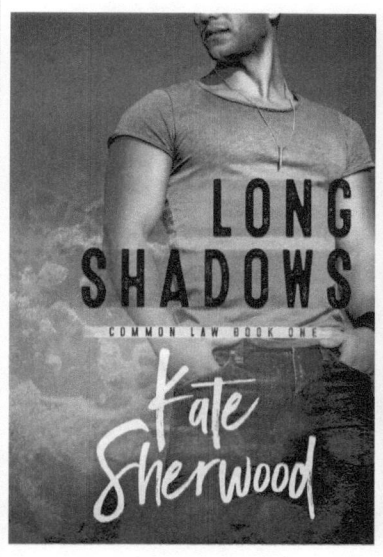